The Sorceress by Margaret Oliphant

In Three Volumes

Margaret Oliphant Wilson was born on April 4th, 1828 to Francis W. Wilson, a clerk, and Margaret Oliphant, at Wallyford, near Musselburgh, East Lothian.

Her youth was spent in establishing a writing style and by 1849 she had her first novel published: Passages in the Life of Mrs. Margaret Maitland.

Two years later, in 1851 Caleb Field was published and also an invitation to contribute to Blackwood's Magazine; the beginning of a life time business relationship.

In May 1852, Margaret married her cousin, Frank Wilson Oliphant. Their marriage produced six children but, tragically, three died in infancy. When her husband developed signs of the dreaded consumption (tuberculosis) they moved to Florence, and then to Rome where, sadly, he died.

Margaret was naturally devastated but was also now left without support and only her income from writing to support the family. She returned to England and took up the burden of supporting her three remaining children by her literary activity.

Her incredible and prolific work rate increased both her commercial reputation and the size of her reading audience. Tragedy struck again in January 1864 when her only remaining daughter Maggie died.

In 1866 she settled at Windsor to be closer to her sons, who were being educated at near-by Eton School.

For more than thirty years she pursued a varied literary career but family life continued to bring problems. Cyril Francis, her eldest son, died in 1890. The younger son, Francis, who she nicknamed 'Cecco', died in 1894.

With the last of her children now lost to her, she had little further interest in life. Her health steadily and inexorably declined.

Margaret Oliphant Wilson Oliphant died at the age of 69 in Wimbledon on 20th June 1897. She is buried in Eton beside her sons.

Index of Contents

CHAPTER XIX
MARGARET OLIPHANT - A SHORT BIOGRAPHY
MARGARET OLIPHANT - A CONCISE BIBLIOGRAPHY

CHAPTER I

It was the most exciting event which had ever occurred in the family, and everything was affected by it.

Imagine to yourselves such a young family, all in the very heyday of life, parents and children alike. It is true that Mrs. Kingsward was something of an invalid, but nobody believed that her illness was anything very serious, only a reason why she should be taken abroad, to one place after another, to the great enjoyment of the girls, who were never so happy as when they were travelling and gaining, as they said, experience of life. She was not yet forty, while Charlie was twenty-one and Bee nineteen, so that virtually they were all of the same age, so to speak, and enjoyed everything together—mamma by no means put aside into the ranks of the dowagers, but going everywhere and doing everything just like the rest, and as much admired as anyone.

To be sure she had not been able to walk about so much this time, and had not danced once, except a single turn with Charlie, which brought on a palpitation, so that she declared with a laugh that her dancing days were over. Her dancing days over! Considering how fond she had always been of dancing, the three young people laughed over this, and did not take the least alarm. Mamma had always been the ringleader in everything, even in the romps with the little ones at home. For you must not think that these three were all of the family by any means.

Bee and Betty were the eldest of I can't at this moment tell how many, who were safe in the big nursery at Kingswarden under the charge (very partial) of papa, and the strict and steady rule of nurse, who was a personage of high authority in the house. Papa had but lately left "the elder ones," as he called them, including his pretty wife—and had gone back to his work, which was that of an official at the Horse Guards, in some military department of which I don't even know the name, for I doubt whether the Intelligence Department, which satisfies all the necessities of description, had been invented in those days.

Colonel Kingsward was a distinguished officer, and the occasion of great—éclatto the little group when he showed himself at their head, drawing round him a sort of cloud of foreign officers wherever he went, which Bee and Betty appreciated largely, and to which Mrs. Kingsward herself did not object; for they all liked the clank of spurs, as was natural, and the endless ranks of partners, attendants in the gardens, and general escort and retinue thus provided. It was not, however, among these officers, red, blue, green, and white—of all the colours in the rainbow—that Bee had found her fate. For I need scarcely say it was a proposal which had turned everything upside down and filled the little party with excitement.

A proposal! The first in the family! Mamma's head was as much turned by it as Bee's. She lay on the sofa in her white dressing gown, so flushed with happiness and amusement and excitement, that you would have supposed it was she who was to be the bride.

And then it was so satisfactory a thing all round. If ever Mrs. Kingsward had held anyone at arm's length in her life it was a certain captain of Dragoons who had clanked about everywhere after her daughters and herself for three weeks past. The moment they had appeared anywhere, even at the springs, where she went to drink her morning glass of disagreeable warm water, at the concert in the afternoon, in "the rooms" at night, not to speak of every picnic and riding party, this tall figure would jump up like a jack-in-a-box. And there was no doubt that the girls were rather pleased than otherwise to see him jump up. He was six foot two at least, with a moustache nearly a yard long, curling in a tawny and powerful twist over his upper lip. He had half-a-dozen medals on his breast; his uniform was a compound of white and silver, with a helmet that literally blazed in the sun, and his spurs clanked louder than any other spurs in the gardens. The only thing that was wanting to him was a very little thing—a thing that an uninstructed English person might not have thought of at all—but which was a painful thing in his own troubled consciousness, and in that of the regiment, and even was doubtful to the English friends who had picked up, as was natural, all the prejudices of the class into which their own position brought them.

Poor Captain Kreutzner, I blush to say it, had no "Von" to his name. Nobody could deny that he was a distinguished officer, the hope of the army in his branch of the service; but when Mrs. Kingsward thought how the Colonel would look if he heard his daughter announced as Madame Kreutzner—tout court—in a London drawing-room, her heart sank within her, and a cold perspiration came out upon her forehead. "And I don't believe Bee would care," she cried, turning to her son for sympathy.

Charlie was so well brought up a young man that he cared very much, and gave his mother all the weight of his support. His office it was to beguile Captain Kreutzner as to the movements of the party, to keep off that bold dragoon as much as was possible; when, lo! all their precautions were rendered unnecessary by the arrival of the real man from quite another quarter, at once, and in a moment cutting the Captain out!

There was one thing Mrs. Kingsward could never be sufficiently thankful for in the light of after events, and that was, that it was Colonel Kingsward himself who introduced Mr. Aubrey Leigh to the family. He was a young man who was travelling for the good of his health, or rather for the good of his mind, poor fellow, as might be seen at a glance. He was still in deep mourning when he presented himself at the hotel, and his countenance was as serious as his hatband. Nevertheless, he had not been long among them before Bee taught him how to smile, even to laugh, though at first with many hesitations and rapid resuming of a still deeper tinge of gravity, as if asking pardon of some beloved object for whom he would not permit even himself to suppose that he had ceased to mourn. This way he had of falling into sudden gravity continued with him even when it was evident that every decorum required from him that he should cease to mourn. Perhaps it was one of the things that most attracted Bee, who had a touch of the sentimental in her character, as all young ladies had in those days, when Mrs. Hemans and L. E. L. were the favourite poets whom young ladies were expected to read. Well brought up girls were not permitted, I need not say, to read Byron. Shelley was a name of fear, and the poems of Mr. Thomas Campbell, not to say Mr. Thomas Moore (carefully selected) were likely to promote that quality.

The pale young man, with his black coat, his hatband, his look of melancholy, drove out the image of the Captain at once from Bee's mind. She had perhaps had enough of captains, fine uniforms, spurs, and all. They had become what modern levity calls a drug in the market. They made—Fenster—parade all day long under her windows; they thronged upon her steps in the gardens; they tore the flounces from her tarlatan into pieces at the balls. It was something far more original to sit out in the moonlight and look at the moon with a sorrowful young hero, who gradually woke up into life under her hand. Poor, poor boy!—so young and so melancholy!—who had gone through so much!—who was really so handsome when the veil of grief began to blow away!—who had such a pretty name!

Bee was only nineteen. She had mocked and charmed and laughed at a whole generation of young officers, thinking of nothing but picnics and dinner parties and balls. She wanted something new upon which to try her little hand—and now it was thrown, just when she felt the need, in her way. She had turned a young fool's head several times, so that the operation had lost its charm. But to bring a sad man back to life, to drive away sorrow, to teach him to hold up his head again, to learn how sweet it was to live and smile, and ride and run about this beautiful world, and wake every day to a new pleasure— that was something she felt worthy of a woman's powers. And she did it with such effect that Mr. Aubrey Leigh went on improving for three weeks more, and finally ended up with that proposal which was to the Kingsward family in general the most amusing, the most exciting, the most delightful incident in the world.

And yet, of course, it was attended with a certain amount of anxiety which in her—temporarily—invalid state was not very good for mamma. Everybody insisted on all occasions that it was a most temporary state, and that by the end of the summer she would be all right—the palpitations quite calmed down, the flush—which made her so pretty—a little subdued, and herself as strong as ever. But in the meantime this delightful romantic incident, which certainly acted upon her like a glass of champagne, raising her spirits, brought her some care as well. Her first interview was of course with Bee, and took place in the privacy of her chamber, where she cross-examined her daughter as much as was compatible with the relations between them—which indeed were rather those of companions and comrades than of mother and daughter.

"Now, Bee, my dear child," she said, "remember you have always been a little rover, and Mr. Leigh is so quiet. Do you think you really, really, can devote yourself to him, and never think of another man all your life?"

"Mamma," said Bee, "if you were not such a dear I should think you were very insulting. Another man! Why, where should I find another man in the world that was fit to tie Aubrey's shoe?"

"Well," said Mrs. Kingsward, dubiously; but she added, after a moment, "You know, darling, that's not quite the question. If you did find in the after ages a man that perhaps was—fit to tie Mr. Leigh's shoe?"

"Why in all this world,—petite mère—, will you go on calling him Mr. Leigh?"

"Well, well," said Mrs. Kingsward; "but I don't feel," she said again, after a moment's hesitation, "that I ought to go so far as to call him Aubrey until we have heard from papa."

"What could papa find to object to?" said Bee. "Why, it was he who introduced him to us! We should not have known Aubrey, and I should never have been the happiest girl in the world, if it had not been for papa. Dear papa! I know what he'll say: 'I can't understand, my dear, why you should hesitate for a moment. Of course, you don't suppose I should have introduced Mr. Leigh to my family without first ascertaining, &c., &c.' That, of course, is what papa will say."

"I dare say you are right, Bee. It is quite what I expect, for, of course, a man with girls knows what it is, though for my part I confess I always thought it would be a soldier—Captain Kreutzner or Otto von—"

"Mamma!" cried Bee, almost violently, light flashing out of the blue eyes, which were so bright even on ordinary occasions as to dazzle the beholder—you may imagine what fire came out of them now—"as if I should ever have looked twice at one of those big, brainless, clinking and clanking Germans. (N.B.—Mr. Aubrey Leigh was not tall.) No! Though I may like foreigners well enough because it's amusing to talk their language and to feel that one has such an advantage in knowing German and all that—yet, when it comes to be a question of spending one's life, an Englishman for me!"

Thus, it will be seen, Bee forestalled the patriotic sentiments of a later generation by resolving, in spite of all temptations, to belong to other nations—to select an Englishman for her partner in life. It is doubtful, however, how far this virtuous resolution had existed in her mind before the advent of Aubrey Leigh.

"I am sure I am very glad, Bee," said her mother, "for I always had a dread that you would be snatched off somewhere to—Styria or Dalecarlia, or heaven knows where—(these were the first out-of-the-way names that came to Mrs. Kingsward's mind; but I don't know that they were altogether without reference or possibilities), where one would have had no chance of seeing you more than once in two or three years. I am very thankful it is to be an Englishman—or at least I shall be," she added, with a sigh of suspense, "as soon as I have heard from papa—"

"One would think,—Mütterchen—, that you were frightened for papa."

"I shouldn't like you ever to try and go against him, Bee!"

"Oh, no," said Bee, lightly, "of course I shouldn't think of going against him—is the inquisition over?—for I promised," she said, with a laugh and a blush, "to walk down with Aubrey as far as the river. He likes that so much better than those noisy blazing gardens, with no shade except under those stuffy trees—and so do I."

"Do you really, Bee? I thought you thought it was so nice sitting under the trees—"

"With all the—gnadige—Fraus knitting, and all the—wohlgeborne—Herrs smoking. No, indeed, I always hated it!" said Bee.

She jumped up from where she had been sitting on a stool by her mother's sofa, and took her hat, which she had thrown down on the table. It was a broad, flexible, Leghorn hat, bought in Florence, with a broad blue ribbon—the colour of her eyes, as had often been said—floating in two long streamers behind. She had a sash of the same colour round the simple waist of her white frock. That is how girls were dressed in the early days of Victoria. These were the days of simplicity, and people liked it, seeing it was the fashion, as much as they liked crinolines and chignons when such ornamental arrangements "came in." It does not become one period to boast itself over another, for fashion will still be lord—or lady—of all.

Mrs. Kingsward looked with real pleasure at her pretty daughter, thinking how well she looked. She wore very nearly the same costume herself, and she knew that it also looked very well on her. Bee's eyes were shining, blazing with brightness and happiness and love and fun and youth. She was not a creature of perfect features, or matchless beauty, as all the heroines were in the novels of her day, and she was conscious of a great many shortcomings from that high standard. She was not tall enough—which, perhaps, however, in view of the defective stature of Mr. Aubrey Leigh was not so great a disadvantage—and she was neither fair enough nor dark enough for a Minna or a Brenda, the definite and distinct blonde and brunette, which were the ideal of the time; and she was not at all aware that her irregularity, and her mingling of styles, and her possession of no style in particular, were her great charms. She was not a great beauty, but she was a very pretty girl with the additional attraction of those blue diamonds of eyes, the sparkle of which, when my young lady was angry or when she was excited in any more pleasurable way, was a sight to see.

"All that's very well, my dear," said Mrs. Kingsward, "but you've never answered my question: and I hope you'll make quite, quite sure before it's all settled that you do like Aubrey Leigh above everybody in the world."

"—A la bonne heure—," said Bee; "you have called him Aubrey at last, without waiting to know what papa will say:" with which words she gave her mother a flying kiss, and was gone in a moment, thinking very little, it must be allowed, of what papa might say.

Mrs. Kingsward lay still for a little, and thought it all over after Bee was gone. She knew a little better than the others what her Colonel was, and that there were occasions on which he was not so easy to deal with as all the young ones supposed. She thought it all over from the moment that young Mr. Leigh had appeared on the scene. What a comfort it was to think that it was the Colonel himself who had introduced him! Of course, as Bee said, before presenting anyone to his wife and family, Colonel Kingsward would have ascertained, &c., &c. It was just how he would write no doubt. Still, a man may introduce another to his wife and family without being ready at once to accept him as a son-in-law. On the other hand, Colonel Kingsward knew well enough what is the possible penalty of such introductions. Young as Bee was, she had already attracted a good deal of attention, though this was the first time it had actually come to an offer. But Edward must surely have thought of that. She was, though it seemed so absurd, and though Bee had laughed at it, a little afraid of her husband. He had never had any occasion to be stern, yet he had it in him to be stern; and he would not hesitate to quench Bee's young romance if he thought it right. And, on the other hand, Bee, though she was such a little thing, such a child, so full of fun and nonsense, had a spirit which would not yield as her mother's did. Mrs. Kingsward drew another long fluttering sigh before she got up reluctantly in obedience to her maid, who came in with that other white gown, not unlike Bee's, over her arm, to dress her mistress. She would have liked to lie still a little longer, to have finished the book she was reading, to have thought over the situation—anything, indeed, to justify her in keeping still upon the couch and being lazy, as she called it. Poor little mother! She had not been lazy, nor had the chance of being lazy much in her life. She had not begun to guess why it was she liked it so much now.

CHAPTER II

I have now to explain how it was that Mr. Aubrey Leigh was so interesting and so melancholy, and thus awoke the friendship and compassion, and secured the ministrations of the Kingsward family. He was in deep mourning, for though he was only eight-and-twenty he was already a widower, and bereaved beside of his only child. Poor young man! He had married with every appearance of happiness and prosperity, but his wife had died at the end of the first year, leaving him with a baby on his inexperienced hands. He was a young man full of feeling, and, contrary to the advice of all his friends, he had shut himself up in his house in the country and dedicated himself to his child. Dedicated himself to a baby two months old!

There was nobody who did not condemn this unnecessary self-sacrifice. He should have gone away; he should have left the child in the hands of its excellent nurse, under the supervision of that charming person who had been such a devoted nurse to dear Mrs. Leigh, and whom the desolate young widower had not the courage to send away from his house. Her presence there was a double reason, people said, why he should have gone away. For though his sorrow and trouble was so great that nobody for a moment supposed that he had any idea of such a thing, yet the presence of a lady, and of a lady still called by courtesy a young lady, though older than himself, and who could not be treated like a servant in his house, was embarrassing and not very seemly, everybody said. Suggestions were made to her that she should go away, but then she answered that she had nowhere to go to, and that she had promised to dear Amy never to forsake her child. The country ladies about who took an interest in the young man thought it was "just like" dear Amy, who had always been a rather silly young woman, to exact such a promise, but that Miss Lance would be quite justified in not keeping it, seeing the child had plenty of people to look after her—her grandmother within reach and her father dedicating himself to her.

Miss Lance, however, did not see her duty in the same way; indeed, after the poor little child died—and there was no doubt she had been invaluable during its illness, and devoted herself to it as she had done to its mother—she stayed on still at Leigh Court, though now at last poor Aubrey was persuaded to go away. The mind of the county was relieved beyond description when at last he departed on his travels. These good people did not at all want to get up any scandal in their midst. They did not very much blame Miss Lance for declining to give up a comfortable home. They only felt it was dreadfully awkward and that something should be done about it, though nobody knew what to do. He had left home nearly six months before he appeared at the Baths with that letter to Mrs. Kingsward in his pocket, and the change and the travel had done him good.

A young man of twenty-eight cannot go mourning all the days of his life for a baby of eight months old, and he had already begun to "get over" the death of his wife before the second event occurred. This troublous beginning of his life had left him very sad, with something of the feeling of a victim, far more badly treated than most in the beginning of his career. But this is not like real grief, which holds a man's heart with a grip of steel. And he was in the stage when a man is ready to be consoled when Bee's blue eyes first flashed upon him. The Kingswards had received him in these circumstances with more—abandon—than they would have done in any other. He was so melancholy; his confidences, when he began to make them, were so touching; his waking up to interest and happiness so delightful to see. And thus, before anyone had thoroughly realized it, the deed was done. They knew nothing about Miss Lance—as how should they?—and what could she have had to do with it if they had known?

So there really was nothing but that doubt of Colonel Kingsward's approval to alloy the pleasure of the party, and it was only Mrs. Kingsward who thought of it. Charlie pooh-poohed the idea altogether. "I think I should know my father better than anyone," the young man said, with much scorn of his mother's hesitation. He was very fond and very proud of his mother, but felt that as a man himself, he probably understood papa better than the ladies could. "Of course he will approve; why shouldn't he approve? Leigh is a very decent fellow, though I don't think all the world of him, as you girls do. Papa, of course, knew exactly what sort of a fellow he was; a little too quiet—not Bee's sort at all. No, you may clamour as you like, but he's not in the least Bee's sort—"

"I'm supposed to prefer a noisy trooper, I believe," said Bee.

"Well, I should have said that was more like it—but mind you, the governor would never have sent us out a man here who was not good enough for anything. Oh, I understand the old boy!"

"Charlie, how dare you?" cried his mother; but the horror was modified by a laugh, for anything more unlike an old boy than Colonel Kingsward it would not have been very easy to conceive.

"Well, mamma, you wouldn't have me call him my honoured father, would you?" the young man said. He was at Oxford, and he thought himself on the whole not only by far the most solid and serious member of the present party, but on the whole rather more experienced in the world than the gentleman whom in the bosom of the family he still condescended to call "papa."

As for little Betty, who up to this time had been Bee's shadow, and who had not yet begun to feel herself—de trop—, she, no more than her sister, was moved by any of these cares. She was wholly occupied in studying the new thing which had suddenly started into being before her eyes. Betty was of opinion that it was entirely got up for her amusement and instruction. When she and Bee were alone, she never ceased in her interrogatory. "Oh, Bee, when did you first begin to think about him like that? Oh, Bee, how did you first find out that he was thinking about you? Oh, Bee, don't you mind that he was once in love before?" Such were the questions that poured in an incessant stream into Bee's ears. That young lady was equal to them all, and she was not unwilling to let her sister share more or less in the new enlightenment that had come to herself.

"When did I first begin to think of him?" she said. "Oh, Betty, the first minute I saw him coming through the garden with Charlie to speak to mamma! There were all those horrid men about, you remember, in those gaudy uniforms, and their swords and spurs, and so forth—such dreadful bad taste in foreigners always to be in uniform—"

"But, Bee," cried Betty, "why, I've heard you say—"

"Oh, never mind what you've heard me say! I've been silly, I suppose, in my day, like almost everybody. Aubrey says he cannot think how they can live, always done up in those hot, stiff clothes—none of the ease of Englishmen about them."

"Papa says they are such soldier-like men," says little Betty, who had not been converted from the—regime—of the officers, like Bee.

"Oh, well, papa—he is an officer himself, but he never wears his uniform when he can help it, you know."

"Well," said Betty, "you may say what you like—for my part, I do love a nice uniform. I don't want ever again to dance with a man in a black coat. But Bee, you're too bad—you won't say a word, and I want so to know how it all came about. What put it into your head? And what did you say to one another? And was it he that began first—or was it you?"

"You little dreadful thing," said Bee; "how could a girl ever begin? It shows how little you know! Of course he began; but we didn't begin at all," she said, after a pause, "it just came—all in a moment when I wasn't thinking, and neither was he."

"Do you mean to say that he didn't intend to propose to you?" said Betty, growing pale.

"Oh!" said Bee, impatient, "as if proposing was all! Do you think he just came out with it point blank—'Miss Kingsward, will you marry me?'"

"Well," said Betty: "what did he say then if he didn't say that?"

"Oh, you little goose!" said Bee.

"I am sure if he had said 'Oh, you little goose' to me," said Betty, "I should never have spoken a word to him again."

"It is no use talking to little girls," said Bee, with a sigh. "You don't understand; and, to be sure, how could you understand—at your age and all?"

"Age!" said Betty, indignant, "there is but fifteen months between us, and I've always done everything with you. We've always had on new things together, and gone to the same places and everything. It is you that are very unkind now you have got engaged; and I do believe you like this big horrid man better than me."

"Oh, you little goose!" said Bee, again.

"No, it isn't a big but a little, horrid man. I made a mistake," said Betty, "not like Captain Kreutzner that you used to like so much. It's small people you care for now; not your own nice people like me and mamma, but a man that you had never heard the name of when you first came here, and now you quote and praise him, and make the most ridiculous fuss about him, even to Charlie, who is far nicer-looking!—and won't even tell your sister what he says!"

This argument came to so high a tone that mamma called out from her room to know what was amiss. "It does not become you girls to carry on your old scuffles and quarrels," she said, "now that one of you, at least, is so grown up and about to take upon herself the responsibilities of life."

"Is Aubrey a responsibility?" Betty whispered in her sister's ears.

"Oh, you little silly thing!" Bee replied; and presently Mrs. Kingsward's maid came in to say that Mr. Leigh was in the sitting-room, and would Miss Bee go to him as her mistress was not ready; for this was the little fiction that was kept up in those days before Colonel Kingsward's letter had been received. It will be seen, however, that it was but a fiction, and that as a matter of fact there was very little restraint put on the young people's intercourse. "You must not consider that anything is settled; you must not think there's any engagement," Mrs. Kingsward had said. "Indeed, indeed, I cannot take upon me to sanction anything till I hear from her papa." But virtually they met as much as they liked, and even indulged in little talks apart, and meetings by themselves, before Mrs. Kingsward was ready; so that as a matter of fact this restriction did very little harm.

And in due time Colonel Kingsward's letter was received, and it was not unfavourable. The Colonel said that, on the whole, he should have preferred it had Mr. Leigh waited till they had all returned home. It would have been a seemly forbearance, and saved Mrs. Kingsward a great deal of anxiety; but as matters stood and as his dear wife approved, and he heard nothing but good of Mr. Leigh, he would not withdraw the provisional consent which she seemed to have given. "It will be expedient in the circumstances that you should all return home as soon as possible, that I may go into matters with the young man," the Colonel added in that part of his letter which was not intended to be read to Aubrey Leigh. And he added, as Bee had prophesied, "You might have been sure that I should not introduce a young man to my family, and to yourself, my dear, without ascertaining previously," etc., etc., just as Bee had said. He added, "Of course I never contemplated anything of this sort: but one can never tell what may happen when young people are thrown together. The property is a good one, and the young man unexceptionable, from all I can hear." Then Mrs. Kingsward's mind was set at ease. It seemed to Bee that her father might have said something on the subject of her happiness, and acknowledged Aubrey to be something more than an unexceptionable young man. It was inconceivable, she thought to herself, how cool people are when they come to that age. The property good, and the young man unexceptionable—was that all? Did papa take no more interest than that? But at all events the engagement was now quite permitted and acknowledged, and they might walk out together all day, and dance together all night, without a word said; for which Bee forgave and instantly forgot—it was really of so little importance—the coolness of papa.

Mrs. Kingsward's "cure" was over, and by this time most people were leaving the Bath. Our party made their preparations for leaving too, in the pleasantest way. It was not to be at all a rapid journey, which would not have been good for Mrs. Kingsward. They were to make their way at leisure from one beautiful old city to another across the breadth of Germany, staying a day here and a day there, travelling for the most part in a large, old-fashioned carriage, such as was the custom then, with a wide-hooded seat in front, like the—banquette—of a French diligence, in which two people could be extremely happy, seeing the scenery much better than those inside could do, or perhaps not seeing the scenery at all, but occupying each other quite as agreeably with the endless talk of lovers, which is not interesting to anybody but themselves. Before they set out upon this journey, however, which was to hold so great a place in Bee's life, a little incident occurred to her which did not appear to be of very much consequence, but which made some impression on her mind at the time, and vaguely appeared afterwards to throw light on various other events. The German Bath at which the little story of her love took place is surrounded with woods—woods of a kind that are never seen anywhere else, though they are the special feature of German Baths. They are chiefly composed of fir trees, and they are arranged upon the most strictly mathematical principles, with that precision which is dear to the German mind, row upon row standing close together, as if they had been stuck in so at their present height, with so many cubit feet of air to each, as in the London lodging-houses. They are traversed by broad roads, with benches at intervals, and at each corner there is a wooden board on which is painted indications how to find the nearest—restauration—where beer is to be had, and the veal of the country—for the German, in his hours of ease and amusement, has continual occasion to be "restored."

Bee had gone out early in the morning to make a little sketch of an opening in the trees through which a village spire was visible. There were not many points for the artist in landscape, especially one of such moderate powers as Bee, and she was very anxious to finish this to present it, I need scarcely say, to Aubrey, as a memento of the place. Probably there was some other sentimental reason—such as that they had first spoken words of special meaning there, or had first exchanged looks that were of importance in their idyll, or some other incident of equal weight. She was seated on one of the benches, with her little colour box and bottle of water, giving the finishing touches to her sketch. Sooth to say, Bee was no great performer, and the ranks of the dark trees standing arithmetically apart to permit of that little glimpse of distance, were too much for her. They looked in her sketch like two dark green precipices rather than like trees, and had come to a very difficult point, when a lady coming along by one of the side walks, round the corner past the—restauration—, suddenly sat down by Bee's side and startled her a little. She was not a girl who was easily frightened, but the suddenness of the apparition out of the silent morning when she had thought nobody was in sight was a little startling and made her hand shake.

"I hope I am not intruding upon you," the lady said.

"Oh, no!" said Bee, looking up with her bright face. She was as fresh as the morning in her broad Leghorn hat with the blue ribbon, and her eyes that danced and sparkled. The stranger by her side was much older than Bee. She was a handsome woman; dark, with fine eyes, too, a sidelong look in them, and a curious half smile which was like La Gioconda, that famous picture Bee had seen in the Louvre, as we all have. She thought of La Gioconda at once, when she looked up into the lady's face. She was entirely dressed in black, and there could not have been found anywhere a more perfect contrast to Bee.

They got into conversation quite easily, for Bee was a girl who loved to talk. The lady gave her several hints about her little picture which Bee knew enough to know were dictated by superior knowledge, and then they got talking quite naturally about the place and the people who were there. After they had discussed the society and the number of English people at the Bath, and Bee had disclosed the hotel at which she was staying, and many details of her innocent life, which she was not at all conscious of disclosing—the stranger began to inquire about various people. It was not by any means at once that she introduced the name of Leigh; not indeed till she had been over the Reynoldses, and the Gainsboroughs, and the Collinses, under Bee's exultant guidance and fine power of narrative; then she said tentatively, that there was she believed, at one of the hotels, a family of Leighs.

"Oh!" cried Bee, her countenance flushing over with a sudden brilliant delightful blush, which seemed to envelop her from top to toe. She had been looking up into her companion's face so that the stranger got the full benefit of this sudden resplendent change of colour. She then turned very demurely to her sketch, and said meekly, "I don't know any family, but there is a Mr. Leigh at our hotel."

"Oh," said the lady, but in a very different tone from Bee's startled "oh!" She said it coldly, as if recording a fact. "I thought," she said, "it was the Leighs of Hurstleigh, friends of mine. I may have been deceived by seeing the name in the lists."

"But I think, indeed I am sure, that Mr. Aubrey Leigh is connected with the Leighs of Hurstleigh," Bee said.

"Oh, a young man, a widower, an inconsolable; I think I remember hearing of him. Is that the man?"

"I don't know if he is an inconsolable," cried Bee, with a quick movement of anger and then she thought how foolish that was, for of course a stranger like this could have no unkind meaning. She added with great gravity, "It is quite true that he has been married before."

Poor little Bee, she was not at all aware how she was betraying herself. She was more vexed and indignant than words can say, when the woman (who after all could not be a lady) burst into a laugh. "Oh! I think I can see how matters stand with Aubrey Leigh," this impertinent intruder cried.

CHAPTER III

It was just two days after the interview in the wood described above, that the Kingsward party got under weigh for home, accompanied, I need not say, by Aubrey Leigh. Bee had not told him of that chance meeting, restrained I do not know by what indefinite feeling that he would not care to hear of it, and also by the sensation that she had as good as told the lady, who was so disagreeable and impertinent as to laugh, what change had taken place in Aubrey's sentiments, and what she had herself to do with that change. It was so silly, oh, so silly of her, and yet she had said nothing, or next to nothing. And there was no reason why she should not have said whatever she pleased, now that the engagement was fully acknowledged and known; indeed, if that woman were in any society at all, she must have heard of it, seeing that, as Bee was aware, not without pleasure, it had afforded a very agreeable diversion to the floating community, a pleasant episode in the tittle-tattle of the gardens and the wells. Bee had no absurd objection to being talked of. She knew that in her condition of life, which was so entirely satisfactory as a condition, everything that concerned a family was talked over and universally known. It was a thing inevitable to a certain position, and a due homage of society to its members. But somehow she did not mention it to Aubrey, nor, indeed, to anyone, which was a very unusual amount of reticence. She did not even give him the sketch, though it was finished. She had been quite grateful for that person's hints at the time, and eagerly had taken advantage of them to improve her drawing; but it seemed to her, when she looked at it now, that it was not her own at all, that the other hand was so visible in it that it would be almost dishonest to call it hers. This, of course, was wholly fantastic, for even supposing that person to have given valuable hints, she had never touched the sketch, and Bee alone had carried them out. But, anyhow, her heart sickened at it, and she thrust it away at the very bottom of the box that Moulsey was packing. She had no desire to see the horrid thing again.

In a day or two, however, Bee had altogether forgotten that interview in the wood. She had so many things to occupy her mind. There were few railways in those days, and the party had a long way to travel before they came to Cologne, where that method of travelling began. They all felt that common life would re-commence there and their delightful wandering would be over. In the meantime, there was a long interval of pleasure before them. The early breakfast at the hotel in the first hours of the autumnal morning, the fun of packing everyone away in the big coach, the books to be brought out to fill up corners, both of time and space, and "Murray" then alone in his glory, with no competitive American, no Badæker, no Joanne, to share his reign—spread out open at the right place, so that mamma inside should be able to lay her finger at once upon any village or castle that struck her—and above all the contrivances to be carried out for securing the—banquette—, as Bee said, for "ourselves," made a lively beginning. Charlie and Betty sometimes managed to secure this favourite place if the attention of the others flagged for a moment, and though mamma generally interposed with a nod or a whisper to restore it to the privileged pair, sometimes she was mischievous too, and consented to their deprivation, and desired them for once to keep her company inside. She generally, however, repented of this before the day was over, and begged that their favourite seat might be restored to them.

"For they are really no fun at all," the poor lady said. "I might as well have two images from Madame Tussaud's."

"It had been a little hard upon Aubrey at the moment of their departure to find half the garrison round the carriage, and bouquets enough to fill a separate vehicle thrust into every corner, the homage of those warriors to the gracious ladies. He had been very cross, and had made a great exhibition of himself, especially when Captain Kreutzner's faggot of forget-me-nots, tied with a ribbon like that on Bee's hat, had been presented with indescribable looks. What did the fellow mean by bringing forget-me-nots? He wanted to pitch it out of the window as soon as they were fairly started.

"What an idiotic custom!" he cried. "What do the fools think you want with such loads of flowers when you are starting on a journey?"

"Why, it is just then you do want them," cried Betty, who had a dozen or so to her own share, "to smell sweet and show us how much our friends think of us."

"They will not smell sweet very long, and then what will your friends think of you?" said the angry lover.

Was it possible that Bee was detaching a little knot of the blue flowers to put in her waistband? Bee, Bee! his own property, who had no right so much as to look at another man's flowers! And what did she do, seeing the cloud upon his face, but arrange another little bouquet, which, with her sweetest smile— the little coquette—she endeavoured to put into his, Aubrey's, button-hole! He snatched them out of her hand in a sort of fury. "Do you want me never to forget that heavy brute of a German?" he cried, in his indignation. "You may put him near your heart, but I should like to kick him!" These very natural sentiments made Bee laugh—which was cruel: but then poor Captain Kreutzner had been blotted out of her life some time ago, and knew his fate, and had really no right whatever to present her with these particular flowers. His lovely bouquet with its blue ribbon was given to a girl in the first village, and awakened the still more furious jealousy of another swain who was less easily appeased than Aubrey; but this—ricochet—was not thought of by the first and principal pair.

There was not perhaps so many remarkable features in that journey as if it had been through Italy. There were great plains to traverse, where the chief sights were cottages and farmhouses, women going by with great loads of freshly cut grass full of flowers on their heads, fodder for the home-dwelling cows—or men carrying their hops clinging to the pole, to be picked at home, or long straggling branches of the tobacco plant; and in the evening the postillion would whip up his horses, and Charlie in the— banquette—, or John, the manservant, in the rumble, would tootle upon a horn which the former had acquired clandestinely before the party set out—as they dashed through a village or little town with lighted windows, affording them many a flying peep of the domestic life of those tranquil places. And in the middle of the day they stopped to rest somewhere, where the invariable veal was to be found at some Guest-house a little better than the ordinary, where perhaps a bigger village stood with all its high peaked stream: and at night rattled into an old walled town with shadowy high houses which belonged to the fourteenth century, and had not changed a whit since that time. There they stayed a day or two, varying the confinement of the coach by a course through everything that was to be seen, setting out in a party through the roughly-paved streets, but parting company before long, so that Aubrey and Bee would find themselves alone in the shelter of a church or in an insignificant corner by the walls, while the others pursued their sightseeing conscientiously.

"As for me, what I like is the general aspect," said Bee, with an air of superiority. "I don't care to poke into every corner, and Aubrey knows the history, which is the chief thing."

"Are they talking all the time of the history?" said Betty, overawed.

But this perhaps, was not the opinion of Charlie and mamma. No, they did not care very much for the history. People are bad travellers in that stage of life. They are too much interested in their own history. They went about like a pair of Philistines through all these ancient streets, talking of nothing but the things of to-day. The most serious part of their talk was about the home in the depths of England in which they were henceforth to spend their lives. Aubrey had ideas about re-furnishing—about making everything new. It would be impossible to tell the reader how bad was the taste of the time, and with what terrible articles of furniture he proposed to replace the spindle legs and marquetry of his grandfathers. But then these things were the fashion, and supposed to be the best things of the time. To hear them talking of sofas and curtains, and of the colour for the boudoir and the hangings of the drawing-room in the midst of all those graceful old places, was inconceivable. You would have said the stupidest, unimpressionable pair, talking of ugly modern English furniture, when they should have been noting the old world of Nuremberg—the unchanging mediæval city. But you must remember that the furniture was only a symbol of their love and their new life, and all the blessedness of being together, and the endless delights of every day. The sofas and the curtains meant the—Vita Nuova—, and the refurnishing of the old house a beautiful fabric of all the honour and the joy of life.

Then came the great river, and the progress down its shining stream, and between those beautiful banks, where again they made several pauses to enjoy the scenery. The Rhine is not now the river it was then. It was still the great river of romance in those days—Byron had been there, and the young people remembered Roland and his tower, with his love in the white convent opposite, and felt a shudder at the thought of the Lorelei as they floated under the high and gloomy bank. I doubt, however, whether the lovers thought much even of these things. They were busy just now about the gardens, which Bee was fully minded to remodel and fill with everything that was new and delightful in the way of flowers.

"I shall have masses of colour about the terrace, and every spot covered. I wonder which you like best, majolica vases or rustic baskets?" Bee was saying, when her mother called her to point out the Platz and Bishop Hatto's tower.

"Oh, yes, mamma, it's very pretty. But you like clematis, Aubrey, for the balustrade—to wind in and out of the pillars. Yes, yes, I can see it well enough. I like every kind of clematis, even the common one, the traveller's joy—and it would hang down, you know, over that old bit of wall you told me of. Do go forward, Aubrey, and let them see you are taking an interest. I do see it all quite well, and it is very romantic, and we are quite enjoying it I can assure you, mamma."

This was how they made their way down stream; in the moonlight nights they ceased to talk of practical matters, and went back to the history of their loves.

"Do you remember, Bee, that first time in the wood—?"

"Oh, Aubrey, don't you recollect that drive coming back in the dark—before I knew—?"

"But you always did know from the very beginning, Bee?"

"Well, perhaps I suspected—and used to think—"

"You darling, what did you think?—and did you really care—as early as that?"

They went on like this whatever happened outside, giving a careless glance at the heights, at the towers, at the robbers' castle above and the little villages below; not so much as looking at them, and yet remembering them ever after, enclosing the flow of their young lives, as it were, in that strong flowing of the Rhine, noting nothing and yet seeing everything with the double sight which people possess at the highest moment and crisis of their career. They came at length to Cologne, where this enchanted voyage was more or less to end. To be sure, they were still to be together; but only in the railway, with all the others round them, hearing more or less what they said. They said good-bye to the Rhine with a little sentiment, a delightful little sadness full of pleasure.

"Shall we ever be so happy again?" said Bee, with a sigh.

"Oh, yes, my sweet, a hundred times, and happier, and happier," said the young man; and thus they were assured it was to be.

I don't think any of them ever forgot that arrival at Cologne. They came into sight of the town just in the evening, when the last glow of sunset was still burning upon the great river, but lights beginning to show in the windows, and glimmering reflected in the water. The Cathedral was not completed then, and a crane, like some strange weird animal stood out against the sky upon the top of the tower. The hotel to which they were going had a covered terrace upon the river with lights gleaming through the green leaves. They decided they would have their table there, and dine with all that darkling panorama before their eyes through the veil of the foliage, the glowing water, the boats moving and passing, with now and then a raft coming down from the upper stream, and the bridge of boats opening to give passage to a fuming fretting steamboat. Aubrey and Bee went hand in hand up the steps; nobody noticed in the half dark how close they were together. They parted with a close pressure of warm hands.

"Don't be long, darling," he said, as they parted, only for a moment, only to prepare a little for the evening, to slip into a fresh dress, to take out a new ribbon, to make one's youthful self as fair as such unnecessary adjuncts permitted.

But what did Aubrey care for a new ribbon? The only blue he thought of was that in Bee's eyes.

I do not think she was more than ten minutes over these little changes. She dressed like a flash of lightning, Betty said, who could not find her own things half so quickly, Moulsey being occupied with mamma. Such a short moment not worth counting, and yet enough, more than enough, to change a whole life!

Bee ran down as light as air to the sitting-room which had been engaged for the party. She felt sure that Aubrey would hurry, too, so as to have a word before dinner, before the rest were ready—as if the whole day had not been one long word, running through everything. She came lightly to the door of the room in her fresh frock and her blue ribbons, walking on air, knowing no shadow of any obstacle before her or cloud upon the joyful triumphant sky. She did not even hear the sound of the subdued voices, her faint little sob, strangest of all sounds at such a moment, which seemed to come out to meet her as she opened the door. Bee opened it wondering only if Aubrey were there, thinking of some jibe to address to him about the length of time men took to their toilettes, if she happened to be ready first.

She was very much startled by what she saw. Her mother, still in her travelling dress, sat by the table with a letter open in her hands. She had not made any preparation for dinner—she, usually so dainty, so anxious to get rid of the cloaks and of the soils of the journey. She had taken off her hat, which lay on the table, but was still enveloped in the shawl which she had put on to keep off the evening chills. As for Aubrey, he was exactly as he had been when they parted with him, except that all the light had gone out of his face. He was very pale, and he, too, had a letter in his hand. He uttered a stifled exclamation when he saw Bee at the door, and, lifting his arms as though in protest against something intolerable, walked away to the other end of the room.

"Oh, Bee," said Mrs. Kingsward, "Oh, go away, my dear, go away! I mean—get something to eat, you and Charlie, and Betty, and then get to bed. Get to bed! I am too tired to take anything, and I am going upstairs at once."

"I thought you had been upstairs, mamma, half-an-hour ago. What is the matter? You look like a ghost, and so does Aubrey. Has anything happened? Mamma, you won't look at me, and Aubrey turns his back. What have I done? Is it anything about me?"

"What nonsense, child!" said Mrs. Kingsward, with a pretence at a smile. "What could you have to do with it? We have both—Mr. Leigh and myself—found letters, and we are busy reading them. I am sure the dinner must be served. We ordered it in the balcony, don't you remember? Run away and make Charlie and Betty sit down at once. I am too tired. Moulsey will run down in a little and get something for me."

"Mamma," said Bee, "you cannot make up a story. Something has happened, I am sure of it; and it is something about me."

"Nonsense, child! Go away and have your dinner. I would come if I could. Don't you see what a budget of letters I have got? And some of them I must answer to-night."

"Have you letters, too, Aubrey?" said Bee, in her amazement, standing still as she had paused, arrested by the sight of them, just within the door.

"Bee, I must beg you will not put any questions; go and do what I tell you; your brother and sister will be coming downstairs. Yes, of course, you can see that Mr. Leigh has his letters to read as well as I."

"Mr. Leigh! I wonder if we have all gone mad, or what is the matter? Aubrey! tell me—you, at least, if mamma won't. You must have had a quarrel. Mamma, why do you call him Mr. Leigh?"

"Oh, for goodness sake, Bee, go away."

"I am not going away," cried the girl. "You have had a quarrel about something. Come, mamma, you must not quarrel with Aubrey—if he has done something wrong or said something silly, I will answer for him, he never intended it. Aubrey, what do you mean, sir, turning your back both on mamma and me? Come here, quick, and ask her pardon, and say you will never do it again."

Poor little Bee's heart was fluttering, but she would not allow herself to believe there was anything really wrong. She went close up to her mother and stood by her, with a hand upon her shoulder. "Aubrey!" she said, "never mind if you are wrong or not, come and beg mamma's pardon, and she will forgive you. There must not—there must not—oh, it is too ridiculous!—be anything wrong between mamma and you. Aubrey!"

He turned round slowly and faced them both with a face so pale that Bee stopped short with a gasp, and could not say a word more. Mrs. Kingsward had buried her face in her hands. Bee looked from one to the other with a dismay which she could not explain to herself. "Oh, what is the matter? What is the matter?" she said.

There was no merry dinner that night in the verandah of the hotel under the clinging wreaths of green. Mrs. Kingsward went up to her room still with her heavy shawl about her shoulders which she had forgotten, though it added something to her discomfort—followed by Bee, pale and rigid, offering no help, following her mother like an angry shadow. Charlie and Betty met them on the stairs and stood aside in consternation, unable to conceive what had happened. Mrs. Kingsward gave them a sort of troubled smile and said: "Get your dinner, dears; don't wait for us. I am too tired to come down to-night."

"But, mamma—" they both began in remonstrance.

"Go down and get your dinner," said Mrs. Kingsward, peremptorily.

As for Bee, she did not look at them at all. Her eyes were fierce with some sentiment which Betty could not divine, and angry, blazing, as if they might have set light to the hotel.

Little Betty pressed against Charlie's side as they went down, startled and alarmed. "Bee has had a quarrel with mamma," she whispered, in tones of awe.

"That's impossible," said Charlie.

"Oh, no, it's not impossible. There was once—"

It comforted them both a little in the awful circumstances that such a thing had perhaps happened before. They went very silently and much cast down to that table in the verandah, whither obsequious waiters beckoned them, and contemplated with dismay all the plates laid, all the glitter of the lamps and the glasses.

"I suppose we must not wait for them as they said so," said Charlie, sitting down in his place at the bottom of the table. "Tell Mr. Leigh—that is the other gentleman—that we are ready."

"The other gentleman, sir," said the waiter, who was the pride of the establishment for his English, "has gone out."

"Gone out!" said Charlie. He could only stare at Betty and she at him, not knowing what to think.

"He has had his letters, too, sir," said the waiter in a significant tone.

His letters! What could that have to do with it? Charlie also had had his letters, one of them a bill which he did not view with any satisfaction; but even at twenty-one a man already learns to disguise his feelings, and sits down to dinner cheerfully though he has received a bill by the post. Charlie's mind at first could not perceive any connection between Bee's withdrawal upstairs and Aubrey's disappearance. It was Betty who suggested, sitting down very close to him, that it looked as if Aubrey and Bee had quarrelled too.

"Perhaps that is what it is," she said, as if she had found out a satisfactory reason. "Lovers always quarrel; and mamma will have taken Aubrey's part, and Bee will be so angry, and feel as if she could never forgive him. There, that is what it must be."

"A man may quarrel with his sweetheart," said Charlie, severely, "but he needn't spoil other people's dinner for that;" however, they comforted themselves that this was the most likely explanation, and that all would come right in the morning. And they were very young and hungry, having eaten nothing since the veal at one o'clock. And these two made on the whole a very satisfactory meal.

The scene upstairs was very different. Mrs. Kingsward sent Moulsey away on pretence of getting her some tea, and then turned to her daughter who stood by the dressing-table and stared blankly, without seeing anything, into those mysterious depths of the glass which are so suggestive to people in trouble. She said, faintly, "Bee, I would so much rather you would not ask me any more questions to-night."

"That is," said Bee, "you would like to send me away to be miserable by myself without even knowing what it is, while you will take your sleeping draught and forget it. How can you be so selfish, mamma? And you have made my Aubrey join in the conspiracy against me—my Aubrey who belongs to me as papa does to you. If you are against us it is all very well, though I can't imagine why you should be against us—but at least you need not interfere between Aubrey and me."

"Oh, my dear child, my poor darling!" said Mrs. Kingsward, wringing her hands.

"It is all very well to call me your poor child, when it is you that are making me poor," said Bee.

She kept moving a little, first on one foot then on the other, but always gazing into the glass which presented the image of an excited girl, very pale, but lit up with a sort of blaze of indignation, and unable to keep still. It was not that girl's face, however, that Bee was gazing at, but at the dim world of space beyond in which there were faint far-away reflections of the light and the world. "And if you think you will get rid of me like this, and hang me up till to-morrow without knowing what it is, you are mistaken, mamma. I will not leave you until you have told me. What is it? What has papa got in his head? What does he say in that horrid—horrid letter? I wish I had known when I gave it to you I should have thrown it into the river instead of ever letting it come into your hands."

"Bee, you must know that this passion is very wrong and very improper. You ought not to face me like that, and demand an answer. I am your mother," said Mrs. Kingsward, but with a falter which was all unlike that assumption of authority, "and I have no need to tell you anything more than I think is for your good."

"Ah! I know where that comes from," cried Bee; "that's papa's thunder! that's what he has told you to say! You don't believe, yourself, that you have a right to hang up a poor girl over some dreadful, dreadful abyss, when she was so happy and never suspected anything." Here Bee's voice faltered for a moment, but she quickly recovered herself. "And to drag her away from the one person that could support her, and to cut the ground from under her feet, and never to tell her what it means!"

It was at this point that Moulsey, with a little discreet cough to herald her approach, came into the room, bearing a tray with tea, and a little cover from which came a faint but agreeable odour. Mrs. Kingsward was in great trouble about her child, but she was much exhausted and in want of physical support, and it did seem to her hard that she might not be permitted to eat the smallest of cutlets before embarking on a scene such as she knew this would be. Oh, why didn't papa come and say it himself, when there was so much that was dreadful to say?

"Shall I fetch something for Miss Bee, too?" said Moulsey. "It ain't a good thing for a young creature to go without her dinner. If she's not going down, ma'am, as would be much the best, I'll just run and fetch a little something for Miss Bee too."

"Indeed, indeed, Bee, Moulsey is right. Think how miserable the others will feel all alone, and thinking something has happened. Do go down, darling, and strengthen yourself with a little food, and take a glass of wine just for once to please me. And after that you shall be told everything—all that I know."

Bee grew paler and paler, standing there before the glass, and her eyes blazed more and more. "It is as bad as that, then!" she said under her breath to herself, and then went away from where she was standing to the further end of the room. "I shall wait here, mamma, till you have had your tea. I know you want it. Oh, go away Moulsey! Let me alone! No, you shall not bring me anything! or, if you do, I will throw it out of the window," she said, stamping her foot. The dark end of the room seemed suddenly lighted up by a sort of aurora borealis, with the fire of poor Bee's burning eyes and the flashes here and there of her white frock—oh, poor white frock! put on in the sunshine of life and happiness to please her love, and now turned into a sort of sacrificial robe.

"Take it away, Moulsey; I can't eat anything—I can't, indeed—no more than Miss Bee—"

"But you must, ma'am," said Moulsey. "Miss Bee's young; she's had nothing to drain away her strength. But it's far different with you, after all your family and so weak as you are. If Miss Bee were a real good girl, as I always thought her, she'd go away and get something herself just for her poor mamma's sake, and leave you alone for a moment to get a little peace and rest."

"There is no rest for me," murmured the poor lady. "Oh, papa, papa, why didn't you come and tell them yourself?"

These piteous tones went to Bee's heart. They moved her half with contempt, half with compassion—with something of that high indignant toleration of weakness which is one kind of pity. If mamma could eat and drink at such a moment, why shouldn't she be left to do it? The girl started up and left the room in the quick flashing impulse of her passion. She walked up and down in the corridor outside, her arms folded over her high-beating, tumultuous heart. Yes, no doubt she was going to be miserable, all her happiness was cut down and withered away, but in her present passionate impulse of resistance and gathering of all her forces to resist the catastrophe, which she did not understand, it could scarcely be said that she was wretched yet. What was it—what was it? she was saying to herself. It might still be something that would pass away, which would be overcome by the determined, impassioned stand against it, which Bee felt that it was in her to make. The thing that was worst of all, that stole away her courage, was that Aubrey had failed her. He should have been there by her side whatever happened. He ought not to have abandoned her. No doubt he thought it was more delicate, more honourable, more something or other; and that it was his duty to leave her to brave it alone. It must have been one of those high-flown notions of honour that men have. Honour! to leave a girl to fight for herself and him, alone—but, no doubt, that was what had seemed right in his eyes. Bee walked up and down in the half-lighted passage, sometimes almost pushing against someone going up or down, waiters or chambermaids or surprised guests, who looked after her when she had passed; but she did not take any notice of them, and she heard as she passed her mother's door little sounds of tea-cups and dishes, and

Moulsey's voice saying "A little more," and her mother's faint replies. Poor mamma! After all, what ever it was, it could not be her affair as it was Bee's. She would be unhappy about it, but not all unhappy. She had the others, who were all right. She had papa. It would not shatter her to pieces even if one of the children was to be shipwrecked. It was the shipwrecked one only who would be broken to pieces. For the first time in her life Bee felt the poignant sensation, the jealous pride, the high, desolate satisfaction of suffering. The others could all eat and do the ordinary things. She was elevated over all that, silent as on a Peak in Darien. She felt almost a kind of dreadful pleasure in the situation, smiling to herself at the sounds of her mother's little meal. She could dine while Bee was miserable. They could all dine—Charlie (which was natural), Betty, even Aubrey. She had no doubt that he, too, must be seated, feeling as a man does that dinner must go on whatever happens, at the table downstairs.

After a while, which seemed a long time to Bee, Moulsey came out with the tray. She was startled, and exclaimed under her breath at the appearance of the girl walking up and down in the corridor: "I did think you would have had the sense to go and join the others, Miss Bee." Bee was too much uplifted, too distant on her high pinnacle of martyrdom, to make any reply, but when Moulsey ventured to add a word of advice, to the effect that she must be careful of her mamma and not weary her with questions and she so tired and so weak, the girl flashed forth all her heart of indignation. "She has eaten her cutlet, it appears," cried Bee. "I should think she may answer my questions."

"Oh!" cried the maid, who had the privileges of an old servant, "you have got a heart without pity. You are just like your papa!"

Bee swept past her into the room, where poor Mrs. Kingsward, who after all had eaten but a morsel, sat lying back in an easy chair awaiting the dreadful conflict which she knew was coming. Poor lady, she had lost all her brightness, that pretty grace of the young mother among her grown up children, which prompted so many compliments. She lay back in her easy chair, feeling as she said "any age"—as old as any woman on the edge of the grave, not knowing how she was to bear the onslaught that was coming, and how she was to say what had to be said. He had borne it far better than Bee—poor Aubrey, poor Aubrey! whom she must not call Aubrey any more. He had not denied anything, he had fallen as it were at her feet, like a house that had been undermined and had no sound foundations, but Bee was different. Bee was a tower that had foundations—a girl that was able to stand up even to papa, and why—why had he not come to give forth his sentence in his own way?

Bee came forward flashing into the light, in that white frock which shone, and with those eyes that blazed through all the neutral tints in the room. She did not sit down, which would have been a little relief, but seized a chair and stood with her hand upon the back, leaning upon it.

"I hope, mamma," she said, pitiless, "that you liked your tea, and ate something—and that you are better now."

"Oh, Bee!" cried the poor lady; if there is one reproach more dreadful than another it is this of being able to eat when you ought to be overwhelmed with trouble." Mrs. Kingsward could scarcely keep from crying at the imputation. And Bee, I fear, knew that it was the unkindest thing that could be said.

"Now, mamma," she resumed, almost stonily, "it is time that you should tell me what has happened. We arrived here all quite happy—it is just an hour ago—" here Bee's voice shook a little, but she commanded it with an effort—"I ran up to dress for dinner, and when I came back in about ten minutes I found you and Aubrey—with your letters—looking as if you had both been dead and buried while I was away. You wouldn't answer me, and he never said a word. You had done something to him in that little time to make him turn away from me, and yet you will not tell me what it is. Here I am alone," said Bee, once more with a quiver in her voice. "Aubrey ought to be standing by me. I suppose he is having his dinner downstairs, too, and thinking no more of me. I just stand alone, nobody caring in all the world. What is the meaning of it, mamma?"

"Bee, you are very hard upon me. And poor Aubrey, he is having no dinner—of that I am sure."

"You called him Mr. Leigh downstairs."

"So I did, and so I must, and all of us; but I cannot have you speaking of him like that, poor, poor fellow; and just for this once—Oh, Bee, my darling, don't stand and look at me so! I would rather have died than say it either to him or to you. Your papa has been hearing I don't know what, and he has changed his mind about Mr. Leigh altogether, and says it must not be."

"What must not be?"

"Oh, Bee! Oh, don't take it so hard! Don't look like that! Your—your—engagement, my darling. Have patience; oh, have patience! He has heard something. Men hear things that we would never hear. And he doesn't deny it. Oh! he doesn't deny it. I had a hope that he would contradict it at once, and flare up in a rage like you, and say it wasn't true. But he doesn't deny it—poor boy, poor boy! And after that, how can I say one word to papa?"

"My engagement?" said Bee, in a hoarse voice. She had been staring at her mother as in a dream—only partially hearing, not understanding at all the rest that was said. "My engagement? He gave his consent. It was all settled. You would not allow us till the letter came, but then it was consent."

"Yes, yes, dear. That was at first. He consented at first because—and now it appears he has heard something—someone has called upon him—he has discovered—and he writes to me that it must be broken off. Oh, Bee, don't think my heart doesn't bleed for you. I think it will kill me. He says it must be broken off at once."

"Who says so?" said Bee, in her passion. "He! One would think you were speaking of God—that can say 'Yes' to-day and 'No' to-morrow, and build things up and then snatch them down. But I will not have it! I am not a doll, to be put in one position and then in another, as anybody pleases. My engagement! It is mine; it is not his."

"Bee, think; it is papa you are speaking of. Dear, I feel for you—I feel for you! but so does he. Oh, my darling, you don't know what you are saying. Do you think he would do anything to make you unhappy if he could help it—your papa, Bee, who has been so good to you all your life?"

"I do not care how good he has been. He is not good now. How will it harm him? He sits at home, and he thinks he can do as he pleases. But not with me. It is my affair more than it is his. He thinks he can break his word and it doesn't matter—but I have given my word, and it does matter. Break my engagement!" cried Bee, her young bosom swelling, the sob rising in her throat that would soon choke her voice. "It is mine and not his; and nobody in the world shall break it. You can tell him so, mamma, or I will write myself and tell him so. I am not a wax image to take any shape he pleases. Who is he? He is not God—"

"Bee—he is your father—"

"Oh, my father! Yes, I do whatever he tells me. If he says I am to fetch anything I run like a little dog. I have never been disobedient. But this—this is different. I am not a child any longer. And, mamma, not for him nor for anyone—not even for you will I take back my word."

"Bee! You make me say a great deal more than I meant to say. I thought you would have been a good child and seen that papa must know best. My poor, poor little girl, there is worse behind. Mr. Leigh, whom we all thought so much of—"

"Aubrey," Bee managed to say, though for no other word could she command her voice.

"Darling, he has deceived us. He is not what he seems. He has done, oh, so wrong—there have been things—that you ought never to hear—"

"Stop!" said Bee. She had to speak in monosyllables with her labouring breath. "Wait!—not behind his back." She rushed to the bell and rung it so wildly that both waiter and chambermaid appeared in alarm, with Moulsey rushing in calling for a doctor, and saying that her lady was going to faint. Bee pushed the woman aside and turned to the waiter, who stood anxious at the door. "Mr. Leigh!" she cried, impatiently; "the gentleman—who was with us: tell him—to come here."

"The tall young gentleman?" said the waiter.

"No—the other: tell him he is to come here—instantly—this moment."

"I beg your pardon, miss," said the man. "The other gentleman? He have been gone away this half-hour."

"Gone away!" she cried. And it seemed to Bee that the blackness of darkness closed over her and the room and everything in it. She did not faint, oh no, no such happiness—but everything grew dark, and through the dark she heard her own voice speaking—speaking, and did not know what she said.

CHAPTER V

But Aubrey had not gone away. He had gone out in the dizziness of a great downfall, scarcely knowing how to keep his feet steady as he wandered along the dark street, not knowing where he went. The landscape that had charmed them all so much—was it scarcely an hour ago?—the lamps reflected in the water; the verandah, with its wreaths of green; the brilliant yet mysterious glimmer of the moon, made his heart sink to look at them now. He strayed off into the darkest of the narrow streets, into the great gloom of the cathedral shadow, where he could see nothing but a poor light twinkling here and there, making the darkness visible. Oh! how certain it is that, however sweet they may seem, your sins will find you out! Oh! how more than certain if you have let yourself be dragged down once, only once, in a spotless life, that the one fault will be made into the central fact of your whole existence. If he had been a bad, dissipated man, it would have been only fair. But this poor young fellow was like the young man whom our Lord loved though he went away. All good things he had kept from his youth up—but once, only once, half distracted by grief, and by the desire which is so natural to escape from grief, and by infernal temptation, he had fallen—oh, there was no need to tell him how he had fallen! Had it not been the canker in his soul ever since? And now this one thing, this miserable, much-repented fault, which revolted, disgusted, horrified himself, was brought up against him as if it were the pattern upon which he had shaped his life.

And now, what was left for him but to fall down, down into the unfathomable abyss? The distracted feelings with which he had broken away from home, the horror and dismay that at once belonged to his natural grief and made the burden of it a thousand times harder to bear, all rushed back upon him, whirling him down and down to dimmer and more awful depths. He had partially healed himself in the intolerableness of his trouble by travel and change, and the arbitrary forgetfulness which comes from absence and the want of any association which could call back to him what was past; and then the touch of Bee's soft, girlish hand, the sound of her voice, had suddenly called him back into an enchanted land where everything had again become possible. He had hesitated for some time, wondering if he might dare—he who had a secret smirch upon him which nobody suspected—to avail himself of this way of salvation. The reader will think that he had not hesitated very long—poor Aubrey—seeing that the introduction, the acquaintance, the love, the engagement had all occurred within the small space of one month; but to the brooding spirit the hours of one interminable day are long enough for a chronicle. Something like the phenomena of love at first sight had occurred in the bleeding yet young heart, which had felt itself cut loose from all the best associations of life. Deliverance, recreation, the new beginning of life and all its possibilities had gleamed upon him in Bee's blue eyes. Her appearance swept away everything that was dark and ominous in his life. Did he dare to ask for her hand, to set out again to make himself a new career? He had worked at that question almost from the first day, discussing it with himself for the three weeks preceding their engagement, waking and sleeping, almost without intermission; and then in a moment he had forgotten all controversy, and let forth without intention the words that had been lying, so to speak, on the threshold of his lips—and in that moment all the clouds had been swept away. He was only eight and twenty after all—so young to have such a past behind him, and what so natural as that his life should begin again—begin now as for the first time? He had hesitated in the first fervour of his betrothal whether he should not tell all his story. But there was no one to tell it to but Mrs. Kingsward—a lady, even a young lady, not looking much older than Bee herself. That is one of the drawbacks of a young mother. She was still in the sphere of the girls, not in that of the old ladies whom Heaven has ordained to represent the mothers of the race. How could he tell to her the story of that entanglement? If Colonel Kingsward had been there, Aubrey was of opinion that he would have made a clean breast of everything to him. But I think it very likely that he might not have done so. He would have intended it, and he would have put it off from day to day; and then he knew how lightly men of the world look upon such matters. What would have horrified Mrs. Kingsward would probably call forth nothing but a pooh-pooh from her husband. Aubrey, as it proved, was mistaken there, for Colonel Kingsward had ideas of his own, not always corresponding to those of the ordinary man of the world; but no doubt had he heard the story from that side and not from the other, he would have regarded it in a very different light.

But it was too late—too late for these reflections now. The fiat had gone forth, the sentence had been pronounced beyond appeal. Oh, Bee, Bee, she was too good for him; too fresh, too bright, unsullied by the world, for a man who had gone through so much already although he was still young enough. He who had loved and married—though, oh, how differently!—poor little Amy, who was nobody, whom he had liked for her yielding sweetness, sweetness which had cost him so dear—he who had been a father, who had lost his way in life amid the fogs of death and grief—how had he now dared to think that such a girl as Bee should dedicate her fresh young life to restore him again to the lost possibilities of his? It seemed to him the greatest presumption, the most dreadful, cynical, almost blasphemous attempt. It was the way of the world—to think that any woman, however good, might be sacrificed to the necessities of a man's restoration whatever he had done; everybody thought so, his own mother even. But he, Aubrey, should have known better—he should have known that even at his best he could never have been good enough for Bee, and to think that he had dared now when he was no longer at his best! What a fool, what a fool he had been! He had come to be able to endure the daylight and "get on" well enough when he had arrived at the Bath and seen her first. Why had he not contented himself with that, knowing that he had no right to expect more? And now there was nothing—nothing before him but a plunge into the unutterable darkness—darker than ever, without any hope—worse almost, if worse were possible, than when he had fled from his home.

He did not know how long he had been roaming about the dark town pondering all these dreadful thoughts. When he went back to the hotel, which he finally did, worn out, not knowing where else to go, one reproachful waiter, with eyes that said he ought to have been in bed long ago, was waiting for him with a curt demand what he would have to eat, and all the house, except that deserted eating-room, where one light twinkled—reproachful, like the waiter—was shut up. He went to his room when he had swallowed some brandy, which was the only thing he could find to put a little warmth into his chilled limbs and despairing heart, and threw himself miserable upon his bed, where I have no doubt he slept, though he was not aware of it—as Bee did, though she had no intention of doing so.

The only one who was really a sufferer in this respect was poor Mrs. Kingsward, who was ill, and who had been far more agitated than her feeble strength could bear. She it was who lay and wondered all through the night what she must do. Was he really gone without a word, thus proving how much he was in the wrong, and how right the Colonel was? It would have saved her from a great deal of embarrassment, but I do not think Mrs. Kingsward wished that Aubrey might have really gone. It was too summary, it was not natural, it would show Colonel Kingsward to have been too right. Oh! she believed he was right! She did not doubt that his decision was for the best any more than she doubted that it was inexorable: but still the heart revolted a little, and she hoped that he might not be proved so unutterably right as that. And poor Bee—poor little Bee! She did not know, poor child, that there were bitters in the sweetest cup—that if she had twenty years of Aubrey she would not probably have thought quite so much of him as now—that nobody was perfect, which was a conviction that had been forced upon Mrs. Kingsward's own mind, though it was not a strong one, by the passage of the years. And then the poor lady went off into perplexed considerations of what she personally must do. Must he leave them all at once, travel home in a different carriage, avoid them at the stations, not venture to come near their table when they dined on the way? It would seem so ridiculous, and it would be so embarrassing after their very close intercourse. But men never thought of these little things. She felt sure that the Colonel would expect her never to let the two meet again. And how could she do that when they were both travelling the same way? Besides, was it fair, was it just, would Bee endure it— never to see him again?

Bee woke up in all the energy of despair. It burst upon her in the first moment of her waking that he had gone away, that it was all over; but her mind, when it had time to think, rejected that idea; he would not, could not have gone without a word, without even saying farewell, without asking her—anything, anything—to forgive him or to forget him, or to be faithful to him, or not to believe what was said against him. One or other of these things Aubrey must say to her before he went away. Therefore, he could not have gone away, and everything was still possible. In her passion and pride she had refused last night to let her mother tell her what it was. She had resolved that Aubrey should be present, that he should hear the accusation against him, that he should give his own explanation—that was only just, she said to herself—the poorest criminal had a right to that! And Aubrey should have it. He should not, whatever papa said and whatever mamma said, be condemned unheard. She dressed in great haste and rang the bell energetically to ascertain if he had come back. But the chambermaid who answered Bee's bell was stupid and could not understand what Herr it was about whom the young lady questioned her so closely. Had he come back? Oh, yes, she believed all the Herren had come back; there was not a bed to be had in the house. But what Herr was it whom the gracious young lady sought. The old gentleman in the next room, who was so ill? She heard that he was a little better this morning—or the young Herr in number ten, or the Herr whose eyes were so bad, who was going to the great doctor at Dusseldorf? Perhaps poor Bee's German was at fault. She was still attempting to make the matter clear when Moulsey came in with the news that Mrs. Kingsward was very poorly, and had not slept at all, a statement which Betty, rushing in half-dressed, confirmed anxiously. "Mamma has had a very bad night; and what is the matter, Bee, that we are all at sixes and sevens, and why did you lock your door? I came up as soon as I could—as soon as Charlie would let me. He said it was dreadful, nobody coming down; and that we must eat through the dinner for the sake of appearances. And Aubrey never showing neither, and me obliged to sleep in mamma's room because you had locked the door."

"I want to know," said Bee, "whether Aubrey came back last night."

"Oh, how should I know?" said Betty, "and why shouldn't he come back? Of course he must have come back. Is he going anywhere else but home? I wish people would not get letters," said the girl. "You are all so ridiculous since those letters came last night. Letters are nice when they are nice. But, oh! how much nicer it was yesterday morning when you had none, and we were all quite happy, and mamma well, and Aubrey and you as funny as you could be!"

There flashed upon Bee as she spoke the whole bright panorama of yesterday. Not a cloud in the sky nor a trouble in the world. Mamma as fresh as the morning, the river shining, the steamboat thrilling through the water with a shiver of pleasure in its wooden sides, every group adding amusement, and they themselves affording it, no doubt, to the rest. How conscious they had been when they laughed under their breath at the young German pairs, that they themselves were lovers too, quite as happy, if not so demonstrative. Oh! yesterday—yesterday! You might as well say last century for anything that resembled it now. Bee turned almost fiercely to Moulsey, who stood looking on with that air of knowing all about it which so often exasperated the girls, and requested her to go downstairs immediately and ask if Mr. Leigh had come back. Moulsey hesitated and protested that the chambermaid would know. "And you that know the language, Miss Bee."

"Go down directly and inquire if Mr. Leigh has come back. You know the waiter that speaks such good English as well as I do," said Bee, peremptorily. And Moulsey could do nothing but obey.

Yes, Mr. Leigh had come back; he had occupied his room, but was not yet up so far as the attendants knew. There came such a change on Bee's face at this news as startled both the curious observers. The light grew less fierce, more like the usual sunny brightness in her eyes. A softening came over her face. Her colour flashed back. "I want to know when mamma is coming downstairs," she said. "Moulsey—or no, stop. I'll go myself and see."

Moulsey was so roused that she caught the young lady by the arm. "If it was your papa himself, my lady shan't be disturbed," she said. "And not by you, Miss Bee, as are the cause of it all; not if you should put a knife into me afore her door."

"How dare you say I am the cause of it all?"

"Because it's the truth," said the enraged maid. "She was worrited enough before by those letters, and you coming in like the wind, like your papa himself, as I always said you were his living image; and stopping her in the middle of her little bit of cutlet that would have given her strength, and questioning of her like a drum-major, and pacing up and down outside the door like a wild beast. Mind my words: you don't know, none of you, how little strength my poor lady's got. And you're all so masterful, every one, with mamma here and mamma there, and you'll not find out till it's too late—"

"But mamma's better," cried Betty. "She has taken her cure, and she's all right till next year."

"I only wish as you may all find it so, miss," said Moulsey, folding her arms across her broad chest and shaking her head.

Bee was awe-struck for a moment by this speech, but she knew that Moulsey was always a croaker, and it was quite true about the cure. She paused a little uncertain, and then she resumed in a subdued voice—

"I never want to disturb mamma. But Moulsey, we've got to leave here to-day."

"That can't be," said Moulsey, decisively. "My lady is not fit to travel after such a bad night, and I won't have it," she said. "The doctor has put my lady into my hands, and he says 'She's not to be overtired. Mind, I don't respond for nothing if she's overtired.' And she just shan't go—that's flat. And you may all say what you like, and your papa, too."

"Not to-day?" said Bee, with another change of countenance. It flashed upon her that another day's delay would give time for all the explanations in which she could not help hoping. Her excited pulses calmed down a little. She was not alarmed about her mother. Had she been so, it would no doubt have given her thoughts another direction. But Bee knew nothing of illness, much less anything of death. She was not afraid of them. In her experience people might be ill occasionally, but they always got better. Mamma, too, would be better presently, when she got up; and then they could all meet, and the letters and the whole matter could be discussed. And it seemed to be impossible—impossible that from this some better conclusion could be arrived at. There had been so much confusion last night, when it burst upon them like a thunderstroke. When looked at calmly, without flurry or haste, the better moment would bring better views, and who could say that all might not yet be well?

CHAPTER VI

Emboldened by this thought Bee went downstairs to breakfast, which was spread again in the verandah in the warm sunshine of the autumnal morning. The new hope, though it were a forlorn one, restored her youthful appetite as well as her courage, and her coffee and roll were a real restorative after the long fast and agitated night. But there was no appearance of Aubrey, neither at the table nor in the passages, nor anywhere about. He seemed to have disappeared as if he had never been. When Charlie came down from his mother's room, where he had been shut up with her for some time, Bee, who had no particular respect for Charlie's opinion or inclination to allow him any authority over herself, such as an elder brother is sometimes supposed to have, began at once to question him. "Where is Aubrey?" she said. "Why doesn't he come to breakfast? Will you go and look for Aubrey, Charlie?"

"Indeed, I will do no such thing," said Charlie, almost roughly. "I hope he has had the sense to go away. I should just like to see him come calmly down to breakfast as if nothing had happened. If he came, then I can answer for it, you should not be allowed to say a word to him, Bee."

"Who should prevent me?" cried Bee, looking up with her eyes on fire and her nostrils dilating. She had not noticed before what a cloud was upon Charlie's face and how heavy and scowling were his brows. She added, springing up, "We shall soon see about that. If you think I shall do what you tell me, or condemn any man unheard—"

"The cad! He never denied it. You can ask mamma."

"I will not ask anyone but Mr. Leigh," said Bee, throwing back her head; "and I advise you to mind your own business, and not to call names that may come back upon yourself."

"Stop where you are, Bee. I never went out into the world under false pretences. A man is a cad when he does that."

"I shall not stop for you, nor anyone but my parents," said Bee, in a splendid flush of anger, her countenance glowing, her eyes blazing. "Stand out of my way. Oh, if that is all, and you want to make a scene for the edification of the tourists, I can go in by the other door."

And she did so, leaving Charlie standing flushed and angry, but quite unable, it need scarcely be said, to coerce his sister. To make an attempt of this kind, which comes to nothing, is confusing and humiliating. He looked round angrily for a moment to see if it were possible to intercept her, then, yielding to necessity, sat down where Betty, eager and full of a thousand questions, sat calling for explanations. That is the good of a family party, there is always someone ready to hear what you have to say.

Bee went at once to the English-speaking waiter, and asked for Mr. Leigh, whom the man, curious as all lookers-on are at a social drama going on under their eyes, declared to be still in his room. She sent him off instantly with a message, and stood in the hall awaiting his return, angry and brave, like the rose in George Herbert's poem, yet soon getting shamefaced and troubled, as the people coming and going, travellers, visitors, attendants, stared at her and brushed against her as they passed. Bee never forgot all her life the gleam of the river at the foot of the steps, of which she had a glimpse through the doorway—the Rhine barges slowly crossing that little space of vision, the little boats flitting across the gleam of the rosy morning, and the strong flowing tide, the figures going up and down breaking the prospect.

The man came back to her after a time, looking half sympathetic, half malicious, with the message that the gentleman was just going out.

"Just going out!" She repeated the words half-consciously. "Was it Aubrey that sent her that message? Aubrey—who yesterday would not let her out of his sight, who followed her everywhere, saw every sign she made, heard every word almost before it was spoken!" The surprise and the pang together made her heart sick. She could not rush upstairs and knock at his door and call him out imperatively, to tell her immediately what it all meant—at least, though it occurred to her that this would be the most natural thing to do, she did not. Intimidated by the circumstances, by the half impertinence of the waiter, by the stare of the people about, she reflected for a moment breathlessly that he must come out this way, and that if she remained there she must see him. But Bee's instinct of a young woman, now for the first time awakened, made her shrink from this. When she was only a little girl, so very short a time ago, she did not mind who looked at her, who pushed past her. But now everything was different!

She went away, still holding her head high that nobody (above all not Charlie, who was watching her through the glass of the verandah) should guess that her courage was drooping, and going into the deserted sitting-room, where last night that blow had fallen upon her, sat down and wrote to her lover a hurried little note:

"Oh, Aubrey, what is the matter? Have you deserted me without a word? Do you think I am like them, to take up any report? I don't know what report there is—I don't know what it is, this terrible thing that has come between us. What is it? I will take your word and nobody else's. I don't believe you have done anything that is wrong. Aubrey! come and tell me out of your own mouth. I told mamma last night I would hear nothing unless you were there; but you were gone away, they said. And now you send me word that you are going out and can't see me. Going out and can't see—me—! What does it all mean?

"If it is some fad of honour, of not seeing me against—their—will—though I do think your first duty is to me, Aubrey, before anyone else in the world—but if it should be so, mamma will be down here at twelve o'clock—and I invite you to meet her, to hear what is said, to answer for yourself and for me. If you have done anything wrong, what does that matter? Don't we all do wrong? And why should it come between you and me? Am I without sin that I should throw stones at you? Aubrey, you can't throw everything away without a word. You can't desert me without a word. I can bear anything—anything, rather than this.

"Your BEE—."

Bee, poor child, shrank from intrusting this to the impertinent waiter, who had a leer in his eye as if he were defending his own side from the importunities of the other. She went out furtively into the hall and studied the numbers of the rooms and the names of the tenants upon the board, necessity quickening her perceptions, and then she stole upstairs and gave her poor little appeal into the hands of the stout chambermaid who watched over that part of the hotel. It was for the Herr in No. 10, and the answer was to be brought immediately to the little salon No. 20 downstairs. "Eine Antwort," she said over and over again in her imperfect speech. "Schnell, schnell!" This, with the aid of a thaler—for it was before the days of the mark—produced perfect understanding in the mind of the maid, who with becks and wreathed smiles accepted the commission, and in a short time brought her back the answer for which she waited with feverish anxiety. It was very much shorter than her own.

"I am not worthy to stand before you. I cannot and I must not take advantage of your innocence; better I should disappear altogether than wound your ears with what they say. But I will not since you will it so. At twelve o'clock then, Bee, my darling, I will stand up before your mother, and say what I can for myself. Bee, my own dearest, my only hope!"

This last was scrawled across the paper as if he had put it in after the despair of the former part. It was this that the poor little girl fixed upon—the sweet words to which she had been accustomed, which her heart was fainting for. It was not, one would have said, a very cheerful note for a love-letter. But Bee was ridiculously cheered by it. So long as she was his own dearest, his hope, his darling—so long as there was no change in his love for her—why then, in the long run, whatever was said, everything must come right.

I need not follow Bee to her mother's bedside, when Mrs. Kingsward woke and for the first moment did not remember what had happened.

"Is that you, Bee?" she said, smiling, not thinking.

"Are you better, mamma?"

"Oh, yes, just in my usual—," said Mrs. Kingsward. And then she caught a fuller sight of her daughter's face. Bee had none of her usual pretty colour, the light in her eyes was like fire. The mother gave a little feeble cry, and in a moment was no longer in her usual, but lost in the feverish mists of a trouble far too great for her to bear. "Oh, Bee! Oh, Bee!"

"We had better not say anything about it, mamma, to agitate you. I have told him you will be ready at twelve o'clock, that I may know what the story is, and what he has to say."

Mrs. Kingsward struggled up to a sitting position. "At twelve o'clock? No! I cannot, I cannot!" Then she dropped back upon her pillows sobbing, "Oh, Bee, spare me; I am not equal to it. There is Charlie can read your papa's letter. Bee! Bee!"

"Charlie!" cried Bee, with a flash of fury. "Who is Charlie, that he should sit in judgment on Aubrey and me? If he has anything to do with it, I tell you, mamma, I will go away. I will go with Aubrey. I will not hear a word."

"Oh, Bee," cried Mrs. Kingsward, holding out her hot, feverish hands, "I am not fit for it! I am not fit for it! If I am to travel to-morrow—ask Moulsey—I ought to stop in bed and be quiet all day."

"I don't see that it matters," said Bee, sternly, "whether we travel to-morrow or in a week. To go home will be no pleasure to me."

"If we were there, then papa could manage it all himself; he is the proper person. On a journey is not the time to settle things so important. I will write and tell him I have put it all off, and have not said anything, till he could do it himself."

"But that will not be true," cried the young Rhadamanthus, inexorable, with her blazing eyes.

"O Bee! you are dreadfully, dreadfully hard upon me!" the poor young mother said. This is the drawback of being so young a mother, just as young as your grown-up children. It is very delightful, when all is sunny and bright, but in a great emergency like this it is trying for all parties when a girl's mother is only, so to speak, a girl like herself. Bee lifted up her absolute young head, and gave forth her ultimatum unmoved.

"Well, mamma, it must be as you choose. If you think my happiness is of less consequence than the chance of a headache to yourself, I have naturally nothing more to say."

A headache! That was all she knew.

Mrs. Kingsward was ready by twelve o'clock, much against Moulsey's will, who dressed her mistress under protest. "I ain't one to interfere with what's going on in a family," said Moulsey, as she combed out the long locks, tangled with the restlessness of a troubled night, which were as silky and as smooth as Bee's. "I'm only a servant, and I knows my place; but you're not fit to struggle among them young ones. The nursery children, it's all very well; if they're naughty you whip them, or you put them in a corner, and there's a good cry and all right again. But when it comes to a business with a young lady and a gentlemen, the Colonel ought to have come himself, or he ought to have put it off till we all got home."

"Oh, I wish, I wish he had!" Mrs. Kingsward said, sighing. "I am not in the least what I used to be, Moulsey; don't you think I am very different from what I used to be? I have not half the strength."

"There often is," said Moulsey, "a time when a lady isn't so strong, after all these children and everything. It takes a deal out of you, it do. And I don't hold much with them foreign cures. I'm one that stands for home. And there's where you ought to be, ma'am, whatever anyone may say."

"I am sure it is where I wish to be," said the poor lady, "but we must not be unjust, Moulsey. My cure did me a great deal of good, and I liked being out and seeing everything just as much as the girls."

"That is just it, ma'am," said Moulsey; "you're a deal too much the same as the young ladies, and can't make up your mind as you haven't the strength for it. I'm not one to ask any questions, but I can't help seeing there's something wrong. Don't you give in to Miss Bee in everything. I wouldn't go down to make up the quarrel if I was you. Leave 'em to themselves, and it'll all come right. Bless us, lovers' quarrels is nothing—it wouldn't be half the fun if it wasn't for that."

Moulsey knew very well this was no lovers' quarrel; but it seemed to her a good way of satisfying herself what it was.

"Oh, if that were all!" sighed the poor lady. "Moulsey, you are an old friend, and take an interest in the family. You have known Miss Bee since ever she was born. I don't know why I shouldn't tell you. It is no quarrel; it's something the Colonel has heard about Mr. Leigh."

"All lies, ma'am, I don't make no manner of doubt."

"Do you think so, Moulsey; oh, do you think so? Have you heard anything? You often know more, hearing the servants speak, than we do. If you have any light to throw on the subject, oh, do so, do! I shall be grateful to you all my life."

"I don't know as I have any light to throw. I knew as there was some trouble at the time the poor young lady died—some friend of hers, as Mr. Leigh, being a kind-hearted gentleman, couldn't turn out of the house—and it made a talk. But if there was anything wrong, you take my word, ma'am, it was none of his fault."

"Ah, it's so easy to say that, Moulsey; but the man must bear the blame."

"I've always heard, ma'am, as it was the woman that got the blame; and right enough, for they often deserve it the most," Moulsey said.

"Oh, I wish—I wish, whoever was to blame, that it was not I that had to clear it up," poor Mrs. Kingsward said.

"Oh, cursed spite,   That ever I was born to set it right."

She would not have said this, poor lady. She would have thought it swearing and unbecoming for a woman's lips; still, Hamlet's sentiment was hers, with much stronger reason. She looked like anything but a strong representative of justice as she went downstairs. Charlie had come to give her his arm, and though he was very tender to her, Charlie had no idea of sparing her any more than Bee. He, too, thought that it was only the risk of a headache, and that a headache was no such great matter. Charlie's idea was, however, that what the governor said was, of all things on earth, the most important to be carried out—especially when it did not concern himself.

Bee was sitting at the window looking out upon the river, seeing the reflections flash and the boats pass. The steamer had just started with its lively freight—the steamboat which had brought them down the stream yesterday, with all its changing groups, and the pairs of German lovers with their arms about each other in the beatitude of the betrothal. All just the same, but how different, how different! She did not rise, but only turned her head when her mother came in. She was on the other side. She did not see, with so many other things in her head, how fragile Mrs. Kingsward looked. Betty was the only one who perceived at all that mamma was less strong than usual, and even Betty took no notice, for she, too, was on the other side. As for Charlie, he stood behind her, a sort of representative of executive force at the back of Justice, backing her authority up. It was he who arranged her chair, her footstool, the shawl Moulsey had insisted she should wear, and which Charlie, who knew nothing about shawls, huddled up about her neck, not unlike the judge's ermine. He did it all, not with sympathetic touches as the girls would have done had they not been on the other side, but rather with an eye to her dignity as a representative of the law.

And then, just as the hour of noon sounded from all the church clocks, Aubrey came in. He was very pale, but dressed with care, no symptoms of neglect about him, with an air of preparation which became a man who was going to stand his trial. Bee jumped up from her seat and went up to him, putting her hand through his arm, and Betty, half-frightened, with a glance at her mother, offered him a timid hand. She sat down behind them, on a chair that was ranged against the wall. The defendant's side was her side. She wanted to show that, and yet not to go against mamma. Charlie took no notice at all of the new comer, but stood scowling, looking at nobody, behind his mother's chair.

Mrs. Kingsward, frightened at her own dignity and breathless with agitation, cried, "Oh, Mr. Leigh!" which was a kind of salutation. She had some papers in her lap, over which her hands fluttered restlessly, her husband's letter, and something else beside, and she looked at the group before her with a little dubious smile, asking pardon of the culprit whom she had come here—oh, so much against her will—to try for his life.

"Now, mamma," said Bee, in a cheerful voice, "we are quite ready, Aubrey and I—"

CHAPTER VII

Mrs. Kingsward's opening speech was a wonder to hear. She sat and looked at them all for a moment, trying to steady herself, but there was nothing to steady her in what she saw before her—Aubrey and Bee, the pair who had been so sweet to see, such a diversion in all circumstances, so amusing in their mutual absorption, so delightful in their romance. It all flashed back to her mind; the excitement of Bee's first proposal, the pleasure of seeing "her bairn respected like the lave," though Mrs. Kingsward might not have understood what these words meant, the little triumph it was to see her child engaged at nineteen, when everybody said there was nobody for the girls to marry—and now to have that triumph turned into humiliation and dismay! And to think of Bee's bright face overcast, and her happiness over, and poor Aubrey thrown out into the uttermost darkness. Had she seen Charlie it might have given her some support, for Charlie was the impersonation of immovable severity; but Betty's wistful little face behind the other pair, coming out from Aubrey's shadow by moments to fix an appealing look upon her mother, was not calculated to make her any stronger. She cleared her throat— she tried hard to steady her voice. She said, "Oh, my dear children," faltering, and then the poor lady ended in a burst of sobbing and tears. It gave her a little sting and stimulant to see through her weeping that though little Betty ran towards her with kisses and soothing, Bee took no notice, but stood hard and unaffected in her opposition, holding close to Aubrey's arm. Mrs. Kingsward indeed got no sympathy except from little Betty. Charlie put his hand imperatively upon her shoulder, recalling her to herself, and Bee never moved, standing by the side of Aubrey Leigh. The mother, thus deserted, plucked up a little spirit in the midst of her weakness.

"Bee," she said, "I do not think it is quite nice of you to stand there as if your own people were against you. We are not against you. There has been, I fear, a great mistake made, which Colonel Kingsward"— here she turned her eyes to Aubrey—"has found out in—in time; though it is a pity, a sad pity, that it was not found out before. If Mr. Aubrey had only been frank and said at once—but I don't see what difference that would have made. Papa says that from what he has heard and discovered things must not go any further. He is sorry, and so am I, that they have gone so far, and the engagement must be broken off at once. You hear what I say, Bee?"

"I heard you say so last night, mamma, but I say it is my engagement, and I have a right to know why. I do not mean to break it off—"

"Oh, how can I make explanations—how can I enter into such a question? I appeal to you, Mr. Aubrey— tell her."

"She ought not to ask any explanations. She is a minor, under age. My father has a right to do whatever he pleases—and she has none to ask why."

This was how Charlie reasoned on the height of his one-and-twenty years. Charlie was the intolerable element in all this question. Aubrey cast a look at him, and forcibly closed his own lips to keep in something that was bursting forth. Bee defied him, as was natural, on the spot. "I will not have Charlie put in his opinion," she cried. "He has nothing to do with me. Even if I obeyed papa, I certainly should not obey him."

"Let Aubrey say, himself," said Mrs. Kingsward, "whether you ought to be told everything, Bee."

"It is cruel to ask me," said Aubrey, speaking for the first time. "If Bee could know all—if you could know all, Mrs. Kingsward! But how could I tell you all? Part of this is true, and part is not true. I could speak to Colonel Kingsward more freely. I am going off to-night to London to see him. It will free you from embarrassment, and it will give me perhaps a chance. I did not want to put you to this trial. I am ready to put myself unreservedly in Colonel Kingsward's hands."

"Then," said Bee, hastily, "it seems I am of no sort of importance at all to anyone. I am told my engagement is broken off, and then I am told I am not to know why, and then—. Go, then, Aubrey, as that is your choice, and fight it out with papa, if you please." She loosed her arm from his, with a slight impulse, pushing him away. "But just mind this—everybody," she cried; "you may think little of Bee— but my engagement shall not be broken by anybody but me, and it shall not be kept on by anybody but me; and I will neither give it up nor will I hold to it, neither one nor the other, until I know why."

Then the judge and the defendant looked each other in the face. They were, as may be supposed, on opposite sides, but they were the only two to consult each other in this emergency. Aubrey responded by a movement of his head, by a slight throwing up of his hand, to the question in Mrs. Kingsward's eyes.

"Then you shall know as much as I can tell you, Bee. Your father had a letter last week, from a lady, telling him that she had a revelation to make. The letter alarmed your father. He felt that he must know what it meant. He could not go himself, but he sent Mr. Passavant, the lawyer. The lady said that she had lived in Mr. Leigh's house for years, in the time of his late wife. She said Mr. Leigh had—had behaved very badly to her."

"That I do not believe," said Bee.

The words flashed out like a knife. They made a stir in the air, as if a sudden gleam had come into it. And then all was still again, a strange dead quiet coming after, in which Bee perceived Aubrey silent, covering his face with his hand. It came across her with a sudden pang that she had heard somebody say this morning or last night—"He did not deny it."

"And that he had promised her—marriage—that he was engaged to her, as good as—as good as married to her—when he had the cruelty—oh, my dear child, my dear child!—to come to you."

Aubrey took his hand away from his white face. "That," he said, in a strange, dead, tuneless voice, "is not true."

"Oh, more shame to you, Aubrey, more shame to you," cried Mrs. Kingsward, forgetting her judicial character in her indignation as a woman, "if it is not true!—" She paused a moment to draw her breath, then added, "But indeed you were not so wicked as you say, for it is true. And here is the evidence. Oh!" she cried, with tears in her eyes, "it makes your conduct to my child worse; but it shows that you were not then, not then, as bad as you say."

Bee had dropped into the chair that was next to her, and there sat, for her limbs had so trembled that she could not stand, watching him, never taking her eyes from him, as if he were a book in which the interpretation of this mystery was—

"Never mind about me," he said, hoarsely. "I say nothing for myself. Allow me to be as bad as a man can be, but that is not true. And what is the evidence? You never told me there was any evidence."

"Sir," said Mrs. Kingsward, fully roused, "I told you all that was in my husband's letter last night."

"Yes—that she," a sort of shudder seemed to run over him, to the keen sight of the watchers—"that she—said so. You don't know, as I do, that—that—is no evidence. But you speak now as if there was something more."

She took a piece of folded paper from her lap. "There is this," she said, "a letter you wrote to her the morning you went away."

"I did write her a letter," he said.

Mrs. Kingsward held it out to him, but was stopped by Charlie, who put his hand on her arm. "Keep this document, mother. Don't put the evidence against him into a man's power. I'll read it if Mr. Leigh thinks proper."

Once more Aubrey and Bee together, with a simultaneous impulse, looked at this intruder into their story.

"Mamma! send him away. I should like to kill him!" said Bee within her clenched teeth.

"Be quiet, Charlie. Mr. Leigh, I am ready to put this or any other evidence against you into your hands."

He bowed very gravely, and then stood once more as if he were made of stone. Mrs. Kingsward faltered very much, her agitated face flushed. "It begins," she said, in a low fluttering voice, "My dear little wife—"

Then there came a very strange sound into the agitated silence, for Aubrey Leigh, on trial for more than his life, here laughed. "What more, what more?" he said.

"No, it is not that. It is—'I don't want my dear little wife to be troubled about anything. It can all be done quite easily and quietly, without giving an occasion for people to talk; a settlement made and everything you could desire. I shall make arrangements about everything to-day.' It is signed A. L., and it is in your handwriting. Bee, you can see it is in his handwriting; look for yourself."

Bee would not turn her head. She thought she saw the writing written in fire upon the air—all his familiar turns in it. How well she knew the A. L.; but she did not look at it—would not look. She had enough to do looking at his face, which was the letter—the book she was studying now.

"No doubt it is my handwriting," he said, "only it was addressed not to any other woman, but to my wife."

"Your wife died two years ago, Mr. Leigh; and that is dated Christmas—this year."

"That is a lie!" he cried; then restrained himself painfully. "You know I don't mean you—but the date and the assumption is entirely a lie. Give me time, and I will tell you exactly when it was written. I remember the letter. It was when I had promised Amy to provide for her friend on condition that she should be sent away—for she made my house miserable."

"And yet—and yet, Mr. Leigh—. Oh, don't you see how things contradict each other? She made your house miserable, and yet—when your wife was dead, and you were free—"

He looked at her, growing paler and paler. "And yet!" he said. "I know what you mean. That is the infernal art of it. My own folly has cut the ground from beneath my feet, and put weapons into every hand against me. I know—I know."

Again there came into Bee's mind the words she had heard last night—"He does not deny it." And yet he was denying it with all his might! Denying, and not denying—what? The girl's brain was all in a maze, and she could not tell.

"You see?" said Mrs. Kingsward, gently. "Oh, I am sorry for you in my heart. Perhaps you were led into—a connection that you feel not to be—desirable. That I can understand. But that you should think you could save yourself by means of an innocent girl, almost a child, and impose yourself on a family that had no suspicions!—oh, Mr. Leigh, Mr. Leigh! you ought to have died sooner than have done that!"

He looked at her piteously for a moment, and then a dreadful sort of smile came upon his face. "I allow," he said, "that that would have been the best."

And there fell a silence upon the room. The sun was shining outside, and the sound of the water gurgling against the sides of boats, and of all the commotion of the landing place, and of the hundreds of voices in the air, and of the chiming of the clocks, came in and filled the place. And just then there burst out a carillon from one of the steeples setting the whole to music, harmonising all the discords, and sweeping into this silence with a sudden rush of sound as if some bodily presence had come in. It was the touch too much for all these excited and troubled people. Mrs. Kingsward lay back in her chair and began to weep silently. Aubrey Leigh turned away from where he was standing and leant his head against the wall. As for Bee, she sat quite still, dazed, not able to understand, but crushed out of all her youthful self-assertion and determination to clear it all up. She to clear it up!—who did not even understand it, who could not fathom what was meant. That there was something more than met the eye, something that was not put into words, seemed to show vaguely through the words that were said. But what it was Bee could not tell. She could not understand it all. And yet that there was a fatal obstacle rising up between her and her lover, something which no one could disperse or clear away, not a mistake, not a falsehood, not a thing that could be passed over triumphantly and forgotten—not as youth is so quick to believe a mere severity, tyranny, arbitrary conclusion of papa—she felt in every fibre of her frame. She could not deny it or struggle against it; her very being seemed paralysed. The meaning went out of her face, the absolute, certain, imperious youthfulness died out of her. She who loved to have her own way, who had just protested that she would neither give up nor hold fast except by her own will and understanding, now sat dumb, vaguely staring, seeing shadows pass before her and hearing of things which were undeniable, mighty things, far more powerful than her little hot resolutions and determinations. Bee had never yet come face to face with any trouble which could not be smoothed away. There was her own naughtiness, there were Charlie's escapades at school and college—some of which she had known were serious. But in a little while they had been passed over and forgotten, and everything had been as before. One time she remembered papa had threatened not to let Charlie go back to Harrow, which was a dreadful thing, exposing him and his naughtiness to all the world. But after a while papa had changed his mind, and everything had gone smoothly as before. Could papa change his mind now? Would time make it, even if he did, as it was before? Bee had not mental power enough to think these things, or ask these questions of her own will. But they went through her mind as people come in and go out by an open door.

It was Aubrey who was the first to speak. The carillon stopped, or else they got used to the sound and took no further notice of it, and he collected himself and came forward again to the middle of the room. He said, "I know it will be a relief that I should go away. There is an afternoon train which I shall take. It is slow, but it does not matter. I shall be as well there as anywhere—or as ill. I shall go direct to Colonel Kingsward and lay my whole case before him. He will perhaps confront me with my accuser—I hope so—if not, he will at least hear what I have to say for myself."

"Oh, Mr. Leigh! Oh, Aubrey! I can't wish you anything but well, whatever—whatever may be done!"

"Thank you, Mrs. Kingsward, I looked for nothing less from your kind heart. Will you give me that letter?"

She put it into his hands without the least hesitation, and he examined it—with a sort of strained smile upon his face. "I should like to take this back to Colonel Kingsward," he said. Then added quickly with a short laugh, "No, I forgot; there might be suspicions. Send it back to him, please, by the first post, that he may have it when I get there." He gave the letter back, and then he looked round wistfully. "May I say good-bye to Bee?"

She got up at the words, feeling herself vaguely called upon—yet quite dull, dumb, with all sorts of thoughts going and coming through those wide-open doors of her mind—thoughts like strays which she seemed to see as they passed. Even Aubrey himself appeared a ghost. She got up and stood awaiting him when he approached her, not putting out a finger. Nobody interfered, not even Charlie, who was fuming internally yet somehow did not move. Aubrey went up to her and put his hands upon her shoulders. Her unresponsiveness sent a chill to his heart.

"Have you given me up, Bee?" he cried, "Already, already!" with anguish in his voice.

She could not say a word. She shook her head like a mute, looking at him with her dazed eyes.

"She does not understand it—not a word!" he said.

Bee shook her head again. It was all she could do. No, she did not understand, except that it was a kind of dying, something against which nobody could struggle. And then he kissed her on her forehead as gravely as though he had been her father; and the next moment was gone—was it only out of the room, or out of the world, out of life?

CHAPTER VIII

It was a slow train. The slowest train that there is, is, of course, far, far quicker than any other mode of conveyance practicable in a land journey, but it does not seem so. It seems as if it were delay personified to the eager traveller, especially on the Continent. In England, when it stops at a multiplicity of stations at which there is nothing to do, it at least goes on again in most cases after it has dropped its half-passenger or taken in its empty bag of letters. But this can never be said of a German or even of a brisker Belgian train. The one in which Aubrey was meandered about Liege, for instance, till he had mastered every aspect of that smoky but interesting place. It stopped for what looked like an hour at every little roadside station, in order, apparently, that the guard might hold a long and excited conversation about nothing at all with the head man of the place. And all the while the little electric bell would go tingling, tingling upon his very brain. Thus he made his slow and weary progress through the afternoon and evening, stopping long at last at a midnight station (where everything was wrapped in sleep and darkness) for the arrival of the express, in which the latter portion of the journey was to be accomplished more quickly. If there had been anything wanted to complete the entire overthrow of a spirit in pain it was such an experience. All was dismal beyond words at the place where he had to wait—one poor light showing through the great universe of darkness, the dark big world that encompassed it around—one or two belated porters wandering through the blackness doing mysterious pieces of business, or pretending to do them. A poor little wailing family—a mother and two children, put out there upon a bench from some other train, one of the babies wailing vaguely into the dark, the other calling upon "mamma, mamma," driving the poor mother frantic—were waiting like himself. It gave Aubrey a momentary consolation to see something that appeared at least to the external eye more forlorn than he. He remembered, too, that there had once been a baby cry that went to his heart, and though all the associations connected with that had now turned into gall and bitterness, so that the sound seemed like a spear penetrating his very being, and he walked away as far as the bounds of the station would allow, to get, if possible, out of hearing of it—yet pity, a better inspiration, at last gained the day. He went up and spoke to the woman, and found that she was an English workman's wife making her way home with her children to a mother who was dying. They had turned her out here, with her babies, to wait—ah, not for the express train which was to carry on the gentleman, but for the slow, slow-creeping third-class which only started in the morning, and which would, after other long waits at other places, reach England sometime, but she could scarcely tell when.

"And must you pass the night here out in the cold?" said Aubrey.

"It isn't not to call a cold night, sir," said the woman, meekly, "and they've got plenty on to keep them warm."

"I'll try and get them to open the waiting-room for you," said Aubrey.

"Oh, no, sir; thank you kindly, but don't take the trouble—the rooms are that stuffy. It's better for them in the open air, and they'll go to sleep in a little while. Baby will be quite warm on my lap, and Johnny's lying against me."

"And what is to become of you in this arrangement?" said Aubrey, looking pitifully, with eyes that had known the experiences both of husband and father, upon this little plump human bed, which was to stand in the place of down pillows for the children.

"Oh, I'll do very well, sir, when they go to sleep," she said, looking up at him with a smile.

"And when does your train go?"

"Not till six in the morning," she replied; "but perhaps that's all the better, for I'll be able to get them some bread and milk, and a good wash before we start."

Well, it was not much of an indulgence for a man who was well off. He might have thrown it away on any trifle, and nobody would have wasted a thought on the subject. He got hold of one of the wandering ghosts of porters, and got him, with a douceur, to change the poor woman's cheap ticket for her into one for the express, and commissioned him, if possible, to get her a place in a sleeping carriage, where, I fear, she was not likely to be at all a warmly welcomed addition to the luxurious young men or delicate ladies in these conveyances. He saw that there was one found for her which was almost empty when the train came up. He scarcely knew if she were young or old—though indeed, as a matter of fact, the poor little mother, bewildered by her sudden elevation among the gentlefolks, and not quite sure that she would not have preferred to remain where she was and pick up in the morning her natural third-class train, was both young and pretty, a fact that was remarked by the one young lady in the carriage, who saw the young man through the window at her side, and recognised him in a flash of the guard's lantern, with deep astonishment to see him handing in such a woman and such children to the privileged places. He disappeared himself into the dark, and indeed took his place in the corner of a smoking carriage, where his cigar was a faint soother of pain. In his human short-sightedness, poor Aubrey also was consoled a little, I think, by the thought that this poor fellow-passenger was comfortable—she and her children—and that instead of slumbering uneasily on a bench, she was able to lay the little things in a bed. It seemed to him a good omen, a little relaxation of the bonds of fate, and he went away cheered a little and encouraged by this simple incident and by the warmth of the kindness that was in his heart.

He spoke to them again on one or two occasions on the way, sent the poor woman some tea in the morning, bought some fruit for the children, and again on the steamboat crossing, when he listened to the account of how they were going on, from Dover, with a certain interest. When they parted at the train he shook hands with the mother, hoping she would find her relation better, and put a sovereign into Johnny's little fat hand. The lady who had been in the sleeping carriage kept her eye upon him all the time. She was not by any means a malicious or bad woman, but she did not believe the poor woman's story of the gentleman's kindness. She was, I am sorry to say, a lady who was apt to take the worst view of every transaction, especially between men and women. People who do so are bound in many cases to be right, and so are confirmed in their odious opinion; but in many cases they are wrong, yet always hold to it with a faith which would do credit to a better inspiration. "I thought young Mr. Leigh was going to marry again," she said to a friend whom she met going up to town.

"Oh, so he is! To the nicest girl—Bee Kingsward, the daughter of one of my dearest friends—such a satisfactory thing in every way."

"Wasn't there something," said the lady of the sleeping carriage, "about a woman, down at his place in the country?"

"Oh, I don't think there was ever anything against him. There was a woman who was a great friend of his poor wife, and lived with them. The wife was a goose, don't you know, and could not be made to see what a foolish thing it was. My opinion is that he never could abide the woman, and I am sure she made mischief between them. But I believe that silly little Mrs. Leigh—poor thing, we should not speak ill of those that are gone—made him promise on her deathbed that this Miss Something-or-other should not be sent away from the house. It was a ridiculous arrangement, and no woman that respected herself would have done it. But she was poor, and it's a comfortable place, and, perhaps, as there was no friendship between them she may have thought it was no harm."

"Perhaps she thought she would get over him in time and make him marry her."

"Oh, I can't tell what she thought! He rushed off in a hurry at a moment's notice, nobody knowing what he intended, after the poor baby died, the very day of its funeral. Not much to be wondered at, poor young man, after all he had gone through. I don't know how things were settled with Miss Lance, but I believe that she has gone at last. And I am delighted to hear of his engagement. So will all his neighbours in the county be."

"I should not like a daughter of mine to marry a man like that."

"Why? I wish a daughter of mine could have the chance. Everybody likes him at home. Do you know anything of Aubrey Leigh?"

He did not know in the least that this talk was going on as the train went rushing on to town; his ears did not tingle. He was in the next carriage, divided only by a plank from these two ladies in their compartment. The woman who took the bad view of everything did not wish him any harm. She did not even think badly of him. She thought it was only human nature, and that young men will do that sort of thing, however nice they may be, and whatever you may say of morals and so forth. I do not think, though she had made that little conventional speech, that she would at all have hesitated to give her own daughter to Aubrey, provided that she had a daughter. His advantages were so evident, and the disadvantages, after all, had so little to do with actual life.

Aubrey did not present himself before Colonel Kingsward that night. He did not propose to follow him to Kingswarden, the old house in Kent, which was the sole remnant of territorial property belonging to the family. He wanted to have all his wits about him, to be cool and self-possessed, and able to remember everything, when he saw the man who had given him Bee and then had withdrawn her from his arms. He already knew Colonel Kingsward a little, and knew him as a man full of—bonhommie—, popular everywhere—a man of experience, who had been about the world, who knew men. By this time Aubrey had recovered his spirits a little. He thought it impossible that such a man, when a younger than himself laid bare his heart to him, could fail to understand. It was true that the Colonel was probably a martinet in morals as he was in his profession, and Aubrey had that behind him which he could not deny. He would not attempt to gloss it over, to make excuses for it. He would lay his life in this man's hand as if he had been his confessor. And surely, surely the acknowledged sin would find absolution, the extenuating circumstances would be considered, the lie with which that accusation was accompanied would recoil upon the accuser. The young man buoyed himself up with these thoughts through the long evening. He did not go out or to his club, or anywhere where he was known. In September there are not so many inducements to stray about London. He sat in his room and thought of Bee, and wrote little letters to her, which were a relief to his mind though he knew he could not send them. By this time he reflected they must have started. They were beginning their journey as he ended his. He hoped that Charlie, that lout, would have the sense to take care of his mother, to see that she suffered as little as possible, to prevent her from having any trouble—which I fear was not the view at all that Charlie took of his duty to his mother. Aubrey, like all outsiders, had a clearer view of Mrs. Kingsward's condition than her family had arrived at. He was very sorry for her, poor, delicate, tender woman—and grieved to the bottom of his heart that this trouble should have come upon her through him. Bee was different. There would be so many ways, please God, if all went well—and he could not bring himself to think that all would not go well—in which he could make it up to his Bee. Finally, he permitted himself to write a little letter to meet his darling on her return, and enclosed in it another to Mrs. Kingsward, directed to Kingswarden. They would receive it when they entered their house—and by that time, surely by that time, his letters would not be any longer a forbidden thing.

That morning it rained, and the London skies hung very low. The world had the effect of a room with a low roof, stifling and without air. He set out to walk to Colonel Kingsward's office. I forget whether the Intelligence Department of the War Office was in existence at that time, or if it has always been in existence only not so much heard of as in our vociferous days. If it did exist then, it was, of course, in Pall Mall, as we all know. Aubrey set out to walk, but soon recollected that muddy boots detracted from a man's appearance, especially in the eyes of a spick and span person like Colonel Kingsward, who never had a speck upon any garment, and accordingly he got into a hansom. It did not go any faster than the beating of his heart, and yet he could have wished that it should only creep along like the heavier cabs. He would have put off this interview now had he been able. To think that you are within an hour at most of the moment when your life shall be settled for you absolutely by another person's will, and that your happiness or unhappiness rest upon the manner in which he will look at the question, the perception he will have of your difficulties, the insight into your heart, is a terrible thing—especially if you know little of the person who has thus become endowed, as it were, with the power of life and death over you—do not know if his understanding is a large or limited one, if he has any human nature in him, or only mere conventionality and the shell of human nature. It is seldom, perhaps, that one man is thus consciously in the power of another—and yet it must come to that more or less, every day.

Colonel Kingsward was in his room, seated at his writing table with piles of books and maps, and masses of newspapers all round him. He was an excellent linguist, and there were French papers and German papers, Russian, Scandinavian—all kinds of strange languages and strange little broadsheets, badly printed, black with excessive ink, or pale with imperfect impression, on the floor and the table. He had a large paper knife at his hand in ivory, with the natural brown upon it, looking like a weapon which could cut a man, not to say a book, in pieces. He looked up with an aspect which Aubrey, whose heart was in his mouth, could not read—whether it was mere politeness or something more—and bade Mr. Leigh be seated, putting aside deliberately as he did so the papers with which he was engaged. And then he turned round with the air of a man who says: Now you have my entire attention—and looked Aubrey in the face. The young man was facing the light which came in from a large high window reaching nearly to the roof. The elder man had his back half turned from it, so that his regard was less easy to read. It was not quite fair. Aubrey had everything against him; his agitation, his anxiety, an expressive tell-tale face, and the light searching every change that took place in it; whilst his opponent was calm as his own paper knife, impassive, with a countenance formed to conceal his emotions, and the light behind him. It was not an equal match in any way.

"I have come direct from Cologne," Aubrey said.

"Ah, yes. I believe my wife says so in her letter."

"You have news from them to-day? I hope that Mrs. Kingsward is better."

"My wife never at any time speaks much of her health. She was a little fatigued and remained another day to rest."

"She is very delicate, sir," said Aubrey. He did not know why, unless it was reluctance to begin what he had to say.

"I am perfectly acquainted with Mrs. Kingsward's condition," said the Colonel, in a tone which was not encouraging. He added, "I don't suppose you took the trouble to come here, Mr. Leigh, in order to speak to me about my wife's health."

"No. It is true. I ought not to waste the time you have accorded me. I do not need to tell you, Colonel Kingsward, what I have come about."

"I think you do," said the Colonel, calmly. "My letter to my wife, which I believe she communicated to you, conveyed all I had to say on the matter. It was not written without reflection, nor without every possible effort to arrive at the truth. Consequently, I have no desire to re-open the subject. It is in my mind concluded and put aside."

"But you will hear me?" said Aubrey. "You have heard one statement, surely you will hear the other. No man is condemned unheard. I have come here to throw myself upon your mercy—to tell you my story. However prejudiced you may be against me—"

"A moment, Mr. Leigh. I have no prejudice against you. I am not the judge of your conduct. I claim the right to decide for my daughter—that is all. I have no prejudice or feeling against you."

"Colonel Kingsward," cried Aubrey, "for God's sake listen! Hear what I have to say!"

The Colonel looked at him again. Perhaps it was the passion of earnestness in the young man's face that touched him. Perhaps he felt that it was unwise to leave it to be said that he had not heard both sides. The end was that he waved his hand and said:

"My time is not my own. I have no right to spend it on merely private interests; but if you will make your story as short as possible I will hear what you have to say."

CHAPTER IX

The story which Aubrey Leigh had to tell was indeed made as short as possible. To describe the most painful crisis in your life, the moment which you yourself shudder to look back at, which awakens in you that fury of self-surprise, horror and wonder which a sudden departure from all the habits of your life brings after it when it is guilt, is not an easy thing; but it supplies terse expressions and rapidity of narration. There is no desire to dwell upon the details, and to tell a story so deeply affecting one's self to a politely unsympathetic listener who does not affect to be much interested or at all moved by the subtle self-defence which runs through every such statement, is still more conducive to brevity. Aubrey laid bare the tempest that had swept over him with a breathless voice and broken words. He could not preserve his equanimity, or look as if it were an easy thing for him to do. He made the most hurried description of the visitor who had taken possession of his house, saying not a word beyond the bare fact. It had been deeply embarrassing that she should be there, though at first in the melancholy of his widowerhood he had not thought of it, or cared who was in the house. Afterwards he was prevented from doing anything to disturb her by his promise to his dying wife. Then had come the anxiety about the baby, the wavering of that little life in which the forlorn young father had come to take a little pleasure. She had been very kind to the child, watching over it, and when the little thing died, when the misery of the fresh desolation, and the pity of it, and the overwhelming oppression of the sad house had quite overcome the spirit of its young master, then she had thrown herself upon him, with all the signs of a sudden passion of sympathy and tenderness. Had any confessor skilled in the accounts of human suffering heard Aubrey's broken tale he could have found nothing but truth in it, and would have recognised the subtle sequence of events which had led to that downfall. But Colonel Kingsward, though not unlearned in men, listened like a man of wood, playing with the large paper-knife, and never looking towards the penitent, who told his story with such a strain of the labouring breast and agonised spirit.

Had a young officer in whom he had no particular interest thus explained and accounted for some dereliction of duty he might have understood or sympathised. But he had no wish to understand Aubrey; his only desire was to brush him off as quickly as possible, to be done with his ridiculous story, to hear of him no more. He might be as little guilty as he described himself. What then? Aubrey's character was nothing to Colonel Kingsward, except as it affected his daughter. He had cut him off from all connection with his daughter, and it was now quite immaterial to him whether the man was a weak fool or a deceiver. Probably from as much as he heard while thus listening as little as he could, Leigh was in the former class, and certainly he did not intend to take a weak fool, who had shown himself to be at the mercy of any designing woman, into his family as the husband of Bee. Give him the benefit of the doubt, and allow that it had happened so, that the woman was much more to blame than the man, and what then? A sturdy sinner on the whole was not less but more easily pardoned than a weak fool.

"This is all very well, Mr. Leigh," Colonel Kingsward said, "and I am sorry that you have thought it necessary to enter into these painful details. They may be quite true. I will not offend you by doubting that you believe them to be quite true. But how, then, do you account for the letter which my wife, I believe, showed you, and which came direct from the lady's own hand to mine?"

"The letter was a letter which I wrote to my wife two years ago. There had been discussions between us on this very subject. I promised, on condition that Miss Lance should leave us, to make such arrangements for her comfort as were possible to me—to settle a yearly income on her, enough to live on."

"Was that arrangement ever carried out?"

"No; my wife became ill immediately after. I found her on my return in Miss Lance's arms, imploring that so long as she lived her friend should not be taken from her. What could I do? And that prayer was changed on my poor Amy's deathbed to another—that I would never send Miss Lance away; that she should always have a home at Forest-leigh and watch over the child."

"I don't wish to arouse any such painful recollections—especially as they can be of no advantage to anyone—but how does this letter come to have the date of last Christmas, more than a year after Mrs. Leigh's death?"

"How can I tell that, sir? How can I tell how the devilish web was woven at all? The note had no date, I suppose, and the person who could use it for this purpose would not hesitate at such a trifle as to add a date."

"Mr. Leigh, I repeat the whole matter is too painful to be treated by me. But how is it, if you regarded this lady with those sentiments, that you should have in a moment changed them, and, to put the mildest interpretation upon your proceedings, thus put yourself in her power?"

The young man's flushed and anxious face grew deadly pale. He turned his eyes from the inquisitor to the high blank light pouring in from the large window. "God knows," he said, "that is what I cannot explain—or rather, I should say, the devil knows!" he cried with vehemence. "I was entirely off my guard—thinking, heaven knows, of nothing less."

"The devil is a safe sort of agency to put the blame on. We cannot in ordinary affairs accept him as the scapegoat, Mr. Leigh—excuse me for saying so. I will not refuse to say that I allow there may be excuses for you, with a woman much alive to her own interests and ready for any venture. You did write to her, however, on the day you left?"

"I wrote to her, telling her the arrangement I had proposed to my wife, in the very letter which she has sent to you—that I would carry it out at once, and that I hoped she would perceive, as I did, that it was impossible we should remain under the same roof, or, indeed, meet again."

"That was on what date?"

"The evening before my child's funeral. Next day, as soon as it was over, I left the house, and have never set foot in it again."

"Yet this lady, to whom you had, you say, sent such a letter, was at the funeral, and stood at the child's grave leaning on your arm."

"More than that," cried Aubrey, with a gasp of his labouring breath, "she came up to me as I stood there and put her arm, as if to support me, within mine."

The Colonel could not restrain an exclamation. "By Jove," he said, "she is a strong-minded woman, if that is true. Do you mean to say that this was after she had your letter?"

"I suppose so. I sent it to her in the morning. I was anxious to avoid any scene."

"And then, on your way to London, on that day, you went to your solicitors, and gave instructions in respect to Miss Lance's annuity—which you say now had been determined on long before?"

"It was determined on long before."

"But never mentioned to any one until that time."

"I beg your pardon; on the day on which I wrote that letter to my wife I went direct to my lawyer and talked the matter over freely with Mr. Morell, who had known me all my life, and knew all the circumstances—and approved my resolution, as the best of two evils, he said."

"This is the most favourable thing I have heard, Mr. Leigh. He will, of course, be able to back you up in what you say?"

"Mr. Morell!" Aubrey sprang to his feet with a start of dismay. "I think," he cried, "all the powers of hell must be against me. Mr. Morell is dead."

They looked at each other for a moment in silence. A half smile came upon the Colonel's face, though even he was a little overawed by the despair in the countenance of the young man.

"I don't know that it matters very much," he said, "for, after all, Mr. Leigh, your anxiety to get rid of your wife's companion might have two interpretations. You might have been sincerely desirous to free yourself from a temptation towards another woman, which would have given Mrs. Leigh pain. A man does not sacrifice two hundred a year without a strong motive. And subsequent events make this a far more likely reason than the desire to get rid of an unwelcome inmate."

"I cannot tell whether my motive was likely or not. I tell you, sir, what it was."

"Ah, yes—but unfortunately without any corroboration—and the story is very different from the other side. It appears from that that you wished to establish relationship during your poor wife's life, and that it was the lady who was moved by pity for you in a moment of weakness—which is much more according to the rule in such matters."

"It is a lie!" Aubrey cried. "Colonel Kingsward, you are a man—and an honourable man. Can you imagine another man, with the same principles as yourself, guilty of such villainy as that? Can you believe—"

"Mr. Leigh," said the other, "it is unnecessary to ask me what I can believe; nor can I argue, from what I would do, as to what you would do. That may be of good Christianity, you know, but it is not tenable in life. Many men are capable enough of what I say; and, indeed, I do you the credit to believe that you were willing to keep the temptation at a distance—to make a sacrifice in order to ease the mind of your wife. I show a great deal of faith in you when I say that. Another man might say that Mrs. Leigh had exacted it from you as a thing necessary to her peace."

Aubrey Leigh rose up again, and began to pace the room from one side to the other. He could not keep still in his intolerable impatience and scorn of the net which was tightening about his feet. Anger rose up like a whirlwind in his mind; but to indulge it was to lose for ever the cause which, indeed, was already lost. When he had gained control over himself and his voice, he said, "We had neighbours; we had friends; our life was not lived in a corner unknown to the world. There is my mother; ask them—they all know—."

"Does anyone outside know what goes on between a husband and wife?" said Colonel Kingsward. "Such discussions do not go on before witnesses. If poor Mrs. Leigh—"

"Sir," cried Aubrey, stung beyond hearing, "I will not permit any man to pity my wife."

"It was beyond my province I allow, but one uses the word for those who die young. I don't know why, for if all is true that we profess to believe they certainly have the best of it. Well, if Mrs. Leigh, to speak by the book, had any such burden on her mind, and really felt her happiness to depend on the banishment of that dangerous companion, it is not likely that she would speak of it either to your neighbours or to your mother."

"Why not? My mother was of that mind, though not for that villainous reason; my mother knew, everybody knew—everybody agreed with me in wishing her gone. I appeal to all who knew us, Colonel Kingsward! There is not a friend I have who did not compassionate me for Amy's insensate affection. God forgive me that I should say a word against my poor little girl, but it was an infatuation—as all her friends knew."

"Don't you think we are now getting into the region of the extravagant?" Colonel Kingsward said. "I cannot send out a royal commission to take the evidence of your friends."

Aubrey had to pause again to master himself. If this man, with his contemptuous accents, his cool disdain, were not Bee's father!—but he was so, and, therefore, must not be defied. He answered after a time in a subdued voice. "Will you allow me—to send one or two of them to tell you what they know.

There is Fairfield, with whom you are acquainted already, there is Lord Langtry, there is Vavasour, who was with us constantly—"

"To none of these gentlemen, I presume, would Mrs. Leigh be likely to unfold her most intimate sentiments."

"Two of them have wives," said Aubrey, determined to hold fast, "whom she saw familiarly daily—country neighbours."

"I must repeat, Mr. Leigh, I cannot send out a royal commission to take the evidence of your friends."

"Do you mean that you will not hear any evidence, Colonel Kingsward?—that I am condemned already?—that it does not matter what I have in my favour?"

Colonel Kingsward rose to dismiss his suitor. "I have already said, Mr. Leigh, that I am not your judge. I have no right to condemn you. Your account may be all true; your earnestness and air of sincerity, I allow, in a case in which I was not personally involved, would go far to making me believe it was true. But what then? The matter is this: Will I allow my daughter to marry a man of whom such a question has been raised? I say no: and there I am within my clear rights. You may be able to clear yourself, making out the lady to be a sort of demon in human shape. My friend, who saw her, said she was a very attractive woman. But really this is not the question. I am not a censor of public morals, and on the whole it is a matter of indifference to me whether you are guiltless or not. The sole thing is that I will not permit my daughter to put her foot where such a scandal has been. I have nothing to do with you but everything with her. And I think now that all has been said."

"That is, you will not hear anything more?"

"Well—if you like to put it so—I prefer not to hear any more."

"Not if Bee's happiness should be involved?"

"My daughter's happiness, I hope, does not depend upon a man whom she has known only for a month. She may think so now. But she will soon know better. That is a question into which I decline to enter with you."

"Men have died and worms have eaten them, but not for love," said Aubrey, with a coarse laugh. He turned as if to go away. "But you do not mean that this is final, Colonel Kingsward—not final? Not for ever? Never to be revised or reconsidered—even if I were as bad as you think me?"

"How needless is all this! I have told you your character does not concern me—and I do not say that you are bad—or think so. I am sorry for you. You have got into a rather dreadful position, Mr. Leigh, for a young man of your age."

"And yet at my age you think I should be cut off for ever from every hope of salvation!"

"Not so; this is all extravagant—ridiculous! And if you will excuse me, I am particularly busy this morning, with a hundred things to do."

Poor Aubrey would have killed with pleasure, knocked down and trampled upon, the immovable man of the world who thus dismissed him; but to be humble, even abject, was his only hope. "I will try, then, to find some moment of leisure another time."

"It is unnecessary, Mr. Leigh. I shall not change my mind; surely you must see that it is better for all parties to give it up at once."

"I shall never give it up."

"Pooh! one nail drives out another. You don't seem to have been a miracle of constancy in your previous relationships. Good morning. I trust to hear soon that you have made as satisfactory a settlement of other claims."

CHAPTER X

Other claims! What other claims? Aubrey Leigh went out of the office in Pall Mall with these words circling through his mind. They seemed to have nothing to do with that which occupied him, which filled every thought. His dazed memory and imagination caught them up as he went forth in the fury of suppressed anger, and the dizzy, stifled sensation of complete failure. He had felt sure, even when he felt least sure, that when it was possible to tell his tale fully, miserable story as it was, the man to whom he humbled himself thus, not being a recluse or a mere formalist—a man of the world—would at least, to some degree, understand and perceive how little real guilt there might be even in such a fault as he had committed. It was not a story which could be repeated in a woman's ears; but a man, who knew more or less what was in man—the momentary lapses, the sudden impulses, the aberrations of intolerable trouble, sorrow, and despair—. Aubrey did not take into account the fact that there are some men to whom such a condition as that into which he himself had fallen in the desolation of his silent house—when death came a second time within the sad year, and his young soul felt in the first sensation of despair that he could not bear it; that he was a man signalled out by fate, to whom it was vain to struggle, to whom life was a waste and heaven a mockery—was inconceivable. Colonel Kingsward was certainly not a man like that. He would have said to himself that the mother being gone it was only a blessing and advantage that the child should go too, and he would have withdrawn himself decorously to his London lodgings and his club, and his friends would all have said that it was on the whole a good thing for him, and that he was young, and his life still before him. So, indeed, they had said of Aubrey, and so poor Aubrey had proved for himself. Had there not been that terrible moment behind him, that intolerable blackness and midnight of despair, in which any hand that gripped his could lead him till the light of morning burst upon him, and showed him whither in his misery he had been led!

Satisfy other claims? The words blew like a noxious wind through his brain. He laughed to himself softly as he went along. What claims had he to satisfy? He had done all that honour and scorn could do to satisfy the harpy who had dug her claws into his life. Should he try to propitiate her with other gifts? No, no! That would be but to prolong the scandal, to give her a motive for continuance, to make it appear that he was in her power. He was in her power, alas, fatally as it proved, if it should be so that she had made an end of the happiness of his life. She had blighted the former chapter of that existence, bringing out all that was petty in the poor little bride over whom she had gained so complete an ascendancy, showing her husband Amy's worst side, the aspect of her which he might never have known but for that fatal companion ever near. And now she had ruined him altogether—ruined him as in old stories the

Pamelas of the village were ruined by a villain who took advantage of their simplicity. What lovely woman who had stooped to folly could be more ruined than this unhappy young man? He laughed to himself at this horrible travesty of that old familiar eighteenth century tale. This was the—fin de siecle—version of it, he supposed—the version in which it was the designing woman who seized upon the moment of weakness and the man who suffered shipwreck of everything in consequence. There was a horrible sort of ridicule in it which wrought poor Aubrey almost to madness. When the woman is the victim, however sorely she may be to blame for her own disgrace, a sort of pathos and romance is about her, and pity is winged with indignation against the man who is supposed to have taken advantage of her weakness. But when it is a man who is the victim! Then the mildest condemnation he can look for is the coarse laugh of contempt, the inextinguishable ridicule, to which even in fiction it is too great a risk to expose a hero. He was no hero—but an unhappy young man fallen into the most dreadful position in which man could be, shut out of all hope of ever recovering himself, marked by the common scorn—no ordinary sinner, a man who had profaned his own home, and all the most sacred prejudices of humanity. He had felt all that deeply when he rushed from his house, a man distraught not knowing where he went. And then morning and evening, and the dews and the calm, and the freshness and elasticity inalienable from youth had driven despair and horror away. He had felt it at last impossible that all his life—a life which he desired to live out in duty and kindness, and devotion to God and man—should be spoiled for ever by his momentary yielding to a horrible temptation. He had thought at first that he never could hold up his head again. But gradually the impression had been soothed away, and he had vainly hoped that such a thing might be left behind him and might be heard of no more.

Now he was undeceived—now he was convinced that for what a man does he must answer, not only at the bar of God, where all the secrets of the heart are revealed, but also before men. There are times in which the former judgment is more easy to think of than the latter—for God knows all, everything that is in favour of the culprit, while men only know what is against him. A man with sorrow in his heart for all his shortcomings, can endure, upon his knees, that all-embracing gaze of infinite understanding and pity. But to stand before men who misconstrue, mis-see, misapprehend, how different a thing it is—who do not know the end from the beginning, to whom the true balance and perfect poise of justice is almost impossible—who can judge only as they know, and who can know only the husk and shell of fact, the external aspect of affairs by the side which is visible to them. All these thoughts went through Aubrey's mind as he went listlessly about those familiar streets in their autumnal quiet, no crowd about, nothing to interrupt the progress of the wayfarer. He went across the Green Park, which is brown in the decadence of summer, almost as solitary as if he had been in his own desolate glades at home. London has a soothing effect sometimes on such a still, sunny autumn day, when it seems to rest after the worry and heat and strain of all its frivolity and folly. The soft haze blurs all the outlines, makes the trees too dark and the sky too pale; yet it is sunshine and not fog which wraps the landscape, even that landscape which lies between Pall Mall and Piccadilly. It soothed our young man a little in the despair of his thoughts. Surely, surely at eight-and-twenty everything could not be over. Bee would in a year or two be the mistress of her own actions. She was not a meek girl, to be coerced by her father. She would judge for herself in such a dreadful emergency. After all that had passed, the whole facts of the case would have to be submitted to her, which was a thought that enveloped him as in flames of shame. Yet she would judge for herself, and her judgment would be more like that of heaven than like that of earth. A kind of celestial ray gleamed upon him in this thought.

And as for these other claims—well, if any claim were put forth he would not shrink—would not try to compromise, would not try to hide his shame under piles of gold. Now he had no motive for concealment, he would face it out and have the question set straight in the eye of day. To be sure, for a man to accuse a woman is against the whole conventional code of honour. To accuse all women is the commonplace of every day; but to put the blame of seduction upon one is what a man dare not do save in the solitude of his chamber—or in such a private inquisition as Aubrey had gone through that day. This is one of the proofs that there is much to be said on both sides, and that it is the unscrupulous of either side who has the most power to humble and to destroy. But the bravado did him good for the moment—let her make her claim, whatever that claim was, and he would meet it in the face of day!

Other ideas came rapidly into Aubrey's mind when he strolled listlessly into his club, and almost ran against the friend in whose house he had first met Colonel Kingsward, and through whom consequently all that had afterwards happened had come about. "Fairfield!" he cried, with a gleam of sudden hope in his eyes.

"Leigh! You here?—I thought you were philandering on the banks of—some German river or other. Well! and so I hear I have to congratulate you, my boy—and I'm sure I do so with all my heart—"

You might have done so a week ago, and I should have responded with all mine. But you see me fallen again on darker days. Fate's against me, it seems, in every way."

"Why, what's the matter?" cried his friend. "I expected to see you triumphant. What has gone wrong? Not settlements already, eh?"

"Settlements! They are free to make what settlements they like so far as I am concerned."

"Kingsward's a very cool hand, Aubrey. You may lose your head if you like, but he always knows what he is about. You are an excellent match—"

"You think so," said poor Aubrey, with a laugh. "Not badly off; a mild, domestic fellow, with no devil in me at all.

"I should not exactly say that. A man is no man without a spice of the devil. Why, what's the matter? Now I look at you, instead of a victorious lover, you have the most miserable hang-dog—"

"Hang-dog, that is it—a rope's end, and all over. Hang it, no! I am not going to give in. Fairfield, I don't want to speak disrespectfully of any woman."

"Is it Mrs. Kingsward who is too young, herself, to think of enacting the part of mother-in-law so soon as this?"

"Mrs. Kingsward is a sort of an angel, Fairfield, if it were not old-fashioned to say so—and, alas, I fear, she will not enact any part long, which is so much the worse for me."

"You don't say so! That pretty creature, with all her pretty ways, and her daughter just the same age as she! Poor Kingsward. Aubrey, if a man shows a little impatience with your raptures in such circumstances, I don't think you ought to be hard upon him."

"I don't believe he knows what are the circumstances, nor any of them. It is not from that cause, Fairfield. You know Miss Lance, poor Amy's friend—"

Once more he grew hot all over as he named her name, and turned his face from his friend's gaze.

"Remember her! I should think so, and all you had to bear on that point, old man. We have often said, Mary and I, that if ever there was a hero—"

"Fairfield! they have got up a tale that it was I who kept her at Forest-leigh against poor Amy's will, and that my poor wife's life was made miserable by my attentions to that fi—." Fiend he would have said, but he changed it to "woman," which meant to him at that moment the same thing.

Fairfield stared for a moment—was he taking a new idea into his commonplace mind? Then he burst into a loud laugh. "You can call the whole county to bear witness to that," he cried. "Attentions! Well, I suppose you were civil, which was really more than anyone expected from you."

"You know, and everybody knows, what a thorn in the flesh it was. My poor Amy! Without that, there would have been no cloud on our life, and it all arose from her best qualities, her tender heart, her faithfulness—"

A dubious shade came over Fairfield's face. "Yes, no doubt; and Miss Lance's flattery and blandishments. Aubrey, I don't mind saying it now that you are well quit of her—that was a woman to persuade a fellow into anything. I should no more have dared to keep her—especially after—in my house, and to expose myself to her wiles—"

"They never were wiles for me," said Aubrey, again turning his head away. It was true, true—far more true than the fatal contradiction of it, which lay upon his heart like a stone. "I never came nearer to hating any of God's creatures than that woman. She made my life a burden to me. She took my wife from me—. She—I needn't get dithyrambic on the subject; you all know."

"Oh, yes, we all know; but you were too soft-hearted. You should have risked a fit of tears from poor Mrs. Leigh—excuse me for saying so now—and sent her away."

"I tried it a dozen times. Poor Amy would have broken her heart. She threatened even to go with her. And they say women don't make friendships with each other!"

Fairfield shrugged his shoulders a little. "I suffer myself from my wife's friends," he said; "there's always some 'dear Clara' or other putting the table out of joint, making me search heaven and earth when there's anybody to dinner to find an odd man. But Mary has some—" Sense, he was going to say, but stopped short. Mrs. Fairfield was one of those who had concluded long ago that dear Amy was a little goose, taken sad advantage of by her persistent friend.

"Fairfield," said Aubrey, "you could do me a great service if you would. Colonel Kingsward has just told me that he can't send out a royal commission to examine my friends on this subject. You see him sometimes, I suppose. I know you belong to one of his clubs. Still more, he's at his office all the morning, and you know him well enough to look in upon him there."

"Well?" said Fairfield, dubiously.

"Couldn't you stretch a point for my sake, and go—and tell him the real state of affairs in respect to Miss Lance, and how untrue it is, how ridiculously untrue, that she was kept at Forest-leigh by any will of mine? Why, it was a thing, as you have just said, that all the county knew! An infatuation—and nothing less than the bane of my whole married life."

"Yes, I know—everybody thought so," Mr. Fairfield said. That new idea—was it perhaps germinating faintly in his mind?—no one had thought of any other explanation, but yet—"

"If you were only to say so—only as much as that—that all my friends recognised the state of the case."

"I could say that," said Fairfield, with hesitation. "Don't think me unfriendly, Aubrey, but it's a little awkward for a man to interfere in another man's affairs, and it's not only your affairs that I know so well, but you see Kingsward's too—"

"I am aware of that, Fairfield; still, to break off what I believe in my heart would be for his daughter's happiness too—"

"To be sure there's the young lady to be taken into consideration," said Fairfield, dubiously.

It will be as well to carry this incident to its completion at once. Mr. Fairfield at the last allowed himself to be convinced, and he went that afternoon to the club, to which he still belonged by some early military experiences, and where Colonel Kingsward was one of those who ruled supreme. He knew exactly when to find him at the club, where he strolled in after leaving his office, to refresh himself with a cup of tea, or something else in its place. The intercessor went up to the table at which the Colonel sat with the evening paper, and conversed for a little on the topics of the day. After these had been run over, and the prospects of war slightly discussed—for Colonel Kingsward had not much respect for Mr. Fairfield's opinion on that subject—the latter gentleman said abruptly—

"I say, Kingsward, I am very sorry to hear there is some hitch in the marriage which I was so glad to hear of last week."

"Ah, oh! So Leigh has been with you, I presume?" the Colonel replied.

"Yes; and, upon my life, Colonel, there is not a word of truth in any talk you may have heard about that Miss Lance—. We all know quite well the whole business. You should hear Mary on the subject. Of course, he can't say to you, poor fellow, that his first wife was a little queer, and that that woman made her her slave."

"No; it wasn't to be expected that he would tell me that."

"But it's true. She got completely the upper hand of that poor little thing. The husband had no influence. I believe he hated her—like the devil."

"You think so," said the Colonel, with a strange smile, "yet it is a curious thing that he endured her all the same, and also that a wife should insist so in keeping another woman in her husband's constant company—and an attractive woman, as I hear."

"Oh! a devil of a woman," cried Fairfield. "I was telling Aubrey I should no more have ventured to expose myself to her blandishments—. One of those sort of women, you know, that you cannot abide, yet who can turn you round their little finger."

"And what did he say to that?" the Colonel asked, still with that smile.

"Oh, he said she never had any charm for him—and I believe it—for what with poor little Mrs. Leigh's whims and vagaries, and the other's flatteries and adulation and complete empire over her, his life was made a burden to him. You should hear Mary on that subject—none of the ladies could keep their patience."

"Yet it appears Mr. Aubrey Leigh kept his—until he got tired," said the Colonel. "Believe me, Fairfield, when there is such an unnatural situation as that, there must be more in it than meets the eye."

Fairfield, a good, steady soul, who generally had his ideas suggested to him, went away very serious from that interview. It was very strange indeed that a woman should prefer her friend to her husband, and make things wretched for him in order to keep herself comfortable—it was very curious that with a woman so much superior to Amy in the house, a woman of the kind that turn men's heads, that mild Aubrey Leigh, who was not distinguished for force of character, should have never sought a moment's relief with her from poor Mrs. Leigh's querulousness. Fairfield accelerated his departure by an hour or two in order not to meet Aubrey again before he had poured those strange doubts and suggestions into his own Mary's ears.

CHAPTER XI

The party of travellers whose progress had hitherto been like that of a party of pleasure, who had been interested in everything they saw, and hailed every new place with delight, as if that had been the haven of all their hopes, travelled home from Cologne in a very different spirit. For one thing, it could not be concealed that Mrs. Kingsward was ill, which was a thing that she herself and the whole family stoutly, one standing by another, had hitherto been able to deny. She had not gone far, not an hour's journey, when she had to abandon her seat by the window—where it had always been her delight to "see the country," and point out every village to her children—and lie down upon the temporary couch which Moulsey prepared for her with shawls and cushions along one side of the carriage. She cried out against herself as "self-indulgent" and "lazy," but she did not resist this arrangement. It effectually took any pleasure that there might have been out of the journey: for Bee, as may be supposed, though she was not melancholy, and would not admit, even to Betty, in the closest confidence, that she was at all afraid of the ultimate issue, was certainly self-absorbed, and glad not to be called upon to notice the scenery, but allowed to subside into a corner with her own thoughts. Charlie was in the opposite corner, exceedingly glum, and not conversible. Bee would not speak to him or look at him, and even Betty, that little thing, had said, "Oh, Charlie, how could you be so nasty to Aubrey?" for her sole salutation that morning. He was not sure even that his mother, though he had stood on her side and backed her up, was pleased with him for it. She talked to him, it is true, occasionally, and made him do little things for her, but rather in the way in which a mother singles out the pariah of the family, the one who is boycotted for some domestic offence, to show him that all are not against him, than in the tone which is used to a champion and defender. So it was not wonderful that Charlie was glum; but to see him in one corner, biting or trying to bite the few hairs that he called his moustache, with his brows bent down to his chin, and his chin sunk in the collar of his coat—and Bee in another, very different—indeed, her face glorified with dreams, and her eyes full of latent light, ready to flash at out any moment—was not cheerful for the others.

Mrs. Kingsward looked at them from one to another, and at little Betty between busied in a little book, with that baffled feeling which arises in the mind of a delicate woman when the strong individualities and wills of her children become first developed before her, after that time of their youth when all were guided by her decision, and mamma's leave was asked for everything. How fierce, how self-willed, how determined in his opposition Charlie looked like his father, not to be moved by anything! And Bee, how possessed by those young hopes of her own, which the mother knew would be of no avail against the fiat gone forth against her! Mrs. Kingsward knew her husband better than her children did. She knew that having taken up his position he would not give in. And Bee, with all that light of resistance in her eyes—Bee as little willing to give in as he! The invalid trembled when she thought of the clash of arms that would resound over her head—of the struggle which would rend her cheerful house in two. She did not at all realise that the cheerful days of that house were numbered—that soon it would be reduced into its elements, as a somewhat clamorous, restless, too energetic brood of children, with a father very self-willed, who hitherto had known nothing of them but as happy and obedient creatures, whose individual determinations concerned games and lessons, and who, so far as the conduct of life was affected, were of no particular account. Mrs. Kingsward was not yet aware that this was the dolorous prospect before her household; she only thought, "How am I to manage them all?" and felt her heart fail before Charlie's ill humour and—parti pris—, and before the bright defiance in Bee's eyes. Poor Aubrey, whom she had learned to look upon as one of her own, half a son, and half a brother—poor Aubrey, who had gone so wrong, and yet had so many excuses for him, a victim rather than a seducer—what was happening to Aubrey this fine September morning? It made her heart sick in her bosom as she thought of all these newly-raised conflicting powers, and she so little able to cope with them. If she did not get strong soon, what would all these children do? Charlie would go back to college, and would be out of it. He had so strong a will, and was so determined to get on, that little harm would happen to him—and besides, he was entirely in accord with his father, which was a great matter. But Bee—Bee! It seemed to Mrs. Kingsward that it was on the cards that Bee might take matters into her own hands, and run away with her lover, if her father would not yield. What else was there for these young creatures? Mrs. Kingsward knew that she herself would have done so in the circumstances had—her—lover insisted; and she knew that he would no more have consented to such a sentence—never, never!—than he had done to anything he disliked all his life. And Bee was like him, though she had never hitherto been anything but an obedient child. Mrs. Kingsward could not help picturing to herself, as she lay there, the elopement—Bee's room found empty in the morning, the note left on the table, the so easy, so certain explanation, which already she felt herself to be reading. And then her husband's wrath, his unalterable verdict on the criminal "never to enter this house again!" Poor mother! She foresaw, as we all do, tortures for herself, which she was never to be called upon to bear.

As for Betty, it was the most tiresome journey in all her little experiences. A long journey was generally fun to Betty. The scuffle of getting away, of seeing that all the little packets were right, of abusing Moulsey for hiding away the luncheon basket under the rugs and the books in some locked bag, the trouble of securing a compartment, arranging umbrellas and other things in the vacant seats to make believe that every place was full, the watch at every station to prevent the intrusion of strangers, the running from one side to another to see the pretty village or old castle, or the funny people at the country stations and the queer names—the luncheon in the middle of the day, which was as good as a pic-nic—all these things much diverted Betty, who loved the rapid movement through the air, and to feel the wind on her face; but none of these delights were to be had to-day. She was in one of the middle places, between Charlie, so glum and in a temper, and Bee, lost in her own thoughts and without a word to say, and opposite to mamma, who was so much more serious than usual, giving little Betty a smile from time to time, but not able to speak loud enough to be heard through the din of the train. She tried to read her book but it was not a very interesting book, and it was short too, and evidently would not last out half the journey. Betty was the only member of the party who had a free mind. The commotion of the romance between Bee and Aubrey had been pure amusement to her. It would be a bore if it did not end in a speedy marriage, with all the excitement of the presents, the trousseau, the dresses (especially the bridesmaids' dresses), the wedding day itself, the increased dignity of Betty as Miss Kingsward, the pleasure of talking of "my married sister," the pleasure of visiting Bee, in her own house, and sharing all her grandeur as a county lady. To miss all this would be a real trial, but Betty had confidence in the fitness of things, and felt it was impossible that she should miss all this. And she was at ease in her little mind, and the present dreariness of this unamusing, unattractive journey hung all the more heavy upon her consciousness now.

They arrived next day, having slept at Brussels to break the journey for Mrs. Kingsward, and the Colonel met them, as in duty bound, at Victoria. He gave Charlie his hand, and allowed Bee and Betty to kiss him, but his whole attention, as was natural, was for his wife.

"You look dreadfully tired," he said, with that half-tone of offence in which a man shows his disappointment at the aspect of an invalid. "You must have been worried on the journey to look so tired."

"Oh, no, I have not been at all worried on the journey—they have all been so good, sparing me every fatigue; but it is a tiresome long way, Edward, you know."

"Yes, of course, I know: but I never saw you look so tired before." He cast a reproachful look round upon the young people, who were all ready to stand on the defensive. "You must have bothered your mother to death," he said. "I am sorry I did not come out for her myself—undoing all the effect of her cure."

"Oh, you will see, I shall be all right when I get home," Mrs. Kingsward said, cheerfully. "As for the children, Edward, they have all been as good as gold."

"You had better see to the luggage and bring your sisters home in a cab. I can't let mamma hang about here," said the Colonel, in his peremptory way. "Moulsey will come with us. I suppose you three have brains enough to manage by yourselves?"

Thus insulting his grown-up children, among whom a flame of indignation lighted up, partially burning away their difficulties between themselves, Colonel Kingsward half carried his wife to the carriage. "I thought at first I should have waited at Kingswarden till you came back. I am glad I changed my mind and came back to Harley Street," he said.

"Oh, is it to Harley Street we are going?" said Mrs. Kingsward, faintly. "I had rather hoped for the country, Edward."

"You don't look much like another twenty miles of a journey," said her husband.

"Well, perhaps not. I own I shall be glad to be quiet," the poor lady said. What he wished had always turned out after a moment to be just what his wife wished for all the years of their union. She even meekly accepted the fact that the children—the nursery children, as they were called—the little ones, who were no trouble but only a refreshment and delight, would have been too much for her that first night. Secretly, she had been looking forward to the touch and sight of her placid smiling baby as the one thing that would do her good—and all those large wet kisses of Johnny and Tommy and Lucy and little Margaret, and the burst of delighted voices at the sight of mamma. "Yes, I believe it would have been too much for me," she said, with a look aside at Moulsey, who, as on many a previous occasion, would dearly have loved to box her master's ears. "And I—do—believe it would have been too much for me," Mrs. Kingsward added, when that confidential attendant put her to bed.

"Perhaps it would, ma'am," Moulsey said. "They would have made a noise, bless them—and baby will not go to anyone when he sees me—and altogether I shall be more fit for them, Moulsey, after a good night's rest—"

"If you get that, you poor dear," said Moulsey, under her breath. But her mistress did not hear that remark any more than many others which Moulsey made in her own mind, always addressed to that mistress whom she loved. "If he said dying would be good for you, you would say you were sure of it, and that was what you wanted most," the maid said within herself.

It must not, however, be supposed from this that Colonel Kingsward was not a good husband. He had always been like a lover, though a somewhat peremptory one, to his wife. And without him her young, gay, pleasure-loving ways, her love of life and amusement might have made her a much less successful personage, and not the example of every virtue that she was. Had Mrs. Kingsward had the upper hand, the family would have been a very different family, and its career probably a very broken, tumultuous, happy-go-lucky career. It was that strong hand which had controlled and guided her, which had been, as people say, the making of Mrs. Kingsward; and though she feared his severity in the present crisis, she yet felt the most unspeakable relief from the baffled, helpless condition in which she had looked at her children, feeling herself all unable to cope with them in the presence of papa.

"I wonder if he thinks we are cabbages," was Bee's indignant exclamation as he turned his back upon them.

"Apparently," said Charlie, coming a little out of his sullenness. "Look here, you girls, get into this omnibus—happily we've got an omnibus—with the little things, while I go to the Custom House to get the luggage through."

"Betty, you get in," said Bee. "I will go with you, Charlie, for I have got mamma's keys."

"Can't you give them to me?" Charlie cast a gloomy look about, thinking that Leigh might perhaps be somewhere awaiting a word, a thought which now for the first time traversed Bee's mind, too.

"Then, Betty, you had better go with him, for he doesn't know half the boxes," she said.

"Oh, you can come yourself if you like," said Charlie, feeling in that case that this was the safest arrangement after all.

"No, Betty had better go. Betty, you know Moulsey's box and that new basket that mamma brought me before we left the Baths."

"Come along yourself, quick, Bee."

"No, I shall stop in the omnibus."

"When you have made up your minds," cried Betty, who had slipped out of the vehicle at the first word. Betty thought it would be more fun to go through the Custom House than to wait all the time cooped up here.

And Bee had her reward; for Aubrey was there, waiting at a distance till the matter was settled. "I should have risked everything and come, even if the penalty had been a quarrel with Charlie," Aubrey said, "but I must not quarrel with anyone if I can help it. We shall have hard work enough without that."

"You have seen papa?"

"Yes, I have seen him: but I have not done myself much good, I fear," said Aubrey, shaking his head. "Bee, you won't give me up whatever they may say?"

"Give you up? Never, Aubrey, till you give me up!"

"Then all is safe, my darling. However things look now they can't hold out for ever. Lies must be found out, and then—in time—you will be able to act for yourself."

"Do you think papa will stand to it like that, Aubrey?"

Aubrey shook his head. He did not make any reply.

"Tell me. Is it a lie?" she said.

He bent down his head upon her hand, kissing it.

"Not all," he said, in an almost inaudible voice. "I said that—at Cologne—"

"I did not understand," said Bee. "No; it does not matter to me, Aubrey—not so very much; but if you promised—"

"I never promised—never! My only thought was to escape—"

"Then I can't think what you have done wrong. Aubrey, is she tall, with dark hair, and beautiful dark eyes, and a way of looking at you as if she would look you through and through?"

"Bee!" he said, gripping her fast, as if someone had been about to decoy her away.

"And a mouth," said Bee, "that is very pretty, but looks as if it were cut out of steel? Then, I have seen her. She sat down by me one day in the wood, when I was doing that sketch, and gave me such clever hints, telling me how to finish it, till she made me hate it, don't you know. Is she horribly clever, and a good artist? and like that—"

"Bee! What did that woman say to you?"

"Nothing very much. Asked me about the people at the hotel, and if there were any Leighs—not you, she pretended, but the Leighs of Hurst-leigh, whom she knew. I thought it very strange at the time why she should ask about the Leighs without knowing anything—and then I forgot all about it. But to-day it came back to my mind, and I have been thinking of nothing else. Aubrey—she is older than you are?"

"Yes," he said.

"And she made you promise to marry her?" said Bee, half unconscious yet half conscious of that wile of the cross-examiner, coming back to the point suddenly.

"Never, Bee, never for one moment in my misery! That I should have to make such a confession to you!—but there was no promise nor thought of a promise. I desired nothing—nothing but to escape from her. You don't doubt my word, Bee?"

"No; I don't doubt anything you say. But I think she is a dreadful woman to get anybody in her power, Aubrey. My little drawing was for you. It was the place we first met, and she told me how to do it and make it look so much better. I am not very clever at it, you know; and then I hated the very sight of it, and tore it in two. I don't know why."

"I understand why. Bee, you will be faithful to me, whatever you are told?"

"Till I die, Aubrey."

"And never, never believe that for a moment my heart will change from you."

"Not till I hear it from yourself," she said, with a woeful smile. The despair in him communicated itself to her, who had not been despairing at all.

"Which will never be—and when you are your own mistress, my darling—"

"Oh, we shan't have to wait for that!" she cried, with a burst of her native energy. "Dear Aubrey, they are coming back; you must go away."

"Till we meet again, darling?"

"Till we meet again!"

CHAPTER XII

Bee stole into her mother's room as she went upstairs before that first dinner at home which used to be such a joyous meal. How they had all enjoyed it—until now. The ease and space, the going from room to room, the delight in finding everything with which they were familiar, the flowers in the vases (never were any such flowers as those at home!), the incursions of the little ones shouting to each other, "Mamma's come home!" Even the little air of disorder which all these interruptions brought into the orderly house was delightful to the young people. They looked forward as to an ideal life, to beginning all their usual occupations again and doing them all better than ever. "Oh, how nice it is to be at home!" the girls had said to each other. Instead of those hotel rooms, which at their best are never more than hotel rooms, a—genre—not to be mistaken, how delightful was the drawing-room at home, with all its corners—Bee's little table where she muddled at her drawings, mamma's great basket of needlework where everything could be thrown under charitable cover, Betty's stool on which she sat at the feet of her oracle of the moment, whoever that might be, and all the little duties to be resumed—the evening papers arranged for papa (as if he had not seen enough of them in the daytime in his office!), the flowers to see after, the little notes to write, all the pleasant common-places of the home life. But to-night, for the first time, dinner was a silent meal, hurried over—not much better than a dinner at a railway station, with a sensation in it of being still on the road, of not having yet reached their destination. The drawing-room was in brown holland still, for they were all going on to Kingswarden to-morrow. The house felt formal, uninhabited, as if they had come home to lodgings. All this was bad enough; but the primary trouble of all was the fact that mamma was upstairs—gone to bed before dinner, too tired to sit up. Such a thing had never happened before. However tired she was, she had always so brightened up at the sensation of coming home.

And papa, though kind, was very grave. The happiness of getting his family back did not show in his face and all his actions as it generally did. Colonel Kingsward was very kind as a father, and very tender as a husband; the severity of his character showed little at home. His wife was aware of it, and so were the servants, and Charlie, I think, had begun to suspect what a hand of iron was covered by that velvet glove. But the girls had never had any occasion to fear their father. Bee thought that the additional gravity of his behaviour was owing to herself and her introduction of a new individual interest into the family; so that, notwithstanding a touch of indignation, with which she felt the difference, she was timid and not without a sense of guilt before her father. Never had she been rebellious or disobedient before; and she was both now, determined not to submit. This made her self-conscious and rather silent; she who was always overflowing with talk and fun and the story of their travels. Colonel Kingsward did not ask many questions about that. What he did ask was all about "your mother."

"She is not looking so well as when she went away," he said.

"Oh, papa, it's only because she's so tired," cried little Betty. Betty taking upon her to answer papa, to take the responsibility upon her little shoulders! But Bee felt as if she could not say anything.

"Do you really think so?" he said, turning to that confident little speaker—to Betty. As if Betty could know anything about it! But Bee seemed paralysed and could not speak.

She stole, as I have said, into her mother's room on her way upstairs, but she had hardly time to say a word when papa came in to see if Mrs. Kingsward had eaten anything, and how she felt now that she was comfortably established in her own bed. It irritated Bee to feel herself thus deprived of the one little bit of possible expansion, and stirred her spirit. With her cheek to her mother's, she said in her ear, "Mamma, I saw Aubrey at the station," with a thrill of pleasure and defiance in saying that, though secretly, in her father's presence.

"Oh, Bee!" said Mrs. Kingsward, with a faint cry of alarm.

"And he told me," continued Bee, breathless in her whisper, "that papa was firm against us."

"Bee! Bee!"

"And we promised each other we should never, never give up, whatever anyone might say."

"Oh, child, how dare you, how dare you?" Mrs. Kingsward said.

How Bee's heart beat! What an enlivening, inspiriting strain of opposition came into her mind, making her cheeks glow and her eyes flame! The whisper was, perhaps, a child's device, perhaps a woman's weakness, but it exhilarated her beyond description to say all this in the very presence of her father. There was a sensation of girlish mischief in it as well as defiance, which relieved all the heavier sentiments that had weighed down her heart.

"What are you saying to your mother, Bee? She must not be disturbed. Run away and let her rest. If we are to go back to Kingswarden to-morrow she must get all the rest that is possible now."

"I was never the one to disturb mamma," said Bee, bestowing another kiss on her mother's cheek.

"Oh, be a good child, Bee!" pleaded Mrs. Kingsward, almost without sound; for by this time the Colonel was hovering over the bed, with a touch of suspicion, wondering what was going on between these two.

"Yes, mamma dear, always," said Bee, aloud.

"What is she promising, Lucy? And what were you saying to her? Bee should know better at her age than to disturb you with talk."

"Oh, nothing, Edward. She was only giving me a kiss, and I told her to be a good child—as I am always doing; thinking to be heard, you know, for so much speaking," the mother said, with a soft laugh.

"Bee has always been a sufficiently good child. I don't think you need trouble yourself on that point. The thing is for you to get well, my dear, and keep an easy mind. Don't trouble about anything; leave all that to me, and try and think a little about yourself."

"I always do, Edward," she said with a smile.

He shook his head, but agitation had brought a colour to her cheeks, and to persuade one's-self that it is only fatigue that makes a beloved face look pale is so easy at first, before any grave alarm has been roused. Yet, Colonel Kingsward's mind was not an easy one that night. He was—au fond—, a severe man, very rigid as to what he thought his duty, taking life seriously on the whole. His young wife, who loved pleasure, had made him far more a man of society than was natural or indeed pleasing to him; but he had thus got into that current which it is so difficult to get out of without a too stern withdrawal, and his large young family had warmed his heart and dressed his aspect in many smiles and graces which did not belong to him by nature. The mixture of the rigid and the yielding had produced nothing but good effects upon his character till now. But there is no telling what a man is till the first conflict of wills arises in his own household. Hitherto there had been nothing of the kind. His children had amused him and pleased him and made him proud. Their health, their prettiness, their infantile gaiety and delight in every favour accorded to them had been all so many tributes to his own supreme influence and power. Their very health was a standing compliment to his own health and vigour, from whom they took their excellent constitutions, and to the wonderful care and attention to every law of health which he enforced in his house. Not a drain escaped trapping, not a gas was left undisposed of where Colonel Kingsward was. He had every new suggestion in his nursery that sanitary science could bring up. "And look at the result!" he was in the habit of saying. Not a pale face, not a headache, not an invalid member there. And among the children he was as the sun in his splendour. Every delight rayed out from him. The hour of his coming home was watched for; it was the greatest treat for the little boys to go in the dogcart with Simmons, the groom, to fetch papa from the station, while the others assembled at the door as at a daily celebration to see him arrive. Charlie was now a man grown, but he was a good boy, full of all right impulses, and there had never been any difficulty with him.

Thus Colonel Kingsward had been kept from all knowledge of those contrarieties of nature which appear even in the most favoured regions. He was of opinion that he surrounded his wife with every care, bore everything for her, did not suffer the winds of heaven to visit her cheek too roughly. And it was true. But he was not at all aware that she saved him anything, or that his joyful omnipotence and security from every fret and all opposition depended upon her more than on anything else in the world. He did not know the little inevitable jars which she smoothed away, the youthful wills growing into individuality which she kept in check. Which was a pity, for the strong man was thus deprived of the graces of precaution, and knew no more than the merest weakling what, as his children grow into men and women, every man has to face and provide against. If Colonel Kingsward was too arbitrary, too trenchant in his measures, too certain that there was no will but his own to be taken into account, the blame must thus be partially laid upon those natural fictions of boundless love and duty and sweet affectionate submission, which grow up in the nursery and reign as long as childhood lasts—until a more potent force of self or will or love, comes in to put the gentle dream to flight.

It was thus that Colonel Kingsward considered the matter about Bee. It had been, of course, necessary to cross Bee two or three times in her life before. It had been necessary, or at least he had thought it necessary, to send her to school; it had been thought expedient to keep her back a year longer than she wished from appearing in the world. These decisions had cost tears and a little struggle, but in a few days Bee had forgotten all about them—or so, at least, her father thought. And a lover—at nineteen— what was that but another plaything, a novelty, a compliment, such as girls love? How could it mean anything more serious? Why, Bee was a child—a little girl, an ornamental adjunct to her mother, a sort of reflection, not to be detached for a long time from that source of all that was delightful in her. Colonel Kingsward had felt with a delighted surprise that the child and the mother did "throw up" each other when he began to go out with them together. Bee's young beauty showing what mamma's had been, and Mrs. Kingsward's beauty (so much higher and sweeter than any girl's wild-rose bloom could be) showing what in the after days her child would grow to. To cut these two asunder for a stranger— another man, an intruding personality thrusting himself between the child and her natural allegiance— was oppressive in any shape. At the first word, indeed, and in the amusement furnished him by the letters that had been poured upon him, Colonel Kingsward's consent had been given almost without thought. Aubrey Leigh was a good match, he had a fine place, a valuable estate, and was well spoken of among men. If Lucy was so absurd as to wish her daughter to marry; if Bee, the silly child, was so foolish as to think of leaving her father's house for another, that was probably as good a one as she could have chosen. I don't know if fathers generally feel it a sort of desecration when their young daughters marry. Some fathers do, and some brothers, as if the creature pure by nature from all such thoughts were descending to a lower place, and becoming such an one as themselves. Colonel Kingsward was not, perhaps, visionary enough for such a view, yet he was slightly shocked in his sentiment about the perfection of his own house by this idea on his child's part of leaving it for another. However, it was true he had a very large family, and to provide so well for one of them at the very outset of her career was a thing which was not to be despised.

But when the second chapter of this romance, all so simple, so natural in its first phase, opened out, and there appeared a dark passage behind—a woman wronged who had a claim upon the man, a story, a scandal—whether it were true or untrue!—Colonel Kingsward, in his knowledge of the world, knew that it did not so much matter whether a story was true or untrue. It stuck, anyhow; and years, generations after, when, if false, it had been contradicted and exploded, and acknowledged to be false, people still would shake their heads and say, "Wasn't there some story?" For this reason he was not very rigid about the facts, part of which, at least, the culprit admitted. There was a woman and there was a story, and all the explanations in the world could not do away with these. What did it matter about the man? He, Colonel Kingsward, was not Aubrey Leigh's keeper. And as for Bee, there would be some tears, no doubt, as when she was sent to school—a little passion of disappointment, as when she was kept back for a whole year, from seventeen to eighteen, in her "coming out"—but the tears and the passion once over, things would go on the same as before. The little girl would go back to her place, and all would be well.

This was the man's delusion, and perhaps it was a natural one, and he was conscious of wishing to do the best thing for her, of saving her from the after tortures which a wife has to endure whose husband has proclivities towards strange women, and capabilities of being "led away." That was a risk that he could understand much better than she could, at her age. The fellow might be proud of her, small blame to him—he might strive to escape from disgraceful entanglements by such an exceptionable connection as that of Colonel Kingsward, of Kingswarden, Harley Street, and the Intelligence Department; he might be very much in earnest and all that. He did not altogether blame the man; indeed, he was willing enough to allow that he was not a bad fellow, and that he was popular among his friends.

But these were not enough in the case of a girl like Bee. And it was certainly for her good that her father was acting. She had known the man a month, what could he be to her in so short a time? This is the most natural of questions, constantly asked, and never finding any sufficient answer. Why should a girl in three or four weeks be so changed in all her thoughts as to be ready to give up her father's house, the place in which she has all her associations, the company in which she has been so happy, and go away to the end of the world, perhaps with a man whom she has known only for a month? It is the commonest thing in the world, but also the most mysterious, and Colonel Kingsward refused to believe in it, as so many other fathers have done. Bee would cry, and her mother would console her. She would fly into a childish passion, and struggle against her fate—for a few days. She would swear that she would never, never give up that new plaything, and the joy of parading it before the other girls, who perhaps had not such toys to play with—but all that nonsense would give way in a little to firm guidance and considerate care, and the fresh course of amusement and pleasure which the winter would bring.

The winter is by no means barren to those who spend it habitually in town. It has many distractions. There is the theatre, there are Christmas gatherings without number, there are new dresses also to be got for the same, perhaps a pretty new bonnet or two thrown in by a penitent father, very sorry even in his own interests to give his little girl pain. If all these pleasant things could not make up for the loss of a man—of doubtful character, too—whom she had only known for a month, Colonel Kingsward felt that it would be a strange thing indeed, and altogether beyond his power to explain.

CHAPTER XIII

It was not possible, however, to remove Mrs. Kingsward to Kingswarden next day. She was too much fatigued even to leave her bed, and the doctor who came to see her, her own familiar doctor who had sent her to Germany to the celebrated bath, looked a little grave when he saw the condition in which she had come home. "No fatigue, no excitement," was what he enjoined. She was to have nothing to excite, nothing to disturb her—to go to the country? Oh, yes, but not for some days. To see the children? Certainly, the children could not be kept from their mother; but all in moderation, with great judgment, not too long at a time, not too often. And above all she must not be worried. Nothing must be done, nothing said to cross or vex her. When he heard from the Colonel a very brief and studiously subdued version of a little family business which had disturbed her—"I need not keep any secrets from you, doctor. The fact is that someone wanted to marry my girl Bee, and that I made some discoveries about him which obliged me to withdraw my consent." The doctor formed his lips into a whistle, to which he did not give vent. "That accounts for it," he said.

"That accounts for—what?" cried Colonel Kingsward, not without irritation.

"For the state in which I find her. And mind my words, Kingsward, you'd better let your girl marry anybody that isn't a blackguard than risk that sort of shock with your wife. Never forget that her life—I mean to say that she's very delicate. Don't let her be worried—stretch a point—have things done as she wishes. You will find it pay best in the end."

"For once you are talking nonsense, my dear fellow," said Colonel Kingsward; "my wife is not a woman who has ever been set upon having her own way."

"Let her have it this time," said the doctor, "and you'll never repent it. If she wants Bee to marry, let her marry. Bee is a dear little thing, but her mother, Kingsward, her mother—is of far more consequence to you than even she—"

"That is a matter of course," said Colonel Kingsward. "Lucy is of more importance to me than all the world beside; but neither must I neglect the interests of my child."

"Oh, bother the child," cried the doctor, "let her have her lover; the mother is what you must think of now."

"You seem tremendously in earnest, Southwood."

"So I am—tremendously in earnest. And don't you work your mind on the subject, but do what I say."

"Do you mean to say that my wife is in a—state of danger?"

"I mean that she must be kept from worry—she must not be contradicted—things must not be allowed to go contrary to her wishes. Poor little Bee! I don't say you are to let her marry a blackguard. But don't worry her mother about it—that is the chief thing I've got to say."

"No, I shan't worry her mother about it," said the Colonel, shutting his mouth closely as if he were locking it up. When Dr. Southwood was gone, however, he stopped the two girls who were lingering about to know the doctor's opinion, and detaching Betty's arm from about Bee's waist drew his eldest daughter into his study and shut the door. "I want to speak to you, Bee," he said.

"Yes, papa." In this call to her alone to receive some communication, Bee, as may be imagined, jumped to a conclusion quite different from what her father intended, and almost for the moment forgot mamma.

"The doctor tells me that above everything your mother must be kept from worry. Do you understand? In the circumstances it is extremely important that you should know this."

"Papa," she cried, half in indignation half in disappointment, "do you think that I would worry her—in any circumstances?"

"I think that girls of your age often think that no affairs are so important as your own, and it is very likely that you may be of that opinion, and I wish you to know what the doctor says."

"Is mamma—very ill?" Bee asked, bewildered.

"He does not say so—only that she is not to be fretted or contradicted, or disturbed about anything. I feel it necessary to warn you, Bee."

"Why me above the rest?" she cried. "Am I likely to be the one to worry mamma?"

"The others have no particular affairs of their own to worry her with. There must be no private talks, no discussions, no endeavours to get her upon what you may suppose to be your side."

Bee gave her father a glance of fire, but she felt that a little prudence was necessary, and kept the tumult of feeling which was within her as much as possible in her own breast. "I have always talked to mamma of everything that was in my mind," she said, piteously. "I don't know how I am to stop. She would wonder so if I stopped talking; and how can I talk to her except of things that are in my mind?"

"You must learn," said the Colonel, "to think of her more than of yourself." He did not at all mean to prescribe to her a course of conduct more elevated than that he meant to pursue himself, but then it was only in action that he meant to carry out his purposes, he was not afraid of committing himself in speech.

Bee looked at him again with a gaze that asked a great many questions, but she only answered, "I will try my very best, papa."

"If you do, I am sure you will succeed, my dear," he said, in a gentler tone.

"Is that all?" she asked, hesitating.

"That is all I want with you just now."

Bee turned away towards the door, and then she paused and made a step back.

"Papa!"

"Yes, Bee."

"Would you mind telling me—I will not say a word to her—but oh, please tell me—"

"What is it?" said the Colonel. He went to his writing table, and sitting down began to turn over his papers. His tone was slightly impatient, his eyebrows slightly raised, as if in surprise.

"Papa, you must know what it is. I know that you have seen—Mr. Leigh!"

"How do you know anything about it? What have you to do with whom I have seen? Run away. I do not mean to enter into any explanations on this subject with you."

"Then with whom will you enter into explanations? You cannot speak to mamma; she must not be worried. Papa, I am not a little girl now, to be told to run away."

"You seem to be determined not to lose a moment in telling me so."

"I should not have told you so," said Bee, looking at him over the high back of his writing-table, "if you had not told me I was not to talk to mamma."

He looked up at her, and their eyes met; both of them keenly, fiercely blue, lit up with fires of combat. It is often imagined that blue eyes are the softest eyes—but not by those who are acquainted with the kind which belonged to the Kingswards, which might have been called sapphires, if sapphires ever flash and cut the air as diamonds do. They were not either so dark as sapphires—they were like nothing but themselves, two pairs of blue eyes that might have been made to order, so like were they to each other, and both blazing across that table as if they would have set the house on fire.

"That's an excellent point," he said. "I can't deny it. What made you so terrifically clever all at once?"

There is nothing more stinging than to be called clever in the midst of a discussion. Bee's eyes seemed to set fire to her face, at least, which flashed crimson upon her father's startled sight.

"When one has someone else to think of, someone's interests to take care of—"

"Which are your own interests—and vastly more important than anything which concerns your father and mother."

"I never said so—nor thought so, papa—but if they are different from yours, that's no reason," said Bee, bold in words but faltering in manner, "is it, why I should not think of them, if, as you say, they're my own interests, papa?"

"You are very bold, Bee."

"What am I to do if I have no one to speak for me? Papa, Aubrey—"

"I forbid you to speak with such familiarity of a man whom you have nothing to do with, and whom you scarcely know."

"Papa, Aubrey—" cried Bee, with astonishment.

Colonel Kingsward jumped up from his table in a fury of impatience. "How dare you come and besiege me here in my own room with your Aubrey?—a man whom you have not known a month; a stranger to the family."

"Papa, you must let me speak. You allowed me to be engaged to him. If you had said 'no' at first, there might, perhaps, have been some reason in it."

"Perhaps—some reason!" he repeated, with an angry laugh.

"Yes, for even then it was not your own happiness that was in question. It was I, after all, that was to marry him."

"And you think that is a reason for defying me?"

"It is always said to be a reason—not for defying anybody—but for standing up for what you call my own interests, papa—when they are somebody else's interests as well. You said we might be engaged—and we were. And how can I let anyone, even you, say he is a stranger? He is my—fiancé—. He is betrothed to me. We belong to each other. Whatever anyone may say, that is the fact," cried Bee, very rapidly, to get it all out before she was interrupted.

"It is not at all a cheerful or pleasant fact—if it changes my little Bee, whom I thought I knew, to this flushed and brazen woman, fighting for her—. Go, child, and don't make an exhibition of yourself. Your mother's daughter! It is not credible—to assault me, your father, in my own room, for the sake of—"

"Papa! don't you remember that it is said in the Bible you are not to provoke your children to wrath? Mamma would have stood up for you, I suppose, when she was engaged to you. I may be flushed," cried Bee, putting her hands to her blazing cheeks, "how could I help it? Forced to talk to you, to ask you—on a subject that gives you a right to speak to me, your own child, like that—"

"I am glad you think I have a right to speak as the circumstances demand to my own child," said the Colonel, cooling down; "but why you should be forced, as you say, to take up such an unbecoming and unwomanly position is beyond my guessing."

"It is because I have no longer mamma to speak for me," Bee said.

The creature was not without skill. Now she came back to the point that was not to be gainsaid.

"We have had quite enough of this," Colonel Kingsward replied. "Your mother, as you are quite aware, never set up her will against mine. She was aware, if you are not, that I knew the world better than she did, and was more competent to decide. Your mother would never have stood up to me as you have done."

"It would have been better, perhaps, sometimes, if she had," cried Bee, carried away by the tide of her excitement. Colonel Kingsward was so astounded that he had scarcely power to be angry. He gazed at his excited child with a surprise that was beyond words.

"Oh, papa, papa! Forgive me! I never meant that; it came out before I was aware."

"The thought must have been there or it could not have come out," he said.

"Oh, no; there was no thought there. It may be so with you, but not with us, papa. Words come into our mouths. We don't think them; we don't mean to say—they only seem to—hook on to—something that went before; and then they come out with a crash. Oh, forgive me, forgive me, papa!"

"I suppose," he said, with a half laugh, "that may be taken as a woman's exposition of her own style of argument."

"Don't call me a woman," she said, with her soft small voice, aggrieved and wounded, drawing closer to him. "Oh, papa! I am only your little girl after all."

"A naughty little girl," he said, shaking his head.

"And without mamma to speak for me," added Bee.

The Colonel laughed aloud. "You wily little natural lawyer!" he said; but immediately became very grave, for underneath this burst of half angry amusement Bee had given him a shock she did not know of. All unaware of the edge of the weapons which she used with a certain instinctive deftness, it did not occur to her that these words of hers might penetrate not only deeper than she thought, but far deeper than her own thoughts had ever gone. His wife's worn face seemed suddenly to appear before Colonel Kingsward's eyes in a light which he had never seen before, and the argument which this child used so keenly, yet so ignorantly, pierced him like a knife. "Without mamma to speak for me!" These words sounded very simple to Bee, a mischievous expedient to trap him in the snare he had laid for her. But if the time should ever come when they should be true! The Colonel was struck down by that arrow flown at a venture. He went back to his table subdued, and sat down there. "That will do," he said, "that will do. Now run away and leave me to my work, Bee."

She came up to him and gave him a timid kiss, which the Colonel accepted quietly in the softening of that thought. She roamed about the table a little, flicking off an imperceptible speck of dust with her handkerchief, arranging some books upon the upper shelf of his bureau, sometimes looking at him over that row of books, sometimes lingering behind him as if doing something there. He did not interfere with her movements for a few minutes, in the—attendrissement—of his thoughts. Without a mother to speak for her! Poor little girl, if that should ever be so! Poor little children unconscious in their nursery crying for mamma; and, oh, worse than all, himself without his Lucy, who had made all the world sweet to him! He was a masterfull man, who would stand to his arms in any circumstances, who would not give in even if his heart was broken; but what a strange, dull, gloomy world it would be to him if the children had no mother to speak for them! He made a sudden effort to shake off that thought, and the first thing that recalled him to himself was to hear Bee, having no other mischief, he supposed, to turn her hand to, heaping coals upon the little bit of fire which had been lighted for cheerfulness only.

"Bee," he cried, "are you still there? What are you doing? The room is like an oven already, and you are making up a sort of Christmas fire."

"Oh, I am so sorry—I forgot," cried Bee, putting down the shovel hastily. "I thought it wanted mending—for you always like a good fire."

"Not in September," he said, "and such weather; the finest we have had since July. Come, cease this fluttering about—you disturb me—and I have a hundred things to do."

"Yes, papa." Bee's little figure stole from behind him in the meekest way. She stopped in her progress towards the door to give a touch to the flowers on a side table; and then she went slowly on, going out. She had got her hand upon the handle of the door, and Colonel Kingsward thanked heaven he had got rid of her for the moment, when she turned round, eyeing him closely again though keeping by that means of escape. "Papa," she said, softly, "after all the talk we have been having—you perhaps don't remember that—you have never—answered my question yet."

"What question?" he said sharply.

Bee put her hands together like a child, she looked at him beseechingly, coaxingly, like that child returning to its point, and then she said still more softly, "About Aubrey, dear papa!"

CHAPTER XIV

I will not attempt to follow in detail the course of that autumn. It was a fine season, and Mrs. Kingsward was taken to her home in the country and recovered much of her lost health in the serene ending of the month and the bright days of October, which was a model October—everything that month ought to be. The trees had scarcely begun to take any autumnal colouring upon them when they reached Kingswarden—a house which stood among the Surrey hills; an old house placed not as modern houses are, pitched upon hillsides, or at points where there is "a view." The old Kingswards had been moved by no such ridiculous modern sentiments. They had planted their mansion in a sheltered spot, where it would be safe from the winds that range over the country and all the moorland heights. The gates opened upon a wild country road with an extravagant breadth of green pathway and grassy bank on either side—enough to have made a farmer swear, but very pleasant to the eye and delightful to a horse's feet, as well as to the pedestrians, whether they were tramps or tourists, who walked or rode on bicycles—the latter class only—from London to Portsmouth. The house was old, red, and straggling, covered with multitudes of creepers. Sheets of purple clematis—the Jackmanni, if anybody wishes to know; intolerable name for such a royal garment of blossom—covered half-a-dozen corners, hanging down in great brilliant wreaths over old ivy and straggling Virginia creeper and the strong stalks of the climbing roses, which still bore here and there a flower. Other sheets of other flowers threw themselves about in other places as if at their own sweet will, especially the wild exuberance of the Traveller's Joy; though I need not say that this wildness was under the careful eye of the gardener, who would not let it go too far. I cannot attempt to tell how many other pleasant and fragrant and flowery things there were which insisted on growing in that luxurious place, even to the fastidious Highland creeper, which in that autumn season was the most gay, luxuriant, and delightful of all. The flowers abounded like the children, not to be checked, as healthy and as brilliant, in the fine, peaty soil and pure air. The scent of the mignonette, which in this late season straggled anywhere, seemed to fill half the country round. The borders were crowned with those autumn flowers which make up as well as they can for their want of sweetness by lavish wealth of colour—the glowing single dahlias, which this generation has had the good sense to re-capture from Nature after the quilled and rosetted artificial things which the gardeners had manufactured out of them, and the fine scarlet and blue of the salvias, and the glory of all those golden tribes of the daisy kind that now make our borders bright, instead of the old sturdy red geranium, which once sufficed for all the supplies of autumn, an honest servant but a poor lord. I prefer the sweetness of the Spring, when every flower has a soul in it, and breathes it all about in the air, that is full of hope. But as it cannot always be Spring, that triumph of bright hues is something to mask the face of winter with until the time when the tortured and fantastic chrysanthemum reigns alone.

This was the sort of garden they had at Kingswarden; not shut off in a place by itself, but bordering all the lawns, which were of the velvet it takes centuries to perfect. The immediate grounds sloped a little to the south, and beyond them was a very extensive, if somewhat flat, prospect, ending on the horizon in certain mild blue shadows which were believed to be hills. There was not much that could be called a park at Kingswarden. The few farms which Colonel Kingsward possessed pressed his little circle of trees rather close; but as long as the farms were let the family felt they could bear this. It gave them a comfortable feeling of modest natural wealth and company; the yeomen keeping the squire warm, they in their farmsteadings, he in the hall.

And the autumn went on in its natural course, gaining colour as it began to lose its greenness and the days their warmth. The fruit got all gathered in after the corn, the apple trees that had been such a sight, every bough bent down with its balls of russet or gold, looked shabby and worn, their season done, the hedges ran over with their harvest, every kind of wild berry and feathery seedpod, wild elderberries, hips and haws, the dangerous unwholesome fruit of the nightshade, the triumphant wreaths of bryony of every colour, green, crimson, and purple. The robins began to appear about Kingswarden, hopping about the lawns, and coming very near the dining-room windows after breakfast, when the little tribe of the nursery children had their accustomed half-hour with mamma, and delighted in nothing so much as to crumble the bread upon the terrace and tempt the redbreasts nearer and nearer. When, quite satisfied and comforted about his wife's looks, Colonel Kingsward went off to the shooting, this little flock of children trailed after mamma wherever she went, a little blooming troop. By this time Charlie had gone back to Oxford, and the little ones liked to have the run of the lawns outside and the sitting rooms within, with nothing more alarming than Betty to keep them in order. It is to be feared that the relaxation of discipline which occurred when papa was absent was delightful to all those little people, and neither was Mrs. Kingsward sorry now and then to feel herself at full ease—with no necessity anywhere of further restraint than her own softened perceptions of family decorum required. It was a moment in which, if that could be said, she was self-indulgent—sometimes not getting up at her usual hour, but taking her breakfast in her room, with clusters of little boys and girls all over her bed, and over the carpet, sharing every morsel, climbing over her in their play. And when she went out to drive she had the carriage full of them; and when she took her stroll about the grounds they were all about, shouting and racing, nobody suggesting that it would be "too much for her," or sending them off because they disturbed mamma. She was disturbed to her heart's content while the Colonel was away. She said, "You know this is very nice for a time, but it would not do always," to her elder daughter: but I think that she saw no necessity, except in the return of her husband, why it should not do, and she enjoyed herself singing to them, dancing (a very little) with them, playing for them as only the mother of a large family ever can play, that simple dance music which is punctuated and kept in perfect time by her heart as much as by her ear. For myself, I know the very touch upon the piano of a woman who is the orchestra of the children, who makes their little feet twinkle to the music. There is no band equal to it for harmony, and precision, and go. They enjoyed the freedom of having no one to say, "Hush, don't make such a noise in the house," of the absence of all the disturbable people, "the gentlemen," as the servants plainly said, "being away" more, Mrs. Kingsward sometimes thought, with a faint twinge of conscience, than it was right they should enjoy anything in the absence of papa. Charlie was quite as bad as papa, and declared that they made his head ache, and that no fellow could work with such a row going on; it made the little carnival all the more joyous that he was out of the way.

Bee had spent the six weeks since their return in a sort of splendour of girlish superiority and elation, of which her mother had not been unobservant, though nothing had been said between them. I am not sure that Bee did not enjoy the situation more than if Aubrey had been at Kingswarden wooing her all day long, playing tennis with her, riding with her—in every way appearing as her accepted lover. Circumstances had saved her from this mere vulgarity of beatitude, and she felt that in the very uncertainty of their correspondence, which was private—almost secret, and yet not clandestine—there was a wonderful charm, a romance and tinge of the unhappy and desperate, while yet everything within herself was happy and triumphant. It had never been said, neither by the Colonel nor by his wife (who had said nothing at all), that Bee was not to write letters to Aubrey nor to receive letters from him. I cannot imagine how Colonel Kingsward, in bidding her understand that all was over between Aubrey and herself, did not make a condition of this. But probably he thought her too young and simple to maintain any such correspondence, and her lover too little determined, too persuadeable, to begin it. When Bee had received her lover's first letter it had been under her father's very eyes. It had come at breakfast between two girl-epistles, and Colonel Kingsward would not have been guilty of the pettiness of looking at his daughter's correspondence for any inducement yet before him. She had the tremendous thrill and excitement of reading it in his very sight, which she did not hesitate to do, for the sake of the bravado, feeling her ears tingle and the blood coursing in her veins, never imagining that he would not observe, and setting her young slight strength like a rock in momentary expectation of a question on the subject. But no question came. Colonel Kingsward was looking at the papers, and at the few letters which came to him at his house. The greater part of his correspondence went to the office. He took it very quietly, and he never remarked Bee at all, which was little less than a miracle, she thought. And it was very well for her that this was one of the mornings on which mamma did not come downstairs.

This immense excitement was a little too strong for ordinary use, and Bee so arranged it afterwards that her letters came by a later post, when she could read them by herself in her room. The servants knew perfectly well of this arrangement—the butler who opened the post bag at Kingswarden, and the maid who carried Miss Bee's letters upstairs—but neither father nor mother thought of it. That is, I will not answer for Mrs. Kingsward. She perhaps had her suspicions; but, if her husband did not forbid correspondence, she said to herself that it was not her business to do so. It seemed to her that nothing else could keep Bee so bright. Her disappointment, the shock of the severance, must have affected her otherwise than appeared if she had not been buoyed up by some such expedient. As for the Colonel, he thought nothing about it. He thought that, as for love, properly so called, the thing was preposterous for a girl of her years, and that the foolish business had been all made up of imaginative novelty, and the charm of the position, which had flattered and dazzled the girl. Now that she had returned to all her old associations and occupations, the pretty bubble had floated away into the air. It had not been necessary even to burst it—it had dispersed of itself, as he said to himself he always knew it would. Thus he deceived himself with the easiest mind and did not interfere.

Mrs. Kingsward had come upon her daughter seated out on the lawn under the great walnut tree, reading one of these letters, one morning when she had gone out earlier than usual, on an exceptionally fine day. Bee had thrust it away hastily into her pocket and came forward with burning cheeks when she heard her mother's voice—but it was not till some time later that Mrs. Kingsward spoke. The day had kept up its morning promise. It was one of those warm days that sometimes come in October, breathing the very spirit of that contented season, when all things have come to fruition and the work of the year is done, and its produce garnered into the barns. Now we may sit and rest, is the sentiment of the much toiling earth—all the labour being over, the harvest done, and no immediate need yet to rise again and plough. The world hangs softly swaying in space, the fields are fallow, the labourer rests. The sunshine lay warm upon the velvet grass, the foliage, thinned by one good blast a week ago, gave just shade enough, not too much; the tea-table was set out upon the lawn—the little horde had gone off shouting and skirmishing through the grounds, Betty at the head of them, supposed captain and controller, virtually ringleader, which comes to much the same thing. The air so hushed and silent in itself, half drowsy with profound peace, was just touched and made musical by their shouts, and Bee and her mother, with this triumphant sound of a multitude close by, were alone.

"Bee," Mrs. Kingsward said, "I have long wanted an opportunity to speak to you."

"Yes, mamma," she said, looking up with a rush of blood to her heart, feeling that the moment had come. But she would not have been Bee if she had not put a little something of her own into the thick of the crisis. "There were plenty of opportunities—we have been together all day."

"You know what I mean," said Mrs. Kingsward. "Bee, I saw you reading a letter this morning."

"Yes, mamma."

"Who was it from?"

Bee looked her mother in the face. "I have never made any secret of it," she said. "I have read them openly before papa—I never would pretend they were anything different. Of course it was from Aubrey, mamma."

"Oh, Bee!" said her mother. "You have never told me what your father said to you that morning. He told me that it was all over and done with—that he would never listen to another word on the subject."

"That was what he told me."

"Oh, Bee, Bee! and yet—"

"Stop a moment, mamma! He never said I was not to write; he never said there was to be no correspondence. Had he said so, I should have, at least, considered what it was best to do."

"Considered what was best! But you were not the judge. I hope you would have obeyed your father, Bee."

"I cannot say, mamma. You must remember that it is my case and not his. I don't know what I should have done. But it was not necessary, for he said nothing about it."

"Bee, my dear child, he may have said nothing; but you know very well that when he said it was entirely broken off he meant what he said."

"Papa is very capable of saying what he means," said Bee. "I did not think it was any business of mine to inquire what might be his secret meaning. Mamma, dear, don't be vexed; but, oh, that would have been too hard! And for Aubrey, too."

"I think much less of Aubrey that he should carry on a clandestine correspondence with a girl like you."

"Clandestine!" cried Bee, with blazing eyes. "No more clandestine than your letters that come by the post with your own name upon them. If Aubrey did not scorn anything that is clandestine, I should. There is nothing like that between him and me."

"I never supposed you would be guilty of any artifice, Bee; but you are going completely against your father—making a fool of him, indeed—making it all ridiculous—when you carry on a correspondence, as if you were engaged, after he has broken everything off."

"I am engaged," said Bee, very low.

"What do you say? Bee, this is out of the question. I shall have to tell your father when he comes back. "Oh! child, child, how you turn this delightful time into trouble. I shall be obliged to tell your father when he comes back."

"Perhaps it will be your duty, mamma," said Bee, the colour going out of her face; "and then I shall have to consider what is mine," she said.

"Oh, Bee, Bee! Oh! how hard you make it for me. Oh! how I wish you had never seen him, nor heard of him," Mrs. Kingsward cried.

CHAPTER XV

This communication made a little breach between Bee and her mother and planted a thorn in Mrs. Kingsward's breast. She had been getting on so well; the quiet (which meant the riot of the seven nursery children and all their troublesome ways) had been doing her so much good, and the absence of every care save that Johnny should not take cold, and Lucy eat enough dinner—that it was hard upon her thus to be brought back in a moment to another and a more pressing kind of care. However, after an hour or two's estrangement from Bee, which ended in a fuller expansion than ever of sympathy between them—and a morning or two in which Mrs. Kingsward remembered as soon as she awoke that it would be her duty to tell her husband and break up the pleasant peace and harmony of the household—the sweetness of that—dolce far niente—swept over her again and obliterated or at least blurred the outline of all such troublous thoughts. Colonel Kingsward sent a hasty telegram to say that he was going on somewhere else for another ten days' shooting, and that, though she exclaimed at first with a countenance of dismay, "Oh, children, papa is not coming home for another week!" in reality gave a pang of relief to her mind. Gliding into her being, she scarcely knew how, was an inclination to take every day as it came without thinking of to-morrow—which was perfectly natural, no doubt, and yet was an unconscious realisation of the fact, which as yet she had never put into words, nor had suggested to her, that those gentle days were numbered. Her husband's delay was in one way like a reprieve to her. She had, like all simple natures, a vague faith in accident, in something that might turn up—"perhaps the world may end to-night"—something at least might happen in another ten days to make it unnecessary for her to disturb the existing state of affairs and throw new trouble into the house. She did not waver at first as to her duty, though nothing in the world could be more painful; and Bee did not say a word to change her mother's resolution. Bee had always been aware that as soon as it was known the matter must come to another crisis—and the scorn with which she regarded the idea of doing anything clandestine prevented her even from asking that her secret should be kept. It was not in her mind but in her mother's that those faint doubtings at last arose—those half entertained thoughts that a letter or two could do no harm; that the correspondence would drop of itself when it was seen between the two that there was no hope in it; and that almost anything would be better than a storm of domestic dispeace and the open rebellion in which Mrs. Kingsward felt with a shudder Bee would place herself. How are you to break the will of a girl who will not be convinced, who says it is not your, but her affair?

No doubt that was true enough. It was Bee, not Colonel Kingsward, whose happiness was concerned. According to all the canons of poetry and literature in general, which in such matters permeate theoretically the general mind when there is no strong personal instinct to crush them, Bee had right on her side—and her mother's instinct was all on the side of poetry and romance and Bee. She had not the courage to cut short that correspondence, not clandestine though unrevealed, which kept the girl's heart alive, and was not without attractions to the mother also, into whose ear it might be whispered now and then (with always a faint protest on her part) that Aubrey had better hopes, that he had a powerful friend who was going to speak for him. If they really meant to be faithful to each other—and there was no doubt that was what they meant—they must win the day in the end; and what harm would it do in the meantime that they should hear of each other from time to time? Whereas, if she betrayed the secret, there would at once be a dreadful commotion in the house, and Bee would confront her father and tell him with those blazing eyes, so like his, that it was her affair. Mrs. Kingsward knew that her husband would never stoop to the manœuvre of intercepting letters, or keeping a watch upon those that his daughter received; and what can you do to a girl who says that? She shrank more than any words could say from the renewal of the conflict. She had been so thankful to believe that it had passed over and all things settled into peace while she was ill. Now that she was better her heart sank within her at the thought of bringing it all on again, which would also make her ill again she was convinced. Yet, at the same time, if she could not persuade Bee to give it up of herself (of which there was no hope whatever), then she must, it was her duty, inform her husband. But her heart rose a little at that ten days' reprieve. Perhaps the world might end to-night. Something might happen to make it unnecessary in those ten days.

And something did happen, though not in any way what Mrs. Kingsward could have wished.

Colonel Kingsward's return was approaching very near when on one of those bright October afternoons a lady from the neighbourhood—nay, it was the clergywoman of the parish, the Rector of Kingswarden's wife, the very nearest of all neighbours—came to call. She had just returned from that series of visits which in the autumn is—with all who respect themselves—the natural course of events. Mrs. Chichester was a woman of good connection, of "private means," and more or less "in society," so that she carried out this programme quite as if she had been a great lady. She had an air of importance about her, which seemed to shadow forth from her very entrance something that she had to say—an unusual gravity, a look of having to make up her mind to a certain action which was not without difficulty. There passed a glance between Mrs. Kingsward and Bee, in which they said to each other, "What is it this time?" as clearly as words could have said; for, to be sure, they were well acquainted with this lady's ways. She sat for a little, and talked of their respective travels since they had last met; and of the pleasant weeks she had passed at Homburg, where so many pleasant people were always to be met after the London season; and then she lightly touched on the fact that she had come over early in September, and since then had been staying at a number of country places, with the dear Bishop, and at Lady Grandmaison's, and with old Sir Thomas down in Devonshire, and so on.

"Or," she concluded, with a disproportionate emphasis on that apparently unimportant word, "I should have been to see you long ago."

There was a significance in this which again made Mrs. Kingsward and Bee exchange a look—a laughing glance—as of those who had heard the phrase before. When, however, she had asked some questions about Mrs. Kingsward's health, and expressed the proper feeling—sorry to hear she had been so poorly; delighted that she was so much better—Mrs. Chichester departed from her established use and wont. Instead of beginning upon the real object of her visit, after she had taken her cup of tea, with a "Now," (also very emphatic) "I want to interest you in something I have very much at heart,"—which was generally a subscription, a society, a bazaar, a missionary meeting, or something of the sort—Mrs. Chichester bent forward and said, in a half whisper, "I have something I want very much to talk to you about. Could I speak to you for a moment—alone?"

Bee was much surprised, but took her part with promptitude. "You want to get rid of me," she said. "I shall go out on to the terrace, mamma, and you can call me from the window when you want me. I shall be sure to hear."

There was another look between them, always with a laugh in it, as she stepped out of the open window, with a book in her hand, a look which repeated, "What can it be, now?" with the same amusement as at first, but with more surprise. Bee made a circuit round the lawn with her book, one finger shut in it to mark the place; looking at the flowers, as one does who knows every plant individually, and notes each bud that is opening, and which are about to fall. She calculated within herself how long the dahlias would last, and that the Gloire de Dijon roses must be cut to-morrow, as she pursued her way towards the walnut tree, under which she meant to place herself. But Bee had not been there many minutes before she felt a little shiver creep over her. It was getting rather cold in this late October to sit out of doors, when the sun was already off the garden, and she had, as girls say, "nothing on." She got up again, and made her way round to a garden bench which was set against the wall of the house, at the spot where the sunshine lasted longest. There was still a level ray of ruddy light pouring on that seat, and Bee forgot, or rather never thought, that it was close to the drawing-room window. Her mind was not much exercised about Mrs. Chichester's secret, which probably concerned the mothers and babies of the parish, and which she certainly had no curiosity to hear. Besides, no doubt, the visitor had told by this time all the private details there were to tell. Bee sat down upon the bench, taking no precautions to disguise the sound of her footsteps, and opened her book. She was not an enthusiastic student, though she liked a novel as well as anyone; but her eyes strayed from it to the great width of the horizon in front of her, and the ruddy glory in the west, in which was just about to disappear that last long golden ray of the sun.

Then she heard a low cry—an exclamation, stifled, yet full of horror. Was it mamma? What could the clergywoman be saying to bring from mamma's lips such a cry? Bee—I cannot blame her—pricked up her ears. Mrs. Kingsward was not strong enough to be disturbed by horrors with which she had nothing to do.

"Oh, I cannot believe it; I cannot believe it!" she said.

"But," said the other voice, with that emphasis at which Bee had laughed so often, "I can assure you it is true. I saw him myself shaking hands with the woman at the station. I might not have believed Miss Tatham's story, but I saw with my own eyes that it was Mr. Leigh. I had met him at Sir Thomas's the year before—when he was still in deep mourning for his wife, you know."

"Mr. Leigh! So it was something about Aubrey! Then it was Bee's business still more than her mother's, and she listened without any further thought.

"But," said Mrs. Kingsward, as if taking courage, "you must be mistaken; oh, not about seeing him shake hands with a woman—why shouldn't he shake hands with a woman? He is very friendly with everybody. Perhaps he knew her, and there is nothing to find fault with in that."

"Now," said Mrs. Chichester, solemnly, "should I have mentioned it had it been confined to that? I only told you of that as a proof. The thing is that he put in this woman—a common woman, like a servant—into a sleeping carriage—you know what those sleeping carriages cost; a perfect fortune; far too much for any comfort there is in them—in the middle of the night, with her two children. The woman behaved quite nicely, Miss Tatham says, and looked shocked to be put in with a lady, and blushed all over her face, and told that ridiculous story to account for it. Poor thing! One can only be sorry for her. Probably some poor thing deceived, and thinking she was to be made a lady of. But I know what you must think of the man, Mrs. Kingsward, who could do such a thing on his way from staying with your own family, even if there had been no more in it than that."

"But Mr. Leigh is very kind—kind to everybody—it might have been nothing but charity."

"Charity—in an express train sleeping carriage! Well, I confess I never heard of charity like that. Gentlemen generally know better than to compromise themselves for nothing in that sort of way. They are more afraid of risking themselves in railway carriages and that kind of thing than girls are—much more afraid. And if you remember, Mrs. Kingsward, what kind of reputation Mr. Leigh had in his poor wife's time—keeping that Miss Lance all the time in her very house under her eyes."

"I have always heard that it was Mrs. Leigh who insisted upon keeping Miss Lance—"

"Is it likely?" said Mrs. Chichester. "I ask you, knowing what you do of human nature? And then a thing to happen like this on his very way home—when he had just left you and poor little Bee. Oh, it is shameless, shameless! I could not contain myself when I heard of it. And then it was said that the Colonel had broken off the engagement, and I thought it would be a comfort to you to know that other things were occurring every day, and that it was the only thing to do."

"It is no comfort to me—and I cannot—I cannot believe it!"

"Dear Mrs. Kingsward, you always take the best view; but if you had seen him, as I did, holding the woman's hand, bending over her with such a look!—I was afraid he would kiss her, there, before everybody. And I, knowing of the engagement, and that he had just left you—before Miss Tatham said a word—I sat and stared, and couldn't believe my eyes. It was the tenth of September, and he had left Bee, hadn't he, the night before?"

"I never remember dates," said Mrs. Kingsward, querulously.

"I do," replied the visitor, "and I took the trouble to find out. At least, I found out by accident, through someone who saw him at the club, and who had just discovered the rights of that story about Miss Lance. Oh, I trust you will not be beguiled by his being a good—parti—, or that sort of thing, to trust dear Bee in such hands! Marriage is always rather a disenchantment; but think what it would be in such a case—a man that can't be trusted to travel between Cologne and London without—"

"I don't believe it! I don't believe it!" said Mrs. Kingsward; and Bee heard that her mother had melted into tears.

"That is as good as saying you don't believe me, who saw it with my own eyes," said the visitor, getting up. "Indeed, I didn't mean at all to distress you, for I thought that, as everything was broken off—I thought only if you had any doubts, as one has sometimes after one has settled a thing—that to know he was a man like that, with no respect for anything, who could leave his—fiancée—, and just plunge, plunge—there is no other word for it—"

It was evident that Mrs. Kingsward, reduced to helplessness, here made no effort either to detain her visitor or to contradict her further, or indeed to make any remark. There was a step or two across the room, and then Mrs. Chichester said again—"Good-bye, dear. I am very sorry to have distressed you— but I couldn't leave you in ignorance of such a thing for dear Bee's sake; that is the one thing to be thankful for in the whole matter, that Bee doesn't seem to mind a bit! She looks just as bright and just as nice as if nothing had happened. She can't have cared for him! Only flattered, I suppose, and pleased to have a proposal—as those little things are, poor things. We should all thank heaven on our knees that there's no question of a broken heart in Bee's case—"

She might not have been so sure of that had she seen the figure which came through the window the moment the door had closed upon her—Bee with her blue eyes blazing wildly out of her white face, and strange passion in every line both of features and form.

"What is the meaning of it?" she said, briefly, with dry lips.

"Oh, Bee, you have heard it all!"

"I have heard enough—what does it mean, mamma?"

Mrs. Kingsward roused herself, dried her eyes, and went forward to Bee with outstretched arms; but the girl turned away. "I don't want to be petted. I want to know what—what it means," she said.

"I don't believe it," cried Mrs. Kingsward.

"Give a reason; don't say things to quiet me. Oh, keep your arms away, mamma! Don't pet me as if I wanted that! Why don't you believe it? And if you did believe it—what does it mean—what does it mean?"

CHAPTER XVI

Bee's look of scared and horrified misery was something new in Mrs. Kingsward's experience. The girl had not known any trouble. Her father's rejection of her lover and the apparent break between them had been in reality only another feature in the romance. She had almost liked it better so. There had been no time to pine, to feel the pain of separation. It was all the more like a poem, like what every love story should be, that this breaking off should have come.

And now, all at once, without any warning! The worst of it was that Bee had only heard a part of the story, the recapitulation of it. Mrs. Chichester had given the accused more or less fair play. She had given an imperfect account of the explanation, the story the woman had told—as was almost inevitable to a third party, but she had given it to the best of her ability, not meaning to deceive, willing enough that he should have the benefit of the doubt, or perhaps that the judgment upon him should be all the more hard, because of his attempt to mingle deceit with his sin, and throw dust in the eyes of any possible spectators. This was the way in which it had appeared to herself, but she was not unfair. She told the story which had been told to the astonished lady upon whose solitude the little party had been obtruded in the middle of the night, and who had heard it perhaps even imperfectly at first hand mingled with the jolting and jarring of the train and the murmur of the children. And yet Mrs. Chichester had repeated it honestly.

But Bee had not heard that part of the tale. She had heard only the facts of the case which had presented to her inexperienced young mind the most wild and dreadful picture. Her lover, who had just left her, whom she had promised to stand by till death, suddenly appeared to her in the pale darkness of the midnight with a woman and children hanging on to him—belonging to him, as appeared. Where had he met them? How had he arranged to meet them? When her hand had been in his, when he had been asking from her that pledge till death, had he just been arranging all that—giving them that rendezvous—settling how they were to meet, and where? A horror and sickness came over poor Bee. It made her head swim and her limbs tremble. To leave her with her pledge in his ears, and to meet, perhaps at the very outset of his journey, the woman with the children—a common sort of woman, like a servant. As if that made any difference! If she had been a duchess it would have been all the same. He must have met her fresh from Bee's presence, with his farewell to the girl whom he had pretended to love still on his lips. She could not think so clearly. Was this picture burnt in upon her mind? She seemed to see the dim, half-lighted carriage, and Aubrey at the door putting the party in. And then at Dover, in the daylight, shaking hands with his companion, bending over her as if he meant to kiss her! These two pictures took possession of Bee's mind completely. And all this just when he had left Bee—between his farewell to her and his interview with her father! If she had heard of the story which the woman had told to the startled Miss Tatham in the dim sleeping carriage, from which, looking out, she had recognised Aubrey Leigh, it might have made a difference. But that story had not been told in Bee's hearing. And Mrs. Kingsward did not know this, but supposed she had heard the whole from beginning to end.

Bee's mother, to tell the truth, after the first shock, was glad of that unconscious eaves-dropping on Bee's part; for how could she have told her? Indeed, the story was too gross, too flagrant to be believed by herself. She felt sure that there must be some explanation of it other than the vulgar one which was put upon it by these ladies; but she knew very well that the same interpretation would be put upon it by her husband, and many other people to whom Aubrey's innocent interference in such a case would have seemed much less credible than guilt. Guilt is the thing that generally rises first as the explanation of everything, to the mind, both of the man and woman of the world. The impossibility of a man leaving a delicate flower of womanhood like Bee, whose first love he had won, in order to fall back at once into the bonds of a common intrigue, and provide for the comfort of his paramour, who had been waiting for him on the journey, would not prove so great to most people as the impossibility that he, as a stranger, would step out of his way to succour a poor little mother and children whom he had never seen before, and risk thereby a compromising situation.

The latter was the thing which would have seemed unutterably ridiculous and impossible to Colonel Kingsward. A first-class sleeping carriage secured for a mere waif upon his way, whom he had never seen before and never would see again! The fellow might be a fool, but he was not such a fool as that. Had the woman even been old and ugly the Colonel would have laughed and shrugged his shoulders at Aubrey's bad taste; but the woman was pretty and young. A long-standing affair, no doubt; and, of course, it was quite possible, nay likely, that she was being sent, poor creature, to some retreat or other, where she would be out of the way with her children.

Mrs. Kingsward knew, as if she had heard him say these words, how her husband would speak. And who was she, with not half his experience of the world, to maintain a different opinion? Yet she did so. She thought it was like Aubrey to turn the poor woman's lingering, melancholy journey into a quick and comfortable one, out of pure kindness, without thought of compromising himself any more than of having any recompense for what he did. But she did not know that Bee knew nothing of this explanation of the story. When she found that her child evidently thought nothing of that, but received at once the darker miserable tale into her mind, she was startled, but not perhaps astonished. Bee was young to think the worst of anybody, but at the same time it is by far the commonest way of thinking, and the offence was one against herself, which gives a sharper edge to everything. And then she knew what was going on in Bee's mind chiefly by guesswork, for the girl said little. The colour went out of her face, her eyes sometimes gave a gleam of their old fire, but mostly had a strange set look, as if they were fixed on something not visible to the ordinary spectator. She sat all the evening through and never spoke. This was not so noticeable while the children were still about with their perpetual flow of observations and flood of questions; but when they went off in detachments to bed, and the two elder girls were left alone with their mother, Bee's silence fell upon the others like a cloud. Betty, who knew nothing, after a few minutes rushed away upstairs to find refuge in the nursery, and then Mrs. Kingsward was left alone, face to face with this silent figure, so unlike Bee, which neither moved nor spoke. She had scarcely the courage to break the dreadful silence, but yet it had to be broken. Poor Mrs. Kingsward's heart began to beat violently against her breast as it had not done since her return home.

"Bee!" she said. "Bee!"

Already the pumping of her heart had taken away her breath.

"Yes, mamma."

"Oh! Bee, what—what are you going to do?"

"To do, mamma?"

"Oh! don't repeat my words after me, but give me some sort of an answer. Betty may be back again in a moment. What are you going to do?"

"What can I do?" the girl said, in a low voice.

"I can't suppose but that you have been thinking about it—what else could you be thinking of, poor child? For my part, I don't believe it. Do you hear me, Bee?"

"Yes—I heard you say that before, mamma."

"And that is all you think of what I say! My darling, you can't remain like this. The first thing your father will ask will be, 'What has happened?' I cannot bear that you should give up—without a word."

Mrs. Kingsward had disapproved of the correspondence, had felt that it would be incumbent upon her to tell her husband of it, but yet in this unforeseen emergency she forgot all that.

"Without a word! What words could I say? You don't suppose I could discuss it with him—ask if it was true? If it's true, there isn't a word to say, is there? And if it isn't true it would be an insult to ask him. And so one way or another it is all just done with and over. And I wish you would leave me quiet, mamma."

"Done with and over! Without a word—on a mere story of something that took place on a journey!"

"Oh! leave me quiet, mamma. Do you think I need to be reminded of that journey? As if I did not see it, and the lamps burning, and hear the very wheels!"

"Bee, dear, how can I leave you quiet? Do you mean just to let it break off like that, without a word, without giving him the chance to explain?"

"I thought," said Bee, with a faint satirical smile, for, indeed, her heart was capable of all bitterness, "that it was broken off completely by papa, and all that remained was only—what you called clandestine, mamma."

"I did not call it clandestine. I knew you would do nothing that was dishonourable. And it is true that it was—broken off. But, Bee! Bee! you don't seem to feel the dreadful thing this is. After all that has passed, to let it drop in a moment, without saying a word!"

"I thought it was what I ought to have done, as soon as papa's will was made known."

"Oh! Bee, you will drive me mad. And I have got no breath to speak. So you ought, perhaps—but you have not, when perhaps there was a reason. And now, for a mere chance story, and without giving him—an opportunity—to speak for himself."

Bee raised her face, now crimson as it had before been pale.

"How could I put any questions on such a thing? How could it be discussed between him and me? To think of it is bad enough, but to speak of it—mamma! How do I know, even, what words to say?"

"In that case, every engagement would be at the mercy of any slanderer, if the girl never could bring herself to ask what it meant."

"I am not any girl," cried poor Bee, with a quiver of her lip. "I am just myself. I don't think very much of myself any more than you do, but I can't change myself. Oh, let me alone, let me alone, mamma!"

Mrs. Kingsward was very much excited. Her nostrils grew pinched and dilated in the struggle for breath; her lips were open and panting from the same cause. She was caught in that dreadful contradiction of sentiment and feeling which is worse than any unmingled catastrophe. She had been rent asunder before this by her desire to shield her daughter, yet the sense of her duty to her husband remained, and now it was the correspondence which she seemed to be called upon to defend almost at peril of her life; that actually clandestine, at least secret correspondence, of which she could not approve, which she was bound to cut short. And yet to cut it short like this was something which she could not bear. She threw aside the work with which she had been struggling and fixed her eyes on Bee, who did not look at her nor see how agitated her expression was.

"If you can do this, I can't," she said. "I will write to him. The other dreadful story may be true, for anything I know. And that, of course, is enough. But this one I don't believe, if an angel from Heaven told it me. He shall at least have the chance of clearing himself!"

"I don't know," said Bee, "what the other dreadful story was. I thought it was only pretending to love—some other woman; and then—pretending to love—me—"—she broke off into a little hoarse laugh. The offence of it was more than Bee could bear. The insult—to suffer (she said to herself) was one thing—but to be insulted! She laughed to think what a fool she had been; how she had been taken in; how she had said—oh, like the veriest credulous fool—"Till death."

"He was not pretending to love you. What went before I know not, but with you he was true."

"One before—and one after," said Bee, rising in an irrepressible rage of indignation. "Oh, mamma, how can we sit quietly and discuss it, as if—as if it were a thing that could be talked about? Am I to come in between—two others—two—I think it will make me mad," the girl cried, stamping her foot. How does a man dare to do that—to insult a girl—who never sought him nor heard of him, wanted nothing of him—till he came and forced himself into her life!"

"Oh! Bee, my darling," cried the mother, going up to her child with outstretched arms.

"Don't touch me, don't touch me, don't pet me; I cannot bear it. Let me stand by myself. I am not a little thing like Lucy to be caught up and kissed till I forget. I don't want to forget. There is nothing that can ever be done to me, if I were to live to an hundred, to put this out of my head."

"Bee, be patient with me for a moment. I have lived longer than you have. What went before could be no offence to you, whatever it was. It might be bad, but it was no offence to you. And this—I don't believe it—"

Bee was far too much self-absorbed to see the labouring breath, the pink spot on each cheek, the panting which made her mother's fine nostrils quiver and kept her lips apart, or that she caught at the back of a chair to support herself as she stood.

"I don't know why—you shouldn't believe it. I don't believe it; I see it, I hear it," cried Bee. "It's like a story—and I thought these things were always stories, things made up to keep up the interest in a book—I'm the—deceived heroine, the one that's disappointed, don't you know, mamma? We've read all about her dozens of times. But she generally makes a fuss over it," the girl said, with her suffocating laugh. "I shall make—no fuss—Mamma! What is the matter, mamma?"

Nothing more was the matter than the doctor could have told Mrs. Kingsward's family long ago—a spasm of the heart. She stumbled backward to the sofa, and flung herself down before consciousness forsook her. Did consciousness forsake her at all? Bee rushing to the bell, making its violent sound peal through the house, then flinging herself at her mother's feet, and calling to her in the helplessness of utter ignorance, "Mamma, mamma!" did not think that she was unconscious. Broken words fell from her in the midst of her gasps for breath, then there was a moment of dread stillness. By this time the room seemed to be full of people—Bee did not know who was there—and then there suddenly appeared out of the mist Moulsey with a glass and teaspoon in her hands.

"Go away, all of you," cried Moulsey, "she'll be better directly—open all the windows and take a fan and fan her, Miss Bee."

The blast of the cold October night air came in like a flood, Bee seemed to come out of a horrible dream in the waft of air brought by the fan which she was herself waving to and fro—and in a little time, as Moulsey said, Mrs. Kingsward was better. The labouring breath which had come back after that awful moment of stillness gradually calmed down and became softer with an occasional long drawn sigh, and then she opened her eyes and said, with a faint smile, "What is it? What is it?" She looked round her for a moment puzzled—and then she said, "Ah! you are fanning me," with a smile to Bee, but presently, "How cold it is! I don't think I want to be fanned, Moulsey."

"No, ma'am, not now. And White is just a-going to shut all the windows. The fire was a bit too hot, and you know you never can bear it when the room gets too hot."

"No, I never can bear it," Mrs. Kingsward said, in a docile tone. She followed the lead of any suggestion given to her. "I must have got faint—with the heat."

"That was just it," said Moulsey. "When you have a fire in the drawing-room so early it looks so cheerful you're apt to pile it too high without thinking—for it ain't really cold in October, not cold enough to have a fire like that. You want it for cheerfulness, ma'am, more than for heat. A big bit of wood that will make a nice blaze, and very little coal, as is too much for the season, is what your drawing-room fire should be."

Mrs. Kingsward gradually came to herself during this long speech, which no doubt was what Moulsey intended. But she said she felt a little weak, and that she would keep on the sofa until it was time to go to bed. The agitation she had gone through seemed to have passed from her mind. "Read me a little of that story," she said, pointing to a book on the table. "We left off last night at a most interesting part. Read me the next chapter, Bee."

Bee sat down beside her mother's sofa and opened the book. It was not a book of a very exciting kind it may be supposed, when it was thus read a chapter at a time, without any one of the party opening it from evening to evening to see how things went on. But as it happened at this point of the story, the heroine had found out that her lover was not so blameless as she thought, and was making up her mind to have nothing to do with him. Bee began to read with an indignation beyond words for both hero and heroine, who were so pale, so colourless, beside her own story. To waste one's time reading stuff like this, while the tide of one's own passion was ten times stronger! She did not think very much of her mother's faint. It was, no doubt, the too large fire, as Moulsey said.

END OF VOLUME I

Margaret Oliphant – A Short Biography

Margaret Oliphant Wilson was born on April 4th, 1828 to Francis W. Wilson, a clerk, and Margaret Oliphant, at Wallyford, near Musselburgh, East Lothian.

She spent her childhood at Lasswade, near Dalkeith, Glasgow before moving to Liverpool.

Her youth was spent in establishing a writing style so much so that, in 1849, she had her first novel published: Passages in the Life of Mrs. Margaret Maitland based on the Scottish Free Church movement. It met with some success and was a good start to her career.

Two years later, in 1851, her third book Caleb Field was published. It was also now that she met the publisher William Blackwood in Edinburgh and was asked to contribute to his well-received Blackwood's Magazine. It was to be a lifetimes endeavor. Over the course of the relationship she would have well over 100 articles published.

In May 1852, Margaret married her cousin, Frank Wilson Oliphant, at Birkenhead, and they settled at Harrington Square, Camden, London. He was an artist working primarily in stained glass. With the marriage she became Margaret Oliphant Wilson Oliphant.

Their marriage produced six children but three tragically died in infancy.

When her husband developed signs of the dreaded consumption (tuberculosis) they moved, on the advice of doctors, to warmer climes. In January 1859 it was to Florence, and then to Rome where, sadly, he died.

Margaret was naturally devastated but was also now left without support and only her income from her writing. She returned to England and took up the task of supporting her three remaining children by her literary activity.

By now she was being published both as an established novelist and regularly in Blackwood's Magazine, amongst others. Her incredible and prolific work rate increased both her commercial reputation and the size of her reading audience.

Against this her domestic life continued to be tragic, full of sorrow and disappointment.

In January 1864 her only remaining daughter Maggie died and was buried in her father's grave in Rome. Her brother, who had emigrated to Canada, was shortly afterwards involved in financial ruin. Margaret generously offered a home to him and his children, adding another demand to her already heavy responsibilities.

In 1866 she settled at Windsor to be closer to her sons, who were being educated at near-by Eton School. That year, her second cousin, Annie Louisa Walker, came to live with her as a companion-housekeeper. Windsor was now to be her home for the rest of her life.

Her literary career for three decades was one of constant delivery and success. Whether she wrote historical works or across several genres in fiction: domestic realism, historical, romance or supernatural she was successful.

For more than thirty years she pursued a varied literary career but family life continued to bring problems.

The literary ambitions she wished for her sons were unfulfilled. Cyril Francis, the eldest, died in 1890, leaving a Life of Alfred de Musset, incorporated in his mother's Foreign Classics for English Readers. The younger, Francis, who she nicknamed 'Cecco', collaborated with her in the Victorian Age of English Literature and won a position at the British Museum, but was rejected by Sir Andrew Clark, a famous physician. Cecco died in 1894.

With the last of her children now lost to her, she had but little further interest in life. Her health steadily and inexorably declined.

Margaret Oliphant Wilson Oliphant died at the age of 69 in Wimbledon on 20th June 1897. She is buried in Eton beside her sons.

At her death, Margaret was still working on Annals of a Publishing House, a record of Blackwood's Magazine with which she had enjoyed such a successful relationship.

Her Autobiography and Letters, which present a thoughtful picture of her domestic anxieties, was published in 1899. Only parts were written with a wider audience in mind: she had originally intended the Autobiography for her son, but he died before she could finish it.

Opinions on Oliphant's work are split, with some critics seeing her as a 'domestic novelist', while others recognize her work as influential and important to the Victorian literature canon. Critical reception from her contemporaries is also divided. John Skelton took the view that Oliphant wrote too much and too quickly. Writing a Blackwood's article called 'A Little Chat About Mrs. Oliphant', he asked, "Had Mrs. Oliphant concentrated her powers, what might she not have done? We might have had another Charlotte Brontë or another George Eliot." However not all of the contemporary reception was negative. The esteemed M. R. James admired Oliphant's supernatural fiction, concluding that "the religious ghost story, as it may be called, was never done better than by Mrs. Oliphant in 'The Open Door' and 'A Beleaguered City'. Mary Butts lavished praise on Oliphant's ghost story 'The Library Window', describing it as "one masterpiece of sober loveliness".

More modern critics of Oliphant's work include Virginia Woolf, who asked in Three Guineas whether Oliphant's autobiography does not lead the reader "to deplore the fact that Mrs. Oliphant sold her brain, her very admirable brain, prostituted her culture and enslaved her intellectual liberty in order that she might earn her living and educate her children."

Whatever the merits of their cases Margaret Oliphant has been shamefully neglected in modern years. She is now becoming more widely recognised as a leading writer of her day.

VOLUME II

CHAPTER I

It was perhaps a very good thing for Bee at this distracting and distracted moment of her life, that her mother's illness came in to fill up every thought. Her own little fabric of happiness crumbled down about her ears like a house of cards, only as it was far more deeply founded and strongly built, the downfall was with a rumbling that shook the earth and a dust that rose up to the skies. Heaven was blurred out to her by the rising clouds, and all the earth was full of the noise, like an earthquake, of the falling walls. She could not get that sound out of her ears even in Mrs. Kingsward's sick room, where the quiet was preternatural, and everybody spoke in the lowest tone, and every step was hushed. Even then it went on roaring, the stones and the rafters flying, the storms of dust and ruin blackening the air, so that Bee could not but wonder that nobody saw them, that the atmosphere was not thick and stifling with those debris that were continually falling about her own ears. For everything was coming down; not only the idol and the shrine he abode in, but heaven and earth, in which she felt that no truth, no faith, could dwell any longer. Who was there to believe in? Not any man if not Aubrey; not any goodness, any truth, if not his—not anything! For it was without object, without warning, for nothing at all, that he had deserted her, as if it had been of no importance: with the ink not dry on his letter, with her name still upon his lips. A great infidelity, like a great faith, is always something. It is tragic, one of the awful events of life in which there is, or may be, fate; an evil destiny, a terrible chastisement prepared beforehand. In such a case one can at least feel one's self only a great victim, injured by God himself and the laws of the universe, though that was not the common fashion of thought then, as it is now-a-days. But Bee's downfall did not mean so much as that it was not intended by anyone—not even by the chief worker in it. He had meant to hold Bee fast with one hand while he amused himself with the other. Amused himself—oh, heaven! Bee's heart seemed to contract with a speechless spasm of anguish and rage. That she should be of no more account than that! Played with as if she were nobody—the slight creature of a moment. She, Bee! She, Colonel Kingsward's daughter!

At first the poor girl went on in a mist of self-absorption, through which everything else pierced but dully, wrapped up and hidden in it as in the storm which would have arisen had the house actually fallen about her ears, perceiving her mother through it, and the doctor, and all the accessories of the scene—but dimly, not as if they were real. When, however, there began to penetrate through this, strange words, with strange meanings in them: "Danger"—danger to whom?—"Strength failing"—but whose strength?—a dull wonder came in, bringing her back to other thoughts. By-and-by, Bee began to understand a little that it was of her mother of whom these things were being said. Her mother? But it was not her mother's house that had fallen; what did it mean? The doctor talked apart with Moulsey, and Moulsey turned her back, and her shoulders heaved, and her apron seemed to be put to her eyes. Bee, in her dream said, half aloud, "Danger?" and both the doctor and Moulsey turned upon her as if they would have killed her. Then she was beckoned out of the room, and found herself standing face to face with that grave yet kindly countenance which she had known all her life, in which she believed as in the greatest authority. She heard his voice speaking to her through all the rumbling and downfall.

"You must be very courageous," it said, "You are the eldest, and till your father comes home—"

What did it matter about her father coming home, or about her being the eldest? What had all these things to do with the earthquake, with the failure of truth, and meaning, and everything in life? She looked at him blankly, wondering if it were possible that he did not hear the sound of the great falling, the rending of the walls, and the tearing of the roof, and the choking dust that filled all earth and heaven.

"My dear Beatrice," he said, for he had known her all his life, "you don't understand me, do you, my poor child?"

Bee shook her head, looking at him wistfully. Could he know anything more about it, she wondered—anything that had still to be said?

He took her hand, and her poor little hand was very cold with emotion and trouble. The good doctor, who knew nothing about any individual cause little Bee could have for agitation, thought he saw that her very being was arrested by a terror which as yet her intelligence had not grasped; something dreadful in the air which she did not understand. He drew her into the dining-room, the door of which stood open, and poured out a little wine for her. "Now, Bee," he said, "no fainting, no weakness. You must prove what is in you now. It is a dreadful trial for you, my dear, but you can do a great deal for your dear mother's sake, as she would for yours."

"I have never said it was a trial," cried Bee, with a gasp. "Why do you speak to me so? Has mamma told you? No one has anything to do with it but me."

He looked at her with great surprise, but the doctor was a man of too much experience not to see that here was something into which it was better not to inquire. He said, very quietly, "You, as the eldest, have no doubt the chief part to play; but the little ones will all depend upon your strength and courage. Your mother does not herself know. She is very ill. It will require all that we can do—to pull her through."

Bee repeated the last words after him with a scared look, but scarcely any understanding in her face—"To pull her—through?"

"Don't you understand me now? Your mother—has been ill for a long time. Your father is aware of it. I suppose he thought you were too young to be told. But now that he is absent, and your brother, I have no alternative. Your mother is in great danger. I have telegraphed for Colonel Kingsward, but in the meantime, Bee—child, don't lose your head! Do you understand me? She may be dying, and you are the only one to stand by her, to give her courage."

Bee did not look as if she had courage for anyone at that dreadful moment. She fell a-trembling from head to foot and fell back against the wall where she was standing. Her eyes grew large, staring at him yet veiled as if they did not see—and she stammered forth at length, "Mother, mother!" with almost no meaning, in the excess of misery and surprise.

"Yes, your mother; whatever else you may have to think of, she is the first consideration now."

He went on speaking, but Bee did not hear him; everything floated around her in a mist. The scenes at the Bath, the agitations, Mrs. Kingsward's sudden pallors and flushings, her pretence, which they all laughed at, of not being able to walk; her laziness, lying on the sofa, the giddiness when she made that one turn with Charlie, she who had always been so fond of dancing; the hurry of bringing her to Kingswarden when Bee had felt they would have been so much better in London, and her strange, strange new fancy, mutely condemned by Bee, of finding the children too much for her. Half of these things had been silently remarked and disapproved of by the daughters. Mamma getting so idle—self-indulgent almost, so unlike herself! Had they not been too busily engaged in their own affairs, Bee and Betty would both have been angry with mamma. All these things seem to float about Bee in a mist while she leaned against the wall and the doctor stood opposite to her talking. It was only perhaps about a minute after all, but she saw waving round her, passing before her eyes, one scene melting into another, or rather all visible at once, innumerable episodes—the whole course of the three months past which had contained so much. She came out of this strange whirl very miserable but very quiet.

"I think it is chiefly my fault," she said, faltering, interrupting the doctor who was talking, always talking; "but how could I know, for nobody told me? Doctor, tell me what to do now? You said we should—pull her through."

She gave him a faint, eager, conciliatory smile, appealing to him to do it. Of course he could do it! "Tell me—tell me only what to do."

He patted her kindly upon the shoulder. "That is right," he said. "Now you understand me, and I know I can trust you. There is not much to do. Only to be quiet and steady—no crying or agitation. Moulsey knows everything. But you must be ready and steady, my dear. Sit by her and look happy and keep up her courage—that's the chief thing. If she gives in it is all over. She must not see that you are frightened or miserable. Come, it's a great thing to do for a little girl that has never known any trouble. But you are of a good sort, and you must rise to it for your mother's sake."

Look happy! That was all she had to do. "Can't I help Moulsey," she asked. "I could fetch her what she wants. I could—go errands for her. Oh, doctor, something a little easier," cried Bee, clasping her hands, "just at first!"

"All that's arranged," he said, hastily, "Come, we must go back to our patient. She will be wondering what I am talking to you about. She will perhaps take fright. No, nothing easier, my poor child—if you can do that you may help me a great deal; if you can't, go to bed, my dear, that will be best."

She gave him a look of great scorn, and moved towards her mother's room, leading the way.

Mrs. Kingsward was lying with her face towards the door, watching, in a blaze of excitement and fever. Her eyes had never been so bright nor her colour so brilliant. She was breathing quickly, panting, with her heart very audible to herself, pumping in her ears, and almost audible in the room, so evident was it that every pulse was at fever speed. "What have you been telling Bee, doctor? What have you been telling Bee? What—" When she had begun this phrase it did not seem as if she could stop repeating it again and again.

"I have been telling her that she may sit with you, my dear lady, on condition of being very quiet, very quiet," said the doctor. "It's a great promotion at her age. She has promised to sit very still, and talk very little, and hush her mamma to sleep. It is you who must be the baby to-night. If you can get a good long quiet sleep, it will do you all the good in the world. Yes, you may hold her hand if you like, my dear, and pat it, and smooth it—a little gentle mesmerism will do no harm. That, my dear lady, is what I have been telling Miss Bee."

"Oh, doctor," said Mrs. Kingsward, "don't you know she has had great trouble herself, poor child? Poor little Bee! At her age I was married and happy; and here is she, poor thing, plunged into trouble. Doctor, you know, there is a—gentleman—"

Mrs. Kingsward had raised herself upon her elbow, and the panting of her breath filled all the room.

"Another time—another time you shall tell me all about it. But I shall take Miss Bee away, and consign you to a dark room, and silence, if you say another word—"

"Oh, don't make my room dark! I like the light. I want my child. Let me keep her, let me keep her! Who should—comfort her—but her mother?"

"Yes, so long as you keep quiet. If you talk I will take her away. Not a word—not a word—till to-morrow." In spite of himself there was a change in the doctor's voice as he said that word—or Bee thought so—as if there might never be any to-morrow. The girl felt as if she must cry out, shriek aloud, to relieve her bursting brain, but did not, overborne by his presence and by the new sense of duty and self-restraint. "Come now," he went on, "I am very kind to let you have your little girl by you, holding your hand—don't you think so? Go to sleep, both of you. If you're quite, quite, quiet you'll both doze, and towards the morning I'll look in upon you again. Now, not another word. Good-night, good-night."

Bee, whose heart was beating almost as strongly as her mother's, heard his measured step withdraw on the soft carpets with a sense of wild despair, as if the last hope was going from her. Her inexperienced imagination had leaped from complete ignorance and calm to the last possibilities of calamity. She had never seen death, and what if that awful presence were to come while she was alone, incapable of any struggle, of giving any help. She listened to the steps getting fainter in the distance with anguish and terror unspeakable. She clasped her mother's hand tightly without knowing it. That only aid, the only man who could do anything, was going away—deserting them—leaving her alone in her ignorance to stand between her mother and death. Death! Every pulse sprang up and fluttered in mortal terror. And she was put there to be quiet—ready and steady, he had said—to look happy! Bee kept silent; kept sitting upon her chair; kept down her shriek after him with a superhuman effort. She could do no more.

"Listen—he's talking to Moulsey now," said Mrs. Kingsward, "about me; they're always—whispering, about me—telling the symptoms—and how I am. That is the worst of nurses—"

"Mamma! Oh, don't talk, don't talk!" cried Bee; though she was more comforted than words can tell by the sound of her mother's voice.

"Whispering: can't you hear them? About temperature—and things. I can bear talking—but whispering. Bee—don't you hear 'em—whis—whispering—"

"Oh, mamma," cried Bee, "I love to hear you speak! But don't, don't, don't, or they'll make me go away."

"My baby," said the mother, diverted in her wandering and weakness to a new subject, "my little thing! He said we were to go to sleep. Put your head there—and I'll sing you—I'll sing you—to sleep—little Bee, little Bee, poor little Bee!"

CHAPTER II

This night was the strangest in Bee Kingsward's life. She had never known what it was to remain silent and awake in the darkness and warmth of a sick room, which of itself is a strange experience for a girl, and shows the young spirit its own weakness, its craving for rest and comfort, the difficulty of overcoming the instincts of nature—with such a sense of humiliation as nothing else could give. Could you not watch with me one hour? She believed that she had lain awake crying all night when her dream of happiness had so suddenly been broken in upon at Cologne; but now, while she sat by her mother's side, and the little soft crooning of the song, which Mrs. Kingsward supposed herself to be singing to put her child to sleep, sank into a soft murmur, and the poor lady succeeded in hushing herself into a doze by this characteristic method. Bee's head dropped too, and her eyelids closed. Then she woke, with a little shiver, to see the large figure of Moulsey like a ghost by the bed, and struggled dumbly back to her senses, only remembering that she must not start nor cry to disturb Mrs. Kingsward, whose quick breathing filled the room with a sensation of danger and dismay to which the girl was sensible as soon as the film of sleep that had enveloped her was broken. Mrs. Kingsward's head was thrown back on the pillow; now and then a faint note of the lullaby which she had been singing came from the parted lips, through which the hot, quick breath came so audibly. Now and then she stirred in her feverish sleep. Moulsey stood indistinguishable with her back to the light, a mass of solid shadow by the bedside. She shook her head. "Sleep's best," she said, in the whisper which the patient hated. "Sleep's better than the best of physic." Bee caught those solid skirts with a sensation of hope, to feel them so real and substantial in her hand. She did not care to speak, but lifted her face, pale with alarm and trouble, to the accustomed nurse. Moulsey shook her head again. It was all the communication that passed between them, and it crushed the hope that was beginning to rise in Bee's mind. She had thought when she heard the doctor go away that death might be coming as soon as his back was turned. She had felt when her mother fell asleep as if the danger must be past. Now she sank into that second stage of hopelessness, when there is no longer any immediate panic, when the unaccustomed intelligence dimly realises that the sufferer may be better, and may live through the night, or through many nights, and yet there may be no real change. Very dim as yet was this consciousness in Bee's heart, and yet the first dawning of it bowed her down.

In the middle of the night—after hours so long!—more like years, when Bee seemed to have sat there half her life, to have become used to it, to be uncertain about everything outside, but only that her mother lay there more ill than words could say—Mrs. Kingsward awoke. She opened her eyes without any change of position with the habit of a woman who has been long ill, without acknowledging her illness. It was Moulsey who saw a faint reflection of the faint light in the softly opening eyes, and detected that little change in the breathing which comes with returning consciousness. Bee, with her head leant back upon her chair and her eyes closed, was dozing again.

"You must take your cordial, ma'am, now you're awake. You've had such a nice sleep."

"Have I? I thought I was with the children and singing to baby. Who's this that has my hand—Bee?"

"Mamma," cried the girl, with a little start, and then, "Oh! I have waked her, Moulsey, I have waked her!"

"Is this her little hand? Poor little Bee! No, you have not waked me, love; but why, why is the child here?"

"The doctor said she might stay—to send for him if you wanted anything—and—and to satisfy her."

"To satisfy her, why so, why so? Am I so bad? Did he think I would die—in the night?"

"No, no, no," said Moulsey, standing by her, patting her shoulder, as if she had been a fretful child. "What a thing to fancy! As if he'd have sent the child here for that!"

"No," said the poor lady, "he wouldn't have sent the child, would he—not the child—for that—to frighten her! But Bee must go to bed. I'm so much better. Go to bed. Moulsey; poor Moulsey, never tires, she's so good. But you must go to bed."

"Oh, mother, let me stay. When you sleep, I sleep too; and I'm so much happier here."

"Happier, are you? Well—but there was something wrong. Something had happened. What was it that happened? And your father away! It never does for anything to happen when—my husband is away. I've grown so silly. I never know what to do. What was it that happened, Bee?"

"There was—nothing," said Bee, with a sudden chill of despair. She had forgotten everything but the dim bed-chamber, the faint light, the quick, quick breathing. And now there came a stab at her poor little heart. She scarcely knew what it was, but a cut like a knife going to the very centre of her being. Then there came the doctor's words, as if they were written in light across the darkness of the room— "Ready, and steady." She said in a stronger voice, "You have been dreaming. There was nothing, mamma."

Mrs. Kingsward, who had raised herself on her elbow, sank back again on her pillow.

"Yes," she said, "I must have been dreaming. I thought somebody came—and told us. Dreams are so strange. People say they're things you've been—thinking of. But I was not thinking of that—the very last thing! Bee, it's a pity—it's a great pity—when a woman with so many children falls into this kind of silly, bad health."

"Oh, mamma," was all that poor Bee could say.

"Oh—let me alone, Moulsey—I want to talk a little. I've had such a good sleep, you said; sometimes—I want to talk, and Moulsey won't let me—nor your father, and I have it all here," she said, putting her hand to her heart, "or here," laying it over her eyebrows, "and I never get it out. Let me talk, Moulsey— let me talk."

Bee, leaning forward, and Moulsey standing over her by the bedside, there was a pause. Their eyes, accustomed to the faint light, saw her eyes shining from the pillow, and the flush of her cheeks against the whiteness of the bed. Then, after a while, there came a little faint laugh, and, "What was I saying?" Mrs. Kingsward asked. "You look so big, Moulsey, like the shadows I used to throw on the wall to please the children. You always liked the rabbit best, Bee. Look!" She put up her hands as if to make that familiar play upon the wall. "But Moulsey," she added, "is so big. She shuts out all the light, and what is Bee doing here at this hour of the night? Moulsey, send Miss Bee to bed."

"Oh, mother, let me stay. You were going to tell me something."

"Miss Bee, you must not make her talk."

"How like Moulsey!" said the invalid. "Make me talk! when I have wanted so much to talk. Bee, it's horrid to go on in this silly ill way, when—when one has children to think of. Your father's always good— but a man often doesn't understand. About you, now—if I had been a little stronger, it might have been different. What was it we heard? I don't think it was true what we heard."

"Oh, mamma, don't think of that, now."

"It is so silly, always being ill! And there's nothing really the matter. Ask the doctor. They all say there's nothing really the matter. Your father—but then he doesn't know how a woman feels. I feel as if I were sinking, sinking down through the bed and the floor and everything, away, I don't know where. So silly, for nothing hurts me—I've no pain—except that I always want more air. If you were to open the window, Moulsey; and Bee, give me your hand and hold me fast, that I mayn't sink away. It's all quite silly, you know, to think so," she added, with again a faint laugh.

Bee's eyes sought those of Moulsey with a terrified question in them; the great shadow only slightly shook its head.

"Do you remember, Bee, the picture—we saw it in Italy, and I've got a photograph—where there is a saint lying so sweetly in the air, with angels holding her up? They're flying with her through the blue sky—two at her head, and other two—and her mantle so wrapped round her, and she lying, oh! so easy, resting, though there's nothing but the air and the angels. Do you remember, Bee?"

"Yes, mamma. Oh, mamma, mamma!"

"That's what I should like," said Mrs. Kingsward; "it's strange, isn't it? The bed's solid, and the house is solid, and Moulsey there, she's very solid too, and air isn't solid at all. But there never was anybody that lay so easy and looked so safe as that woman in the air. Their arms must be so soft under her, and yet so strong, you know; stronger than your father's. He's so kind, but he hurries me sometimes; and soft—you're soft, Bee, but you're not strong. You've got a soft little hand, hasn't she, Moulsey? Poor little thing! And to think one doesn't know what she may have to do with it before she is like me."

"She'll have no more to do with it, ma'am, than a lady should, no more than you've had. But you must be quiet, dear lady, and try and go to sleep."

"I might never have such a good chance of talking to her again. The middle of the night and nobody here—her father not even in the house. Bee, you must try never to begin being ill in any silly way, feeling not strong and that sort of foolish thing, and say out what you think. Don't be frightened. It's—it's bad for him as well as for you. He gets to think you haven't any opinion. And then all at once they find out—And, perhaps, it's too late—."

"Mamma, you're not very ill? Oh, no; you're looking so beautiful, and you talk just as you always did."

"She says am I very ill, Moulsey? Poor little Bee! I feel a great deal better. I had surely a nice sleep. But why should the doctor be here, and you made to sit up, you poor little thing. Moulsey, why is the doctor here?"

"I never said, ma'am, as he was here. He's coming round first thing in the morning. He's anxious—because the Colonel's away."

"Ah! you think I don't know. I'm not so very bad; but he thinks—he thinks—perhaps I might die, Bee."

"Mamma, mamma!"

"Don't be frightened," said Mrs. Kingsward, drawing the girl close to her. "That's a secret; he doesn't think I know. It would be a curious, curious thing, when people think you are only ill to go and die. It would surprise them so. And so strange altogether—instead of worries, you know, every day, to be all by yourself, lying so easy and the angels carrying you. No trouble at all then to think whether he would be pleased—or anything; giving yourself to be carried like that, like a little child."

"But mamma," cried Bee, "you could not, would not leave us—you wouldn't, would you, mamma?—all the children, and me; and I with nobody else, no one to care for me. You couldn't, mother, leave us; you wouldn't! Say you wouldn't! Oh! Moulsey! Moulsey! look how far away she is looking, as if she didn't see you and me!"

"You forget, Bee," said Mrs. Kingsward, "How easy it looked for that saint in the picture. I always liked to watch the birds floating down on the wind, never moving their wings. That's what seems no trouble, so easy; not too hot nor too cold, nor tiring, neither to the breath nor anything. I shouldn't like to leave you. No—But then:" she added, with a smile, "I should not require to leave you. I'd—I'd—What was I saying? Moulsey, will you please give me some—more—"

She held out her hand again for the glass which Moulsey had just put down.

"It makes me strong—it makes me speak. I'm—sinking away again, Bee. Hold me—hold me tight. If I was to slip away—down—down—down to the cellars or somewhere." The feeble laugh was dreadful for the listeners to hear.

"Run," cried Moulsey, in Bee's ear, "the doctor—the doctor! in the library."

And then there was a strange phantasmagoria that seemed to fill the night, one scene melting into another. The doctor rousing from his doze, his measured step coming back; the little struggle round the bed; Moulsey giving place to the still darker shadow; the glow of Mrs. Kingsward's flushed and feverish countenance between; then the quiet, and then again sleep—sleep broken by feeble movements, by the quick panting of the breath.

"She'll be easier now," the doctor said. "You must go to bed, my dear young lady. Moulsey can manage for the rest of the night."

"Doctor," said Bee, with something in her throat that stopped the words, "doctor—will she—must she? Oh, doctor, say that is not what it means? One of us, it would not matter, but mother—mother!"

"It is not in our hands," the doctor said. "It is not much we can do. Don't look at me as if I were God. It is little, little I can do."

"They say," cried poor Bee, "that you can do anything. It is when there is no doctor, no nurse that people—Oh, my mother—my mother! Doctor, don't let it be."

"You are but a child," said the doctor, patting her kindly on the shoulder, "you've not forgotten how to say your prayers. That's the only thing for you to do. Those that say such things of doctors know very little. We stand and look on. Say your prayers, little girl—if they do her no good, they'll do you good. And now she'll have a little sleep."

Bee caught him by the arm. "Sleep," she said, looking at him suspiciously. "Sleep?"

"Yes, sleep—that may give her strength for another day. Oh, ask no more, child. Life is not mine to give."

What a night! Out of doors it was moonlight as serene as heaven—the moon departing in the west, and another faint light that was day coming on the other side, and the first birds beginning to stir in the branches; but not even baby moving in the house. All fast asleep, safe as if trouble never was, as if death could not be. Bee went upstairs to her chill, white room, where the white bed, unoccupied, looked to her like death itself—all cold, dreadful, full of suggestion. Bee's heart was more heavy than could be told. She had nothing to fall back upon, no secret strength to uphold her. She had forgotten how wretched she had been, but she felt it, nevertheless, behind the present anguish. Nevertheless, she was only nineteen, and when she flung herself down to cry upon her white pillow—only to cry, to get her passion out—beneficent nature took hold of the girl and made her sleep. She did not wake for hours. Was it beneficent? For when she was roused by the opening of the door and sat up in her bed, and found herself still dressed in her evening frock, with her little necklace round her throat, there pressed back upon Bee such a flood of misery and trouble as she thought did not exist in the world.

"Miss Bee, Miss Bee! Master's come home. He's been travelling all night—and I dare not disturb Mrs. Moulsey in Missis's room; and he wants to see you this minit, please. Oh, come, come, quick, and don't keep the Colonel waiting," the woman said.

Half awakened, but wholly miserable, Bee sprang up and rushed downstairs to her father. He came forward to meet her at the door, frowning and pale.

"What is this I hear?" he said. "What have you been doing to upset your mother? She was well enough when I went away. What have you been doing to your mother? You children are the plague of our lives!"

CHAPTER III

The week passed in the sombre hurry yet tedium of a house lying under the shadow of death—that period during which when it is night we long for morning, and when it is morning we long for night, hoping always for the hope that never comes, trembling to mark the progress which does go on silently towards the end.

Colonel Kingsward was rough and angry with Bee that first morning, to her consternation and dismay. She had never been the object of her father's anger before, and this hasty and imperious questioning seemed to take all power of reply out of her. "What had she been doing to her mother?" She! to her mother! Bee was too much frightened by his threatening look, the cloud on his face, the fire in his eyes, to say anything. Her mind ran hurriedly over all that had happened, and that last terrible visit, which had changed the whole aspect of the earth to herself. But it was to herself that this stroke of misfortune had come, and not to her mother. A gleam of answering anger came into Bee's eyes, sombre with the unhappiness which had been pushed aside by more immediate suffering, yet was still there like a black background, to frame whatever other miseries might come after. As for Colonel Kingsward, it was to him, as to so many men, a relief to blame somebody for the trouble which was unbearable. The blow was approaching which he had never allowed himself to believe in. He had blamed his wife instinctively, involuntarily, at the first hearing of every inconvenience in life; and it had helped to accustom him to the annoyance to think that it was her fault. He had done so in what he called this unfortunate business of Bee's, concluding that but for Mrs. Kingsward's weakness, Mr. Aubrey Leigh and his affairs would never have become of any importance to the family. He had blamed her, too, and greatly, for that weakening of health which he had so persistently endeavoured to convince himself did not mean half so much as the doctors said. Women are so idiotic in these respects. They will insist on wearing muslin and lace when they ought to wear flannel. They will put on evening dresses when they ought to be clothed warmly to the throat, and shoes made of paper when they ought to be solidly and stoutly shod, quite indifferent to the trouble and anxiety they may cause to their family. And now that Mrs. Kingsward's state had got beyond the possibility of reproach, he turned upon his daughter. It must be her fault. Her mother had been better or he should not have left her. The quiet of the country was doing her good; if she had not been agitated all would have been well. But Bee, with all her declarations of devotion to her mother; Bee, the eldest, who ought to have had some sense; Bee had brought on this trumpery love business to overset the delicate equilibrium which he himself, a man with affairs so much more important in hand, had refrained from disturbing. It did him a little good, unhappy and anxious as he was, to pour out his wrath upon Bee. And she did not reply. She did not shed tears, as her mother had weakly done in similar circumstances, or attempt excuses. Even if he had been sufficiently at leisure to note it, an answering fire awoke in Bee's eyes. He had not leisure to note, but he perceived it all the same.

Presently, however, every faculty, every thought, became absorbed in that sick chamber; things had still to be thought of outside of it, but they seemed strange, artificial things, having no connection with life. Then Charlie was summoned from Oxford, and the younger boys from school, which increased the strange commotion of the house, adding that restless element of young life which had no place there, nothing to do with itself, and which roused an almost frenzied irritation in Colonel Kingsward when he saw any attempt on the part of the poor boys to amuse themselves, or resume their usual occupations. "Clods!" he said; "young brutes! They would play tennis if the world were falling to pieces." And again that glance of fire came into Bee's eyes, marked unconsciously, though he did not know he had seen it, by her father. The boys hung about her when she stole out for a little air, one at each arm. "How is mother, Bee? She's no worse? Don't you think we might go over to Hillside for that tournament? Don't you think Fred might play in the parish match with Siddemore? They're so badly off for bowlers. Don't you think—"

"Oh, I think it would be much better for you to be doing something, boys; but, then, papa might hear, and he would be angry. If we could but keep it from papa."

"We're doing mother no good," said Fred.

"How could we do mother good? Why did the governor send for us, Bee, only to kick our heels here, and get into mischief? A fellow can't help getting into mischief when he has nothing to do."

"Yes," repeated Fred, "what did he send for us for? I wish mother was better. I suppose as soon as she's better we'll be packed off again."

They were big boys, but they did not understand the possibility of their mother not getting better, and, indeed, neither did Bee. When morning followed morning and nothing happened, it seemed to her that getting better was the only conclusion to be looked for. If it had been Death that was coming, surely it must have come by this time. Her hopes rose with every new day.

But Mrs. Kingsward had been greatly agitated by the sight of Charlie when he was allowed to see her. "Why has Charlie come home?" she said. "Was he sent for? Was it your father that brought him?

Charlie, my dear, what are you doing here? Why have you come back? You should have been going on with—Did your father send for you? Why—why did your father send for you, my boy?"

"I thought," said Charlie, quite unmanned by the sight of her, and by this unexpected question, and by all he had been told about her state, "I thought—you wanted to see me, mother."

"I always like to see you—but not to take you away from—And why was he sent for, Moulsey? Does the doctor think?—does my husband think?—"

Her feverish colour grew brighter and brighter. Her eyes shone with a burning eagerness. She put her hot hand upon that of her son. "Was it to say good-bye to me?" she said, with a strange flutter of a smile.

At the same time an argument on the same subject was going on between the doctor and the Colonel.

"What can the children do in a sick room? Keep them away. I should never have sent for them if you had consulted me. It is bad enough to have let her see Charlie, summoned express—do you want to frighten your wife to death?"

"There can be no question," said the Colonel, "if what you tell me is true, of frightening her to death. I think, Benson, that a patient in such circumstances ought to know. She ought to be told—"

"What?" the doctor said, sharply, with a harsh tone in his voice.

"What? Do you need to ask? Of her state—of what is imminent—that she is going to—"

Colonel Kingsward loved his wife truly, and he could not say those last words.

"Yes," said the doctor, "going to—? Well, we hope it's to One who has called her, that knows all about it, Kingsward. Doctors are not supposed to take that view much, but I do. I'd tell her nothing of the sort. I would not agitate her either with the sight of the children or those heathenish thoughts about dying. Well, I suppose you'll take your own way, if you think she's in danger of damnation; but you see I don't. I think where she's going she'll find more consideration and more understanding than ever she got here."

"You are all infidels—every one of you," said Colonel Kingsward; "you would let a soul rush unprepared into the presence of—"

"Her Father," said Doctor Benson. "So I would; if he's her Father he'll take care of that. And if he's only a Judge, you know, a Judge is an extraordinarily considerate person. He leaves no means untried of coming to a right decision. I would rather trust my case in the hands of the Bench than make up my own little plea any day. And, anyhow you can put it, the Supreme Judge must be better than the best Bench that ever was. Leave her alone. She's safer with Him than either with you or me."

"It's an argument I never would pardon—in my own case. I shudder at the thought of being plunged into eternity without the time to—to think—to—to prepare—"

"But if your preparations are all seen through from the beginning? If it's just as well known then, or better, what you are thinking, or trying to think, to make yourself ready for that event? You knew yourself, more or less, didn't you, when you were in active service, the excuses a wretched private would make when he was hauled up, and how he would try to make the worse appear the better cause. Were you moved by that, Colonel Kingsward? Didn't you know the man, and judge him by what you knew?"

"It seems to me a very undignified argument; there's no analogy between a wretched private and my—and my—and one of us—at the Judgment Seat."

"No—it's more like one of your boys making up the defence—when brought before you—and the poor boy would need it too," Dr. Benson added within himself. But naturally he made no impression with his argument, whether it was good or bad, upon his hearer. Colonel Kingsward was in reality a very unhappy man. He had nobody to blame for the dreadful misfortune which was threatening him except God, for whom he entertained only a great terror as of an overwhelming tyrannical Power ready to catch him at any moment when he neglected the observances or rites necessary to appease it. He was very particular in these observances—going to church, keeping up family prayers, contributing his proper and carefully calculated proportion to the charities, &c. Nobody could say of him that he was careless or negligent. And now how badly was his devotion repaid!—by the tearing away from him of the companion of his life. But he felt that there was still much more that the awful Master of the Universe might inflict, perhaps upon her if she was not prepared to meet her God. He was wretched till he had told her, warned her, till she had fulfilled everything that was necessary, seen a clergyman, and got herself into the state of mind becoming a dying person. He had collected all the children that she might take leave of them in a becoming way. He had, so far as he knew, thought of everything to make her exit from the world a right one in all the forms—and now to be told that he was not to agitate her, that the God whom he wished to prepare her to meet knew more of her and understood her better than he did! Agitate her! When the alternative might be unspeakable miseries of punishment, instead of the acquittal which would have to be given to a soul properly prepared. These arguments did not in the least change his purpose, but they fretted and irritated him beyond measure. At the bottom of all, the idea that anybody should know better than he what was the right thing for his own wife was an intolerable thought.

He went in and out of her room with that irritated, though self-controlled look, which she knew so well. He had never shown it to the world, and when he had demanded of her in his angry way why this was and that, and how on earth such and such things had happened, Mrs. Kingsward had till lately taken it so sweetly that he had not himself suspected how heavy it was upon her. And when she had begun to show signs of being unable to bear the responsibility of everything in earth and heaven, the Colonel had felt himself an injured man. There were signs that he might eventually throw that responsibility on Bee. But in the meantime he had nobody to blame, as has been said, and the burden of irritation and disturbance was heavy upon him.

The next morning after his talk with Dr. Brown he came in with that clouded brow to find Charlie by her bedside. The Colonel came up and stood looking at the face on the pillow, now wan in the reaction of the fever, and utterly weak, but still smiling at his approach.

"I have been telling Charlie," she said, in her faint voice, "that he must go back to his college. Why should he waste his time here?"

"He will not go back yet," said Colonel Kingsward; "are you feeling a little better this morning, my dear?"

"Oh, not to call ill at all," said the sufferer. "Weak—a sort of sinking, floating away. I take hold of somebody's hand to keep me from falling through. Isn't it ridiculous?" she said, after a little pause.

"Your weakness is very great," said the husband, almost sternly.

"Oh, no, Edward. It's more silly than anything—when I am not really ill, you know. I've got Charlie's hand here under the counterpane," she said again, with her faint little laugh.

"You won't always have Charlie's hand, or anyone's hand, Lucy."

She looked at him with a little anxiety.

"No, no. I'll get stronger, perhaps, Edward."

"Do you feel as if you were at all stronger, my dear?"

She loosed her son's hand, giving him a little troubled smile. "Go away now, Charlie dear. I don't believe you've had your breakfast. I want to speak to—papa." Then she waited, looking wistfully in her husband's face till the door had closed. "You have something to say to me, Edward. Oh, what is it? Nothing has happened to anyone?"

"No, nothing has happened," he said. He turned away and walked to the window, then came back again, turning his head half-way from her as he spoke. "It is only that you are, my poor darling—weaker every day."

"Does the doctor think so?" she said, with a little eagerness, with a faint suffusion of colour in her face.

He did not say anything—could not perhaps—but slightly moved his head.

"Weaker every day, and that means, Edward!" She put out her thin, hot hands. "That means—"

The man could not say anything. He could do his duty grimly, but when the moment came he could not put it into words. He sank down on the chair Charlie had left, and put down his face on the pillow, his large frame shaken by sobs which he could not restrain.

These sobs made Mrs. Kingsward forget the meaning of this communication altogether. She put her hands upon him trying to raise his head. "Edward! Oh, don't cry, don't cry! I have never seen you cry in all my life. Edward, for goodness' sake! You will kill me if you go on sobbing like that. Oh, Edward, Edward, I never saw you cry before."

Moulsey had darted forward from some shadowy corner where she was and gripped him by the arm.

"Stop, sir—stop it," she cried, in an authoritative whisper, "or you'll kill her."

He flung Moulsey off and raised his head a little from the pillow.

"You have never seen me with any such occasion before," he said, taking her hands into his and kissing them repeatedly.

He was not a man of many caresses, and her heart was touched with a feeble sense of pleasure.

"Dear!" she said softly, "dear!" feebly drawing a little nearer to him to put her cheek against his.

Colonel Kingsward looked up as soon as he was able and saw her lying smiling at him, her hand in his, her eyes full of that wonderful liquid light which belongs to great weakness. The small worn face was all illuminated with smiles; it was like the face of a child—or perhaps an angel. He looked at first with awe, then with doubt and alarm. Had he failed after all in the commission which he had executed at so much cost to himself, and against the doctor's orders? He had been afraid for the moment of the sight of her despair—and now he was frightened by her look of ease, the absence of all perturbations. Had she not understood him? Would it have to be told again, more severely, more distinctly, this dreadful news?

CHAPTER IV

Mrs Kingsward said nothing of the communication her husband had made to her. Did she understand it? He went about heavily all day, pondering the matter, going and coming to her room, trying in vain to make out what was in her mind. But he could not divine what was in that mind, hidden from him in those veils of individual existence which never seemed to him to have been so baffling before. In the afternoon she had heard, somehow, the voices of the elder boys, and had asked if they were there, and had sent for them. The two big fellows, with the mud on their boots and the scent of the fresh air about them, stood huddled together, speechless with awe and grief, by the bedside, when their father came in. They did not know what to say to their mother in such circumstances. They had never talked to her about herself, but always about themselves; and now they were entirely at a loss after they had said, "How are you, mamma? Are you very bad, mamma? Oh, I'm so sorry;" and "Oh, I wish you were better." What could boys of twelve and fourteen say? For the moment they felt as if their hearts were broken; but they did not want to stay there; they had nothing to say to her. Their pang of sudden trouble was confused with shyness and awkwardness, and their consciousness that she was altogether in another atmosphere and another world. Mrs. Kingsward was not a clever woman, but she understood miraculously what was in those inarticulate young souls. She kissed them both, drawing each close to her for a moment, and then bade them run away. "Were you having a good game?" she said, with that ineffable, feeble smile. "Go and finish it, my darlings." And they stumbled out very awkwardly, startled to meet their father's look as they turned round, and greatly disturbed and mystified altogether, though consoled somehow by their mother's look.

They said to each other after a while that she looked "jolly bad," but that she was in such good spirits it must be all right.

Their father was as much mystified as they; but he was troubled in conscience, as if he had not spoken plainly enough, had not made it clear enough what "her state" was. She had not asked for the clergyman—she had not asked for anything. Was it necessary that he should speak again? There was one thing she had near her, but that so fantastic a thing!—a photograph—one of the quantities of such rubbish the girls and she had brought home—a woman wrapped in a mantle floating in the air.

"Take that thing away," he said to Moulsey. It irritated him to see a frivolous thing like that—a twopenny-halfpenny photograph—so near his wife's bed.

"Don't take it away," she said, in the whisper to which her voice had sunk; "it gives me such pleasure."

"Pleasure!" he cried; even to speak of pleasure was wrong at such a moment. And then he added, "Would you like me to read to you? Would you like to see—anyone?"

"To see anyone? Whom should I wish to see but you, Edward, and the children?"

"We haven't been—so religious, my dear, as perhaps we ought," stammered the anxious man. "If I sent for—Mr. Baldwin perhaps, to read the prayers for the sick and—and talk to you a little?"

She looked at him with some wonder for a moment, and then she said, with a smile, "Yes, yes; by all means, Edward, if you like it."

"I shall certainly like it, my dearest; and it is right—it is what we should all wish to do at the—" He could not say at the last—he could not say when we are dying—it was too much for him; but certainly she must understand now. And he went away hurriedly to call the clergyman, that no more time might be lost.

"Moulsey," said Mrs. Kingsward, "have we come then quite—to the end now?"

"Oh, ma'am! Oh, my dear lady!" Moulsey said.

"My husband—seems to think so. It is a little hard—to leave them all. Where is Bee?"

"I am here, mamma," said a broken voice; and the mother's hand was caught and held tight, as she liked it to be. "May Betty come too?"

"Yes, let Betty come. It is you I want, not Mr. Baldwin."

"Mr. Baldwin is a good man, ma'am. He'll be a comfort to them and to the Colonel."

"Yes, I suppose so; he will be a comfort to—your father. But I don't want anyone. I haven't done very much harm—"

"No! oh, no, ma'am, none!" said Moulsey, while Betty, thrown on her knees by the bedside, tried to smother her sobs; and Bee, worn out and feeling as if she felt nothing, sat and held her mother's hand.

"But, then," she said, "I've never, never, done any good."

"Oh! my dear lady, my dear lady! And all the poor people, and all the children."

"Hush! Moulsey. I never gave anything—not a bit of bread, not a shilling—but because I liked to do it. Never! oh, never from any good motive. I always liked to do it. It was my pleasure. It never cost me anything. I have done no good in my life. I just liked the poor children, that was all, and thought if they were my own—Oh, Bee and Betty, try to be better women—different from me."

Betty, who was so young, crept nearer and nearer on her knees, till she came to the head of the bed. She lifted up her tear-stained face, "Mother! oh, mother! are you frightened?" she cried.

Mrs. Kingsward put forth her other arm and put it freely round the weeping girl. "Perhaps I ought to be, perhaps I ought to be!" she said, with a little thrill and quaver.

"Mother," said Betty, pushing closer and closer, almost pushing Bee away, "if I had been wicked, ever so wicked, I shouldn't be frightened for you."

A heavenly smile came over the woman's face. "I should think not, indeed."

And then Betty, in the silence of the room, put her hands together and said very softly, "Our Father, which art in Heaven—"

"Oh, children, children," cried Moulsey, "don't break our hearts! She's too weak to bear it. Leave her alone."

"Yes, go away, children dear—go away. I have to rest—to see Mr. Baldwin." Then she smiled, and said in gasps, "To tell the truth—I'm—I'm not afraid; look—" She pointed to the picture by her bedside. "So easy—so easy! Just resting—and the Saviour will put out his hand and take me in."

Mr. Baldwin came soon after—the good Rector, who was a good man, but who believed he had the keys, and that what he bound on earth was bound in Heaven—or, at least, he thought he believed so—with Colonel Kingsward, who felt that he was thus fulfilling all righteousness, and that this was the proper way in which to approach the everlasting doors. He put away the little picture in which Catherine of Siena lay in the hold of the angels, in the perfect peace of life accomplished, the rest that was so easy and so sweet—hastily with displeasure and contempt. He did not wish the Rector to see the childish thing in which his wife had taken pleasure, nor even that she had been taking pleasure at all at such a solemn moment; even that she should smile the same smile of welcome with which she would have greeted her kind neighbour had she been in her usual place in the drawing-room disturbed her husband. So near death and yet able to think of that! He watched her face as the Rector read the usual prayers. Did she enter into them—did she understand them? He could scarcely join in them himself in his anxiety to make sure that she felt and knew what was her "state," and was preparing—preparing to meet her God. That God was awaiting severely the appearance of that soul before him, the Colonel could not but feel. He would not have said so in words, but the instinctive conviction in his heart was so. When she looked round for the little picture it hurt him like a sting. Oh, if she would but think of the things that concerned her peace—not of follies, childish distractions, amusements for the fancy. On her side, the poor lady was conscious more or less of all that was going on, understood here and there the prayers that were going over her head, prayers of others for her, rather than anything to be said by herself. In the midst of them, she felt herself already like St. Catherine, floating away into ineffable peace, then coming back again to hear the sacred words, to see the little circle round her on their knees, and to smile upon them in an utter calm of weakness without pain, feeling only that they were good to her, thinking of her, which was sweet, but knowing little more.

It was the most serene and cloudless night after that terrible day. A little after Colonel Kingsward had left the room finally and shut himself up in his study, Moulsey took the two girls out into the garden, through a window which opened upon it. "Children, go and breathe the sweet air. I'll not have you in a room to break your hearts. Look up yonder—yonder where she's gone," said the kind nurse who had done everything for their mother. And they stole out—the two little ghosts, overborne with the dreadful burden of humanity, the burden which none of us can shake off, and crept across the grass to the seat where she had been used to sit among the children. The night was peace itself—not a breath stirring, a young moon with something wistful in her light looking down, making the garden bright as with a softened ethereal day. A line of white cloud dimly detached from the softness of the blue lay far off towards the west amid the radiance, a long faint line as of something in the far distance. Bee and Betty stood and gazed at it with eyes and hearts over-charged, each leaning upon the other. Their young souls were touched with awe and an awful quiet. They were too near the departure to have fallen down as yet into the vacancy and emptiness of re-awakening life. "Oh," they said, "if that should be her!" And why should it not be? Unless perhaps there was a quicker way. They watched it with that sob in the throat which is of all sounds and sensations the most overwhelming. It seemed to them as if they were watching her a little further on her way, to the very horizon, till the soft distance closed over, and that speck like a sail upon the sea could be seen no more. And when it was gone they sank down together upon her seat, under the trees she loved, where the children had played and tumbled on the grass about her, and talked of her in broken words, a little phrase now and then, sometimes only "Mother," or "Oh, mamma, mamma," now from one, now from another—in that first extraordinary exaltation and anguish which is not yet grief.

They did not know how long they had been there when something stirred in the bushes, and the two big boys, Arthur and Fred, came heavily into sight, holding each other by the arm. The boys were bewildered, heavy and miserable, not knowing what to do with themselves nor where to go. But they came up with a purpose, which was a little ease in the trouble. It cost them a little convulsion of reluctant crying before they could get out what they had to say. Then it came out in broken words from both together. "Bee, there's someone wants to speak to you at the gate."

"Oh! who could want to speak to me—to-night? I cannot speak to anyone; you might have known."

"Bee," said Arthur, the eldest, "it isn't just—anyone; it's—we thought you would perhaps—"

"He told us," said Fred, "who he was; and begged so hard—"

Then there came back upon poor Bee all the other trouble that she had pushed away from her. Her heart seemed to grow hard and cold after all the softening and tenderness of this dreadful yet heavenly hour. "I will see no one—no one," she said.

"Bee," said the boys, "we shut the gate upon him; but he took hold of our hands, and—and cried, too." They had to stop and swallow the sob before either could say any more. "He said she was his best friend. He said he couldn't bear it no more than us. And if you would only speak to him."

Bee got up from her mother's seat; her poor little heart swelled in her bosom as if it would burst. Oh! how was she to bear all this—to bear it all—to have no one to help her! "No, no, I will not. I will not!" she said.

"Oh, Bee," cried Betty, "if it is Aubrey—poor Aubrey! She was fond of him. She would not like him to be left out. Oh, Bee, come; come and speak to him. Suppose one of us were alone, with nobody to say mother's name to!"

"No, I will not," said Bee. "Oh! Betty, mother knows why; she knows."

"What does she know?" cried Betty, pleading. "She was fond of him. I am fond of him, without thinking of you, for mother's sake."

"Oh, let me go! I am going in; I am going to her. I wish, I wish she had taken me with her! No, no, no! I will never see him more."

"I think," said Betty to the boys, pushing them away, "that she is not quite herself. Tell him she's not herself. Say she's not able to speak to anyone, and we can't move her. And—and give poor Aubrey—oh, poor Aubrey!—my love."

The boys turned away on their mission, crossing the gravel path with a commotion of their heavy feet which seemed to fill the air with echoes.

Colonel Kingsward heard it from his study, though that was closed up from any influence outside. He opened his window and came out, standing a black figure surrounded by the moonlight. "Who is there?" he said. "Are there any of you so lost to all feeling as to be out in the garden, of all nights in the world on this night?"

CHAPTER V

Aubrey Leigh had been living a troubled life during the time which had elapsed since the swallowing up in the country of the family in which he had become so suddenly interest, of which, for a short time, he had felt himself a member, and from which, as he felt, he could never be separated, whatever arbitrary laws might be made by hits head. When they disappeared from London, which was done so suddenly, he was much cast down for the moment, but, as he had the fullest faith in Bee, and was sustained by her independence of character and determined to stand by him whatever happened, he was, though anxious and full of agitation, neither despairing nor even in very low spirits. To be sure there were moments in which his heart sank, recalling the blank countenance of the father, and the too gentle and yielding disposition of the mother, and Bee's extreme youth and habits of obedience to both. He felt how much there was to be said against himself—a man who had been forced into circumstances of danger which nobody but himself could fully understand, and against which his whole being had revolted, though he could say but little on the subject. And, indeed, who was to understand that a man might yield to a sudden temptation which he despised and hated, and that he could not even explain that this was so, laying the blackest blame upon another—to a man, and still less to a woman; which last was impossible, and not even to be thought of. He might tell it, perhaps, to his mother, and there was a possibility of help there; though even there a hundred difficulties existed. But he was not wound up to that last appeal, and he felt, at first, but little fear of the eventual result He was assured of Bee's faithfulness, and how could any parent stand out against Bee? Not even, he tried to persuade himself, the stern Colonel, who had so crushed himself. And she had received his first letters, and had answered them, professing her determination never to be coerced in this respect.

He was agitated, his life was full of excitement, and speculation, and trouble. But this is nothing dreadful in a young man's life. It was perhaps better, more enlivening, more vivid, than the delights of an undisturbed love-making, followed by a triumphant marriage. It is well sometimes that the course of true love should not run smooth. He thought himself unhappy in being separated from Bee; but the keen delight of her determination to stand by him for good or evil, her faith in him, her championship, and the conviction that this being so all must come right in the end, was like a stream of bright fresh water flowing through the somewhat sombre flat of his existence. It had been very sombre in the early days of what people thought his youthful happiness—very flat, monotonous, yet with ignoble contentions in it. Bee's sunshiny nature, full of lights and shadows, had changed the whole landscape, and now the excitement of this struggle for her, changed it still more. It might be a hard battle, but they would win in the end. Whether he, a somewhat unlucky fellow, would have done so was very doubtful—but for her the stars would fight in their courses. Everything would be overturned in the world, rather than that Bee should be made miserable, and since she had set her dear heart on him, on his behalf too the very elements would fight, for how otherwise could Bee be made happy? The argument was without a flaw.

This was his reasoning, never put, I need not say, into any formula of words, yet vaguely believed in, and forming a source of the brightest exhilaration in his life, rousing all combative influences by the power of that hope of success which was a certainty in such a case. This exhilaration was crossed by the blackest of disappointments, and threatened to become despair when for days he had no sign of existence from Bee: but that after all was only a keener excitement—the sting of anxiety which makes after satisfaction more sweet. And then he was consoled to hear of Mrs. Kingsward's illness, which explained everything. Not that Aubrey was selfish enough to rejoice in that poor lady's suffering. He would have been shocked and horrified by the thought. But then it was no unusual thing for Mrs. Kingsward to be ill; it is not unusual, a young man so easily thinks, for any middle-aged person to be ill—and in so many cases it does not seem to do them much harm; whereas it did him much good—for it explained the silence of Bee!

And then it came to Aubrey's ears that Mrs. Kingsward was very ill—worse than she had ever been before; and then that all the family had been summoned that she was dying. Such rumours spread like wildfire—they get into the air—nobody knows how they come. He went down to the village nearest Kingswarden, and found a lodging there, when this news reached him, and endeavoured to send a note to Bee, to let her know he was at hand. But in the trouble of the house this note, sent by a private hand—always in these days an unsafe method—was somehow lost and never reached her. He hung about the house in the evenings, avoiding on various occasions an encounter with Charlie, who was not friendly, and with the Colonel, who was his enemy. These two were the only members of the family visible outside the gates of Kingswarden—until he managed to identify the two boys, whose disconsolate wanderings about pointed them out to him, and who did not know, therefore had no hostility or suspicion of the stranger who inquired after their mother so anxiously. Everybody inquired after their mother. It was nothing strange to them to be stopped on the road with this question. It was thus at last, hearing the final blow had fallen, Aubrey had ventured to send a message, to ask for a word from Bee. The thought of what the girl must be suffering in her first grief, and to feel himself so near her—almost within hearing—yet altogether shut out, was more than he could bear. He pushed in within the gate, into the shelter of the shrubbery, and there he stopped short, bound by invisible restraints. It was the home of his love, and yet it was the house of his enemy. He could not take advantage of the darkness of the night and of the misery of the moment to violate the sanctuary of a man soul-stricken by such trouble. But from where he stood he could see the little group of shadows under the tree. And how could he go away and not say a word to her—not take her in his arms, tell her his heart was with her, and that he was a mourner too? "Ask Bee to speak to me. Ask her to speak to me—only for a moment. I am Aubrey Leigh," he said to the two brothers, taking an arm of each, imploring them. The boys did not know much about Aubrey Leigh, but still they had heard the name. And they were overawed by his earnestness; the sound of his voice which, full of passion and feeling as it was, was strange to their undeveloped consciousness. They took his message, as we have seen, and then there came a mysterious moment which Aubrey could not understand. He could not hear what was said, but he was conscious of a resistance, of denial, and that Bee did not make a step towards him; that she recoiled rather than advanced. Though he could scarcely see anything distinctly, he could see that—that there was no impulse towards him, but rather the reverse; that Bee did not wish to come. And then the harsh voice of the Colonel broke the spell of the quiet, of the mournful, tranquil night, which it was so easy for a roused imagination to think was penetrated, too, by the sentiment of sorrow and of peace. The Colonel's voice put every gentler vision to flight. "Is it possible that any of you are out here in the garden—of all nights in the world on this night?" Oh! the very night of all nights to be there—in the first awe and silence, watching her pass, as it were, to the very gates of Heaven! Perhaps, it was unawares from Bee's mind that this idea came to his—"to watch her ascending, trailing clouds of glory," as the poet said; but that was the spirit coming and not going. These thoughts flew through his mind in the shock and irritation of the Colonel's voice. And then the shadows under the tree seemed to fly away and disperse, and silence fell upon all around, the great ghostly trees standing up immovable like muffled giants in the moonlight, their shadows making lines and heavy clumps of blackness on the turf, the late roses showing pale in the distance, the garden paths white and desolate. A moment more, and the harsh sound, almost angry, of the Colonel's window shutting, of bolts and bars, and a final closing up of everything came unkindly upon the hushed air. And then the moonlight reached the shut up house, all unresponsive, with death in it, with one faint light burning in the large window upstairs, showing where the gentle inmate lay who needed light no more. Strange prejudice of humanity that put out all the lights for sleep, but surrounds death with them, that no careless spirit may mistake for a common chamber the place where that last majesty lies.

Aubrey stood alone in this hushed and silent world. His heart was as heavy as a stone, heavy with grief for the friend who had passed for ever out of his life. He had not known perhaps till now what he too had lost—a friend, who would not have forsaken him not a very strong champion to fight for him; but a friend that never, whatever might be said, would have refused to hear him, refused to give him her sympathy. Had Bee, his own Bee, refused? The young man was bewildered beyond the power of thought. Was it his fault to have come too soon? Was it an outrage to be there on the night of the mother's death? But there was no outrage in his thoughts, not even any selfishness. It was her he had been thinking of, not himself; that she might feel there was someone whose thoughts were all hers, who was herself, not another, feeling with her, mourning with her, her very own to take the half of her burden. He had felt that he could not be far away while Bee was in trouble—that even to stand outside would be something, would somehow lighten her load, would make her feel in the very air a consciousness of the mighty love that would

—cleave in twain
The lading of a single pain
And part it giving half to him.

His heart, which had so gone out to her, seemed to come back confused, with all the life out of it, full of wonder and dismay. Had she rejected him and his sympathy? Was it the fault of the others, the boys who did not know what to say? Was she angry that he should come so soon? But it was now, immediately on the very stroke of the distress, that love should come. He stood for a long time silent, bewildered, not knowing what to think. Was it possible that she could have misunderstood him, have thought that he had come here only to beguile her into his arms, to take advantage of an opportunity? It pained poor Aubrey to the heart to think that she might have thought so. Ah! Mrs. Kingsward would not have done it, would not have let Bee do it. But she lay there, where the light was, never to say anything more: and Bee—Bee!

He got out of the little park that surrounded Kingswarden by the stile near the village, some time after, he did not know how long. He thought it was in the middle of the night. The moon had set, everything was dark, and all the cottagers asleep. But time is long to watchers unaccustomed to long vigils, and the lights were not out at the small inn in the village where he was lodging. He found the master of the house and his wife talking at the door in subdued tones, over the event of the evening. "She was always a weakly body, but she'll be sore missed," the woman said. "She kept everything going. The Colonel, he'll not have a servant left as will put up with him in three months. You take my word. She kept all straight. Lord, that's how women mostly is—no account as long as they're living—and then you finds the want o' them when they're gone."

"Here you are, mister," said the landlord; "we thought as you was lost. It was a fine night, tempting for a walk. But it's clouding over now."

"Oh, no, sir, nought of the sort," said the woman. "My master here, he never goes to bed afore the middle of the night, he don't, and it's an excuse for not getting up in the mornin'. But you'll have to be early to-morrow, Gregg, you take my word, for there'll be undertakers' men and that sort down from London, and I'll not be bothered with them, mind you that."

"I suppose you're right this time," said the man. "They drinks a deal to keep up their spirits, being as it is a kind of depressing trade."

"If I hear you laugh again like that!—and the missis lying in her coffin! Don't you think, sir, as he's got no feeling. He puts it off like with a laugh not to cry. I was kitchen-maid up there, and he was groom in the old days, and many and many's the kindness she done to me and mine. Oh, and such a pretty lady and sweet—and a young family left just at the ages that most need a mother's care."

"They're all ages, Molly, if you come to that."

"Well, and don't they want a mother's care at all ages? What would you do with my children if I was took, John Gregg? And the Colonel, he's just a helpless man like you are. The only hope is as Miss Bee will turn out like her mother. I always thought she favoured Missis, though some said it was the Colonel she was like. It's a dreadful charge for her, poor thing, at her age; but if she takes after the Missis there will be some hope for them," the woman said.

"I thought as Miss Bee was going to be married?" said the landlord.

"Oh, that's all broken off," she said, "and a good thing too, seeing what's happened, for what could ever little Miss Betty do?"

Aubrey, who had lingered listening, went slowly up the narrow wooden stair to his shabby little room as the pair locked the door and put out their lights. He heard them carrying on the conversation in the kitchen underneath for a few minutes before they, too, in their turn clambered upstairs to bed. "Oh, that's all broken off, and a good thing too." He kept saying these words over and over miserably, as if they had been the chorus of some dreadful song of fate.

Aubrey stayed at the village public-house day after day, hoping for some sign or message. He wrote to Bee, this time by the post; but he had no better success. Was it only because of her grief that she took no notice? Terrible as that grief must be, and rigorous as evidently were the rules of the closed-up house, from which no one came forth, even for a mouthful of air, it did not seem to him that this was reason enough for putting him from her—he who was to share her life, and whose sympathy was so full and overflowing. Surely it was the moment when all who loved her should gather round her, when she most wanted solace and support. It could not be that her heart was so wrapped up in sorrow that she should push from her the man who had the best right to share her tears—whom her mother approved and liked, whose acceptance she had ratified and confirmed. It could not be that. He felt that, had he been in the same circumstances, his cry would have been for Bee to stand by him, to comfort him. Was she so different, or was she overwhelmed by what was before her—the charge of her father's house, the dreadful suggestion that it was to him and the children she should dedicate herself henceforward, giving up her own happiness? It seemed to Aubrey, after long thinking, that this must be the cause of her silence; the burden which surely was not for her young shoulders, which never could be intended for her, must have come down upon her, crushing her. She was the eldest girl. She must have, like so many girls, an exaggerated sense of what was her duty. Her duty! Could anything be more fantastic, more impossible? To take her mother's place—and her mother had been killed by it!—to humour the stern father—to take care of the tribe of children, to be their nurse, their ruler—everything that a creature of nineteen could not, should not be! And for this she would throw aside her own life—and him, whose life it was also. He would never, never consent to such a sacrifice, he said to himself. Bee was not soft and yielding, like their mother. She was a determined little thing. She would stand to it, and sacrifice him as she sacrificed herself, unless he made a bold stand from the first. No, no, no! Whatever was to be done, that must not be done. He would not have it—he must let her know from the very first—if it were not that she knew already, and that this was the reason why she was silent, feeling that if ever they met she could not hold out against him. Poor little Bee! Poor, poor little Bee! Her mother dead, and her father so stern; and thinking it her duty—her duty, God bless her!—to take all that household upon her little shoulders. The tears came into his eyes with a sudden softening. She thought it better to keep him at arm's length, the darling, knowing that she never could stand against him, that he would never, never consent; the little, sublime, unreasonable girl! The things they took into their heads, these inexperienced, generous creatures! But, thank heaven, he was here; even though she held him at bay—here, to make all right.

The reader knows that poor Bee was not actuated by such lofty feelings, but then Aubrey had no knowledge in his mind of that strange story which had destroyed her faith in him. When a man is guilty he knows all that can be brought against him, in which, in its way, there is a certain advantage. He cannot be taken by surprise. He knows that this or that is lying ready like a secret weapon apt to be picked up by any man who may wish to do him harm. But the innocent man has not that safeguard. It is not likely to occur to him that harmless circumstances may be so twisted as to look like guilt. For his own part he had forgotten all about that little episode on the railway—or if he remembered it, it was with a smile and a glow of momentary pleasure, to think how, with a little money—so small a matter—he had been able to make comfort take the place of misery to the poor little family, whom perhaps he would never have noticed at all had not his thoughts been full of Bee. He had done that for her with the feeling with which he might have given her an ornament or a basket of flowers; the only drawback to the pleasure of it being that he could not tell her off-hand, and get the smile of thanks she would give him for it—far more than he deserved, for he liked doing it—kindness coming natural to this young man. It was hard on Aubrey in the complications of fate that this innocent, nay praiseworthy, incident should be made the occasion of his trouble. But he had no suspicion of it—forgot the fact, indeed, altogether—and would have laughed at the idea that such an accidental occurrence could in any way influence his fate.

He went to the funeral, unnoticed in the crowd of people who were there—some for love and some for conventional necessity, but almost all with a pang of natural sympathy to see the train of children who followed their mother to her last rest. The Colonel, rigid in all things, had insisted at last, that all, except the very youngest, should be there—having wavered for a moment whether it would not be more in order that the girls should remain at home, and only the boys be present at the melancholy ceremony. To see the little wondering faces two-and-two that followed the elder children up the aisle, and were installed in the mourners' places, some of them scarcely tall enough to see over the edge of the pew, brought many a gush of tears to sympathetic eyes. Bee and Betty, the two inseparable "eldest,"—slim, black figures—drooping under the heavy veils that covered them from the daylight, almost touched Aubrey with their clinging black garments as they passed. Did they see him? He saw, wherever he was, at whatever distance, any movement they made. He saw that Bee never raised her head; but Betty was younger, and less self-restrained—that she had seen him at least he felt sure. And he felt the Colonel's eyes upon him, penetrating the thickest of the crowd. Colonel Kingsward had a glance that saw everything. He was a man bereaved, the light of his eyes taken from him, and the comfort of his life— and yet he saw everything at his wife's funeral, saw and noted the faces that were dull and tired of the tension, and those that were alive with sympathy—making notes for or against them in his memory, and, above all, he saw Aubrey Leigh. Charlie saw him more accidentally, without any conscious observation, and the boys who had cried all they were capable of, and now could not help their eyes straying a little, conscious of the spectacle, and of the important part they played in it, everybody looking at them. All of them saw him, but Bee. Was it only Bee who was so little in sympathy with him that she did not know he must be there?

He went back to his lodging a little angry through his emotion. It was too much. Even in the interval between her mother's death and funeral he felt that a girl who loved him should not be so obdurate as that, and he listened with a very sombre face to all the landlady's discussion of the proceedings. "It was a shame," she said, "to bring those little children there, not much more than babies—what could they know? I'd have kept them safe in the nursery with some quiet game to play, the poor little innocents! And so would Missis. Missis would have thought what was best for them, not for making a display. But God knows what will become of them children now."

"What should become of them?" said the husband. "They'll get the best of everything and servants to wait on them hand and foot. The Colonel, he ain't like a poor man who could do nothing for them. When the mother's gone the children had better go too—in a poor man's house."

"It's little you know about it," said the woman with contempt. "Rich house or poor house, it don't make no such great difference. Nurses is a long way different from mothers. Not as I'm saying a word against Sarah Langridge, as is a good honest woman, that would wrong her master not by a candle end or a boot lace, not she. But that's not like being a mother. The Lord grant that if I die and there's a baby it may go too, as you say. You're more than a nurse, you're their father, and you're part of them; but Lord forbid that I should leave a poor little baby on your hands."

The man turned on his heel with a tremulous laugh. "Well, I ain't wishing it, am I?" he said.

"But," said Aubrey, "there are the—elder sisters—the young ladies."

"Miss Bee! Lord bless us, sir, do ye know the age that child is? Nineteen, and no more. Is that an age to take the charge of a nursery full of children? Why, her mother was but forty as has been laid in her grave to-day. I wish to goodness as that marriage hadn't been broke off. He was a widower—and I don't much hold with widowers—but I wish that I could give him a sign to come back, if he has any spirit in him, and try and get that poor young lady away."

"If he has been sent about his business," said Aubrey, forcing a smile, "he could have no right to come back."

"I don't know whose fault it was," said the landlady. "None o' missis's, you take my word; but, Lord, if a gentleman loves a young lady, what's to hinder him putting his pride in his pocket? A man does when he's real fond of a woman in our rank of life."

"I don't know about that," said her husband. "If I had been sent away with a cuff on the side of my head, blessed if I'd ever have come back."

"You're a poor lot, all of you," the woman said.

Aubrey could not but smile at the end of the argument, but he asked himself when he was alone—Was he a poor lot? Was he unwilling to put his pride in his pocket? Walking about his little room, turning over and over the circumstances, remembering the glare from Colonel Kingsward's eye, which had recognised him, he at last evolved out of his own troubled feelings and imagination the idea that it was his part to offer sympathy, to hold out an olive branch. Perhaps, after all, the stern man's heart was really touched; perhaps it would soothe him in his grief to hear that "when the eye saw her, then it blessed her," which was Aubrey's sincere feeling at this moment in respect to Bee's mother. It seemed to him that it was best to act upon this impulse before other arguments came in; before the sense of wounding and pain in Bee's silence got the upper hand. He spent most of the afternoon in writing a letter, so carefully put together, copied over and over again, that there might be nothing in it to wound the most sensitive feelings; offering to Colonel Kingsward his profound sympathy, telling him with emotion of her kindness to himself, her sweetness, her beauty, with that heightening of enthusiastic admiration, which, if it is permissible anywhere, is so over a new-made grave. And at the end he asked, with all the delicacy he could, whether in these new circumstances he might not ask a hearing, a renewed consideration, for her dear sake who had been so good to him, and who was gone.

I am not sure that his judgment went fully with this renewed effort, and his landlady's remarks were but a poor reason for any such step. But his heart was longing after Bee, angry with her, impatient beyond words, disturbed, miserable, not knowing how to support the silence and separation while yet so near. And to do something is always a relief, even though it may be the worst and not the best thing to do. In the evening after dark, when there was no one about, he went up to Kingswarden, and himself put his letter into the hands of the butler, who did not know him, and therefore knew no reason why the letter should either be carried in haste to his master or delayed. Aubrey heard that the young ladies were quite as well as could be expected, and the Colonel very composed, considering—and then he returned to the village. How silent the house was! Not a creature about, and how disturbing and painful to the anxious spirit even the simple noises and commotion of the village street.

Next morning a letter came, delivered by the postman, from Kingswarden. It contained only a few words.

"Colonel Kingsward is obliged to Mr. Aubrey Leigh for his message of sympathy, but, on consideration of the whole circumstances, thinks it better that no pretence at intercourse should be resumed. It could be nothing but painful to both parties, and Colonel Kingsward, with his compliments, takes the liberty to suggest that Mr. Aubrey Leigh would do well to remain in the neighbourhood as short a time as suits his convenience.

"Kingswarden, October 15."

Inside were the two or three notes which Aubrey on different occasions—twice by post and once by a private messenger—had sent to Bee. They had not been opened. The young man's colour rose with a fiery indignation—his heart thumped in his ears. This was an explanation of which he had not thought. To keep back anyone's letters had not occurred to him as a thing that in the end of the eighteenth century any man would dare to do. It seemed to bring him back face to face with old-fashioned, forgotten methods, of all sorts of antiquated kinds. He put down the papers on the table with a sort of awe. How was he to struggle against such ways of warfare? Bee might think he had not written at all—had shown no sympathy with her in her trouble. How likely that it was this that had made her angry, that kept her from saying a word, from vouchsafing a look! She might think it was he who was deficient, who showed no feeling. What was he to do? The landlady coming up with his breakfast broke in upon this distracting course of thought.

"I didn't know, sir, as you were acquainted with the Colonel's family," the woman said.

"A little," said poor Aubrey. The letters were all lying on the table, giving to a sharp observer a very good clue to the position. Mrs. Gregg had noted the unopened letters returned to him in the Colonel's enclosure at the first glance.

"You didn't ought to have let us talk. Why, we might have been saying, without thinking, some ill of the Colonel or of Miss Bee."

He smiled, though with little heart. "You were once in their service," he said, "do you ever go there now?"

"Oh, yes, now and again," said Mrs. Gregg. "Sarah Langridge, as is in the nursery, is a cousin of mine, and I do go just to see them all now and again."

"Would you venture to take a letter from me to—Miss Kingsward?"

"Sir," said Mrs. Gregg, "is it about the marriage as was broke off? Is it?" she added quickly, as he answered her by nodding his head, "likely to come on again? That's what I want to know."

"If it does not," said Aubrey, "it will not be my fault."

"Then I will and welcome," the landlady said. "It's natural I should want to go the day after the funeral, to see about everything. Give me your letter, sir, and I'll get it put safe into Miss Bee's own hands."

All that he sent was half-a-dozen words of appeal.

"Bee, these have been sent back to me. Was it by your will? I have   been here since ever I heard of her illness, longing to be with   you, to tell you what I felt for her and you. And you would not   speak to me! Bee, dearest, say you did not mean it. Tell me what I   am to do.

"A.L."

How long the woman was in getting ready—how long in going! Before she came back it was almost night again of the lingering, endless day. She brought him a little note, not returning the enclosures—that was always something—with a reproach. "Oh, sir, and you very near got me into terrible trouble! I'll never, never carry anything from you again." The note was still shorter than his own:—

"It was not by my will. I have never seen them till now. But please—please let this be the last. We can't meet again. There can never more be anything between us—not from my father's will, but my own. And this for ever—and your own heart will tell you why.

"BEE."

"My own heart will tell me why! My heart tells me nothing—nothing!" poor Aubrey said to himself in the silence of his little room. But there was little use in repeating it to himself, and there was no other ear to hear.

CHAPTER VII

It was with a sort of stupified bewilderment that Aubrey read over and over the little letter of Bee's. Letter! To call it a letter. Those straggling lines without any beginning, no name of him to whom they were addressed, nothing even of the most superficial courtesy, nothing that marked the link that had been—unless it were, perhaps, the abruptness, the harshness, which would have used to no other. This was a kind of painful comfort in its way, when he came to think of it. To nobody but him would she have written so—this was the little gleam of light. And she had retained his letters, though she had forbidden him from sending more. These lights of consolation leaped into his mind with the first reading, but the more he repeated that reading, the darker grew the prospect, and the less comfort they gave him. "Not by my father's will, but my own; and your own heart will tell you why." What did she mean by his own heart? She had begun to write conscience, and then drew her pen through it. Conscience! What had he done? What had he done? The real trouble of his life Bee had forgiven. Her father had stood upon it, and nothing had changed his standing ground so far as the Colonel was concerned; but Bee, who did not understand—how should any girl understand?—had forgiven him, had flung his reproach away and accepted him as he was. How was it that she should thus go back on her decision now? "Not my father's will, but mine. And your conscience will tell you why." Aubrey's conscience reproached him with nothing, with no thought of unfaithfulness to the young and spotless love which had re-created his being. He had never denied the old reproach. But what was it, what was it which she bid him to remember, which would explain the change in her? "Your heart will tell you why"—why his heart? and what was there that could be told him, which could explain this? He walked about his little room all night, shaking the little rickety little house with his tread, asking himself, "What was it, what was it?" and finding no answer anywhere.

When he got up from a troubled morning sleep, these disturbed and unrefreshing slumbers, full of visions which turn the appearance of rest into the most fatiguing of labour, Aubrey formed a resolution, which he said to himself he should perhaps have carried out from the first. He had an advocate who could take charge of his cause without any fear of betrayal, his mother, and to her he would go without delay. Of all things in the world to do, after the reception of Bee's note, giving in was the last thing he could think of. To accept that strange and agitated decision, to allow that there was something in his own heart that would explain it to him, was what he would not and could not do. There was nothing in his own consciousness, in his heart or conscience, as she had said, that could explain it. Nothing! It was not to his credit to accept such a dismissal, even if he had been unaffected by it. He could not let a mystery fall over this, leaving it as one of those things unexplained which tear life in pieces. That would be mere weakness, not the mode of action of a man of sense who had no exposure to face. But if his letters were intercepted—miserable folly!—by the father, a man of the world who ought to have known that such proceedings were an anachronism—and rejected by herself, it was little use that he should continue writing. Against two such methods of silencing him no man could contend. But there was still one other great card to play. He went out and took a last view of the sheltered and flowery dwelling of Kingswarden, as it could be seen among the trees at one part of the road. The windows were open and all the blinds drawn up. The house had come back out of the shadow of death into the every-day composure of living. White curtains fluttered in the wind at the upper windows. The late climbing roses and pretty bunches of clematis seemed again to look in. It was still like summer, though the year was waning, and the sun still shone, notwithstanding all sorrow. Aubrey saw no one, however, but a housemaid, who paused as she passed to put up a window, and looked out for a moment. That was all. He had not the chance of seeing any face that he wished to see. In the village he met the two boys, who recognised him sheepishly with their eyes, and a look from one to another, but were about to shuffle past, Reginald on the heels of Arthur, to escape his notice—when he stopped them, which was a fact they were unprepared for, and had not calculated how to meet. He told them that he was going away, a definite fact upon which they seized eagerly. "Oh, so are we," they said, both together, one of them adding the explanation that there was always something going on at school. "And there's nothing to do here," the other added. "I hope we'll, sometime or other, know each other better," said Aubrey, at which the boys hung their heads. "There is a good deal of shooting down at my little place," he added. He was not above such a mean act; whereupon the two heads raised themselves by one impulse, as if they had been upon wires, and two pairs of eyes shone. "Try if you can do anything for me, and I'll do everything I can for you," this insidious plotter said. The boys shook hands with him with a warmth which they never expected to have felt for any such "spoon," and said to each other that he didn't seem such a bad fellow at bottom—as if they had searched his being through and through. Mr. Leigh met Charlie when on his way to the railway station, but he had no encouragement to say anything to Charlie. They passed each other with a nod, very surly on Charlie's part, whose anger at the sight of him—as if that man had anything to do with our trouble—was perhaps not so unnatural. Charlie, too, was going back to Oxford next day, and thankful to be doing so, out of this dreary place, where there was nothing to do.

It was the afternoon of the next day when Aubrey arrived at his mother's house. It was at some distance from his own house, much too far to drive, and only to be got at by cross-country railways, with an interval of an hour or two of waiting at several junctions, facts which he could not help remembering his poor little wife and her companion had congratulated themselves upon in those old, strange days, which had disappeared so entirely, like a tale that is told. He wondered whether she would equally think it an advantage—if she ever was the partner of his home. There seemed to him now something wrong in the thought, a mean sort of petty feeling, unworthy of a fine nature. He wondered if Bee—Bee! How unlikely it was that she would ever consider that question, or know anything further about his house or his ways of living—she who had thrust him away from her at the very moment when her heart ought to have been most soft—when love was most wanted to strengthen and uphold. Not her father's will, but her own. And your own heart will explain it. His own heart! in which there was nothing but truth and devotion to her.

He arrived thus at his mother's house very depressed in spirits. Mrs. Leigh was not the ordinary kind of mother for a young man like Aubrey Leigh. She was not one of those mothers wholly wrapped up in their children, who are so general. She had all along made an attempt at an independent life of her own. When Aubrey married she was still a comparatively young woman, by no means disposed to sink her identity in him or his household. Mrs. Aubrey Leigh might possess the first place in the family as the queen regnant, but Mrs. Leigh, in her personality a much more important person, had no idea of being swamped, and giving up her natural consequence. She was still a considerable person, though she was not rich, and inhabited only a sort of jointure-house, a "small place" capable of holding very few visitors. Aubrey was her only son, and she was, of course, very fond of him—of course, she was very fond of him—but she had no intention of sinking into insignificance or living only in the reflection of Aubrey, still less of his wife.

Hurstleigh, where Mrs. Leigh lived, was near the sea, and near also to the county town, which was a brisk and thriving seaport. It was an old house that had known many fluctuations, an ancient manor house, inhabited once by the Leighs when they were of humbler pretentions than now; then it became a farm-house, then was let to a hunting man, who greatly enlarged the stables; and now it was a jointure-house, the stables veiled by a new wing, the place in that trim order which denotes a careful master, and more particularly mistress; with large lattice windows, heavy mullions, and a terrace with stone balustrades running all the length of the house. Mrs. Leigh generally sat in a room opening upon this terrace, with the windows always open, except in the coldest weather, and there it was that Aubrey made his way, without passing through the house. His mother was sitting at one of her favourite occupations—writing letters. She was one of those women who maintain a large correspondence, chiefly for the reason that it amuses them to receive letters and to feel themselves a centre of lively and varied life; besides that, she was considered a very clever letter writer, which is a temptation to everyone who possesses, or is supposed to possess, that qualification. She rose quickly, with a cry of "Aubrey!" in great surprise.

"You are the last person I expected to see," she said, when she had given him a warm welcome. "I saw the death in the papers, and I supposed, of course, you would be there."

"I have just come from Kingswarden," he said, with a little nod of his head in assent; "and yet I was not there."

"Riddle me no riddles, Aubrey, for I never was good at guessing. You were there and yet you were not there?"

"I am afraid—I am no longer a welcome visitor, mother," he said, with a faint smile.

"What!" Mrs. Leigh's astonishment was so great that it seemed to disturb the afternoon quiet which reigned over the whole domain. "What! Why, Aubrey! It was only the other day I heard of your engagement."

"It is quite true, and yet it has become ancient history, and nobody remembers it any more."

"What do you mean?" she cried. "My dear Aubrey, I do not understand you. I thought you were dangling about after your young lady, and that this was the reason why I heard so little of you; and then I was much startled to see that announcement in the papers. But you said she was always delicate. Well, but what on earth is the meaning of this other change?"

"I told you, mother. For some time I was but half accepted, pending Colonel Kingsward's decision."

"Oh, yes; one knows what that sort of thing means! And then Colonel Kingsward generously consented—to one of the best matches in England—in your condition of life."

"I am not a young duke, mother."

"No, you are not a young duke. I said in your condition of life, and the Kingswards are nothing superior to that, I believe. Well—and then? That was where your last letter left me."

"I am ashamed not to have written, mother; but it wasn't pleasant news—and I always hoped to change their mind."

"Well? I suppose there was some cause for it?" she said, after waiting a long minute or two for his next words.

He got up and walked to the window, which, as has been intimated, was also a door opening and leading out on to the terrace. "May I shut this window?" he said, turning his back on her; and then he added, still keeping that attitude, "it was of course because of that old affair."

"What old affair?"

"You generally understand at half a word, mother; must I go into the whole nauseous business?"

She came up to him and laid her hand on his shoulder. "Miss Lance," she said.

"What else? I haven't had so many scandals in my life that you should stand in any doubt."

"Scandals!" she exclaimed; and again was silent for a moment. "Aubrey, explain it to me a little. How did that business come to their ears?"

"Oh, in the easiest way, the simplest way!" he cried, "The injured woman called on the father of the girl who was going to be given to such a reprobate as me." He laughed loudly and harshly, preserving the most tragic face all the time.

"The injured woman! Good heavens! And was the man such an ass—such an ass—?"

"He is not an ass, mother; he is a model of every virtue. My engagement, if you like to call it so, lasted about a week, and then I was suddenly turned adrift."

"Aubrey, when did all this happen?"

"I suppose about three weeks ago. Pardon me, mother, for not having written, but I had no heart to write. I left them at Cologne, and travelled home by myself, and the first thing I did, of course, was to go and see Colonel Kingsward."

"Well?"

"No, it wasn't well at all. He refused to listen to me. Of course, I got it out from my side as well as I could, but it made no difference. He would not hear me. He would understand no excuse."

"And the ladies?"

"Mrs. Kingsward was too gentle and yielding. She never opposed him, and—"

"Aubrey, the girl whom you loved, and had such faith in—Bee, don't you call her?—"

"Bee—stood by me, mother; never hesitated, gave me her hand, and stood by me."

"Ah, well," said Mrs. Leigh, with a little sigh of relief, "then that's all right. The father will soon come round—"

"So I should have said yesterday. I left them in that full faith. But since they came back to Kingswarden something has happened. I wrote to her, but I got no answer—I supposed it was her mother's illness—now I have found that he stops my letters; but something far worse—wait a moment—she, Bee herself, wrote to me yesterday, dismissing me without a word of explanation—declaring she did it by her own will, not her father's—and adding, my conscience would tell me why."

Mrs. Leigh looked her son straight in the face for a full minute. "Aubrey—and does your conscience tell you why?"

"No, mother. I am too bewildered even to be able to think—I have not an idea what she means. She knew all there was to know—without understanding it in the least, it needn't be said—and held fast to her word; and now I know no more what she means than you do. Mother, there's only one thing to be done—you must take it in hand."

"I—take your love affairs in hand!" she said.

CHAPTER VIII

But though Mrs. Leigh said this it is by no means certain that she meant it even at the first moment. It is only a very prudent woman who objects to being asked to interfere in a young man's love affairs. Generally the request itself is a compliment, and not less, but perhaps more so, when made to a mother by her son. And Mrs. Leigh, though a sensible and prudent person enough in ordinary affairs, did not attain to the height of virtue above indicated. When she went upstairs to change her gown for dinner, after talking it over and over with Aubrey in every possible point of view, her mind, though she had not yet consented in words, had begun to turn over the best methods of opening the question with the

Kingswards, and what it would be wisest in the circumstances to do. That Aubrey should be beaten, that he should have to give up the girl whom he loved, and of whom he gave so exalted a description, seemed the one thing that must not be permitted to be. Mrs. Leigh was very anxious that her son should marry, if it were only to wipe out the episode of that little, silly Amy, who was fonder of her friend than of her husband; and the half ludicrous, half tragic chapter of that woman, staying on, resisting all efforts to dislodge her for so long, until she had as she thought acquired rights over the poor young man, who was not strong-minded enough to turn her out of his house. To obliterate these circumstances from the mind of the county altogether, as could only be done by a happy and suitable marriage, Mrs. Leigh would have done much, and, to be sure, her son's happiness was also dear to her. Poor Aubrey! His first adventure into life had not been a happy one, and his descriptions of Bee and all her belongings had been full of a young lover's enthusiasm, not tame and tepid as she had always felt his sentiments towards Amy to be. What would it be best to do if I really undertake this business, she said to herself. Herself replied that it was not a business for her to meddle with, that she would do no good, and many other dissuasions of the conventional kind; but, when her imagination and feelings were once lit up, Mrs. Leigh was not a woman to be smothered in that way. After dinner, without still formally undertaking the mission, she talked with Aubrey of the best ways of carrying it out. If she did interfere, how should she set about it? "Mind, I don't promise anything, but supposing—" Should she write? Should she go? Which thing would it be best to do? If she made up her mind to go, should she write beforehand to warn them? What, on the whole, would be most appropriate to do?

The method finally decided upon between them—"if I go—but I don't say that I will go—" was that Mrs. Leigh should first, without warning or preparation, endeavour to see Bee, and ascertain whether any new representations had been made to her to change her mind; and then, according to her success or non-success with Bee, decide whether she should ask an interview with her father. Aubrey slept under his mother's roof with greater tranquility and refreshment than he had known for some time, and with something of the vague hope of his childhood that she could set everything right, do away with punishment or procure pleasure, when she took it in hand. It had always been so in the childish days, which seemed to come near him in the sight of the old furniture, the well-known pictures and ornaments and curiosities which Mrs. Leigh had brought with her when she settled in this diminished house. How well he remembered them all!—the old print of the little Samuel on his knees, the attitude of which he used half-consciously to copy when he said his prayers; the little old-fashioned books in blue and brown morocco on the shelves, the china ornaments on the mantel-piece. He smiled at their antiquity now-a-days, but he had thought them very grand and imposing once upon a time.

In the morning Mrs. Leigh coquetted a little, or else saw the whole subject in a colder light. "Don't you think it is possible that I might do more harm than good," she said; "things might settle of themselves if you only give them a little time. Colonel Kingsward would come to his senses, and Miss Bee—"

"Mother," cried Aubrey, pale with alarm, "on the contrary. Do you forget the circumstances? Mrs. Kingsward is dead, there is a large family of little children, and Bee is of the race of the Quixotes. Don't you see what will happen? She will get it into her mind, and everybody will persuade her, that as the eldest daughter she is wanted at home. It will be impressed upon her on all sides, and unless there is a strong influence to counteract it, and at once, Bee is lost to me for ever."

"My dear, don't be so tragical. These dreadful things don't happen in our days."

"You may laugh, mother, but it is no laughing matter to me."

"I don't laugh," she said. "I see the strength of your argument; but, my dear boy, nothing will be so effectual in showing your Bee the happiness that is awaiting her as a little trial of the troubles of a large family on her shoulders. I know what it is."

Aubrey sprang from his seat though it was in the middle of his breakfast. "Mother," he said, "there is one thing that I believe you will never know—and that is, Bee. The burden is exactly what will hold her fast beyond any argument—the sense of duty—the feeling that she is bound to take her mother's place."

What was in Mrs. Leigh's mind was the thought: Ah, that's all very well at first, till she has tried it. But what she said was: "I beg your pardon, Aubrey. Of course, that is a much more elevated feeling. Sit down, my dear, and take your breakfast. It is not my fault that I don't know Bee."

Upon which Aubrey had to beg her pardon and sit down, commiserating her for that deficiency, which was indeed her misfortune and not her fault.

At the end Mrs. Leigh was wound up to take the strongest step possible. She joined her son in London after about a week had elapsed. He chafed at the delay, but allowed that to leave Bee in quiet for a few days after all the storms that had gone over her head was necessary. Mrs. Leigh went down early on a bright October morning to Kingswarden with much more excitement than she had expected to feel. She was herself inclined to take a lighter view, to laugh at the idea of interrupted letters or parental cruelty, and to believe that poor Bee was worn out, her nerves all wrong, and possibly her temper affected by the irritability which is so apt to accompany unaccustomed grief, and that in a little time she would of herself come round. Seeing, however, that these suggestions only made Aubrey angry, she had given them up, and was in fact more influenced than she cared to show by his emotion and anxiety when she thus sallied forth into the unknown to plead her son's cause. They had ascertained that Colonel Kingsward had returned to his office, so the coast was clear. Only the two girls and the little children were at home. Mrs. Leigh said to herself as she walked to the gate that it was a shame to take the little girl, poor little thing, thus unprotected, with nobody to stand by her. If it were not that it was entirely for her good—nobody that knew Aubrey would deny that he would make the best husband in the world, and surely to have a good house of her own, and a good husband, and distinct place in the world was better than to grow to maturity a harassed woman at the head of her father's house, acting mother to a troop of children who would not obey her, nor even be grateful for her kindness to them. Surely there could not be two opinions as to what it would be best for the girl to do. Yet she felt a little like a wolf going down into the midst of the lambkins when she opened the unguarded gate.

Mrs. Leigh was a clever woman, and a woman of the world. She had a great deal of natural understanding, and a considerable knowledge of life, but she was not unlike in appearance the ordinary British matron, who is not much credited with these qualities. That is to say, she was stout—which is a calamity common with the kind. She had white hair, considerably frizzed on the top of the forehead, as it is becoming to white hair to be, and dark eyes and good complexion. These things were in her favour; still, it is impossible to deny that when Bee and Betty saw coming towards them, following the footman across the lawn, a stout figure, not very tall, nor distinguishable from various ladies in both country and town whom they knew, and with the natural impertinence of youth set down as bores, they had both a strong revolt in their minds against their visitor. "Oh, who is it—who is it?" they said to each other. "Why did James let her in? Why did he let anyone in?"

It was a warm morning, though the season was far advanced, and they were seated again on that bench under the tree where they had watched the white cloud floating away on the night of their mother's death. They went there instinctively whenever they went out. "Mother's tree," they began to call it, and sat as she had been used to do, with the children playing near, and nurse walking up and down with the baby in her arms. They had been talking more that morning than ever before. It was little more than a week since Mrs. Kingsward's funeral, but they were so young that their hearts now and then for a moment burst the bondage of their sorrow, and escaped the length of a smile or two. It was not much; and, to be sure, for the children's sake it was indispensable that they should not be crying and miserable always, as at first they had felt as if they must continually be. But it was another thing to receive visitors and have perhaps to answer questions about the circumstances of their loss.

"Mrs.—? what did James say?" Neither of them were sure, though a thrill ran through Bee's veins. It was a stranger. Who could it be?

"I have to apologise for coming—without knowing you—and at such a time," said Mrs. Leigh, making a little pause till the nurse had got to the end of the gravel walk with the baby, and James was out of hearing. "It is you who are Bee, is it not?" she said, suddenly taking the girl's hands. "I am the mother of Aubrey Leigh."

All the colour went out of Bee's face; she drew away her hands hurriedly, and dropped upon her mother's seat. She felt that she had no power to say a word.

"Oh, I thought it was Mrs. Leigh he said," cried Betty, "but I could not suppose—oh, Mrs. Leigh, whatever Bee may say, I am so glad, so glad to see you—perhaps you will be able to make things right."

"I hope I shall," said Mrs. Leigh, "and I shall always be obliged to you, my dear, for giving me your countenance. But your sister does not look as if she meant to let me put things right."

"I am sorry if I seem rude," said Bee, gathering herself together, "but—I don't think that papa would like us to receive visitors."

"I am not a common visitor," said Mrs. Leigh. "I hope you will do me the credit to think that it is with a very different feeling I come. I am very, very sorry for you, so young as you are—more sorry than I can say. And, Bee, if indeed I am to hope to be one day your mother—"

Bee did not speak; but she fixed her blue eyes upon her visitor with a sort of entreaty to be left alone, and mournfully shook her head.

"We can't think just now of that name," said little Betty, with the tears standing in her eyes.

"My dear children, I came to try to comfort you, not to open your wounds. Dear," she said, putting her hand on Bee's shoulder, "you would not see Aubrey, nor let him have a word from you. But he said you had heard everything an evil woman could say, and did not give him up for that—and he is heart-broken. He thought perhaps you would tell me if he had done anything to displease you—or if it was only the effect of your grief, to which he would be submissive at once. All he wanted was to share your trouble, my dear child."

This was not at all what Mrs. Leigh intended to say. She had meant to represent her visit as one of sympathy solely, without at first referring to the hard case of Aubrey; but Bee's looks had confused even this experienced woman. The girl's pale face put on an expression of determined decision, or rather of that blank of resistance to entering upon the question, which is a kind of defence which it is almost impossible to break down.

"I would rather, if you please, not say anything of Mr. Leigh."

"Dear child! Do not take that tone. If he has done anything that does not please you, how is he ever to clear himself if you will not tell him what it is."

"She is like this all the time," cried Betty; "she will not say what is wrong—and yet she is just as miserable herself as anyone could be."

Bee gave her sister a look in which Mrs. Leigh, closely watching, saw the lightening of the glance, the brilliancy and splendour of the blue eyes of which Aubrey had raved. Poor little Betty was illuminated as if with a great flame. It was all that she could do to restrain a very inappropriate smile. "You know nothing, and how do you dare to say anything?" Bee said.

"I am sure that Bee is just," said the older lady. "She would not condemn anyone unheard. Aubrey Leigh is my son, but we have been separated for many years, and I think I judge him impartially. He does not always please me, and I am sure that at some time or other he has much displeased you. Your eyes tell me, though you have not said a word. But, my dear, I have never, since he was a child, found him out in anything except the one thing you know, in which he was so sorely, sorely tried. He has always been kind. He gets into trouble by his kindness as other men do by ill-behaviour. I don't know what you have against him, but I feel sure that he will clear himself if you will let him speak. Bee—"

"I do not want," cried Bee, "to seem rude. Oh, I don't want to be rude! I am sure, quite sure, that you are kind; but I have nothing to say, oh! nothing to say to anyone. I am not able to discuss any subject, or enter into things. I have a great deal to think of, for I am the eldest and it will not do for me to—to break down, or to have any more to bear. I am very, very sorry—and you are so kind. But I must go in now—I must go in now."

"Bee, Bee—"

"You can stay, Betty, and talk to the lady. You can stay, but—oh, forgive me—I cannot—cannot help it! I must go in now."

This was the end of Mrs. Leigh's embassy. She had a long talk with Betty, who was but too glad to pour into this kind woman's bosom all her troubles. Betty could not tell what had happened to Bee. She was not the Bee of old, and she did not know what it was that had happened about Aubrey, or if Bee had heard anything against him. She was as much in the dark as Mrs. Leigh herself. But she made it very evident that Bee had a grievance, a real or supposed ground of complaint which made her very angry, and which she resented bitterly. What was it? But this Betty did not know.

CHAPTER IX

Mrs Leigh went back to her son with a sense of humiliation which was rare in her consciousness. She had been completely unsuccessful, which was a thing which had very rarely happened to her. She had expected if she got admission at all that anything which so young a girl might have on her mind must have burst forth and all have been made clear. She had expected at once to overawe and to soothe a young creature who loved Aubrey, and who had some untold grievance against Aubrey. But she was not prepared for the dual personality, so to speak, of Bee, or the power she had of retreating, herself, and leaving her little sister as her representative to fulfil all necessary civilities without the power of betraying anything that the visitor wanted to know. She went back to town very angry with Bee; turned against her; very little disposed to sympathise with Aubrey, which she had so freely done before. "My dear boy," she said, "you have made a mistake, that's all. The elder sister has a temper like her father. Everybody will tell you that Colonel Kingsward is a sharp-tempered man. But Betty is a little darling. It is she that should have been the mistress of Forest-leigh."

In answer to this, Aubrey simply turned his back upon his mother. He was deeply disappointed, but this speech turned his disappointment into a kind of rage. She had mismanaged the whole matter. That was as clear as daylight, and such a suggestion was an added insult. Betty! a child—a little girl—a nobody. His Bee seemed to tower over her in his imagination, so different, so high above her, another species. It was some minutes before he could trust himself to speak.

"Of course, you think me a fool," said Mrs. Leigh, "and so I am, to tell a young man that there is another in the world equal to the object of his fancy."

"Mother," said Aubrey, in a choked voice, "you mistake the matter altogether. That is not what is in question. What I want to know is, what has been said against me, what new thing she has heard, or in what new light she has been taught to see me. You might as well suggest," he cried, angrily, "that another person might have been better in your place—as in hers."

"If that is all I don't mind allowing it," said Mrs. Leigh, with an aggravation peculiar to mothers. "You might have had some one who would have been, all round, of more use to you as a mother—only it's a little late to think of that. However, without any persiflage, here is one thing evident, that she has some grievance against you, something new, something definite, which she believes you to be conscious of, which she is too proud to discuss—I suppose?" said Mrs. Leigh, looking at him with the look of the too-profoundly experienced, never sure how far human weakness may go.

"Mother!" Aubrey cried. He was as indignant as she was unassured.

"Well, my dear, don't be angry. I am not imagining anything. I only ask whether you are quite sure that there is nothing which might be twisted into a new accusation against you? There might be many incidents, in which you were quite blameless, which an enemy might twist—"

"You need not be melo-dramatic, mother. I have nothing in the world that could be an enemy—so far as I know."

"Oh, as for that, there are people who make up stories out of pure devilry. And I had no intention of being melo-dramatic," said Mrs. Leigh with displeasure. She added, after a moment, "Examine—I don't say your conscience, which probably has nothing to do with it—but what has occurred for the last six months? See if there is anything which admits of a wrong interpretation, which could be, as I say, twisted."

Aubrey paused a moment to attempt to do as she said, but the little episode of the railway station, the poor woman and her babies, he did not think of. If truth must be told, he thought that incident was one of the most creditable things in his life. He felt a little pleased with himself when he thought of it. It was one of those things which to mention might seem like a brag of his own generosity. He felt that it was really one of the few incidents in his life which modesty kept him from telling, one of the things in which the right hand should not know what the left hand did. Had he thought of it that would have been his feeling; but when he was asked suddenly to endeavour to recollect something which might be twisted to his disadvantage, naturally this good deed—a deed of charity if ever one was—did not come into his mind at all. He shook his head. "You know whether I am that kind of man, mother."

"Don't refer it to me, Aubrey—a young man's mother probably is the very last person to know. I know you, my dear, au fond. I know a great deal about you; but I know, too, that you have done many things which I never could have supposed you would have done: consult your own recollection. Probably it is something so insignificant that you will have difficulty in recalling it. One can never calculate what trifle may move a young girl's imagination. A grain of sand is enough to put a watch all wrong."

Thus it will be seen that Mrs. Leigh's long experience was after all good for something. She divined the character of the dreadful obstacle which had come in her son's way and shattered all his hopes. If he had recounted to her that incident which it would have seemed ostentation to him to refer to, probably she would have pierced the imbroglio at once—or could she have seen into his life and his memory, she would, no doubt, have put her finger at once on that place. But there they stood, two human creatures in the closest relation to each other that nature can make, anxious to find out between them the key to a puzzle which neither of them could divine, but the secret of which lay certainly between them, could they but find it—and could make out nothing. A word from the son might have set the keen-witted mother, better acquainted than he with the manner in which scandals arise, on the scent. But it never occurred to him to say that word. They looked into each other's faces and made out nothing. Strange veil of individuality which is between two human creatures, as the sea is between two worlds, and more confusing, more impenetrable still than any distance! Aubrey made the most conscientious efforts to lay bare his heart, to discover something that might be twisted, as she said; but he found nothing. His thoughts since he met the Kingswards first had been full of nothing but Bee—his very dreams had been full of her. He wandered vaguely through his own recollections, not knowing what to look for—what was there? There was nothing. His mother sat by, and, notwithstanding her anxiety, could scarcely refrain from smiling at his puzzled, troubled endeavour to find out something against himself. But there was nothing to find out. He shook his head at last, with a sort of appeal to her out of his troubled eyes. He was distressed not to find what he sought. "I know nothing," he said, shaking his head. "One never does anything very good indeed—but not very bad either. I have just been as I always am—not much to brag of—but nothing to be ashamed of, between one man and another."

"The question is between one man and one woman, Aubrey, which is different."

"Then," he cried, with a short laugh, "I defy discovery. There has been nothing in all my thoughts that need have been hidden. You do me grievous wrong, mother, if you can think—even if I had been inclined that way."

"I don't think. I have the most complete faith in you, Aubrey. I say—anything that could be twisted by a malign interpretation?"

He shook his head again. "And who would take the trouble to make a malign interpretation? I assure you, I have no enemy."

"Colonel Kingsward is enemy enough."

"Ah! Colonel Kingsward. I have no reason, however, to think that he would do a dishonourable action."

"What do you call intercepting letters, Aubrey?"

"It is very antiquated and out of date, but I don't know that it need be called dishonourable; and he has a high idea of his authority; but to make a false representation of another man—"

"Aubrey, these distinctions are too fine for me. There is only one thing that I can do. I will now go and interview Colonel Kingsward. If he knows of anything new, he will soon reveal it to me. If he goes only over the old ground, then we may be sure that your fiancée has been told something in her own ear—something apart from her father—which she has betrayed to no one. Unless, perhaps, it was got from the mother—"

"Not a word about the mother. She is dead, and she is sacred; and besides she was the last, the very last—"

"You have yourself said she was very weak, Aubrey."

"Weak so far as resisting her husband was concerned, but incapable of an unkind word; incapable of any treachery or falsehood; a creature, both in body and soul, whom you could almost see through."

Mrs. Leigh shook her head a little.

"I know those transparent people," she said. "They are not always so—But never mind; I am going to interview Colonel Kingsward now."

Colonel Kingsward was very courteous to his visitor. He received her visit of sympathy with polite gratitude, accepting her excuse that so nearly connected as the families had been about to be, she could not be in town without coming to express her great regret and feeling for his family left motherless. Colonel Kingsward was very digne. He had the fullest sense of what was expected in his position, and he did not allow any other feeling to come in the way of that. He thanked Mrs. Leigh for her sympathy, and exaggerated his sense of her goodness in coming to express it. It was more, much more, than he had any right to expect. If there was any alleviation to his grief it was in the sense of the great kindness of friends—"and even of strangers," he said, with a grave bow, which seemed to throw Mrs. Leigh indefinitely back into the regions of the unknown. This put her on her mettle at once.

"I do not feel like a stranger," she said. "I have heard so much of your family—every member of it—through my son, Aubrey. I regret greatly that the connection which seemed to be so suitable should hang at all in doubt—"

"It does not hang in doubt," said Colonel Kingsward, "I am sorry if you have got that impression. It is quite broken off—once for all."

"That is a hard thing to say to Aubrey Leigh's mother," she said; "such a stigma should not be put upon a young man lightly."

"I am sorry to discuss such matters with a lady. But I don't know what you call lightly, Mrs. Leigh. I do not believe for a moment that you would give a daughter of your own—I do not know whether you have daughters of your own—"

"Two—happily married, thank heaven, and off my hands."

"You will understand me so much the better. (Colonel Kingsward knew perfectly well all about Mrs. Leigh's two daughters). I do not believe that you would have given one of them to a man—to whom another lady put forth a prior claim."

"I am not at all sure of that. I should have ascertained first what kind of person put forth the claim—"

"We need not go into these details," said Colonel Kingsward, waving his hand.

"It is most important to go into these details. I can give you every particular about this lady, Colonel Kingsward; and so can a dozen people, at least, who have no interest in the matter except to tell the truth."

"The question is closed in my mind, Mrs. Leigh. I have no intention of opening it again."

"And this is the sole ground upon which my son is rejected?" she said, fixing her keen eyes upon his face.

"It is the sole ground; it is quite enough, I believe. Supposing even that the lady was everything you allege, an intimacy between a woman of that character and your son is quite enough to make him unsuitable for my daughter."

"Who is not of your opinion, however," Mrs. Leigh said.

Colonel Kingsward was confused by this speech. He got up and stood before the fire. He avoided meeting her eye. "My daughter is very young and very inexperienced," he said. "She is at present more moved by her feelings than her reason. I believe that with an increase of maturer judgment she will fully adopt my view."

Colonel Kingsward believed that he had altogether crushed his visitor, but he was not so right as he thought. Mrs. Leigh went back to her son with triumph in her eyes. "He knows nothing more," she said. "He does not know that she has turned against you. Whatever is her reason, it is something different from his, and she has not confided it to him. I thought as much when you told me of the letters stopped. A man does not intercept a girl's letters when he knows she has come round to his way of thinking. Now you have got to find out what she has heard, and to set her right about it whatever it may be."

To set oneself to find out without any clue or guidance what it is which has affected the thoughts of a girl for or against her lover—without any knowledge of her surroundings, or from what quarter an adverse influence, an ill report, could have come—who could have spoken to her on the subject of Aubrey, or what kind of story to his disadvantage (for this was what Mrs. Leigh convinced herself must have happened) she had heard—to discover everything and counteract it, was a mission that might well have frightened anyone who undertook it. And I don't doubt that Mrs. Leigh, to encourage her son, spoke a great deal more confidently than she felt, and that she really intended to give herself up to this discovery, and to take no rest until she had made it, and cleared up the matter which threatened to separate these two young people for ever, and make havoc in both their lives.

Aubrey himself shook his head and declared himself to have little hope; but he was not really more hopeless than his mother was the reverse. While he shook his head there was a warm sensation of comfort at his heart. That she should have undertaken to find it out seemed like half the battle. When a man retains any confidence in his mother at all, which is by no means always the case, he is apt to be influenced more than he is aware by the old prejudice of childhood that she can do anything that is wanted. She by no means felt herself to be so powerful as he did, though she professed her certainty of success, and he was much more held up and supported by her supposed convictions than he himself allowed to appear. Thus they separated, Aubrey remaining in town, ready to take advantage of any occasion that might present itself, while she returned to her home, to make every exertion to discover the cause of Bee's estrangement. Very easy words to say—but how to do it? She had not a notion even what kind of story had been told to Bee. She did not know any special point of weakness on the part of Aubrey which could have been exaggerated or made to appear worse than it was. There was no inclination towards dissipation about him; he did not gamble; he was not addicted to bad company. What was there to say about him? The episode of Miss Lance—and that was all. And it was not the episode of Miss Lance which had revolted Bee. Had Mrs. Leigh ever heard of Aubrey's adventure at the railway station, it is possible that her mind, excited in that direction, would have been keen enough to have divined that the mystery was somehow connected with that; for it was certainly Quixotic of a young man to put a poor woman and her children into a sleeping-carriage—the most expensive mode of travelling, and wholly beyond her condition—by a mere charitable and kindly impulse. And the world, which believes that nothing is given without an equivalent, might easily have made a story out of it. But then, Mrs. Leigh was quite ignorant on this point, which, as has been said, had never occurred again to Aubrey himself, except as one of the few actions in his life which he could look back upon with entire satisfaction and even a little complacence. And thus the only way of setting things right was hermetically closed.

Mrs. Leigh went back to her jointure-house. It was near the sea, as has been said, and near a lively seaside town, where, in the summer, there were many visitors and a great deal going on, strangers appearing and disappearing from all parts of the country. But in winter there was nothing of the kind; the world closed up without, leaving only the residents, the people who were indigenous, the contracted society of neighbours who knew all about each other, and were acquainted with the same pieces of news, and, excepting by long intervals, heard but little of the outside gossip, or the doings of other circles. Mrs. Leigh returned to her natural surroundings, which knew no more of Colonel Kingsward and his family than people in what is called "a certain position" know of each other—something of his name, something of his connections, but nothing of his immediate circumstances. There were indeed many questions about Aubrey's marriage which she had to answer as she could. The news of his engagement had been received with many congratulations. Everybody felt that poor Aubrey's first essay at matrimony had been a very unfortunate one. The sooner he brings a nice wife to Forest-leigh the better, everybody had said. And when Mrs. Leigh returned after her brief absence, the many callers whom she received daily were full of inquiries about the marriage. It was generally supposed that his mother's hasty expedition had been in some way connected with it. She had gone about the refurnishing, about the household linen, which perhaps wanted renewing, and which was not in a man's sphere—about something in the settlements; at all events, whatever it was, her object must have been connected with the approaching marriage. They came down upon her full of the most eager questions. "I suppose the day is fixed? I suppose all the arrangements are made? How nice it will be to see the house opened, and a new, lively, young married couple to put a little life in everything"—matrons and little maids all concurred in this speech.

"You have not heard then?" said Mrs. Leigh, with a very grave countenance—"everything, alas, is postponed for the moment. Mrs. Kingsward, a most charming woman, adored by her family, died last week."

"I told you it was those Kingswards!" one of the ladies said to another.

"There are no other Kingswards that I know of," said Mrs. Leigh, who always held her head so high. "I went up with Aubrey to pay them a visit of sympathy. There is a very large young family. I found them quite broken down with grief. Of course we had not the heart, either Aubrey or I, to press an arrangement in these dreadful circumstances. I confess I am rather down about it altogether. Poor little Bee, my future daughter-in-law, is the eldest. I am quite terrified to hear that she has taken some tragic resolution, such as girls are so apt to do now-a-days, and think it her duty to dedicate herself to her little brothers and sisters."

"Oh, but surely she would not be permitted to do that—when everything was settled!"

"I hope not. I most sincerely hope not," said Mrs. Leigh. "Naturally, I have not said a word to Aubrey. But girls now-a-days are so full of their ideas, their missions, and their duty, and all that!"

"Not when they are engaged to be married," said a scoffing lady.

"I wish I could be sure of that. Miss Kingsward is only nineteen, just the self-sacrificing age. I wish I could be sure—. There was something in her eye. But, however, not a word, not a word about this. I still hope that as soon as a reasonable time has passed—"

"It is such a pity," said another, "where unnecessary delays are made. I am sure no mother would wish her daughter's marriage to be put off—things are so apt to happen. I think it's tempting Providence when there is unnecessary delay."

"Colonel Kingsward is a very particular man. He will allow nothing to be done that the most punctilious could object to. He will not have anything spoken of even. All the arrangements are in abeyance. It is most trying. Of course, I am very sorry for the family, and for him, who has lost so excellent a wife. But, at the same time, I can't help thinking of my own son kept hanging in suspense, and all his plans broken up."

There was a chorus of regrets from all the visitors, one party after another; but from more than one group of ladies as they drove away there arose the most gloomy auguries, spoken amid much shaking of heads. "I don't believe it will ever come to a marriage after all," some said, "if Colonel Kingsward is so very particular a man, and if he hears of all that took place at Forest-leigh in the first wife's time." "Whatever took place," said another, "it was her fault, as everybody knows." "Ah, yes," said the first speaker, who represented more or less the common voice, "I know the first wife was a little fool, and whatever happened, brought it all on herself. But there is never any business of that sort without blame on both sides." Thus the world generally judges, having half forgotten what the facts of the case were, though most of the individuals who constitute the world could have recalled them very easily with an effort of memory. Still, the blurred general view is the one that prevails after a time, and works out great injustices without any evil intention at all.

It was thus that Mrs. Leigh thought it prudent to forestall all remarks as to the postponement of her son's marriage. She succeeded well enough, perhaps too well. Mrs. Kingsward's death accounted for everything. Still, the impression got abroad that Aubrey Leigh, that unlucky fellow, had somehow broken down again. And as the days went on and silence closed around, further and further did Aubrey's mother find herself from making any discovery. Indeed, she did not try, strong as her resolves to do so had been. For, indeed, she did not know what to do. How was she to clear up such a mystery? Had she known the neighbours about Kingswarden, and heard their talk among themselves, she might have been able to form some plan of action. But her own neighbours, who did not even know of Mrs. Kingsward's death—how could she find out anything from them? She thought it over a great deal, and when any friend of her son's drifted near her expended a great deal of ingenuity in endeavouring to ascertain whether there was anything in Aubrey's life which could have injured him in Bee's estimation. But Mrs. Leigh was perfectly aware, even while cautiously making these inquiries, that whatever his friends might know against him, his mother was the last person who was likely to be told. As a matter of fact, however, there was nothing to tell, and gradually this very fruitless quest died from her mind, and she did not even dream of pursuing it any more.

And Aubrey remained in town disconsolately getting through the winter as best he could, neglecting all his duties of hospitality, keeping his house shut up, and leaving his game to be shot by the gamekeepers—indifferent to everything. He could not bear the place with which he had so many painful associations, sharpened now by the loss of all the hopes that had fallen so quickly of taking Bee to it, and beginning a real life of happiness and usefulness. What he wanted most in life was to fulfil all his duties—in the happiest way in which such duties can be fulfilled, after the methods of an English country gentleman with sufficient, but not too great position, money, and all that accompanies them. He was not an enragé foxhunter, or sportsman, but he was quite disposed to follow all the occupations and recreations of country life, to maintain a hospitable house, to take his part of everything that was going on in the county, and above all, to efface the recollection of that first chapter of his life which had not been happy. But all these hopes and intentions seemed to have been killed in him by the cutting off of his new hopes. He kept up his confidence in his mother until he went to her at Christmas to spend with her those days of enforced family life which, when they are not more, are so much less happy than the ordinary course of life. He went down still full of hope, and though Mrs. Leigh received him with professions of unimpaired confidence, he was quick to see that she had in reality done nothing—for that best of all reasons, that there was nothing to do. "You don't seem to have made progress, however," he said, on the first night.

"No, perhaps I have not made much progress. I don't know that I expected to make much progress—at this time of the year. You know in winter one only sees one's neighbours, who know nothing. Later on, when the weather improves, when there is more coming and going, when I have more opportunities—"

This did not sound very cheerful, but it was still less cheerful when he saw how little even his mother's mind was occupied with his affairs. It was not her fault; all the thinking in the world could not make Bee's motives more clear to a woman living at a distance of three or four broad counties from Bee. And one of Aubrey's married sisters was in some family difficulty which occupied all her mother's thoughts. Aubrey did not refuse to be interested in his sister. He was willing to give anything he could, either of sympathy or help, to the solving of her problem; but, conscious of so much in his own fate that was harder than could fall to the lot of any comfortable, middle-aged person, it must be allowed that he got very tired of hearing of Mary's troubles. He answered rather curtly on one or two occasions, and chilled his mother, whose heart was full of Mary, and who was already disposed to blame herself in respect to Aubrey, yet to be irritated by any suspicion of blame from him. On the last morning of his stay he had begged her, if she could abstract her thoughts for a moment from Mary, to think of him. "I don't want to trouble you further, mother. I only want you to tell me if you think my whole business so hopeless that I had better give every expectation up?"

"Think your business hopeless, Aubrey? Oh, no; I don't think that."

"But we know just as much now as we did in October. I do not think we have advanced a step—"

"If you mean to reproach me with my want of success, Aubrey!"

"No—I don't mean to reproach you with anything, mother. But I think it seems just as hopeless as ever—and not a step nearer."

"Things cannot be done in a moment," she said, hurriedly. "I never expected—When the summer comes round, when one sees more people, when one can really pursue one's inquiries—." Mrs. Leigh was very conscious that she had pursued few inquiries, and the thought made her angry. "Rome," she added, "was not built in a day."

Aubrey Leigh said no more—but he went back to London feeling that he was a beaten man, and the battle once more lost.

CHAPTER XI

There is nothing more curious in life than the way in which it closes over those great incidents that shape its course. Like a stone disappearing in a pool, the slow circles of commotion widen and melt away, the missile sinks into the depths of the water, and tranquility comes back to its surface. Every ripple is gone, and yet the stone is always there.

This curious calm came into the life of Bee Kingsward after the incidents related above. The man with whom she had expected to share everything disappeared from her existence as if he had never entered into it, and a dead peace fell over her, and all things around her. It was at once better for Bee and worse that the mourning for her mother swept her away out of all the coming and going of ordinary life for a time—better because she was saved the torment of a perpetual struggle with her trouble, and worse because it shut her up to a perpetual recollection of that trouble. The Kingsward family remained at Kingswarden for the whole of that winter and spring. When the season began there was some question of removing to town, which Bee opposed strongly. "I have no wish to go out," she said. "I could not, papa, so soon—And we have no one to take us."

"You will find plenty of people ready to take you," he said.

And then Bee took refuge in tears. "Nobody—that we could endure to go with—so soon, so soon!—not yet a year," she said. Betty followed her sister dubiously. It was natural that she should always echo what Bee said, but this time she was not quite so sure as usual. Not to balls? Oh, not to balls! was Betty's secret comment, but—Betty felt that to speak occasionally to some one who was not of her own family—not the Rector or the Rector's wife, the Curate or the Doctor—would be an advantage; but she did not utter that sentiment. After all, what was one season to the measureless horizon of eighteen? Bee renounced her season eagerly, and uttered exclamations of content when Colonel Kingsward announced that, in those circumstances, he had let their house in town. But I am not sure that she was so completely satisfied as she professed to be. She had dismissed Aubrey "for ever"—and yet, when the deed was done, a longing seized her sometimes to hear his name, that someone should speak of him in her presence, that she should hear accidentally where he was, and what he was doing. She had imagined little scenes to herself in which she had heard strangers saying to each other that Aubrey Leigh had soon got over his disappointment, that he was going to be married to So-and-So; or that he was going to make the tour of the world, or to shoot big game in Africa; or, anything in short, so long as it was about him. Even when she had been so determined against going out, there had been a hope in her mind that somehow, she did not know how, some news of him and what he was doing might be wafted her way accidentally. She did not want, she said to herself passionately, ever to hear his name again! Yet she had calculated on hearing as much as that, hearing quite accidentally, at the Royal Academy, perhaps, or somewhere where she might happen to be calling, that he was going to the ends of the earth, or that he was going to be married—things which the speakers might suppose were not of the slightest interest to her. She said all the same that she was delighted when Colonel Kingsward informed them that he had let the house in town—very glad! before it had time to get shabby, the poor old house; yet, when she retired to her room for the night, Bee cried, shedding many salt tears.

But nothing of this was apparent in her life. The circles had all melted away from the still bosom of the pool. The household resumed its former regularity, quickened a little, perhaps, by the energetic sweeping of the new broom. Mrs. Kingsward had been an easy mistress about many trifles, which Bee, new to authority, and more enterprising than her mother, exacted a rigid account of. At the beginning she set all the servants by the ears, each of them being anxious to show that their own conscientiousness was perfect, and their desire to consider their master's interests; but, by degrees, matters settled down with an increased strictness of order. "As mamma would have wished it," Bee said; and she herself changed in a way that would be almost miraculous were it not a transformation commonly visible from time to time, from a light-hearted girl, full of little amusing misdemeanours and mistakes, into that sweet serious figure of the eldest daughter, the mother-sister, so often visible in England when the mistress of the household has been removed in early life. There is no more beautiful or more tender vision; it is fine at all ages, but in the first bloom of youth it has a pathetic grace which goes to the heart. Bee underwent this change quite suddenly, after a period of trouble and agitation and over activity. It might not perhaps have come but for the letting for the season of the town house, which seemed to make so complete a severance between her and the ordinary current of life.

It was perhaps this that opened what might almost be called a new relationship between Bee and her brother Charlie, who was the nearest to her in the family, though there had not been hitherto an unusual sympathy between them. For one thing, Betty feeling herself a little forlorn in the country with all the echoes of London, which occasionally came to her ears, had been permitted to accept an invitation to Portman Square to visit a quiet elderly family, not likely to lead her into any dissipation out of keeping with her black frock, and Bee was virtually alone with the children, to whom she gave herself up with a devotion which was the very quintessence of motherhood. Colonel Kingsward also was in town—a man cannot shut himself up (this was what he said) whatever his private griefs may be. He must keep a calm face before the world, he must not allow himself to be hustled out of the way. For this reason, he remained in London, living in chambers, to which he had an official right, in the dingy official grandeur of Pall Mall, and coming to Kingswarden only now and then from Saturday to Monday. This sundered Bee still more completely from the world. And when Charlie came back from Oxford she was more eager to meet him, more pleased with his company than ever before. This was not perhaps entirely the young man's mind. That he should choose to shut himself up in the country in June was perhaps scarcely to be expected. According to the curious rule which prevails in England he "did not mind" the country in January. But in June! However, it was soon apparent that there were other things than the season in Charlie's mind. He began a series of lamentations to Bee upon the situation of the family and things in general, by the usual complaint of a young man in the country of having "nothing to do."

"A man cannot sit at home and dot up the accounts like you," he said, "though I don't say but that it's hard upon you, too. Still, women like to tie up children's sashes and that sort of thing, and calculate how much their boots cost in a year. I say, mother can't have had half such an easy life as we all thought."

"I never thought she had an easy life," said Bee, which was perhaps not exactly true, but the things that Bee had thought a year ago were so unlike the things she thought now that she did not believe life had ever appeared to her in a different light.

"Well," said Charlie, "she had a way of making it appear so. Do you remember that last time at the Baths? What a little thing you seemed then, Bee, and now here I am talking to you quite seriously, as if you were mother. Look here, I want you to speak to the governor for me. I am doing no good here. In fact, there's nothing to do—unless I am to drop into drinking and that sort of thing in the village."

"Charlie!"

"Well," he said, "I can't sit and sew strings on pinafores like you. A man must do something at my age."

"And what should you do at Oxford? And why do you want to go there when everybody is away?"

"Everybody away! That is all you know. The dons are away, if that is what you mean. There are no lectures going on. But lectures are a mere loss of time. There are lots of fellows up there reading. If you want to read hard, now is the best time."

"How curious," said Bee, in genuine surprise, "when all the people who teach are away! And I never knew that you wanted to read hard."

"No. I never was made to think that I ought to," said Charlie, with rising colour. "In this house nobody thinks of anything more than just getting through."

Bee was a little angry as well as surprised by this censure upon the family. She said, "The rest of us may not be clever—but everybody says there are few men that know as much as papa."

"Oh, in his special subjects, I suppose, but I am not going in for the army, Bee," said Charlie, the colour rising higher on his young face, which was still an ingenuous face, though not of a very high order. "It is such a wonderful thing to have your duty set before you, and how you ought to make the best of your life. I, for one, never thought of it before. I was always quite satisfied to get through and to have plenty of time to amuse myself; but if you come to think of it that's a very poor sort of ideal for a life."

Bee looked up at Charlie with more and more surprise. He was pulling his young moustache nervously, and there was a great deal of emotion in his face. It seemed amazing to his sister that Charlie—Charlie who had always been on the unemotional side, should take this heroic tone, or do anything but laugh at the suggestion of an ideal in life. She gazed at him in some bewilderment. "What are you going to read?" she asked, with doubt and wonder in her voice.

"It is just like a girl to ask a man what he is going to read! Why, everything. I just pushed through my mods., you know—a pass—which it covers me with shame to think of now. I must do something better than that. I don't know that I'm very good at anything, but work, after all, steady work, is the great thing; and if work can do it—!" cried Charley, breaking off, a little breathless, with a strange light in his eyes.

"You almost frighten me, Charlie. You were never meant for honours or a high degree, were you? Papa said you need not go in for honours, it would lose time; and you thought so, too."

"I have changed my mind," said Charlie, nervously. "I thought, like other asses, that in diplomacy you don't want much; but now I think differently. How are you to understand how to conduct national affairs and all that, and reconcile conflicting claims, and so forth, and settle the real business of the world—"

"But Charlie, I thought it was languages, and great politeness, and—and even dancing, and that sort of thing, that was wanted in an attaché—"

"Attachés," said the young man, with a gravity which, serious as she also was, almost made Bee laugh, "are the material out of which ambassadors are made. Of course, it takes time—"

Here Bee burst, without meaning it, into a nervous laugh.

"You are so dreadfully serious about it," she cried.

"And what should a man be serious about, if not that?" the young man replied.

Here for the moment, in great impatience on his part, and in the call of some little household necessity on hers, the conversation closed; but it was resumed as soon as the brother and sister were together again. The big boys were still at school, the little ones engaged with their lessons, and baby walking up and down in his nurse's arms, did not interrupt the talk which went on between the elders of the family. And there is nothing with which it is so easy to indoctrinate a girl than enthusiasm about an ideal, whatever that may be, or sympathy in a lofty view of duty such as this, which had dawned, it seemed, upon her brother. Bee took fire, as was so natural. She said to herself, that in the utter downfall of her own life, it would be a fine thing to be able to further his, and kept to the idea of Charlie as ambassador, settling all sorts of difficulties and deciding the fortunes of the world for war or for peace, as easily as if the question had been one of leading a cotillion. How splendid it would be! She thought of herself as an old lady, white-haired, in a cap and shawl—for, in an imagination of twenty, there are few gradations between youth and that pathetic, yet satisfactory ultimate period—seated in a particular corner of a magnificent room at the Embassy, looking on at her brother's triumph. These sort of reflected successes were the only ones she thought that would ever come to Bee.

CHAPTER XII

"Charlie wishes to go up to Oxford to read. Why does he wish to go up to Oxford to read? And what reading is it necessary to do there?"

"He says, papa, that it is easier to get on when you have all your books about you—and when you can arrange all your way of living for that, instead of the interruptions at home."

"Oh, there are too many interruptions at home? I should have thought you were quiet enough here. I hope you have not thrown yourself into lawn tennis parties, and tea parties, and that sort of thing—so soon, Bee."

Her father looked at her with a seriously reproachful air. He had begun to dine out pretty freely, though only in serious houses, and where, he explained, it would be prejudicial to him in his profession not to appear.

The undeserved reproach brought quick tears to Bee's eyes. "I have thrown myself into no parties," she said, hastily. "Nobody has been here. What Charlie means is the meal times, and hours for everything, and all the children about. I have often heard you say that you couldn't work when the children were playing about."

"My work and Charlie's are rather different," Colonel Kingsward said, with a smile.

"Well, papa! but to read for a good degree, so that you may distinguish yourself, must want a great deal of application—"

"Oh, he wants a good degree, does he? He should have thought of it a little earlier. And what use will that be to him in the Foreign Office? Let him learn French and German—that's what he has got to do."

"But even for French and German," said Bee. "German is dreadfully difficult, and Charlie does not pick up a language easily; and, besides," she added, "he has nobody to teach him at home—"

"And who would he have at Oxford? Why, in the Long, even the shopkeepers go away!"

"But that is just the time for good, hard reading," said Bee, acting on her instructions, "when there are no lectures or anything formal to interrupt you."

"He means, I suppose, when he can do whatever he likes, and there are no proctors nor gate bills to keep him right."

"Papa," said Bee, earnestly, "I don't think that is at all what Charlie means. I am sure that he has a real desire to get on. He says that he feels he has been wasting his time, and—and not—not responding properly to all you have done for him. He wants to make himself fit for anything that may happen. If you will think, papa," she added, with the deepest gravity, "what a great deal of study and reading an ambassador must require—"

"An ambassador!" Colonel Kingsward was not given to laughter, but he laughed now. "He may think himself fortunate if he is anything but an unpaid attaché for the next ten years—which is an office which does not require a great deal of study."

"But, papa—"

"Nonsense, Bee. He wants, I suppose, complete freedom, and to amuse himself as he pleases, with no control. I know what it means to stay up at Oxford to read during the Long. Oh, yes. I don't doubt men who know how to grind, grind, but Charlie is not one of them. Let him stay at home. You are a great deal sharper than he is at languages; you can help him with his German as well as anyone."

"Oh," cried Bee, from the bottom of her heart, "not with German, not with German, papa!"

And there came over her a sudden vision of the gardens at the Baths, the murmur of talk in the air, the German officers with their spurs, and one Englishman coming forward among them, an Englishman without spurs, without uniform, so much more distinguished, it had been Bee's pride to think, in his simplicity, than all these bedizened warriors—and now! A gush of hot tears came to her eyes. There was reason enough for them without Aubrey Leigh, and Colonel Kingsward, whose heart was still tender to every recollection of his wife, did not think of the other memory that thrilled poor Bee's heart. He walked up and down through the room for a moment saying nothing, and then he paused by her side and put his hand with an unusual caress upon his daughter's bowed head.

"You are right, you are right," he said. "I could not ask that of you, Bee."

Oh! if I had but known! Bee felt not only miserable, but guilty, when her father's touch came upon her hair. To think how little the dear mother's presence told in that picture, and how much, how much! that of the man—who had been vulgarly untrue to her, a man without sense of purity or honour! One whose name she never desired to hear again. She could hardly accept the imputation of so much higher and nobler feeling which her father's touch conveyed. The dear mother! who never condemned, who was always kind. She was moved to cry out in self-abasement, "It was not mamma I was thinking of, it was him! him!" But she did not do this. She raised her head and took up her work again with a trembling hand.

"I suppose," said Colonel Kingsward, as anxious as his daughter was to get away from a subject which was too moving for discussion, "that Charlie finds Kingswarden dull. It is not unnatural at his age, and I shall not object if he wishes to come to town for a week or so. His own good feeling, I hope, would keep him from anything unbecoming in the circumstances. But I must hear no more of this going to Oxford. It is quite out of the question. If he had shown any desire to go in for honours at the right time—. But now it is worse than folly. He must get through as quickly as he can, and take advantage of his nomination at once. Who can tell how soon it may be of no value? The Foreign Office may be thrown open, like all the rest, to every costermonger in the country, in a year or two, for anything one knows."

Charlie received this conclusion with disappointment, rapidly turning into rage and rebellion. "I should have thought the most old-fashioned old fogey in the world would have known better," he cried. "What, prevent a man from reading when he is at the University! Did you ever hear of such a thing, Bee? Why, even a military man, though they are the most obstinate in the world, must know that to be really educated is everything in these days. A week in town! What do I care for a week in town? It is exactly like the man in the Bible who, being asked for bread, gave a stone."

Bee was greatly impressed by her brother's anxiety to continue his studies. It filled her with a respect and admiration which up to this time she had never entertained for Charlie, and occupied her mind much with the question how, if her father were obdurate, he might be aided at home in those studies. She remembered suddenly that Mr. Burton's curate had been spoken of as a great scholar when he came first to the parish. He had taken tremendous honours she had heard. And why might not he be secured as an aid to Charlie in his most laudable ambition? She thought this over a great deal as she moved about her household duties. Bee as a housekeeper was much more anxious than her mother had been for many years. She thought that everything that was done required her personal attention. She had prolonged interviews every morning with the cook, who had been more or less the housekeeper for a long time, and who (with a secret sense of humour) perplexed Bee with technicalities which she would not allow that she did not understand. The girl ordered everything minutely for dinner and lunch and breakfast, and decided what was to be for the nursery as if she knew all about it, and reproved cook gravely when she found that certain alterations had been made in the menu when those meals were served. "I assure you as that is what you ordered, miss," cook said, with a twinkle in her eye. All this Bee did, not only because of her strong determination to do her duty, but also because preoccupation with all these details was her great salvation from thoughts which, do what she would, claimed her attention more than nursery puddings and the entrées that pleased papa. But while she pursued these labours there was still time for other thoughts, and she occupied herself very much with this question about Charlie. Why could not Mr. Delaine come to read with him? Mr. Delaine had shown an inclination to flirt with Betty, but Betty was now absent, so that no harm could be done in that direction. She thought it all out during the somewhat gloomy days which Colonel Kingsward spent with his family in the country. It rained all the Sunday, which is a doleful addition to the usual heaviness of a day in which all usual occupations are put away. Colonel Kingsward himself wrote letters, and was very fully occupied on Sunday afternoon, after the Church parade on Sunday morning, which was as vigorously maintained as if the lessening rows of little ones all marshalled for morning service had been a regiment—but he did not like to see Bee doing anything but "reading a book" on Sunday. And it had always been a rule in that well-ordered house that the toys should be put away on Saturday evening, so that the day hung rather heavily, especially when it rained, on the young ones' heads. Colonel Kingsward did not mean to be a gloomy visitor. He was always kind to his children, and willing to be interested in what they did and said; but, as a matter of fact, those three days were the longest and the most severe of any that passed over the widowed and motherless house. When Bee came downstairs from the Sunday lesson, which she gave in the nursery, she found her brother at the writing-table in the drawing-room, composing what seemed a very long letter. His pen was hurrying over the page; he was at the fourth side of a sheet of large paper—and opened out on the table before him were several sheets of a very long, closely-written letter, to which he was evidently replying. When Bee appeared, Charlie snatched up this letter, and hastily folding it, thrust it into its envelope, which he placed in his breast pocket. He put the blotting paper hastily over the letter which he was himself writing, and the colour mounted to his very forehead as he turned half round. It was not any colour of guilt, but a glow of mingled enthusiasm and shamefacedness, beautiful upon the face of a youth. Bee was too young herself to admire and appreciate this flush of early feeling, but she was so far sympathetic in her own experience, that she divined something at least of what it meant.

"Oh, Charlie!" she said, "you are writing to someone—"

"Most assuredly, I am writing to someone," he said, with the half pride, half shame of a young lover.

"Who is she?" cried Bee. "Oh, Charlie, tell me! Oh, tell me! Do I know who it is?"

"I don't know," he said, "what you are making such a fuss about. I am writing to—a friend." He paused a moment, and then said with fervour—"the best friend that ever man had."

"A friend," cried Bee, a little disappointed. "But isn't it a lady?" she asked.

"I hope," he said, with a haughty air, "that you are not one of those limited people that think there can be no friendship between a man and a woman, for if that's so I've got nothing to say."

Bee was scarcely philosophical enough to take up this challenge. She looked at him, bewildered, for a moment, and then said, "Oh, tell me about her, Charlie! It would do me good—it would, indeed, to hear about somebody whom there could not be any objection to, who would be, perhaps, happier than me," cried poor little Bee, the tears coming to her eyes.

"Happier than you? And why shouldn't you be happy?" said the elder brother. He made an effort to turn away in dignified silence, but the effort was too much for the young man, longing to talk of the new thing in his life. "There is no comparison at all between a little thing like you and—and the lady I was writing to," he said, holding his head high. "If you think it is any sort of nonsense you are very much mistaken. Why, she—she is as much above me as heaven is from earth. That she should take the trouble to show any interest in me at all, just proves what an angel she is. I, an idle, ordinary sort of fellow, and she!—the sort of woman that one dreams of. Bee, you can't think what she has done for me already," Charlie cried, forgetting his first defiance. "I'm another fellow ever since she began to take notice of me."

Bee stole to her brother's side and gave him a sympathetic stroke upon his shoulder. "Oh! Charlie! what is her name?"

"You wouldn't know her name if I were to tell you," he said. And then, after a moment's hesitation: "Her name," he went on, "her real name as I call it, is Laura, like Petrarch's Laura, don't you know, Bee? But I don't suppose you do know."

"Yes, indeed, I do," said Bee, eagerly. She added in her turn, "I shouldn't have thought you would know anything like that."

"No; I'm not up to it," said Charlie, with unexpected humility; "but I read it all up as soon as she said it. Don't you think it's a beautiful name?"

"Yes," said Bee, yet not with enthusiasm. "But, oh!" she added, "I hope she is not married, Charlie; for that would not be nice at all."

"Married!" cried Charlie. "I wish you were not such a horrid little—Philistine. But she is not married, if that is any satisfaction to you."

"And is she—beautiful, Charlie? and are you very, very fond of her? Oh, Charlie!" Bee clasped his arm in both her hands and sobbed. It made her feel wretched, yet filled her with a delicious tender sense of fellow-feeling. If he would only tell her all! It would be hard upon her, and yet it would be a sort of heavenly pang to hear another, and, oh! surely, this time, a happy love tale. Bee sat down close by him, and clasped his arm, and sometimes leaned her head upon it in the warmth of her tenderness and sympathy. And Charlie was persuaded, by degrees, to speak. But his tale was not like Bee's. It was a tale of a lady who had stooped as from her throne to the young fellow of no account—the ordinary young man, who could not understand how she had come to think of him at all. It was she who had inspired him with his new ambition, who had made him so anxious to distinguish himself, to make something of his life. She had taken the trouble to write to him, to keep him up to it since he had come "down." She had promised to let him come to see her when he came "up" again, to inspire him and encourage him. "One look at her is better than a dozen coaches," Charlie cried, in the fervour of his heart.

"Do you mean that you are going to see her—in town?" asked Bee, doubtfully.

"In town? No. She detests town. It's all so vain and so hollow, and such a rush. She came to live in Oxford at the beginning of last term," Charlie said.

"Oh," said Bee, and she found no more to say. She did not herself understand how it was that a little chill came upon her great sympathy with Charlie and this unknown lady of his—friendship, if not love.

CHAPTER XIII

Colonel Kingsward, however, could not be moved either by Bee's representations or by anything said by his son to grant to Charlie the permission, and the funds necessary, to pursue his studies in Oxford by going "up" to read "in the Long." It was indeed very little that Charlie said to his father on the subject. He responded somewhat sullenly to the Colonel's questions.

"So I hear you want to go back to Oxford to read?"

"Yes," said the young man.

"You have generally found before this that by the end of the term you had had too much reading."

No reply.

"I suppose you want to be free of supervision and do exactly what you please. And you find it dull at home?"

"I have never said so," said Charlie.

"You ought to feel that in the circumstances it was appropriate that it should be dull. Good heavens! Were you contemplating amusing yourself, rioting with your comrades, when your poor mother—"

"I have never thought of rioting with comrades," said Charlie, with averted head.

"One knows what that means—going up to read in the Long: boats and billiards and hotels, bands of young men in flannels lounging about, and every decorum thrown to the winds."

The Colonel looked severely at his son, who stood before him turning over the pages of a book in his hand, with lowering brows and closed mouth.

"You think I don't know," he said, sharply; "but you are mistaken. What would have been best for you would have been the discipline of a regiment. I always thought so, but at least I'm not going to permit every decent bond to be broken through."

"I think, sir," said Charlie, "that it's enough to say 'No,' without accusing me of things I never thought of."

"I am the best judge of what is enough," said the angry father. "If you want a week or so in town, I don't object; but Oxford in the Long—No. I only hope," he added severely, "that there's no woman in the case."

Charlie's countenance flushed crimson. He gave his father a furious glance. "If that's all," he said, "I may now go, perhaps?"

"Yes, go," said the Colonel, angrily. He was himself sorry for that last insinuation as soon as his son had left the room. His angry suspiciousness had carried him too far. Not that he blamed himself for the suspicion, but he was aware that to speak of it was a false step and could do no good. If there was a woman in the case, that flying dart would not move the young man to penitence or turn him from any dangerous way. Colonel Kingsward, however, quickly forgave himself for this inadvertence, and reflected with satisfaction that, at least, he had prevented the young fool from making an ass of himself for this summer. And in such cases absence is the best remedy and hinders much mischief. Charlie rejected with indignation the week in town which his father offered. "A week in town!" he said to Bee, contemptuously, "to waste my time and debase all my ideas! What does he think I want with a week in town? That's the way a fellow's father encourages him to do the best he can. Cuts off all inspiration, and throws one on the dregs of life! It's enough to make a man kick over the traces altogether."

"But, Charlie," said Bee, with timidity, "don't you think it's very, very quiet here. We have nothing to disturb us. If you were to try to do your work at home?—you would have the library to sit in all the week while papa is in town."

"Out of reach of books, out of reach of any coach—it's like telling a mason to build a wall without any stone."

"The library is full of books," said Bee, with a little indignation.

"What kind of books? Military books, and travels, and things for reference—old peerages, and so forth—and some of the heavy old reviews, and a few novels. Much good a man who is going in for real reading would get out of those!"

"But you have your own books—all those that you carry about with you, Charlie."

"Oh!" he said, with impatience, "What are they? Horrible cribs and things, that I promised not to use any more."

"Does Laura," said Bee, with a little awe, "say you are not to use cribs?"

"And as for the quiet," said Charlie, continuing his strain of complaint, "if you call that quiet! When you never know that next moment there may not be a rush down the nursery stairs like wild horses let loose, and shrieks all over the house for Bee or for nurse, sending every idea out of a man's head; or else baby screaming fit to bring down the house. You know nothing about it, to be sure; it is like talking to the wind to talk to a little thing like you. A man can't work unless he's in the right place for working. If any difficulty arises in a passage, for instance, what do you think I am to do here?"

"Do you go to—Laura, when there is a difficulty about a passage, Charlie?"

"No, you little fool!" With a flush of anger and shame he begged her pardon next minute. "But it is so hard to explain things to you, Bee. You are so ignorant—naturally, for, of course, you never were taught anything. Don't you know that Oxford is full of coaches?" he said.

"That was just what I was thinking of, Charlie—if you will not be angry, but let me speak."

"Speak away," he said. This was on Monday, after Colonel Kingsward had left. The days which he spent at Kingswarden were the heaviest, as has been said, to the young party; nevertheless when he went away the blank of that long world of a week, without any communication to speak of from without, closed down alarmingly upon the elders of the family. Even when papa was cross, when he was dissatisfied with his dinner or found fault with the noise of the children, it was more or less an event. But when he departed there was a sense of being cut off from all events, separated from the world altogether, shut out from the news and the hum of society, which was very blank and deadening. Bee and Charlie dined alone, and it was dreary; they spent the evening together, or else—one in the library, one in the garden, where the beauty of the summer evening was terrible to the one poor little girl with her recollections, incapable of shutting them out in that utter stillness, and trying very ineffectually not to be unhappy. When Charlie threw open the window of the library and strolled forth to join her, as he generally did, it was a little better. Bee had just done very conscientiously all her duties in the nursery—had heard the children say their prayers, in which they still, with a little pause of awe, prayed God to bless dear mother—and had made all the valorous little efforts she could to keep down the climbing sorrow. When she heard the sound of the library window she quickly dried her eyes and contrived to smile. And she was a very good listener. She suffered Charlie to talk about himself as much as he pleased, and was interested in all he said. She made those little allusions to Laura which pleased him, though he generally answered with a scornful word, as who should say that "a little thing like you" was incapable of comprehending that lady. But this was the sole diversion of these young people in the evening. People called in the afternoon, and there was occasionally a game of tennis. But in the evening they were almost invariably alone.

They were strolling about the garden on this occasion when the young man bewailed himself. Bee, though she made those allusions to Laura, had never got over that little chill in respect to her which had arisen in the most capricious, causeless way when she knew that Laura lived in Oxford. Nothing could be more unreasonable, but yet it was so. It suggested something fictitious in her brother's eagerness to get back, and in his supposed devotion to his work. Had his Egeria been anywhere else Bee would not have felt this; but she did feel it, though she could not tell why. She was very anxious to please him, to content him, if possible, with his present life, to make her sympathy sweet to him, seeing that he had nobody but herself to console him, and must be separated from Laura until October. Poor Charlie! It was hard indeed that this should be the case, that he should have so dull a home and no companion but his sister. But it could not be helped; his sister, at least, must do what she could.

"You must not be angry," said Bee, very humbly. "It is only an idea that has come into my head—there may be nothing at all in it—but don't please shut me up as you do sometimes—hear me out. Charlie! there is Mr. Delaine."

"Mister—what?" said Charlie, which indeed did not show a very complaisant frame of mind—but a curate in the country is of less importance in the horizon of the son of a house who is at Oxford than he is in that of the daughter at home.

"Mr. Delaine," repeated Bee. "You don't remember him, perhaps, at all. He is the curate. When he came first he was said to be a great scholar. He took a first class. You need not say, pooh! Everybody said so, and it is quite true."

"A first in theology, I suppose," said Charlie, disdainfully.

"No, not that—that's not what people call a first. Mr. Burton, I have always heard, is a good scholar himself, and he said a first; of course you know better than I do what that means."

"Well," said Charlie, "and supposing for the sake of argument that he took a first—what then?"

"Why, Charlie dear! He is an Oxford man too; he must know all the things you want to know—difficult passages and all that. Don't you think, perhaps—"

"Oh, a coach!" cried Charlie. Then he paused, and with withering satire, added "No doubt, for little boys—your curate might do very well, Bee."

"He is not my curate," said Bee, with indignation; "but I have always heard he was a great scholar. I thought that was what you wanted."

"It is not to be expected," said her brother, loftily, "that you should know what I want. It is not a coach that is everything. If that were all, there need be no such things as universities. What a man needs is the whole machinery, the ways of thinking, the arrangements, the very atmosphere."

He strolled along the walk with his hands in his pockets and his shoulders up to his ears.

"I do not think it is possible," he added, turning to her with a softened tone, "that I could make you understand; for it is so different from anything you have ever known."

"I hope I am not so dreadfully stupid!" said Bee, incensed. "If Laura understands, why should it be so impossible for me?"

"Oh, for goodness' sake talk of things you can know something about; as if there was any comparison between her and you."

"I think you are very uncivil," said Bee, ready to weep. "I may not be clever, but yet I am your sister, and it is only because I wanted to help you that I took the trouble to speak at all."

"You are very well meaning, Bee, I am sure," said Charlie, with condescension; "I do full justice to your good intentions. Another fellow might think you wanted to have Delaine here for yourself."

"Me!" cried Bee, with a wild pang of injured feeling and a sense of the injustice, and inappropriateness, the cruel wrong of such a suggestion. And that Charlie could speak like that—who knew everything! It was almost more than she could bear.

"But I don't say that," he went on in his lofty tones. "I know you mean well. It is only that you don't— that you can't understand." How should she? he said to himself with amusing superiority, and a nod of his head as if agreeing to the impossibility. Bee resented the tone, the assumption, the comparison that was implied in every word.

"I wonder," she cried, "if you ever tell Laura that she doesn't and can't understand?"

He stopped short opposite to her, and grasped her arm. "Bee," he said almost solemnly, "Don't! If you knew her you would know what folly it is and presumption to compare yourself for one moment!—and do me the favour not to profane that name, as if it were only a girl's name like your own."

"Is she a princess, then?" cried Bee, "or an angel? Or what is she?"

"She is both, I think," said Charlie, in a voice full of awe, "at least to me. I wish you wouldn't talk of her in that way. I am sorry I ever told you her name. And please just let my affairs alone. You haven't been able to do anything for me with my father, which is the only thing you might have done—and I don't want to discuss other things with you. So please just let my concerns alone from this day."

"It was not I that ever wished to interfere!" cried Bee, with great mortification and resentment, and after a few minutes' silent walk together in much gloom and stateliness the brother and sister bade each other an offended and angry good-night.

CHAPTER XIV

This made, however, but a very temporary breach between Bee and her brother. They were a little stiff next morning at breakfast, and elaborately refrained from talking on any but the most trivial things, but by noon this reserve had broken down, and in the evening, though Bee proudly refrained from any reference to Laura, they were as confidential as ever. Bee's mind had passed through various vicissitudes in respect to the object of Charlie's adoration. Her first overwhelming interest had given way to a little doubt, and this was naturally strengthened by the over-weaning estimate of the unknown which Charlie thrust upon her. A girl is very willing to admire at second-hand her brother's love, but when she is told that it is presumption to compare herself with that divinity, her sympathy is strained too far. Bee began to have an uneasy feeling about this unknown Laura. It was one thing to stimulate Charlie to work, to stir up all that was best in him, to urge him to distinguish himself, for Charlie's sake or for their joint sakes, if they married and became one—which was the only thing that could happen in Bee's idea—but it was quite another thing to pretend an enthusiasm for this in order that Charlie should be kept within her reach and at her feet during that quiet time of the long vacation. Bee knew enough to know that severe work is not compatible with much love-making. She imagined her brother strolling away from his books to take Laura out on the river, or lie at her feet in the garden, which had become the habit of his life, as he betrayed to her accidentally. Bee thought, with a little indignation, that the lofty intentions which would probably end in these proceedings were of the nature of false pretences, and that the girl whom Charlie endowed with the most superlative qualities should not attempt to take him from his home for such reason; or, at least, if she did should do it frankly for love's sake—which was always a thing to be forgiven—and not on any fictitious pretence.

For Charlie, being refused that heroic way of working, "going up to read," did not read at all, as was apparent to his sister's keen eyes. He did not attempt to do the best he could, being prevented from doing what he desired. He settled himself, it is true, in the library after breakfast, with his books, as if with the intention of working, but before Bee got through the little lesson which she gave every morning to the little ones, Charlie was out strolling about the garden, or lying on the grass in the shade with a book, which was usually a novel, or one which lay closed by his side while he abandoned himself to thought—to thought, not about his books it was to be feared, for Bee, with tremors of sympathy in her heart, recognised too well the dreamy look, the drooped eyelids, the air astray from anything going on around. From questions of study, as far as Bee had perceived in her short experience, the merest footstep on a path, the dropping of a leaf, was enough to rouse the student. Charlie's thoughts were of a far more absorbing kind.

Colonel Kingsward suggested once more the week in town, when he came on another Saturday evening to Kingswarden. He was a man not very open to a perception of the wants of others, but as time went on, and he himself became more and more sensible of the ameliorating influences of society and occupation, the stagnant atmosphere at home, where his two elder children were vegetating, so much against all their previous habits, struck him with a sensation which he could not wholly get the better of. It was only right that Bee, at least, should remain in the country and in retirement the first summer after her mother's death. It would have been most unbecoming had she been in town seeing people, and necessarily, more or less, been seen by the world. But yet he felt the stillness close round him like a sensible chill, and was aware of the great quiet—aggravated by his own presence, though of this he was scarcely aware—as if it had been a blight in the air. It made him angry for the moment. In other times his house in the country had always been refreshing and delightful to him. Now, the air, notwithstanding that it was full summer, chilled him to the bone.

When you are escaping from the atmosphere of grief, anything that draws you back to it feels like an injury. He was very cross, very impatient with the silence at table, the subdued looks of the young people, and that they had nothing to say. Was it not worse for him than for them? He was the one who had lost the most, and to whom all ministrations were due, to soften the smart of sorrow. But afterwards his thoughts towards his children softened. It was very dull for them. On the Sunday evening he took the trouble to press that week in town upon Charlie. "There's a spare closet you can have at my rooms at the office," he said. "It's very central if not much else, and I daresay your friends will ask you out quietly as they do me. I think even you might bring up Bee for the day to see the pictures. She could stay the night with the Hammonds and see Betty."

"Oh, don't think of me, papa," cried Bee. "I would rather, far rather, stay at home. I don't care for the pictures—this year."

"That is foolish, my dear," said the Colonel. "There is nothing in the least unbecoming to your mourning in going there. Indeed, I wish you to go. You ought not to miss the pictures, and it will be a little change. Of course, I cannot go with you myself, but Charlie will take you, and you can go to Portman Square to sleep. You will see Betty, who must be thinking of coming home about now; indeed, it is quite necessary you should settle that with her. She can't stay there all the season, and it is rather heartless leaving you like this alone."

"Oh, no, papa. It is I that wish her to stay. She would have come back long ago but for me."

Bee's generous assumption of the blame, if there was any blame, excited her father's suspicion rather than admiration. He looked at her somewhat severely. "I cannot conceive what object you can have in preferring to be alone," he said. "It is either morbid, or—In either case it makes it more desirable that Betty should come back. You can arrange that. We will say Wednesday. I suppose you will not be nervous about returning home alone?"

"But, papa—"

"I consider the question settled, Bee," said Colonel Kingsward, and after that there was nothing more to be said.

Poor Bee wept many tears over this compulsory first step back into the world—without her mother, without—She did not mean (as she said in her inmost thoughts) anyone else; but it made the whole world vacant around her to think that neither on one side nor the other was there anyone to walk by her side, to take her hand, to make her feel that she was not alone. Nevertheless, it cannot be denied that, in the morning, this was the first thought that came into her mind, with a faint expansion of her young being. The change, though it was not joyful, was still something; and when she set out with Charlie on Wednesday morning her heart, in spite of herself, rose a little. To see the pictures! The pictures are not generally very exciting, and there was not, as it happened, a sensation in any one of them in this particular year, even had Bee been capable of it, which she was not. But yet she had a sensation, and one of the most startling description. As she was going languidly along, looking at one picture after another, mechanically referring to the catalogue, which conveyed very little idea to her mind, her attention was suddenly attracted by a lady standing in front of one of the chief pictures of the year. She was talking with great animation to some friends who surrounded her, pointing out the qualities and excellencies (or non-excellencies, for Bee was not near enough to hear) of the picture. She was picturesquely dressed in black, a tall and commanding figure, with a great deal of lace about her, and a fine profile, clearly cut and impressive. Bee's whole attention was called to her as by a charm. Where had she seen her before? She seemed acquainted with every detail of her figure, and penetrated by a vague reminiscence as of someone who had been of personal importance to herself, though she could not tell when or how. "Who is she? Oh, who is she?" Bee asked herself. She was very handsome— indeed Bee thought her a beautiful woman; not young, which is a thing always noted with a certain pain and compassion by a young girl—but full of grace and interest. While Bee gazed, open-eyed, forgetful of herself—a young figure, very interesting, too, to behold, in her deep mourning, and with the complete forgetfulness of herself involved in that wistful, inquiring, and admiring gaze—the lady turned round, presenting her full face to the girl's troubled vision. Bee felt her breath come short, her heart beat. She fell back hurriedly upon a vacant place on one of the benches which someone had charitably left empty. Bee did not know who the woman was, nor what possible connections she could have with her own fate, and yet there was a conviction in the girl's heart that she had to do with it, that somehow or other her life was in this woman's hands. It was the lady whom she had met that autumn morning last year in the firwoods round the Baths, where Bee had gone to finish her sketch—the lady who had appeared suddenly from among the trees, who had sat down by her, and pointed out the errors in the little picture, and advised her how to put them right. The black lace which was so conspicuous in the stranger's dress, seemed to sweep over Bee as she passed, with the same faint, penetrating odour, the same thrill of unaccountable sensation. Bee could not take her eyes from this figure as it moved slowly along, pausing here and there with the air of a connoisseur. Who was she? Who was she? Bee turned as she turned, following her with her eyes.

And then there occurred the most wonderful incident, so strange, so unsuspected, so unaccountable, that Bee could scarcely suppress a cry of astonishment. Charlie had been "doing" the pictures in his way, going faster than his sister, and had been roaming down the whole side of the long gallery while Bee occupied herself with one or two favourites. He appeared now at a little distance, having made the round of the room, and Bee was the involuntary, much surprised witness of the effect produced upon Charlie by the sudden appearance which had so much excited herself. He stopped short, with it seemed a sudden exclamation, let the book in his hands drop in his amazement, then, cleaving the crowd, precipitated himself upon the group in which the lady stood. Bee watched with consternation the hurried, eager greeting, the illumination of his boyish face, even the gesture—both hands put forth, and the quiver of his whole eager figure. She even heard a little cry of surprise from the lady, who presently separated herself from her friends and went on with Charlie in the closest conversation. It seemed to Bee as she watched, following them as well as she could through the crowd which got between her and these two figures, that there were no two heads so close together in all the throng. They seemed to drift into a corner where the pictures were of no importance, where they were comparatively undisturbed as if for the most confidential talk. It was not mere acquaintanceship, a chance meeting with some one he knew, it was utter forgetfulness of everything else, complete absorption in this new interest that seemed to move her brother. For a time Bee formed no conclusion, thought of no explanation, but watched them only with all her faculties. The catalogue which Charlie had dropped was shuffled and kicked to her feet by the passers by, a visible sign that something unusual had happened. What was it? Who was she?

And then there darted into Bee's mind a suggestion, an idea which she could not, would not entertain. Laura! Was it possible that this could be Laura? The thought sent a thrill through and through her. But no! no! no! she cried within herself; impossible! This lady was years older than Charlie—of another generation altogether—not a girl at all. She gazed through the crowd at the two heads in the corner of the room, standing as if they were looking at the pictures. They had their backs to Bee, and she could see nothing but occasionally a side glimpse of Charlie's cheek and the lace bonnet, with the unusual accompaniment of a floating veil, which covered his companion's head. She had remembered the veil at once—not primly fastened over her face, as most ladies wore them, but thrown back and falling behind, a head-dress such as nobody else wore. It distinguished from every other head that of the woman who, Bee now felt sure, was like somebody in a tragedy of Fate—somebody who had to do, she could not tell how, with the shipwreck of her own life—for had she not appeared mysteriously, from she knew not where, on the very eve of misery and ruin?—and now was overshadowing Charlie's, bringing him some calamity. Bee shivered and trembled among all the crowding people on the seat which so many people envied her, and felt that she was retaining far longer than her share. She was too much frightened to do as she could have wished to do, to rush after them, to draw her brother away, to break the spell. Such a dark lady had been known in story long before Bee was born. Could it be true that hateful beings were permitted to stray about even in the brightest scenes, bringing evil augury and all kinds of trouble with them? Many a time had Bee thought of this lady—of her sudden appearance, and of her questions about the Leighs; of something in her look, an air of meaning which even at the moment had confused the unsuspicious, unalarmed girl. And now, What was she? Who was she? Laura? Oh, no, no; a hundred times no. If Bee could have supposed that her respectable father or any member of her innocent family could have wronged anyone, she would have thought it was a ghost-lady ominous of trouble. Oh, what a silly thought in broad daylight, in the Academy of all places in the world! There was very little that was visionary or superstitious in such a place.

Charlie came back to join his sister after a considerable time with a glowing face. "Oh, you are there!" he cried. "I've been looking everywhere for you. I couldn't think where you could have gone—"

"I should have seen you had you been looking for me," said Bee.

"Well, never mind, now that I have found you. Have you seen as much as you wish? It's time to be moving off if you mean to get to Portman Square in time for tea."

"Charlie," said Bee, very gravely, getting up and moving with him towards the door, "who is that lady you were talking to with the black lace about her head?"

"What lady?" said Charlie, with a very fictitious look of surprise, and the colour mounting all over his face. "Oh, the lady I met—that lady? Well, she is a lady—whom I have met elsewhere—"

"I have met her, too," cried Bee, breathless, "down at the Baths just before—Oh, who is she—who is she, Charlie? I think she is one of the Fates."

"You little goose," cried her brother, and then he laughed in an unsteady way. "Perhaps she is—if there was a good one," he cried. "She is," he added, in a different tone, and then paused again; "but I couldn't tell you half what she is if I were to talk till next week—and never in such a noisy, vulgar place as this."

Then Bee's mind, driven from one thought to another, came suddenly back with a jar and strain of her nerves to the question about Laura; was it possible that this should be she?—for it was the tone sacred to Laura in which her brother now spoke. "Oh! tell me about her, tell me about her!" she cried, involuntarily clasping her hands—"she isn't—is she? Oh, Charlie, you will have time to tell me when we get into the park. Didn't she want to speak to me? Why didn't you introduce me to her if she is such a great friend of yours?"

"Hush! for goodness' sake, now; you are making people stare," said Charlie. He hurried down the stairs and across the road outside, making her almost run to keep up with him. "I say, Bee," he cried hurriedly, when he had signalled to a hansom, "should you mind going by yourself? I hate driving when I can walk. Why, you've been in a hansom by yourself before! You're not going to be such a little goose as to make a fuss about it now."

"Oh, but Charlie—I'd rather walk too, and then you can tell me—"

"Oh, nonsense," he cried, "you're tired already. It would be too much for you. Portman Square, No. —. Good-bye, Bee. I'll look up later," he cried, as, to Bee's consternation, the wheels of the hansom jarred upon the curb and she felt herself carried rapidly away.

CHAPTER XV

Portman Square had seemed to Bee the first step into the world, after all that had happened, but when she was there this gentle illusion faded. It was not the world, but only another dry and faded corner out of the world, more silent and recluse than even Kingswarden had become, for there were no voices of children within, and no rustle of trees and singing of birds without. The meeting with Betty was sweet, but the air of the little old-fashioned tea-table, the long, solemn dinner, with the butler and the footman stealing like ghosts about the table, which was laid out with heavy silver and cut glass, with only one small bunch of flowers as a sacrifice to modern ideas in the middle, and the silence of the great drawing-room afterwards, half lighted and dreary, came with a chill upon the girl who had been afraid of being dazzled by too much brightness. There were only the old lady and the old gentleman, Betty and herself, around the big table, and only the same party without the old gentleman afterwards. Mrs. Lyon asked Bee questions about her excellent father, and she examined Bee closely about her dear mother, wishing to know all the particulars of Mrs. Kingsward's illness.

"I can't get a nice serious answer from Betty. She is such a little thing; and she tells me she was not at home through the worst," Mrs. Lyon said.

It was not a subject to inspire Bee, or enable her to rise above the level of her home thoughts. Betty did not seem to feel it in the same way. She was in a white frock with black ribbons, for Mrs. Lyon did not like to see her in black, "such a little thing, you know." Bee wondered vaguely whether she herself, only a year-and-a-half the elder, was supposed to be quite middle-aged and beyond all the happier surroundings of life. Mrs. Lyon gave her a great deal of advice as to what she ought to do, and talked much of the responsibilities of the elder sister. "You must teach them to obey you, my dear. You must not let down the habit of obedience, you must be very strict with them; a sister has more need even than a mother to be very strict, to keep them in a good way." Bee sat very still, while the old lady prosed. It was so silent but for that voice, that the ticking of the clock became quite an important sound in the large dim room. And Bee strained her ears for the sound of a hansom drawing up, for Charlie's step on the pavement. Many hansoms stopped at neighbouring houses, and footsteps sounded, but Charlie did not make his appearance. "My brother said he would look in later," she had told Mrs. Lyon when she arrived. "Well, my dear, we shall hope he will," the old lady had said, "but a young man in London finds a hundred engagements." And Betty, who had been so serious, who had been so sweet, a perfect companion at the time of their mother's death, more deeply penetrated by all the influences of the time than Bee herself, now flitted about in her white frock, with all her old brightness, and sang her little song without faltering, to show Bee what progress she had made since she had been taking lessons. Bee could scarcely yet sing the hymns in church without breaking down, though to be sure a girl who was having the best lessons would be obliged to get over that. After the long evening when they were at last alone together, Betty did not respond warmly to Bee's suggestion that she should now be thinking of returning home. "You seem to think of nothing but the children," she said; "you can't want me," to which Bee could only reply that there were more things than the children to think of, and that she was very lonely and had no one to talk to—

"But you have Charlie," said Betty.

"Charlie is very full of his own concerns. He has not much sympathy with me. All that he wants is to get back to Oxford."

"To Oxford in the vacation? What would he do there?"

"He says he would work," said Bee.

"Oh, Bee, how nice of Charlie! I know they do sometimes, Gerald Lyon tells me; but I never thought that Charlie—"

"No," said Bee, "and I don't feel very sure now, there is someone—to whom he writes such long letters—"

"Oh, Bee! This is far, far more interesting than reading! Do you know who she is? Does he tell you about her?"

"Her name is Laura," said Bee, "that is all I know."

"Oh," cried Betty, "Charlie too!" And then a flush came over the girl's uplifted face. Bee, poor Bee, absorbed in the many things which had dawned upon her which were beyond Betty, did not observe the colour nor even that significant "too" which had come to Betty's lips in spite of herself.

"I think he met her or someone belonging to her—at the Academy to-day; and that's why he hasn't come—Oh, Betty, I am not happy about it—I am not happy at all!"

Betty put her arms round Bee and kissed her. She thought it was the remembrance of her own disappointment and disaster which made her sister cry out in this heart-broken way. Betty looked very wistfully in Bee's eyes. She was more sorry than words could say. If she could have done anything in the world "to make it all come right" she would have done so, and in the bottom of her heart she still had a conviction that all would "come right." "Oh, Bee, Bee!" she cried, "cannot anything be done? If only— only you would have listened to his mother!—Bee—"

Bee held up a warning finger. "Do you think it is myself I am thinking of?" she said, and then, wringing her hands, she added, "I don't know what harm we have done to bring it on, but, oh! I think we are in the hands of fate."

What did this mean? Betty thought her sister had gone out of her mind, and Bee would make no explanation. But I think this strange conversation made Betty rather less willing to return home. She was the darling of the house in Portman Square; though they did not go into society, they had all manner of indulgences for Betty, and took her to the Park, and encouraged the visits of their nephew, Gerald, who was a very merry companion for the girl. He was permitted to take her to see various sights, and the old people, as usual, did not perceive what was beginning to dawn under their very eyes. Betty was such a little thing. The consequence was that, though Bee thought Portman Square still duller than Kingswarden, her little sister was not of that opinion. Bee accordingly went back alone next day, Betty accompanying her to the railway station. Neither at Portman Square nor at the railway station did Charlie appear, and it was with a heavy heart that Bee went home. It seemed to her as she travelled alone, for, I think, the first time in her life—she was not yet quite twenty—that everyone was following his or her own way, and that only she was bearing the whole burden of the family. Her father had returned to his own world, his club, his dinners, official and otherwise. It was indispensable that he should do so. Bee had understood, it being impossible for a man in his position to withdraw from the world on account of any private feeling of his own. And Betty had flashed back again into her music, and her white frock, and was seeing everything as of old. And Charlie—oh, what was Charlie doing, drifting off into some tragic enchantment? The poor girl's heart was very heavy. There seemed only herself to think of them all in their separate paths, one here and another there, going further and further off in so many different directions from the event which had broken the unity of the family, yet surely should have held them together in their common trouble. That event had gone into the regions of the past. The time of the mother was over, like a tale that is told. There were still the children in the nursery, and Bee, their guardian, watching over them—but the others all going off, each at their separate angle. It is hard enough to realise this, even when age has gained a certain insensibility, but to the girl, this breaking up of the family was terrible. "I—even I alone remain," she was inclined to say with the prophet, and what could she do to stop the closing of these toils of Fate? Her mind gradually concentrated on that last and most alarming theme of all—the woman, the lady, without a name or history, or any evident link with the family, who had thus, for the second time, appeared in the path. Bee tried to fall back upon her reason, to represent to herself that she had no real cause for assuming that the stranger of whom she knew nothing, who might simply have been walking through that German wood, and have stopped by chance to speak to the little English girl with her stupid sketch, had anything to do with the disaster which so soon overtook that poor little English girl in the midst of her happy love. She had no reason, none, for thinking so. She tried to represent to herself how foolish she had been to entertain such a notion, how natural and without meaning the incident had been. And now again, for the second time, what reason had she to believe that anything fatal or even dangerous to Charlie was in this lady's appearance now? She was a distinguished-looking woman, much older than Charlie. What was more likely than that such a woman, probably by her looks a married lady, a person of importance, should have a great deal of influence over a youth like Charlie if she took notice of him at all? All this was very reasonable. There was far more sense in it than in that foolish terror and alarm which had taken possession of her mind. She had almost persuaded herself that these apprehensions were foolish before she reached home, and yet the moment after she had succeeded in reasoning it all out, and convincing herself how foolish they had been, they had risen up in a crowd and seized her anxious mind again.

It was some days beyond the week which Charlie had been allowed in town when he came back. He was in agitated spirits, with a look of mingled excitement and exhaustion, which gave Bee many alarms, but which she was not sufficiently skilled or experienced to interpret. Colonel Kingsward had not come home in the interval, having gone somewhere else to spend his weekly holiday, and when he did come there were various colloquies between him and his son, which were evidently of a disturbing kind. Some of these were about money, as was to be made out by various allusions. Charlie had either been spending too much, or had set up a claim to more in the future, a claim which his father was reluctant to allow. But it seemed that he had come out triumphant in the end, to judge by their respective looks, when they issued from the library together, just before Colonel Kingsward left for town.

"I hope, at least, you'll make good use of it," were the father's last words—and "you may trust me, sir," said Charlie, with all the elation of victory.

He was in great spirits all day, teasing the children, and giving Bee half confidences as to the great things he meant to do.

"They shan't put me off with any of their beastly Governorships at the end of the world," said Charlie. "I shall play for high stakes, Bee, I can't afford to be a mere attaché long, but they shan't shelve me at some horrible African station, I can tell you. That's not a kind of promotion that will suit me."

"But you will have to go where you are sent," said Bee.

"Oh, shall I?" cried Charlie, "that is all you know about it. Besides, when a man has a particularly charming wi—" He stopped and coughed over the words, and laughed and grew red.

"Do you think your manners are so particularly charming?" said Bee, with familiar scorn, upon which Charlie laughed louder than ever and walked away.

Next day he left home hurriedly, saying he was going to make a run for a day or two to "see a man," and came back in the same excited, exhausted state on Saturday morning, before his father returned—a process which was repeated almost every week, to the great consternation and trouble of Bee. For Charlie never mentioned these absences to his father, and Bee felt herself spell-bound, as if she were incapable of doing so. How could she betray her brother? And the letters to Laura ceased. He had no time now to write these long letters. Neither did he receive them as used to be the case. Had the correspondence ceased, or was there any other explanation? But Charlie talked but little to his sister now, and not at all on this subject, and thus the web of mystery seemed to be woven more and more about his feet—Bee alone suspecting or fearing anything, Bee alone entirely unable to make it clear.

CHAPTER XVI

The year went on in its usual routine, the boys came back from school, there was the usual move to the seaside, all mechanically performed under the impulse of use, and when the anniversary came round of the mother's death, it passed, and the black dresses were gradually laid aside. And everything came back, and everybody referred to Bee as if there had always been a slim elder sister at the head of affairs. Betty came home at the end of the season with a sentiment in respect to Gerald Lyon, and with the prospect of many returns to Portman Square, but nothing final in her little case, nothing that prevented her from being one of the ringleaders in all the mischief which inevitably occurred when the family were gathered together. Bee had become so prematurely serious, so over-wrought with the cares of the family, that Betty, who was too energetic to be suppressed, gradually came to belong rather to the faction of the boys than to share the responsibilities of the elder sister, which might have been her natural place. The second Christmas, instead of being forlorn, like the first, was almost the gayest that had been known in Kingswarden for many years. For the boys were growing, and demanded invitations for their friends, and great skating while the frost lasted, which, as the pond at Kingswarden was the best for a great number of miles round, brought many cheerful youthful visitors about the house. Colonel Kingsward was nothing if not correct; he did not neglect the interests of any of his children. He perceived at once that to have Bee alone at the head of affairs, without any support, especially when his own time at home was so much broken by visits, would be bad at once for her "prospects," and for the discipline of the family. He procured a harmless, necessary aunt accordingly, a permanent member of the household, yet only a visitor, who could be displaced at any time, to provide for all necessary proprieties, an arrangement which left him very free to go and come as he pleased. And thus life resumed its usual lightness, and youth triumphed, and things at Kingswarden went on as of old, with a little more instead of less commotion and company and entertainment as the young people developed and advanced.

It was perhaps natural enough, too, in the circumstances that Charlie, though the oldest son, should be so little at home. He came for Christmas, but he did not throw himself into the festivities with the spirit he ought to have shown. He was in a fitful state of mind, sometimes in high spirits, sometimes overclouded and impatient, contemptuous of the boys, as having himself reached so different a line of development, and indifferent to all the family re-unions and pleasures. Sometimes it seemed to Bee, who was the only one in the family who concerned herself about Charlie's moods, that he was anxious and unhappy, and that the air of being bored which he put on so readily, and the hurried way in which he rushed out and in, impatient of the family calls upon him, concealed a secret trouble. He complained to her of want of money, of his father's niggardliness, of the unhappy lot of young men who never had any "margin," who dared not spend an extra shilling without thinking where it was to come from. But whether this was the only trouble, or how it came about that he had discovered himself to be so poor, Bee, poor child, who knew so little, could not divine. How miserable it was that it was she who was in the mother's place! Mamma would have divined, she would have understood, she would have helped him through that difficult passage, but what could Bee do, who knew nothing about life, who thought it very likely that she was making mountains out of molehills, and that all young men were bored and uneasy at home—oh, if people would only be all good, all happy with each other, all ready to do what pleased the whole, instead of merely what pleased themselves!

To Bee, so prematurely introduced into the midst of those jars and individual strivings of will and fancy, it seemed as if everything might be made so easy in life by this simple method. If only everybody would be good! The reader may think it was a nursery view of human life, and yet what a solution it would give to every problem! Colonel Kingsward then would have been more at home, would have been the real father who commanded his children's confidence, instead of papa, whose peculiarities had to be studied, and in whose presence the children had to be hushed and every occasion of disturbance avoided, and of whom they were all more or less afraid. And Charlie would have been more or less a second to him, thoughtful of all, chivalrous to the girls, fond of home, instead of, as he was, pausing as it were on one foot while he was with his family, anxious only to get away. And Bee—well, Bee perhaps would have been different too had that new, yet old, golden rule come into full efficacy. Oh, if everybody, including always one's own self, would only be good!

It makes the head go round to think what a wonderful revolution in the world generally the adoption of that simplest method would produce. But in poor Bee's experience it was the last rule likely to be adopted in Kingswarden, where, more and more to the puzzled consciousness of the girl not able to cope with so many warring individualities, everyone was going his own way.

It was in the early spring that Colonel Kingsward came down from town to Kingswarden, looking less like the adoption of this method than ever before. The children were in the hall when he came, busy with some great game in which various skins which were generally laid out there were in use as properties, making, it must be allowed, a scene of confusion in that place. The Colonel was not expected. He had walked from the station, and the sound of his voice stopped the fun with a sudden horror of silence and fright, which, indeed, was not complimentary to a father. Instead of greetings, he asked why the children were allowed to make such a confusion in the place, with a voice which penetrated to the depths of the house and brought Bee and Betty flying from the drawing-room.

"Papa!" they both cried, in surprise, mingled with alarm. Colonel Kingsward walked into the room they had left, ordering peremptorily the children to the nursery, but finding certain friends of Betty's there, in full enjoyment of talk and tea, retreated again to his library, Bee following nervously.

"Is your brother here?" he asked, harshly, establishing himself with his back to the fire.

"My brother?" echoed Bee, for indeed there were half-a-dozen, and how was she to know on the spur of the moment which he meant.

Colonel Kingsward looked, in the partial light (for a lamp which smoked had been brought in hurriedly, to make things worse), as if he would have liked to seize his daughter and wring her slender neck. He went on with additional irritation: "I said your brother. The others, I have no doubt, will provide trouble enough in their turn. For the moment it is, of course, Charlie I mean. Is he here?"

"Papa! Why, he is at Oxford, you know, in the schools—"

Colonel Kingsward laughed harshly. "He was going in for honours, wasn't he? Wanted to go up to read in the long vacation—was full of what he was going to do? Well, it has all ended in less than nothing, as I might have known it would. Read that!" he cried, tossing a letter on the table.

Bee, with her heart sick, took up and opened the letter, and struggled to read, in her agitation, an exceedingly bad hand by an indifferent light. She made out enough to see that Charlie had not succeeded in his "schools," that he had not even secured a "pass," that he had incurred the continual censure of his college authorities by shirking lectures, failing in engagements, and doing absolutely no work. So far as was known there was nothing against his moral character, but—Bee, to whom the censure of the college sounded like a sentence of death, put down the dreadful letter carefully, as if it might explode, and raised large eyes, widened with alarm and misery, to her father's face.

"Oh, papa!" was all that she could say.

"I telegraphed to him to come home at once and meet me here. The fool," said Colonel Kingsward, pacing about the room, "is capable of not doing that—of going away—of—"

"Papa, they say there is nothing against his character. Oh! you couldn't think that he would—do anything dreadful; not disappear, not—" Bee said the rest in an anguish of suspicion and ignorance with her eyes.

"God knows what an idiot like that may do! Things are bad enough, but he will, of course, think them worse than they are. There is one thing we may be sure of," he said, with a fierce laugh, "Charlie will do nothing to make himself uncomfortable. He knows how to take care of himself." Colonel Kingsward walked up and down the room, gnawing the end of his moustache. The lamp smoked, but he took no notice of it. "There is one thing certain," he said, "and that is, there's a woman in it. I remember now, he was always thinking of something; like an ass, I supposed it was his studies. No doubt it was some Jezebel or other."

"Papa," said Bee.

"Speak out! Has he told you anything?" He stopped in front of her, and stood looking with threatening eyes into her face. "If you keep back anything from me," he said, "your brother's ruin will be on your head."

"Papa," said Bee, faltering, "it is not much I know. I know that there was a lady who lived in Oxford—"

"Ah! The long vacation," he exclaimed, with another angry laugh.

"He used to write long letters to her, and he told me her name."

"That is something to the purpose. What was her name?"

"He said," said Bee, in a horror of betraying her brother, yet impelled to speak, "he said that she was called—Laura, papa."

"What?" he cried, for Bee's voice had sunk very low; and then he turned away again with an impatient exclamation, calling her again a little fool. "Laura, confound her! What does that matter? I thought you had some real information to give."

"Papa," said Bee, timidly, "there is a little more, though perhaps it isn't information. When he took me to the Academy in summer I saw him meet a lady. Oh, not a common person, a beautiful, grand-looking lady. But it could not be the same," Bee added, after a pause, "for she was much older than Charlie—not a young lady at all."

"Why didn't you tell me this at the time?" cried Colonel Kingsward. "Can one never secure the truth even from one's own children? I should have sent him off at once had I known. What do you mean by not young at all?"

"I should think," said Bee, with diffidence and a great anxiety not to exaggerate such a dreadful statement, "that she might perhaps have been—thirty, papa."

"You little idiot," her father kindly replied.

Why was she a little idiot? But Bee had not time to go into that question. The evening was full of agitation and anxiety. The poor little girl, unused to such sensations, sat through dinner in a quiver of anxious abstraction, listening for every sound. There were several trains by which he might still come, and at any moment when the door opened Charlie might present himself, pale with downfall and distress, to meet his father's angry look, whose eyes were fixed on the door whenever it opened with as much preoccupation as Bee's—with this difference, that Bee's eyes were soft with excuses and pity, while those brilliant steely eyes which shone from beneath her father's dark brows, and which were the originals of her own, blazed with anger. When dinner was over, which he hurried through, disturbing the servants in their leisurely routine, Colonel Kingsward again called Bee to him into the library. She was the only person to whom he could talk of the subject of which his mind was full, which was the sole reason for this great distinction, for he had very little patience with Bee's trembling remarks. "Don't be a little fool," was the answer he made to any timid suggestion upon which she ventured; but yet there was a necessity upon him to discuss it with someone, and Bee, however inadequate, had this burden to bear.

"If the woman is the kind you say, and if she thinks there's anything to be made by it—why the fool may have married her," he cried. "Heavens! Think of it; married at three and twenty, without a penny! But," he added, colouring a little, "they are very knowing, these women. She would find out that he was not worth her while, and probably throw him off in time."

"Oh, papa!" cried Bee, horrified by the thought that her brother might be deserted in the moment of his downfall.

"That is the best we can hope. He will have Kingswarden, of course, when I die, but not a penny—not a penny in the meantime to keep up any such ridiculous—Listen! Is that the train?"

There was a cutting near Kingswarden through which the thundering of the train was heard as it passed. This had been a great grievance at first, but it was not without its conveniences to the accustomed ears of the household now. They both listened with anxiety, knowing that by this time it must have stopped at the station and deposited any passenger, and for the next half-hour watched and waited; Bee, with all her being in her ears, listened with an intensity of attention such as she had never known before, holding her breath; while Captain Kingsward himself, though he kept walking up and down the room, did so with a softened step which made no sound on the thick carpet, not uttering a word, listening too. To describe all the sounds they heard, or thought they heard, how often the gate seemed to swing in the distance, and the gravel start under a quick foot, would be endless. It was the last train; if he did not come now it would be clear that he did not mean to come. And it was now too late for any telegram. When it was no longer possible to believe that he could have been detained on the way, Colonel Kingsward drew a long breath of that disappointment which, in the yielding of nervous tension, is almost for the moment a relief.

"If there is no letter to-morrow morning I shall go up to Oxford," he said, "and, Bee, if you like, you can come with me. You might be of use. Don't say anything to Betty or your aunt. Say you are going with me to town by the early train, and that you may possibly not return till next day. There is no need for saying any more."

"Yes, papa," said Bee, submissively. That was all he knew! No need for saying any more to Betty, who had known every movement her sister made since ever she was born! But, at all events, Bee made up her mind to escape explanation so far as she could to-night. She paused for a moment at the door of the drawing-room as she passed. No more peaceful scene could have been presented. Betty was at the piano singing one song after another, half for practice, half to amuse the aunt, who sat dozing in her chair by the fire. The others had gone to bed, and careless youth and still more careless age, knowing nothing of any trouble, pursued their usual occupations in perfect composure and calm. The aunt knitted mechanically, and dozed in the warmth and quiet which she loved, and Betty went on singing her songs, indifferent to her audience, yet claiming attention, breaking off now and then in the middle of a line to ask "Do you like that, Aunt Ellen? Are you paying any attention, Aunt Ellen?" "Yes, my dear, I like it very much," the old lady said, and dozed again. Bee turned away with a suppressed sob. Where was Charlie? In disgrace, perhaps heart-broken, deserted by his love, afraid to meet his father! It was foolish to think that he was out in the night, wandering without shelter, without hope, for there was no need of any such tragic circumstances, but this was the picture that presented itself to Bee's aching and inexperienced heart.

Charlie was not in his rooms at College, he had not been there for some days, and nobody could furnish any information as to where he was. Colonel Kingsward had left Bee in the hotel while he went on to make his inquiries. He was very guarded in the questions he asked, for though he was himself very angry with his son, he was still careful for Charlie's reputation, explaining even to the college porter, who was very well acquainted with the eccentricities of the gentlemen, that he had no doubt his son had returned home, though they had unfortunately crossed each other on the way. The Colonel tried to keep up this fiction even with the sympathetic Don, who made matters so much worse by his compassion, but who was very full and detailed in his relation of poor Charlie's backslidings, the heaviness of whose gate bill and the amount of whose sins and penalties were terrible to hear. He had attended no lectures, he had written no essays, he had been dumb and blank in every examination.

"Out of consideration to you, Colonel Kingsward, the College has been very forbearing, and shut its eyes as long as possible."

"I wish, sir, the College had shown more common sense and let me know," the Colonel cried, in wrath; but that did not throw any light upon the subject.

As it turned out, Charlie had not "gone in" for his "schools" at all. He had done nothing that he ought to have done. What things he had done which he ought not to have done remained to be discovered. His stern father did not doubt that a sufficient number of these actual offences would soon be found to add to the virtues omitted. He went back to the hotel where Bee had been spending a miserable morning, and they sat together in gloom and silence.

"You had better go home," he said to her. "He may have got home by this time, and I don't see what use you can be here."

Bee was very submissive, yet begged hard to return as far as London, at least, with her father; to wait for another day, in case some trace of the prodigal might be found. Many such parties have occupied the dreary hotel rooms and stared in vain out of the windows, and watched with sick hearts the passing throng, the shoals of undergraduates, to their eyes all dutiful and well-doing, while the one in whom they are concerned is absent, in what evil ways they know not. Poor Bee was too young to feel the full weight of such alarms but she was as miserable as if she had known everything that could happen in the vagueness of her consciousness of despair and pain. What Charlie could have done, what would become of him, what his father would do or could do, were all hidden from Bee. But there was in it all a vague misery which was almost worse than clear perception. Colonel Kingsward, with all his knowledge of the world, was scarcely less vague. He did not know how to find out the secrets of an under-graduate. Charlie had friends, but all of them protested that they had seen very little of him of late. He had fallen off from sports and exercise as much as from study. He had scarcely been on the cricket ground all the summer; he had given up football; "boating on the river with ladies," he had been seen, but not recently, for the floods were out and such amusements were no longer practicable. At night the Colonel knew almost as little about his son as when he had arrived full of certainty that the whole matter could be cleared up in a few hours.

Next day began gloomily with another visit to the Don, whom Colonel Kingsward hoped to have seen the last of on their former exasperating interview. As he had discovered nothing elsewhere, he went back again to the authority, who had also hoped on his side to be free from the anxious but impatient father, and they had another long talk, which ended like the first in nothing. The college potentate had no idea where the youth could have gone. Charlie had left most of his property still in his rooms; he had gone out with only a little bag, nobody suspecting him of an intention to "go down." After they had gone over the question again, the Don being by no means as sympathetic as the first time, and contributing a good deal to Colonel Kingsward's acquaintance with his son's proceedings—a sudden light was for the first time thrown upon the question by a chance remark. "You know, of course, that he had friends in Oxford?"

"Like other young men, I suppose. I have seen several of them, and they can give me no information."

"I don't mean undergraduates: people living in the town—ladies," said the Don, who was a young man, almost with a blush. And after sending for Charlie's scout, and making other inquiries, Colonel Kingsward was furnished with an address. He went back to the hotel quickly, in some excitement, to inform Bee of the new clue he had obtained, but he scarcely reached the room where she was awaiting him when he was told that a lady had just asked for him downstairs. Bee was sent off immediately to her room while her father received this unexpected visitor. Bee had been watching at the window all the morning, looking down upon that world of young men, all going about their work or their pleasure, all in their fit place, while Charlie was no one knew where. The poor girl had been breaking her heart over that thought, wistfully watching the others among whom he ought to have been, feeling the pang of that comparison, sometimes imagining she saw a figure like his in the distance, and watching, as it approached, how every trace died away. Where was he? Bee's young heart was very sore. The vacancy was appalling to her, filling itself with all kinds of visionary shapes of terror. She could not think of him only as wandering away in misery and despair, feeling himself to have failed, ashamed and afraid to look anyone in the face. She scarcely understood her father when he hurried her out of the sitting-room, but obeyed him with a sense of trouble and injury though without knowing why.

Bee spent a very forlorn hour in her room. She heard the sound of the voices next door. Her father's well known tones, and a low voice which she felt must be a woman's. She would have been much tempted to listen to what they said if it had been possible, but there was no door between the rooms, and she could only hear that a long and close conversation was going on, without making out a word of it. She was very restless in her anxiety, wandering from the window to the door, which she opened with a desire to hear better, which defeated itself—and to see better, though there was nothing to be seen. It seemed to Bee that half the day was over before the sound of movement in the sitting-room warned her that the conference was breaking up. Even after that there was a long pause, and the talking went on, though it moved closer to the door. Bee had gradually grown in excitement as those sounds went on. She stole to her own half-open door, as the one next to it was opened, and the visitor came forth attended with the greatest courtesy by Colonel Kingsward, who accompanied her to the stairs. There the lady turned round and gave him her hand, turning her face towards the spot where the unsuspected watcher stood gazing with eyes of wonder and terror.

"Not another step," she said, with a sweet but decided voice. "The only thing I will ask from you, Colonel Kingsward, will be a line, a single line, to say that all is well."

"You may rely upon that," the Colonel said, bowing over the hand he held, "but may not I see you to your carriage, call your servant?"

"I am walking," she said, "and I am alone; come no further, please; one line to say that all is well." He still held her hand and she gave it a little, significant pressure, adding in a low tone: "And happy—and forgiven!"

Bee stood as if she had been turned to stone; a little, clandestine figure within the shelter of the door. It was a beautiful face that was thus turned towards her for a minute, unconscious of her scrutiny, and the voice was sweet. Oh, not a woman like any other woman! She said to herself that she remembered the voice and would have known it anywhere; and the look, half kind, yet with a touch of ridicule, of mockery in it. This was evidently not what the Colonel felt. He descended a few of the stairs after her, until turning again with a smile and with her hands extended as if to drive him back, she forbade his further attendance. He returned to the sitting-room thoughtfully, yet with a curious, softened expression upon his face, and a few minutes afterwards, not at once, he came to the door again and called Bee. There was still a smile lingering about his lips, though his mouth had stiffened back into its usual somewhat stern composure.

"Come in," he said, "I have something to tell you. I have had a very strange visit—a visit from a lady."

"I saw her," said Bee, under her breath, but her father was too much pre-occupied to hear.

"If this was, as I suppose, the lady whom you and your brother met, you are right, Bee, in thinking her very remarkable. She is one of the handsomest women I ever saw, and with a charm about her, which—. But, of course what you want to hear is about Charlie. I am glad to tell you that she has very much relieved my mind about Charlie, Bee."

Bee stood before her father with her hands folded, with the most curious sense of revolt and opposition in her mind—looking at him, a spectator would have said, with something of the sternness that was habitual to him, but so very inappropriate on her soft brow. She made no reply to this. Her countenance did not relax. Relieved about Charlie? No! Bee did not believe it. Pity and terror for Charlie seemed to take stronger and stronger possession of her heart.

"It is a long story," he said. "Sit down, you have got a way of standing staring, my dear. I wish you had more womanly models like the lady I have just been talking to—perfectly clear and straightforward in what she said, but with a feminine grace and sweetness. Well, it appears that Charlie had the good luck to get introduced to this lady about a year ago. Sit down, I tell you, I won't have you staring at me in that rude way."

There was a little pause, and Bee sat down abruptly, and not very gracefully. Colonel Kingsward could not but remark the difference. He followed her movements for a moment with his eyes, and then he began again—

"For all I can make out, he has been treated with a kindness which should have done everything for a young man. He has been invited to the house of these ladies—he has met all sorts of people who ought to be of use to him, whom it was a distinct advantage to meet—he has been kept out of the usual foolish diversions of young men. So far as I can make out, there is nothing against his character except what these Don-fellows call idleness—a thing that scarcely tells against a young man in after-life, unless he is a parson, or a schoolmaster, or something of that kind. Even the missing of his degree," said the Colonel, pulling his moustache reflectively, "is of little importance among practical men. So long as he can get through in his modern languages, and so forth, of what importance are the classics? I am very much relieved in my mind about Charlie. She thinks he must have gone straight down to London, instead of going home."

"Who is the lady, papa?"

Bee's interest in Charlie seemed to have dropped, as the Colonel's had done, for the moment. His advocate had made herself the first person on the horizon.

"The lady? So far as I can make out she is living here with some friends, up in the district called the Parks, where a great many people now live. She says she has always taken an interest in the undergraduates, who are left so sadly to themselves, and that, being of an age to make it possible, she has wished very much to devote herself to do what she could for these boys. Unfortunately, with her unusual personal attractions—." The Colonel stopped short and bit his moustache. "After all her kindness to your brother, encouraging him in his work and setting his duty before him—and no elder sister, no mother, could have been kinder, from all she tells me—the foolish boy repaid her good offices by—what do you think? But you will never guess."

"And I will never, never believe it," cried Bee, "if it was anything—anything that was not nice on Charlie's part!" Her voice was quite hoarse in her emotion, her secret fury against this woman, of whom she knew nothing, rising more and more.

"You little fool!" her father said, rising and standing up against the mantel-piece. He laughed angrily, and looked at her with his most contemptuous air. "One would think that even in their cradles women must begin to hate women," he said.

Bee, who hated no one unless it was this woman whom she feared but did not know, grew angry red. Her blue eyes flashed and shone like northern lights. The cruel and contemptuous assumption which touched her pride of sex, added vehemence to the other emotion which was already strong enough, and roused her up into a kind of fury.

"If she says anything bad of Charlie I don't believe it," she cried, "not a word, not a word! Whatever he has done she has driven him to it!" Then Bee was suddenly silent, panting, terrified or afraid that her little outburst of passion would close all further revelations.

"It seems unnecessary to add another word in face of such fierce prejudice!"

"Oh, papa, forgive me. Tell me; I shall say nothing more."

"You have said a great deal too much already. After this," he said, sarcastically, "you will perhaps think that your brother—of three and twenty, without a penny or a prospect—did Miss Lance honour by forcing a proposal upon her, making love to her at the end of all—"

"Miss Lance!" Bee said, with a sharp cry.

The Colonel took no notice of the interruption. He went on with a kind of disdainful comment to himself rather than to her.

"After all, there are things which a lady has to put up with, which we don't take into consideration. A young fool whom she has been kind to, knowing he has nobody near to look after him, no mother"—his voice even grew a little tender at this point—"and by way of reward the idiot falls in love with her, asks a woman like that to share his insignificant little life! Jove! What a piece of impertinence!" the Colonel said, with an angry laugh.

"Did you say," said Bee, with faltering lips, "Miss Lance, papa?"

He turned upon her with a look of extreme surprise.

"Why shouldn't I have said Miss Lance? What is there unusual in the name?"

Bee looked at him with a dumb rebellion, an almost scorn and passion far greater than his own. He had forgotten the name—but Bee had not forgotten it. The fact that Bee's own young life had suffered shipwreck had perhaps escaped from his memory altogether, though it was she who had done it. Bee looked at him with her blue eyes blazing, remembering everything that he had forgotten. Her brother had gone out of her mind, and all the history of his Laura, and the way in which he had been enfolded in this fatal web. She went back to her own wrongs—forgetting that she had keenly confirmed her father's decision and rejected Aubrey on what she thought to be other and sufficient grounds. She thought only of the moment when sudden darkness had fallen upon her in the first sunshine of her life, and she had struggled against the rigid will of her father, who would listen to no explanations—who would not understand. And all for the sake of this woman—the spider who dragged fly after fly into her net; the witch, the enchantress of whom all poems and stories spoke! Her exasperation was so intense that she forgot all the laws of respect and obedience in which her very being had been bound, and looked at her father as at an equal, an enemy whom she scorned as well as feared.

"What is the meaning of these looks," he said, "I am altogether at a loss to understand you, Bee. Why this fury at a name—which you have never heard before, so far as I know."

"You think I have never heard it before?" said Bee, in her passion. "It shows how little you think of me, or care for anything that has happened to me. Oh, I have heard it before, and I shall hear it again, I know. I know I shall hear it again. And you don't mind, though you are our father! You don't remember!" Bee was still very young, and she had that fatal woman's weakness which spoils every crisis with inevitable tears. Her exasperation was too great for words. "You don't remember!" she cried, flinging the words at him like a storm; and then broke down in a passion of choking sobs, unable to say more.

CHAPTER XVIII

To do Colonel Kingsward justice, he was taken entirely by surprise by Bee's outburst. He had no remembrance of the name. The name had been wholly unimportant to him even at the time when it had come under his notice. The previous claimant to Aubrey Leigh's affections had been "the woman," no more, to his consciousness. He did not remember anything about the business now, except that there was a story about a woman, and that he would not permit his young daughter to marry a man concerning whom such a story existed. Even after Bee had left him, when he really made an effort to pursue into the recesses of his mind anything that was connected with that name, he could not make it out. Was it perhaps a tyrannical governess? but that would not explain the girl's vehement outcry. He had not thought for a long time of Bee's interrupted love, and broken-off engagement. Of what consequence is such an episode to so young a girl? And there were other matters in his mind of what seemed a great deal more importance. Whatever was the source of Bee's previous knowledge of Miss Lance, she hated that singularly attractive woman, as it is usual for the sex—Colonel Kingsward thought—to hate instinctively every other woman who is endowed with unusual attractions.

What a magnificent creature that woman was! How finely she had talked of the undeveloped boy to whom she had hoped to be of service, and with what genuine feeling, half-abashed, distressed, yet not without a gleam of amusement, she had told him of the wonderful scene at the end, when Charlie had asked her to marry him.

"Me! A woman who might be his mother!" she had said, with beautiful candour; though it was not candour, it was more like jest, seeing that she was still young—young enough to turn any man's head. And she had added hastily, "It must have been my fault. Somehow I must have led him astray, though I was so far from intending it. A boy like your son would not have done such a wild thing had he not supposed—" She put up her hands to her face to hide a blush. "That is the worst of us, poor women," she had said, "we cannot show an interest even in a boy but he supposes—oh, Colonel Kingsward, can't you imagine what I felt, wishing solely to be of use to your son, who is such a good, ingenuous, nice boy—and finding in a moment, without the least warning, that he had mistaken me like that!"

Colonel Kingsward was of opinion, and so was everybody who knew him, that he was by no means an impressionable man; but it would be impossible to say how touched he had been by that explanation. And she was so sorry for Charlie. She avowed that, after what had happened, she would have considered herself inexcusable if she had not come to his father, however unpleasant it might be to herself, to show him how little, how very little, Charlie was to blame.

"You must not—must not be angry with him," she had said, joining her hands in appeal. "Oh, forgive him; it is so much my fault. If I could but bear the penalty! But I cannot endure to think that the poor boy should be punished when all the time I, who am so much older than he is, am the one to blame. I ought to have known better. I am at your mercy, Colonel Kingsward. You cannot say anything worse to me than I have done to myself; but he, poor boy, is really not to blame."

The Colonel had no wish to say anything to her that was uncomplimentary. He entered into her position with the most unusual sympathy. Perhaps he had never had so warm a feeling of understanding and affection for anyone before. The compassion and the appeal was something quite new and original to him. He was not a man to be sympathetic with the troubles of a middle-aged spinster—an elderly flirt, as he would probably have called her, had he heard the story at second hand; in such a case he would have denounced the mature siren in the terms usual to men of experience. But the presence of this lady made all the difference. She was not like anyone else. The usual phrases brought forward on such occasions were meaningless or worse in respect to her. He was softened to Charlie, too, by the story, though he could have raved at his son's folly. The puppy!—to think a woman like that could care for him! And yet, as she said, there was no harm in the boy; only absurdity, presumption, the last depths of fatuity. Poor young fool! But it was a different thing from racing towards the bottomless pit for the mere indulgence of his own appetites, as so many young men did, and if this was the only reason of Charlie's downfall it involved no loss of character and need make no breach in his career, which was the chief thing. He could make up his lost ground, and the F.O. would care very little for what the Dons said. The idleness of a boy in love (the puppy! inexcusable in his presumption, but yet with plenty of justification at least) could do him no more than temporary harm in any case.

These thoughts passed through the Colonel's mind with a great sense of relief. It did not occur to him that Charlie, when he saw his folly, could have much difficulty in getting over such a misplaced sentiment. It must be done, and the boy must feel that such a hope was as much above him as was the moon in the skies. He must make up his mind to apply himself, to get through his examination, to begin his real life—which his father would certainly impress upon him was not mere amusement or happiness, if he liked to call it so, but work and a sharp struggle to secure his standing. As for his degree, that was a matter of complete indifference to Colonel Kingsward. The boy had his experience of Oxford life to talk of and fall back upon; he was a University man all the same, though he had not been crowned by any laurels he had made some friends, and he had gained the necessary familiarity with that phase of a young man's existence. What did the details matter, and who would ever ask about his degree? An attaché does not put B.A. or M.A. (which was which, or if there was any difference, or on what occasion such vanities should be displayed the Colonel was quite unaware) to his name like a schoolmaster. Nothing could be of less importance than this. He dismissed Charlie from his mind accordingly with much relief. It was not at all unnatural that the boy should have gone to town instead of going to Kingswarden. No doubt by this time he had made his way home, and this reminded the Colonel that it would be as well to send his sister off at once to meet Charlie there. He called Bee again accordingly from her room, where she had taken refuge, and instructed her in what he desired.

"There is a train in an hour," he said. "You had better get ready. I wish you to go home at once. Charlie will be there by this time, I have no doubt, and I should like you to let him know that if he is reasonable and drives all folly from his mind, and addresses himself at once to his preparation for the exam., he shall hear no more from me about the Oxford business. It depends upon himself whether it is ever alluded to again."

"Papa," said Bee, faltering a little, "am I to go alone?"

"Why shouldn't you go alone? Are you afraid of getting into a cab at Paddington and driving to Victoria, the most ordinary everyday business? Why, I thought the girls of your period revolted against being protected, and were able to take care of themselves wherever they went?"

Now Colonel Kingsward had always insisted on surrounding his daughters with quite unnecessary care, being, as he prided himself, on all questions in respect to women, of the old school.

"Oh, no," said Bee, very tremulous, looking at him with eyes full of meaning, "I am not afraid."

"Then why do you make any fuss about it?" he said. "I shall stay behind for a few hours, perhaps for another night. I must see whether he has left any debts, and square accounts with the College, and—settle everything." Bee was still looking at him with that troubled air of meaning, and he looked at her with a stern look, putting her down; but there was in his eyes a certain understanding of her meaning and a shrinking from her scrutiny all the same. "You have just time to get ready," he said, pulling out his watch and holding it up to her. And Bee had nothing to do but to obey. It was not the drive from Paddington to Victoria, the change from one railway to another, which frightened her, though for a girl who had never done anything alone, that was not a pleasant thought; but the girl was deeply disturbed to leave her father there within the power of the woman whom more than ever she looked upon with terror as if she had been an embodied Fate. How ludicrous was the idea that a girl of twenty should be disturbed and anxious at the thought of leaving her father unprotected by her poor little guardianship—and such a father as Colonel Kingsward! Bee saw at once the folly and futility of such a notion, but she could not rid herself of the alarm. Her terror of this woman, now fully evident as the same who had wrecked her own life, was more than ever a superstitious panic.

Bee's mind was wholly possessed with this idea. She thought of the beautiful, dreadful lady in Christabel. She thought of that other shuddering image in the poem, of "the angel, beautiful and bright," who looked the hero in the face; "And how he knew it was a fiend, that miserable knight—" Aubrey had not known she was a fiend, nor Charlie; and now papa! What could such a woman do to papa? He was old (Bee thought) beyond the reach of the influences which had moved the others. What could Fate do to him? She asked herself this question in her great alarm, trying to beat down the terror in her bosom, and persuade herself that it was foolishness. But the more she thought the more her heart beat with fright and apprehension. It seemed to her, somehow, as if the former dangers had been nothing in comparison with this, although she did not know what it was that she feared.

Colonel Kingsward walked with his daughter to the station, and he was very affable and kind to her, taking unusual pains to make her feel that there was nothing to fear. He selected carefully a carriage which was reserved for ladies, and put her into the charge of the guard, whom he desired to find a cab for her at Paddington, and look after her in every way. Nothing could be more fatherly, more thoughtful than he was; but all these precautions, instead of reassuring Bee, increased her sensation of danger. For the Colonel, though he had always insisted upon every precaution, had not been in the habit of personally seeing to the comfort of his children. She followed him with her eyes as he occupied himself with all these little cares, and explained to the guard what was to be done. And then he went to the bookstall and bought her illustrated papers and a book to amuse her on the journey, Bee watching all the time with growing wonder. She gave a hurried glance now and then around her, sweeping the station from one end to another, with a terror of seeing somewhere appear the woman who had brought such pain and trouble into her life—though this, too, was folly, as she was aware. And when at last the carriage door was closed, and the train almost in motion, Bee gave her father a last look, in which there were unutterable things. He had not met her eyes hitherto, whether by chance or precaution. But now he was off his guard and did so. Their looks encountered with a clash, as if they had been meeting swords, the same eyes, brilliant with that blue blaze, flashing like lightning. But it was the father's fiery eyes which gave way. The girl's look penetrated into his very being; his dropped, almost abashed. How did this strange change of position come about? It was anything but reassuring to Bee. It seemed to her as if already a new chapter of misery and dismay had opened in life, although her fears had taken no shape, and she could not tell what calamity was possible. The very vagueness made it all the more appalling to her inexperienced heart.

As for Colonel Kingsward, he saw his little daughter go away with a relief which he felt to be ridiculous. That Bee's looks should affect his movements one way or another was beyond measure absurd, and yet he was relieved that she was gone, and felt himself more at ease. He had a great many things to do—to settle his son's accounts, to take his name off the college books, to wind up that early unsuccessful chapter of Charlie's life. But he now felt very little real anger against Charlie—this shipwreck of his had suddenly introduced his father to what seemed a new view and new objects, which indeed he did not in any way define to himself, but of which he felt the stimulus with vague exhilaration to the bottom of his heart.

When Charlie Kingsward fled from Oxford, half mad with disappointment and misery, he had no idea or intention about the future left in his mind. He had come to one of those strange passes in life beyond which the imagination does not go. He had been rejected with that deepest contumely which takes the aspect of the sweetest kindness, when a woman affects the most innocent suspicion at the climax to which, consciously or unconsciously, she has been working up.

"Oh, my poor boy, was that what you were thinking of?" There is no way in which a blow can be administered with such sharp and keen effect. It made the young man's brain, which was only an ordinary brain, and for some time had exercised but small restraining power upon him in the hurry and sweep of his feelings, reel. When he pulled the door upon him of those gardens of Aminda, that fool's paradise in which he had been wasting his youth, and which were represented in his case by a very ordinary suburban garden in that part of Oxford called the Parks, his rejected and disappointed passion had every possible auxiliary emotion to make it unbearable. Keen mortification, humiliation, the sharp sense of being mocked and deceived; the sudden conviction of having given what seemed to the half-maddened boy his whole life, for nothing whipped him like the lashes of the Furies. In most of the crises of life the thought what to do next occurs with almost the rapidity of lightning after a great catastrophe, but Charlie felt as if there was nothing beyond. The whole world had crumbled about him. There was no next step; his very footing had failed him. He rushed back to his rooms by instinct, as a wounded creature would rush to its lair, but on his way was met by eager groups returning from the "Schools," in which he ought to have been, discussing among each other the stiffness of the papers, and how they had been done. This would scarcely add to his pain, but it added to that sickening effort of absolute failure of the demolition of everything around and before him, which was what he felt the most. They made the impossible more impossible still, and cut off every retreat. When he stood in his room, amid all the useless books which he had not opened for days or weeks, and heard the others mounting the staircase outside his locked door, it seemed to the unhappy young man as though the floor under his feet was the last spot on which standing ground was possible, and that beyond and around there was nothing but chaos. For what reason and on what impulse he rushed to London it would be difficult to tell. He had little money, few friends—or rather none who were not also the friends of his family—no idea or intention of doing anything.

"Perhaps the world will end to-night."

He did not even think so much as that, though perhaps it was in some sort the feeling in his mind. Yet no suggestions of suicide, or of anything that constitutes a moral suicide, occurred to him. These would have been something definite, they would have provided for a future, but Charlie was stupefied and had none. He had not so much sense of any resource as consisted in a pistol or a plunge into the river. He flung himself into the train and went to London, because after a time the sound of his comrades, or of those who ought to have been his comrades, became intolerable to him. They kept pacing, rushing up and down the staircase, calling to each other. One or two, indeed, talked at his own closed door, driving him into a silent frenzy. As soon as they were gone he seized a travelling bag, thrust something, he did not know what, into it, and fled—to the desert—to London, where he would be lost and no one would drive him frantic by calling to him, by making believe that there was something left in life.

It occurred to him somehow, by force of that secondary consciousness which works for us when our minds are past all exertion, to fling himself into the corner of a third-class carriage as the place where he was least likely to meet anyone he knew, though indeed the precaution was scarcely necessary, since he could not have recognised anyone, as he sat huddled up in his corner, staring blankly at the landscape that flew past the window and seeing nothing. When he arrived in the midst of the din and bustle of the great railway station, he fled once more through the crowd into the greater crowd outside, clutching instinctively at the bag which lay beside him, but seeing no one, nor whither he went nor where he was going. He walked fast, and in a fierce unconsciousness pushing his way through everything, and though he had in reality no aim, took instinctively the way to his father's house—his home—though it was at that time no home for him, being occupied by strangers. When he got into the park a vague recollection of this penetrated through the maze in which he was enveloped, and for a moment he paused, but then went on walking at the same pace, making the circuit of the park which lay before him in the mists of the afternoon, the frosty sun setting, the hay taking a rosy tint. He went all round the silences of the half-deserted walks, beginning to feel vaguely the strange desolate sentiment of not knowing where to go, though only in the secondary phase of his consciousness. Until all at once his strength seemed to fail him, his limbs grew feeble, his steps slow, and he stopped short, mechanically, as he had walked, not knowing why, and flung himself upon a bench, where he sat long, motionless, as if that had now become the only thing solid in the world and there was no step remaining to him beyond.

A young man, though he may have numberless friends, may yet make a despairing transit like this from one place to another through the midst of a crowd without being seen by anyone who knows him; if the encounters of life are wonderful, the failures to encounter, the manner in which we walk alone with friends on all hands, and in our desperate moments, when help is most necessary, do not meet or come within sight of any, is equally wonderful. The Kingswards had a large circle of acquaintance, and Charlie himself had the numberless intimates of a public school boy, a young university man, acquainted with half the youth of his period—yet nobody saw him, except one to whom he would scarcely have accorded a salutation in ordinary circumstances. Aubrey Leigh, who had been so strangely and closely connected for a moment with the Kingsward family, and then so swiftly and peremptorily cut off, arrived in London from a short visit to a suburban house by the same train which brought Charlie, and caught sight of him as he jumped out of his compartment with his bag in his hand. A very cool, self-possessed, and trim young man young Kingsward had always appeared to the other, with whose brightest and at the same time most painful recollections his figure was so connected. To see him now suddenly, with that air of desperation which had triumphed over all his natural habits and laws, that abstracted look, clutching his bag, half leaping, half stumbling out of the carriage, going off at a swift, unconscious pace, pushing through every crowd, filled Aubrey with surprise which soon turned into anxiety. Charlie Kingsward, with a bag in his hand, rushing through the London streets conveyed an entirely new idea to the minds of the spectators. What such an arrival would have meant in ordinary circumstances would have been the rattling up of a hansom, the careless calling out of an address, the noisy progress over the stones, of the driver expectant of something more than his fare, and keenly cognisant of the habits of the young gentlemen from Oxford.

Aubrey quickened his own pace to follow the other, whose arrival this time was in such different guise. A sudden terror seized his mind, naturally quite unjustified by the outward circumstances. Was anyone ill?—which meant, was Bee ill? Had anything dreadful happened? A moment's reflection would have shown that in such a case the hansom would be more needed than usual, as conveying her brother the more quickly to his home. But Aubrey did not pause on probabilities. A moment more would have made him sure of the unlikelihood that Charlie would be sent for in case of Bee's illness, unless, indeed, the question had been one of life and death.

But he had not even heard of his love for many months. His heart was hungry for news of her, and in that case he would have done his best to intercept Charlie, to extract from him, if possible, some news of his sister. He followed, accordingly, with something of the same headlong haste with which Charlie was pushing through the streets, and for a long time, up to the gates of the park, indeed, kept him in sight. At the rate at which the young man was going it was impossible to do more.

Then Aubrey suddenly lost sight of the figure he was pursuing. There was a group of people collected for some vulgar, unsupportable object or other at that point, and it was there that Charlie deflected from the straight road for home, which he had hitherto taken, and which his pursuer took it for granted he would follow for the rest of the way. When Aubrey had pushed his way through the little crowd Charlie was no longer visible. He looked to left and to right in vain, scrutinised the short cut over the park, and the broad road full of passing carriages and wayfarers, but saw no trace of the figure he sought. Aubrey then walked quickly to the point where Charlie, as he supposed, must be going, and soon came to the gate on the other side and the street itself in which the house of the Kingswards was. But he saw no sign of Charlie, nor of anyone looking for him. He himself had no acquaintance with that house, to which he had never been admitted, but he had passed it many times in the vain hope of seeing Bee at a window, not knowing that it was occupied by strangers. While he walked down the street, however, anxiously gazing to see if there were any signs of illness, asking himself whether he dared to inquire at the door, he saw a gentleman come up and enter with a latch key, who certainly did not belong to the Kingsward family. This changed the whole current of Aubrey's thoughts. It was not here then that Charlie was coming. His rapid and wild walk could not mean any disaster to the family—any trouble to Bee. The discovery was at once a disappointment and a relief; a relief from the anxiety which had gradually been gaining upon him, a disappointment of the hope of hearing something of her. For if Charlie was not going home, who could trace out where such a young man might be going? To the dogs, Aubrey thought, instinctively; to the devil, to judge by his looks. Yet Charlie Kingsward, the most correct of modern young men, had surely in him no natural proclivity towards that facile descent. What could it be that had driven him along like a leaf before the wind?

Aubrey was himself greatly disturbed and stirred up by this encounter. He had schooled himself to quiet, and the pangs of his overthrow, though not quenched, had been kept under with a strong hand. The life which he desired for himself, which he had so fully planned, so warmly hoped for, had been broken to pieces and made an end of, leaving the way he had chosen blank to him, as he thought, for evermore. He had been very unfortunate in that way, his early venture ending in bitter disappointment; his other, more wise, more sweet, cut off before it had ever been. But he was a reasonable being, and knew that life had to be put to other uses, even when that sole fair path which the heart desired was closed. He had given it up definitely, neither thinking nor hoping again for the household life, the patriarchal existence among his own fields, his own people, under his own roof, and was now doing his best to conform his life to a more grey and monotonous standard.

But the sight of Charlie, or rather the sight of Bee's brother, evidently under the influence of some strong feeling, and utterly carried away by it so as to ignore all that regard for appearance and decorum which had been his leading principle, came suddenly like a touch upon a wound, reviving all the questions and impatiences of the past. Aubrey felt that he could not endure the ignorance of her and all her ways which had fallen over him like a pall, cutting off her being from him as if they were not still living in the same world, still within reach of each other. He might endure, he said to himself, to be parted from her, to give up hope of her, since she willed it so—yet, at least, he must know something of her, find out if she were ill or well, what she was doing, where she was even; for that mere outside detail he did not know. How was it possible he should bear this—not even to know where she was? This thought took hold of him, and drove him into a fever of sudden feeling. Oh! yes; he had resigned himself to live without her, to endure his solitary existence far from her, since she willed it so; but not even to know where she was, how she was, what she was doing!

Suddenly, in a moment, the fiery stinging came back, the sword plunged into the wound. He had not for a moment deluded himself with the idea that he was cured of it, but yet it had been subdued by necessity, by the very silence which now he felt to be intolerable. He went back into the park, where the long lines of the misty paths were now almost deserted, gleams of the lamps outside shining through the dark tracery of the branches, and all quiet except in the broad road, still sounding with a diminished stream of carriages. He dived into the intersections of the deserted paths, something as Charlie had done, seeking instinctively a silent place where he could be alone with the newly-aroused torment of his thoughts.

When he came suddenly upon the bench upon which Charlie had flung himself, his first movement was to turn back. He had been walking over the grass, and his steps were consequently noiseless, and he was in the mood to which any human presence—the possible encounter of anyone who might speak to him and disturb his own hurrying passions—was intolerable. But as he turned, his eye fell on the bag—the dusty, half-empty thing still clutched by a hand that seemed more or less unconscious. This insignificant detail arrested Aubrey. He moved a little way, keeping on the grass, to get a fuller view of the half-reclining figure. And then he made out in the partial light that it was the same figure which he had pursued so long.

What was Charlie doing here in this secluded spot—he, the most unlike any such retirement, the well-equipped, confident, prosperous young man of the world, subject to so few delusions, knowing his way so well, both in the outer and the inner world?

Aubrey was more startled than tongue can tell. He thought no longer of family disaster, of illness, or trouble. Whatever was amiss, it was evidently Charlie who was the sufferer. He paused for a minute or more, reflecting what he should do. Then he stepped forward upon the gravel, and sitting down, put his hand suddenly upon that which held the half-filled bag.

"Kingsward!" he said.

CHAPTER II

Meanwhile Colonel Kingsward had remained in Oxford. It was necessary that he should regulate all Charlie's affairs, find out and pay what bills he had left, and formally sever his connection with the University. It is a thing which many fathers have had to do, with pain and sorrow, and a sense of premature failure, which is one of the bitterest things in life; but Colonel Kingsward had not this painful feeling to aggravate the annoyance and vexation which he actually felt. The fact that his son had been idle in the way of books, and was leaving Oxford without taking his degree, did not affect his mind much. Many young fellows did that, especially in the portion of the world to which Charlie belonged. The Colonel was irritated by having to interfere, by the trouble he was having, and the deviation from salutary routine, but he felt no humiliation either for himself or his son. And Charlie's liabilities were not large, so far as he could discover. The fellow, at least, had no vices, he said to himself. Even the unsympathetic Don had nothing to say against him but that charge of idleness, which the Colonel rather liked than otherwise. Had he been able to say that it was his son's social or even athletic successes which were the causes of the idleness he would have liked it altogether. He paid Charlie's bills with a compensating consciousness that these were the last that would have to be paid at Oxford, and he was not even sorry that he could not get back to town by the last train. Indeed, I think he could have managed that very well had he tried. He remained for the second night with wonderful equanimity, finding, as a matter of course, a man he knew in the hotel, and dining not unpleasantly that day. Before he went back to town, he thought it only civil to go out to the Parks to return, as politeness demanded, the visit of the lady who had so kindly and courageously gone to see him, and from whom he had received the only explanation of Charlie's strange behaviour. He went forth as soon as he had eaten an early luncheon, in order to be sure to find Miss Lance before she went out, and stopped only to throw a rapid glance in passing at a band of young ruffians—mud up to their eyes, and quite undistinguishable for the elegant undergraduates which some of them were—who were playing football in the Parks. The Colonel had, like most men, a warm interest in athletic sports, but his soldierly instincts disliked the mud. Miss Lance's house was beyond that much broken up and down-trampled green. It was a house in a garden of the order brought into fashion by the late Randolph Caldecott, red with white "fixings" and pointed roof, and it bore triumphantly upon its little gate post the name of Wensleydale, Oxford Dons, and the inhabitants of that district generally, being fond of such extension titles. Colonel Kingsward unconsciously drew himself together, settled his head into his collar, and twisted his moustache, as he knocked at the door, and yet it was not an imposing door. It was opened, not by a solemn butler, but by a neat maid, who showed Colonel Kingsward into a trim drawing-room, very feminine and full of flowers and knick-knacks. Here he waited full five minutes before anyone appeared, looking about him with much curiosity, examining the little stands of books, the work-tables, the writing-tables, the corners for conversation. It was not a large room, and yet space had been found for two little centres of social intercourse. There were, therefore, the Colonel divined, two ladies who shared this abode. Colonel Kingsward had never been what is called a ladies' man. The feminine element in life had been supplied to him in that subdued way naturally exhibited by a yielding and gentle wife in a house where the husband is supreme. He was quite unacquainted with it in its unalloyed state, and the spectacle amused and pleasantly affected him with a sense at once of superiority and of novelty. It was pleasant to see how these little known creatures arranged themselves in their own private dominion, where they had everything their own way, and the touch of the artificial which appeared in all these dainty particulars seemed appropriate and commended itself agreeably to the man who was accustomed to a broader and larger style of household economy. A man likes to see the difference well marked, at least a man who holds Colonel Kingsward's ideas of life. He had gone so far as to note the "Laura" with a large and flowing "L" on the notepaper, which "L" was repeated on various pretty articles about. When the door opened and Miss Lance appeared, she came up to him holding out both her hands as to an old friend.

"Will you forgive me for keeping you waiting, Colonel Kingsward? The fact is we have just come in, and you know that a woman has always a toilette to make, not like you lucky people who put on or put off a hat and all is done."

"I did not think you were likely to be out so early," the Colonel said.

"My friend has a son at Oriel," replied Miss Lance. "He is a great football player as it happens, and we are bound to be present when he is playing; besides, the Parks are so near."

"I did not think it was a game that would interest you."

"It does not, except in so far that I am interested in everything that interests my surroundings. My friend goes into it with enthusiasm; she even believes that she understands what it is all about."

"It seems chiefly mud that is about," said the Colonel, with a slight tone of disapproval, for it displeased him to think that a woman like this should go to a football match, and also it displeased him after his private amusement and reflections on the feminine character of the house to find, after all, a man connected with it, even if that man were only a boy.

"Come," said Miss Lance, indicating a certain chair, "sit down here by me, Colonel Kingsward, and let us not talk commonplaces any longer. You have been obliged to stay longer than you intended. I had been thinking of you as in London to-day."

"It was very kind to think of me at all."

"Oh, don't say so—that is one of the commonplaces too. Of course, I have been thinking of you with a great deal of interest, and with some rather rebellious, undutiful sort of thoughts."

"What thoughts?" cried the Colonel, in surprise.

"Well," she said, "it is a great blessing, no doubt, to have children—to women, perhaps, an unalloyed blessing; and yet, you know, an unattached person like myself cannot help a grudge occasionally. Here are you, for instance, in the prime of life; your thoughts about everything matured, your reason more important to the world than any of the escapades of youth, and yet you are depleted from your own grave path in life; your mind occupied, your thoughts distracted; really your use to your country interrupted by—by what are called the cares of a family," she concluded, with a short laugh.

She spoke with much use of her hands in graceful movement that could scarcely be called gesticulation—clasping them together, spreading them out, making them emphasise everything. And they were very white and pretty hands, with a diamond on one, which sparkled at appropriate moments, and added its special emphasis too.

The Colonel was flattered with this description of himself and his capacities.

"There is great truth," he said, "in what you say. I have felt it, but for a father at the head of a family to put forth such sentiments would shock many good people."

"Fortunately there are no good people here, and if there were I might still express them freely. It is a thing that strikes me every day. In feeble specimens it destroys the individuality; in strong characters like yourself—"

"You do me too much honour, Miss Lance. My position, you are aware, is doubly unfortunate, for I have all upon my shoulders. Still, one must do one's duty at whatever cost."

"That would be your feeling, of course," said Miss Lance, with a sort of admiring and regretful expression. "For my part, I am the most dreadful rebel. I kick against duty. I think a man has a duty to himself. To stint a noble human being for the sake of nourishing some half-dozen secondary ones, is to me—Oh, don't let us talk of it! Tell me, dear Colonel Kingsward, have you got everything satisfactorily settled, and heard of the arrival—? Oh," she cried, clasping those white hands, "how can I sit here calmly and ask, seeing that I have a share in causing all this trouble—though, heaven knows, how unintentionally on my part!"

"Don't say so," said the Colonel, putting his hands for a second on those clasped white hands. "I am sure that you can have done nothing but good to my foolish boy. To be admitted here at all was too much honour."

"I shall never be able to take an interest in anyone again," she said, drooping her head. "It is so strange, so strange to have one's motives misunderstood, but you don't do so. I am so thankful I had the courage to go to you. My friend dissuaded me strongly from taking such a step. She said that a parent would naturally blame anyone rather than his own son—"

"My dear Miss Lance, who could blame you? I don't know," said the Colonel, "that I blame poor Charlie so much either. To be much in your company might well be dangerous for any man."

"You must not speak so—indeed, indeed, you must not! I feel more and more ashamed! When a woman comes to a certain age—and has no children of her own. Surely, surely—"

"Come!" he cried. "You said a parent's cares destroyed one's individuality—"

"Not with a woman. What individuality has a woman? The only use of her is to sink that pride in a better—the pride of being of some use. What I regretted was for you—and such as you—if there are enough of such to make a class—. Yes, yes," she added, looking up, "I acknowledge the inconsistency. I have not sense enough to see the pity of it in all cases—but my real principle, my deep belief is that to draw a man like you away from your career, to trouble and distress you about others, who are not of half your value—is a thing that ought to be prevented by Act of Parliament," she cried, breaking off with a laugh. "But you have not told me yet how everything has finished," she added, in a confidential low tone, after a pause.

Then he told her in some detail what he had done. It was delightful to tell her, a woman so sympathising, so quick to understand, with that approving, consoling, remonstrating action of her white hands which seemed at the same moment to applaud and deprecate, with a constant inference that he was too good, that really he ought not to be so good. She laughed at his description of the Don, adding a graphic touch or two to make the picture more perfect—till Colonel Kingsward was surprised at himself to think how cleverly he had done it, and was delighted with his own success. This gave a slightly comic character to his other sketches of poor Charlie's tradesmen, and scout, and an unutterable cad of a young fellow who had met the Colonel leaving the college and had told him of a small sum which Charlie owed him.

"The little beast!" the Colonel said.

"Worse!" cried Miss Lance, "I would not slander any gentlemanly dog by calling him of the same species."

Altogether, her interest and sympathy changed this not particularly lively occasion into one of the brightest moments of Colonel Kingsward's life. He had not been used to a woman so clever, who took him up at half a word, and enhanced the interest of everything. Had he been asked, indeed, he would have said that he did not like clever women. But then Miss Lance had other qualities. She was very handsome, and she had an evident and undisguised admiration for him. She was so very frank and sure of her position as a woman of a certain age—a qualification which she appropriated to herself constantly, though most women thought it an insult—that she did not find it needful to conceal that admiration. When he thanked her for her kindness for the patient hearing of all his story, and the interest she had shown, to which he had so little claim, Miss Lance smiled and held out those white hands.

"I assure you," she said, "the benefit is all on my side. Living here among very young men, you must think what it is to talk to, to be treated confidentially, by a man like yourself. It is like a glance into another life." She sighed, and added, "The young are delightful. I am very fond of young people. Still, to meet now and then with someone of one's own age, of one's own species, if I may say so—"

"You do me too much honour," said Colonel Kingsward, feeling with a curious elation, how superior he was. She went with him to the garden gate, not afraid of the wintry air, showing no sense of the chill, and though she had given him her hand before, offered it again with the sweetest friendliness.

"And you promised," she said, looking in his face while he held it, "that you would send me one line when you got home, to tell me how you find him—and that all is well—and forgiven."

"I shall be too happy to be permitted to write," Colonel Kingsward said.

"Forgiven," she said, "and forgotten!" holding up a finger of the other hand, the hand with the diamond. She stood for a moment watching while he closed the low gate, and then, waving her hand to him, turned away. Colonel Kingsward had never been a finer fellow, in his own estimation, than when he walked slowly off from that closed door.

CHAPTER III

I will not repeat the often described scene of anxiety which existed in Kingswarden for some time after. Colonel Kingsward returned, as Bee had done, to find that nothing had been seen or heard of Charlie, whom both had expected to find defiant and wretched at home. It is astonishing how quickly in such circumstances the tables are turned, and the young culprit—whom parents and friends have been ready to crush the moment he appears with well-deserved rebuke—becomes, when he does not appear, the object of the most eager appeals; forgiveness, and advantages of every kind all ready to greet him if only he will come back. The girls were frightened beyond description by their brother's disappearance, and conjured up every dreadful image of disaster and misery. They thought of Charlie in his despair going off to the ends of the earth and never being seen more. They thought of him as in some wretched condition on shipboard, sick and miserable, reduced to dreadful work and still more dreadful privations, he who had lain in the lilies and fed on the roses of life. They thought of him, Colonel Kingsward's son, enlisted as a private soldier, in a crowded barrack-room. They thought of him wandering about the street, cold, perhaps hungry, without a shelter. The most dreadful images came before their inexperienced eyes. The old aunt who was their companion told them dreadful stories of family prodigals who disappeared and were never heard of again, and terror took hold of the girls' minds.

Their constant walk was to the station, with the idea that he might perhaps come as far as the village, and that there his heart might fail him. Except for that melancholy indulgence, they would not be out of the house at any time together, lest at that moment Charlie might arrive, and no one be there to welcome him. There was always one who ran to the door at every sound, scandalising the servant, who could never get there so fast but one of the young ladies was before him. They had endless conversations and consultations on the subject, forming a hundred plans as to how they should go forth into the world to seek for him, all rendered abortive by the reflection that they knew not where to go. Bee and Betty were very unhappy during these lingering, chilly days of early spring. The tranquillity of the family life seemed to be destroyed in a moment. Where was Charlie? Was there any news of Charlie? This was the question that filled their minds day and night.

Colonel Kingsward was not less affectionate, but he was more practical and experienced. He knew that now and then it does happen that a young man disappears, sinks under the stream, and goes, as people say, to the dogs, and is heard of no more—or, at least, only in a shipwrecked condition, the shame and trouble of his friends. It did not seem to him, at first, that there could be any such danger for his son. He anticipated nothing more than a few days' sullenness, perhaps in some friend's house, who would make cautious overtures and intercede for the rebellious but shame-stricken boy. When, however, the time passed on, and a longer interval than any judicious friend would permit had elapsed, a deep anxiety arose also in Colonel Kingsward's mind. The esclandre of an Oxford failure did not trouble him much, but, in view of Charlie's future career, he could not employ detectives, or advertise in the papers, or take any steps which might lead to a paragraph as to the anxiety of a distinguished family on account of a son who had disappeared. Colonel Kingsward might not be a very tender parent, but he was fully alive to the advantage of his children, and would allow no stigma to be attached to them which he could prevent. He went a great deal about London in these days, going into many a spot where a man of his dignity was out of place, with an anxious and troubled eye upon the crowds of young men, the familiars of these confused regions, among whom, however, no trace was to be found of his son.

Nobody ever knew how much the Colonel undertook, in how many strange scenes he found himself, or half of what he really did to recover Charlie, and save him from the consequences of his folly. The most devoted father could scarcely have done more, and his mind was almost as full of the prodigal as were the minds of the girls, who thought of so many grievous dangers, yet did not think of those that filled their father's mind. Colonel Kingsward went about everywhere, groping, saying not a word to betray his ignorance of Charlie's whereabouts. To those who had any right to know his family affairs, he explained that he had decided not to press Charlie to undergo any examination beyond what was necessary, that he had given up the thought of taking his degree, and was studying modern languages and international law, which were so much more likely to be useful to him. "He is a steady fellow—he has no vices," he said, "and I think it is wise to let him have his head." Colonel Kingsward was by nature a despotic man, and his friends were very glad to hear that he was, in respect to Charlie, so amiable—they said to each other that his wife's death had softened Kingsward, and what a good thing it was that he was behaving so judiciously about his son.

A pause like this in the life of a family—a period of darkness in which the life of one of its members is suspended, interrupted, as it were, in mid career, cut off, yet not with that touch of death which stills all anxieties—is always a difficult and miserable one. Some, and the number increases of these uncontrolled persons, cry out to earth and heaven, and make the lapse public and set all the world talking of their affairs. But Colonel Kingsward sternly put down even the tears of his young daughters.

"If you cannot keep a watch over yourselves before the servants, you had better leave the house," he said, all the more stern to them that he was soft to Charlie; but indeed it was not so much that he was soft to Charlie as that he was concerned and anxious about Charlie's career.

"Betty, I suppose, can go back to the Lyons' in Portman Square, and Bee—"

"If you think that I can go visiting, papa, and no one with the children, and poor Charlie—"

"I think—and, indeed, I know, that you can and will do what I think best for you," said Colonel Kingsward.

Bee looked up at him quickly and met her father's eyes. The two looked at each other suspiciously, almost fiercely. Bee saw in her father's look possibilities and dangers as yet undeveloped, mysteries which she divined and feared, yet neither could nor would have put into words, while he looked at her divining her divinations, defying unconsciously the suspicion which he could not have expressed any more than she.

"Let it be understood once for all," he said, "that the children have their nurses and governess, and that your presence is by no means indispensable to them. You are their eldest sister, you are not the mistress of the house. Nothing will happen to the children. In considering what is best for you—"

"Papa!" cried Bee, almost fiercely; but she did not pour out upon him that bitterness which had been collecting in her heart. She paused in time; but then added, "I have not asked you to consider what was best for me."

"That is enough to show that it is time for me to consider it," he said.

And then, once more their looks met, and clashed like the encounter of two armies. What did she suspect? What did he intend? They both breathed short, as if with the impulse of battle, but neither, even to themselves, could have answered that question. Colonel Kingsward cried "Take care, Bee!" as he went away, a by no means happy man, to his library, while she threw herself down upon a sofa, and—inevitable result in a girl of any such rising of passion—burst into tears.

"Bee," said the sensible Betty, "you ought not to speak like that to papa."

"I ought to be thankful that he has considered what was best for me, and spoilt my life!" cried Bee, through her tears. "Oh, it is very easy for you to speak. You are to go to the Lyons', where you wish to go—to be free of all anxiety—for what is Charlie to you but only your brother, and you know that you can't do him any good by making yourself miserable about him? And you will see Gerald Lyon, who is doing well at Cambridge, and listen to all the talk about him, and smile, and not hate him for being so smug and prosperous, while poor Charlie—"

"How unjust you are!" cried Betty, growing red and then pale. "It is not Gerald Lyon's fault that Charlie has not done well—even if I cared anything for Gerald Lyon."

"It is you who ought to take care," said Bee, "if papa thinks it necessary to consider what is best for you."

"There is nothing to consider," said Betty, with a little movement of her hands.

"But it can never be so bad for you," said Bee, with a tone of regret. "Never! To think that my life should be ruined and all ended for the sake of a woman—a woman—who has now ruined Charlie, and whom papa—oh, papa!" she cried, with a tone indescribable of exasperation and scorn and contempt.

"What is it about papa? You look at each other, you and he, like two tigers. You have got the same dreadful eyes. Yes, they are dreadful eyes; they give out fire. I wonder often that they don't make a noise like an explosion. And Bee, you said yourself that there was something else. You never would have given in to papa, but there was something of your own that parted you from Aubrey—for ever. You said so, Bee—when his mother—"

"Is there any need for bringing in any gentleman's name?" cried Bee, with the dignity of a dowager. And then, ignoring her own rule, she burst forth, "What I have got against him is nothing to anyone—but that Aubrey Leigh should be insulted and rejected and turned away from our door, and that my heart should be broken because of a woman whom papa and Charlie—whom papa—! He writes to her, and she writes to him—he tells her everything—he consults her about us, us, my mother's children! And yet it was on her account that Aubrey Leigh was turned from the door—Oh, if you think I can bear that, you must think me more than flesh and blood!" Bee cried, the tears adding to the fire and sparkle of her blazing eyes.

"It isn't very nice," said little Betty, sagely, "but I am not so sure that it was her fault, for if you had stuck to Aubrey as you meant to do at first, your heart would not have been broken, and if Charlie had not been very silly, a person of that age could not have done him any harm; and then papa—. What can she do to papa? I suppose he thinks as she is old he may write to her as a friend and ask her advice. There is not any harm that I can see in that."

Bee was too much agitated to make any reply to this. She resumed again, after a pause, as if Betty had not spoken: "He writes to her, and she writes to him, just as she did to Charlie, for I have seen them both—long letters, with that ridiculous "Laura," and a big L, as if she were a girl. You can see them, if you like, at breakfast, when he reads them instead of his papers, and smiles to himself when he is reading them, and looks—ridiculous"—cried Bee, in her indignation. "Ridiculous! as if he were young too; a man who is father of all of us; and not much more than a year ago—. Oh, if I were not to speak I think the very trees would, and the bushes in the shrubbery! It is more than anyone can bear."

"You are making up a story," said Betty, wonderingly. "I don't know what you mean." Then she cried, carrying the war into the enemy's country, "Oh, Bee, if you had not given him up, if you had been faithful to him!—now we should have had somebody to consult with, somebody that could have gone and looked for poor Charlie; for we are only two girls, and what can we do?"

Bee did not make any reply, but looked at her sister with startled eyes.

"Mamma was never against Aubrey Leigh," said Betty, pursuing her advantage. "She never would have wished you to give him up. And it is all your own doing, not papa's doing, or anyone's. If I had ever cared for him I never, never should have given him up; and then we should have had as good as another brother, that could have gone into the world and hunted everywhere and brought Charlie home."

The argument was taken up at hazard, a chance arrow lying in the young combatant's way, without intention—but it went straight to its mark.

CHAPTER IV

The house that had been so peaceful was thus full of agitation and disturbance, the household, anxious and alarmed, turning their weapons upon each other, to relieve a little the gnawing of that suspense which they were so unaccustomed to bear. It was true what Bee's keen and sharply aroused observation had convinced her, that Colonel Kingsward was in correspondence with Miss Lance, and that her letters were very welcome to him, and read with great interest. He threw down the paper after he had made a rush through its contents, and read eagerly the long sheets of paper, upon which the great L, stamped at the head of every page, could be read on the other side of the table. How did that woman know the days he was to be at home, that her letters should always come on those mornings and never at any other time? Bee almost forgot her troubles, those of the family in respect to Charlie, and those which were her very own, in her passionate hatred and distrust of the new correspondent to whom Colonel Kingsward, like his son, had opened his heart.

He was not, naturally, a man given to correspondence. His letters to his wife, in those days which now seemed so distant, had been models of concise writing. His opinions, or rather verdicts, upon things great and small had been conveyed in terse sentences, very much to the purpose; deliverances not of his way of thinking, but of the unalterable dogmas that were to rule the family life; and her replies, though diffuse, were always more or less regulated by her consciousness of the little time there would be given to them, and the necessity of making every explanation as brief as possible—not to worry papa, who had so much to do.

Why it was that he found the long letters, which he read with a certain defiant pride in the presence of his daughters at the breakfast table, so agreeable, it would be difficult to tell. They were very carefully adapted to please him, it is true; and they were what are called clever letters—such letters as clever women write, with a faux air of brilliancy which deceives both the writer and the recipient, making the one feel herself a Sevigné and the other a hero worthy the exercise of such powers. And there was something very novel in this sudden inroad of sentimental romance into an existence never either sentimental or romantic, which had fallen into the familiar calm of family life so long ago with a wife, who though sweet and fair enough to delight any man, had become in reality only the chief of his vassals, following every indication of his will, when not eagerly watching an opportunity of anticipating his wishes. His new friend treated the Colonel in a very different way. She expounded her views of life with all the adroitness of a mind experienced in the treatment of those philosophies which touch the questions of sex, the differences between a man's and a woman's view, the sentiment which can be carried into the most simple subjects. There is nothing that can give more entertaining play of argument, or piquancy of intercourse, than this mode of correspondence when cleverly carried out, and Miss Laura Lance was a mistress of all its methods. It was all entirely new to Colonel Kingsward. He was as much enchanted with it as his son had been, and thought the writer as brilliant, as original, as poor Charlie had done, who had no way of knowing better. The Colonel's head, which generally had been occupied by professional or public matters—by the intrigues of the service or the incompetencies of the Department—now found a much more interesting private subject of thought. He was a man full of anxiety and annoyance at this particular crisis of his career, and his correspondent was by way of sharing his anxiety to the utmost and even blaming herself as the cause of it; yet she contrived to amuse him, to bring a smile, to touch a lighter key, to relieve the tension of his mind from time to time, without ever allowing him to feel that the chief subject of their correspondence was out of her thoughts. He got no relief of this description at home, where the girls' anxious questions about Charlie, their eagerness to know what had been done, seemed to upbraid him with indifference, as if he were not doing everything that was possible. Miss Lance knew better the dangers that were being run, the real difficulties of the case, than these inexperienced chits of children; but she knew also that a man's mind requires relief, and that, in point of fact, the Colonel's health, strength and comfort, were of more importance than many Charlie's. This was a thing that had to be understood, not said, and the Colonel indeed was as anxious and concerned about Charlie as it was almost possible to be. He did not form dreadful pictures as Bee and Betty did of what the boy might be suffering. The boy deserved to suffer, and this consideration, had he dwelt upon it, would have afforded a certain satisfaction. But what did make him wretched was the fear of any exposure, the mention in public of anything that might injure his son's career. An opportunity was already dawning of getting him an appointment upon which the Colonel had long kept his eye, and which would be of double importance at present as sending him out of the country and into new scenes. But of what use were all a father's careful arrangements if they were thus balked by the perversity of the boy?

Things were still in this painful suspense when Miss Lance announced to Colonel Kingsward her arrival in town. She described to him how it was that she was coming.

"My friend is absent with her son till after Easter, and I am understood to be fond of town, and am coming to spend a week or two to see the first of the season, the pictures, &c., as well as a few friends whom I still keep up, the relics of brighter and younger days—this is the reason I give, but you will easily understand, dear Colonel Kingsward, that there is another reason far more near to my heart. Your poor boy! Or may I for once say our poor boy? For you are aware that I have never ceased to upbraid myself for what has happened, and that I shall always bear a mother's heart to Charlie, dear fellow, to whom, in wishing him nothing but good, I have been so unfortunate as to do such dreadful wrong. Every word you say about your hopes for him, and the great chance which he is so likely to miss, cuts me to the heart. And it has occurred to me that there are some places in which he may have been heard of, to which I could myself go, or where I might take you if you wished, which you would not yourself be likely to know. I wish I had thought of them before. I come up now full of hope that we may hear something and find a reliable clue. I shall be in George Street, Hanover Square, a place which is luckily in the way for everything. Please come and see me. I hope you will not think I am presuming in endeavouring to solve a difficulty for which I am, alas, alas! partially to blame. To assure me of this at least if no more, come, do come to see me to-morrow, Tuesday afternoon. I shall do nothing till I have your approval."

This letter had an exciting effect upon the Colonel, more than anything he had known for years. He held it before him, yielding himself up to this pleasurable sensation for some minutes after he had read it. The Easter recess had left London empty, and he had been deprived of some of the ordinary social solaces which, though they increased the difficulty of keeping his son's disappearance a secret, still broke the blank of his suspense and made existence possible. Hard to bear was the point blank shock which he had sometimes received, as when an indiscreet but influential friend suddenly burst upon him, "I don't see your son's name in the Oxford lists, Kingsward." "No," the Colonel had replied, with a countenance from which all expression had been dismissed, "we thought it better that he should keep to his special studies." "Quite right, quite right," answered that great official, for what is a mere degree to F. O.? Even to have such things as this said to him, with the chance of putting in a response, was better than the stagnation, in which a man is so apt to feel that all kinds of whispers are circulating in respect to the one matter which it is his interest to conceal.

And his heart, though it was a middle-aged, and no longer nimble organ given to leaping, jumped up in his breast when he read his letter. There was the possible clue which it was good to hear of—and there was the listener to whom he could tell everything, who took such an entire and flattering share in his anxieties, with whom there was no need to invent excuses, or to conceal anything. Perhaps there were other reasons, too, which he did not put into words. The image which had dazzled him at Oxford rose again before his eyes. It was an image which had already often visited him. One of the handsomest women he had ever seen, and so flattering, so confidential, so deeply impressed by himself, so candid and anxious to blame herself, to place herself in his hands. He went back to town with agreeable instead of painful anticipations. To share one's cares is always an alleviation—to be able openly to take a friend's advice. The girls, to whom alone he could be perfectly open on this matter, were such little fools that he had ceased to discuss it with them, if, indeed, he had ever discussed it. And to nobody else could he speak on the subject at all. The opportunity of pouring forth all his speculations and alarms, of hearing the suggestions of another mind—and such a mind as hers—of finding a new clue, was balm to his angry, annoyed and excited spirit. There were other douceurs involved, which were not absent from his thoughts. The pleasure of the woman's society, who was so flatteringly pleased with his, her mature beauty, which had so much attraction in it, the look of her eyes, which said more than words, the touch—laid upon his for a moment with so much eloquent expression, appeal, sympathy, consolation, provocation—of her beautiful hands. All this was in the Colonel's mind. He had scarcely known what was the touch of a woman's hand, at least in this way, during the course of his long, calm domestic life. He had been very fond of his wife, of course, and very tender, as well as he knew how, during her illness, though entirely unconscious of how much he demanded from her even in the course of that illness. But this was utterly different, apart from everything he had ever known. Friendship—that friendship between man and woman which has been the subject of so much sentimental controversy. Somebody whom Miss Lance had quoted to him, some great man in Oxford, had said it was the only real friendship; many others, amongst whom Colonel Kingsward himself had figured when at any moment so ridiculous an argument had crossed his path, denounced it as a mere unfounded fiction to conceal other sentiments. Dolts! It was the Oxford great man who was in the right of it. The only friendship!—with sweetness in it which no man could give, a more entire confidence, a more complete sympathy. He knew that he could say things to Laura—Miss Lance—which he could say to no man, and that a look from her eyes would do more to strengthen him than oceans of kind words from lips which would address him as "old fellow." He had her image before him all the time as he went up in the train; it went with him into the decorous dulness of his office, and when he left his work an hour earlier than usual his steps were as light as a young man's. He had not felt so much exhilaration of spirit since—; but he could scarcely go back to a date on which his bosom's lord had sat so lightly on his throne. Truth to tell, Colonel Kingsward had fallen on evil days. Even the course of his ordinary existence, when he had gone through life with his pretty wife by his side, dining out constantly, going everywhere, though enjoyable in its way, and with the satisfaction of keeping up to the right mark, had not been exciting. She no doubt told for a great deal in his happiness, but there were no risks, no excitements, and not as much as the smart of an occasional quarrel between them. He had known what to expect of her in every emergency; there was nothing novel to be looked for, no unaccustomed flavour in anything she was likely to do or say. He did not make this comparison consciously, for indeed there was no comparison at all between his late wife (he called her so already in his mind) and Miss Lance—not the slightest comparison! The latter was a far more piquant thing—a friend—and the most delightful friend, surely, that ever man had!

He found her in a little drawing-room on the first floor of what looked very much like an ordinary London lodging-house; but within it had changed its character completely, and had become, though in a different, more subtle way than that of the drawing-room in Oxford, the bower of Laura, a special habitation marked with her very name, like the notepaper on her table. He could not for the first moment avoid a bewildering idea that it was the same room in which he had seen her in Oxford transported thither. There seemed the same pictures on the walls, the same writing-table, or at least one arranged in precisely the same way, the same chairs placed two together for conversation. What a wonderful creature she was, thus to put the stamp of her own being upon everything she touched. Once more he had to wait for a minute or two before she came, but she made no apology for her delay. She came in with her hand extended, with an air of sympathy yet satisfaction at the sight of him which went to Colonel Kingsward's heart. If she had been sorry only it would have displeased him, as showing a mind occupied wholly with Charlie, but the delicate mingling of pleasure with concern was exactly what the Colonel felt to be most fit.

"I am so glad to see you," she said. "How kind of you to come so soon, to pay such prompt attention to my wish."

"Considering that it was my own wish," he said, "and what I desired most, I should say how good of you to come, but I can't venture to hope that it was entirely for me."

"It was very much for you, Colonel Kingsward. You know what blame I take to myself for all that has happened. And I think, perhaps, I may have it in my power to make some inquiries that would not suggest themselves. But we must talk of this after. In the meantime, I can't but think first of you. What an ordeal for you—what weary work! But what a pull over us you men have! You keep your great spirit and command over yourself through everything, while, whatever little trouble we may have, it shows immediately. Oh," said Miss Lance, clasping her hands, "a calm strong man is a sight which it elevates one only to see."

"You give me far too much credit. One is obliged to keep a good face to the world. I don't approve of people who wash their dirty linen in public."

"Don't try to make yourself little with all this commonplace reasoning. You need not explain yourself to me, dear Colonel Kingsward. I flatter myself that I have the gift of understanding, if nothing else."

"A great many things else," he said; "and indeed my keeping up in this emergency has been greatly helped by your great friendship and moral support. I don't know what you have done to this room," he added, changing the theme quickly, "did you bring it with you? It is not a mere room in London—it is your room. I should have known it among a thousand."

"What a delightful compliment," she said. "I am so glad you think so, for it is one of the things I pride myself on. I think I can always make even a lodging-house look a bit like home."

"It looks like you," he repeated. "I don't notice such matters much, but no one could help seeing. And I hope you are to be here for some time, and that if I can be of any use—"

"Oh! Colonel Kingsward, don't hold out such flattering hopes. You of use! Of course, to a lone woman in town you would be far more than of use—you would simply be a tower of strength. But I do not come here to make use of you. I come—"

"You could not give me greater pleasure than by making use of me. I am not going much into society, my house is not open—my girls are too young to take the responsibilities of a season upon themselves; but anything that a single individual can do to be of service—"

"Your dear girls—how I should like to see them, to be able to take them about a little, to make up to those poor children as far as a stranger could! But I can scarcely hope that you would trust them to me after the trouble I have helped to bring on you all. Dear Colonel Kingsward, your chivalrous offer will make all the difference in my life. If you will give me your arm sometimes, on a rare occasion—"

"As often as you please—and the oftener the more it will please me," he cried, in tones full of warmth and eagerness. Miss Lance raised her grateful eyes to him full of unspeakable things. She made no further reply except by one of those light touches upon his arm less than momentary, if that were possible, like the brush of a wing, or an ethereal contact of ideas.

And then she said gravely, "Now about that poor, dear boy; we must find him, oh, we must find him. I have thought of several places where he may have been seen. Do you know that I met him once by chance in town last year? It was at the Academy, where I was with some artist friends. I introduced him to them, and you know there is great freedom among them, and they have a great charm for young men. I think some of them may have seen him. I have put myself in communication with them."

"I would not for a moment," said the Colonel, somewhat stiffly, "consent to burden you with inquiries of this kind!"

"You do not think," she said, sweetly, "that I would do anything, or say anything to compromise him or you?"

The Colonel looked at her with the strangest sudden irritation. "I was not thinking either of him or myself. Why should you receive men, who must be entirely out of your way, for our sakes?"

"Oh," she said, with a soft laugh, "you are afraid that I may compromise myself." She rose with an unspoken impulse, which made him rise also, in spite of himself, with a feeling of unutterable downfall, and the sense of being dismissed. "Don't be afraid for me, Colonel Kingsward, I beg. I shall not compromise anyone." Then she turned with a sudden illumination of a smile. "Come back and see me to-morrow, and you shall hear what I have found out."

And he went away humbly, relieved yet mortified, not holding his head as high as when he came, but already longing for to-morrow, when he might come back.

CHAPTER V

Colonel Kingsward had been flattered, he had been pleased. He had felt himself for a moment one of the exceptional men in whom women find an irresistible attraction, and then he had been put down and dismissed with the calmest decision, with a peremptoriness which nobody in his life had ever used to him. All these sweetnesses, and then to be, as it were, huddled out of doors the moment he said a word which was not satisfactory to that imperial person! He could not get it out of his mind during the evening nor all the night through, during which it occurred to him whenever he woke, as a prevailing thought does. And he had been right, too. To send for men, any kind of men, artists whom she herself described as having so much freedom in their ways, and have interviews with them, was a thing to which he had a good right to object. That is, her friend had a right to object to it—her friend who took the deepest interest in her and all that she was doing. That it was for Charlie's advantage made really no difference. This gave a beautiful and admirable motive, but then all her motives were beautiful and admirable, and it must be necessary in some cases to defend her against the movements of her own good heart. Evidently she did not sufficiently think of what the world would say, nor, indeed, of what was essentially right; for that a woman of her attractions, still young, living independently in rooms of her own, should receive artists indiscriminately, nay, send for them, admit them to sit perhaps for an hour with her, with no chaperon or companion, was a thing that could not be borne. This annoyance almost drove Charlie out of Colonel Kingsward's head. He felt that when he went to her next day he must, with all the precautions possible, speak his mind upon this subject. A woman with such attractions, really a young woman, alone; nobody could have more need of guarding against evil tongues. And artists were proverbially an unregulated, free-and-easy race, with long hair and defective linen, not men to be privileged with access under any circumstances to such a woman. Unquestionably he must deliver his soul on that subject for her own sake.

He thought about it all the morning, how to do it best. It relieved his mind about Charlie. Charlie! Charlie was only a young fellow after all, taking his own way, as they all did, never thinking of the anxiety he gave his family. And no doubt he would turn up of his own accord when he was tired of it. That she should depart from the traditions which naturally are the safeguards of ladies for the sake of a silly boy, who took so little trouble about the peace of mind of his family, was monstrous. It was a thing which he could not permit to be.

When he went into his private room at his office, Colonel Kingsward found a card upon his table which increased the uneasiness in his mind, though he could not have told why. He took it up with great surprise and anger. "Mr. Aubrey Leigh." He supposed it must have been a card left long ago, when Aubrey Leigh was Bee's suitor, and had come repeatedly, endeavouring to shake her father's determination. He looked at it contemptuously, and then pitched it into the fire.

What a strange perversity there is in these inanimate things! It seemed as if some malicious imp must have replaced that card there on that very morning to disturb him.

Colonel Kingsward did not remember how it was that the name, the sacred name, of Miss Lance was associated with that of Aubrey Leigh. He had been much surprised, as well as angry, at the manner in which Bee repeated that name, when she heard it first, with a vindictive jealousy (these words came instinctively to his mind) which was not comprehensible. He had refused indignantly to allow that she had ever heard the name before. Nevertheless, her cry awakened a vague association in his mind. Something or other, he could not recollect what, of connection, of suggestion, was in the sound. He threw Aubrey's card into the fire, and endeavoured to dismiss all thought on the subject. But it was a difficult thing to do. It is to be feared that during those morning hours the work which Colonel Kingsward usually executed with so much exactitude, never permitting, as he himself stated, private matters—even such as the death of his wife or the disappearance of his son—to interfere with it, was carried through with many interruptions and pauses for thought, and at the earliest possible moment was laid aside for that other engagement which had nothing to do either with the office or the Service, though it was, he flattered himself, a duty, and one of the most lofty kind.

To save a noble creature, if possible, from the over generosity of her own heart; to convince her that such proceedings were inappropriate, inconsistent with her dignity, as well as apt to give occasion for the adversary to blaspheme—this was the mission which inspired him. If he thought of a natural turning towards himself, the friend of friends, in respect to whom the precautions he enforced were unnecessary, in consequence of these remonstrances, he kept it carefully in the background of his thoughts. It was a duty. This beautiful, noble woman, all frankness and candour, had taken the part of an angel in endeavouring to help him in his trouble. Could he permit her to sully even the tip of a wing of that generous effort. Certainly not! On the contrary, it became doubly his duty to protect her in every way.

This time Miss Lance was in her drawing-room, seated in one of the pair of chairs which were arranged for intimate conversation. She did not rise, but held out her hand to him, with a soft impulse towards the other—in which Colonel Kingsward accordingly seated himself, with a solemnity upon his brow which she had no difficulty in interpreting, quick-witted as she was. She did not loose a shade upon that forehead, a note of additional gravity in his voice. She knew as well as he did the duty which he had come to perform. And she was a woman—not only quick-witted and full of a definite aim, but one who took real pleasure in her own dexterity, and played her rôle with genuine enjoyment. She allowed him to open the conversation with much dignified earnestness, and even to begin, "My dear Miss Lance," his countenance charged with warning before she cut the ground from under his feet in the lightest, yet most complete way.

"I know you are going to say something very serious when you adopt that tone, so please let me discharge my mind first. Mrs. Revel kindly came to me after you left yesterday, and she has made every inquiry—indeed, as she compelled me to go back with her to dinner, I saw for myself—"

"Mrs. Revel?" said the Colonel.

"Didn't you know he was married? Oh, yes, to a great friend of mine, a dear little woman. It is in their house I meet my artists, whom I told you of. Tuesday is her night, and they were all there. I was able to make my investigations without any betrayal. But I am very, very sorry to say, dear Colonel Kingsward, equally without any effect."

"Without any effect," Colonel Kingsward repeated, confused. He was not so quick-witted as she was, and it took him some time to make his way through these mazes. Revel, the painter, was a name, indeed, that he had heard vaguely, but his wife, so suddenly introduced, and her "night," and the people described as my artists, wound him in webs of bewilderment through which it was very difficult to guide his steps. It became apparent to him, however, after a moment, that whatever those things might mean, the ground had been cut from under his feet. "Does Mrs. Revel know?" he added after a moment, in his bewilderment.

"Know—our poor dear boy? Oh, yes; I took him there—in my foolish desire to do the best I could for him, and thinking that to see other circles outside of his own was good for a young man. I couldn't take him the round of the studios, you know—could I? But I took him to the Revels. She is a charming little woman, a woman whom I am very fond of, and—more extraordinary still, don't you think, Colonel Kingsward?—who is fond of me."

The Colonel was not up to the mark in this emergency. He did not give the little compliment which is expected after such a speech. He sat dumb, a dull, middle-aged blush rising over his face. He had no longer anything to say; instead of the serious, even impassioned remonstrance which he was about to address to her, he could only murmur a faint assent, a question without meaning. And in place of the generous, imprudent creature, following her own hasty impulses, disregarding the opinion of the world, whom he had expected to find, here was female dignity in person, regulated by all the nicest laws of propriety. He was struck dumb—the ground was cut from beneath his feet.

"This is only an interruption on my part. You were going to say something to me? And something serious? I prize so much everything you say that I must not lose it. Pray say it now, dear Colonel

Kingsward. Have I done something you don't like? I am ready to accept even blame—though you know what women are in that way, always standing out that they are right—from you."

Colonel Kingsward looked at her, helpless, still without a word to say. There was surely a laughing demon in her eyes which saw through and through him and knew the trouble in his mind; but her face was serious, appealing, a little raised towards him, waiting for his words as if her fate hung upon them. The colour rose over his middle-aged countenance to the very hair which was beginning to show traces of white over his high forehead.

"Blame!" he stammered, scarcely knowing what he said, "I hope you don't think me quite a fool."

"What," she cried, picking him up as it were on the end of her lance, holding him out to the scorn—if not of the world, yet of himself. "Do you think so little of a woman, Colonel Kingsward, that you would not take the trouble to find fault with her? Ah! Don't be so hard! You would not be a fool if you did that— you should find that I would take it with gratitude, accept it, be guided by it. Believe me, I am worthy, if you think me in the wrong, to be told so—I am, indeed I am!"

Were these tears in her fine eyes? She made them look as if they were, and filled him with a compunction and a shame of his own superficial judgment impossible to put into words.

"I—think you wrong!" he said, stammering and faltering. "I would as soon think that—heaven was wrong. I—blame you! Dear Miss Laura, how, how can you imagine such a thing? I should be a miserable idiot indeed if—"

"Come," she said, "I begin to think you didn't mean—now that you have called me by my name."

"I beg you a thousand pardons. I—I—It was a slip of the tongue. It was—from the signature to your letters—which is somehow so like you—"

"Yes," she said. "It pleases me very much that you should think so—more like me than Lance. Lance! What a name! My mother made a mésalliance. I don't give up my father, poor dear, though he has saddled me with such a family—but Laura is me, whereas Lance is only—an accident."

"An accident that may be removed," he said, involuntarily. It was a thing that might be said to any unmarried woman, a conventional sort of half compliment, which custom would have permitted him to put in even stronger terms—but to her! When he had said it horror seized his soul.

"No," she said, gently shaking her head. "No. At my age one does not recover from an accident like that; one must bear the scar all one's days. And you really had nothing to find fault with me about?"

"How monstrous!" he cried, "to entertain such a thought." Then, for he was really uneasy in his sense of guilt, he plunged into a new snare. "My little daughter, Betty," he said, "is coming to town to-day to visit some friends in Portman Square. I wonder if I might bring her to see you."

"Your daughter!" cried Miss Lance, clasping her hands, "a thing I did not venture to ask—the very first desire of my heart. Your daughter! I would go anywhere to see her. If you will be so nice, so sweet, so kind as to bring her, Colonel Kingsward!"

"I shall, indeed, to-morrow. It will do her good to see you. At her susceptible age the very sight of such a woman as you—"

"No compliments," she cried, "if I am not to be blamed I must not be praised either—and I deserve it much less. Is she the eldest?" There was a gleam under her half-dropped eyelids which the Colonel was vaguely aware of but did not understand.

"The second," he said. "My eldest girl is Bee, in many respects a stronger character than her sister, but on the other hand—"

"I know," said Miss Lance, "a little wilful, fond of her own way and her own opinion. Oh, that is a good fault in a girl! When they are a little chastened they turn out the finest women. But I understand what a man must feel for this little sweet thing who has not begun to have a will of her own."

It was not perhaps a very perfect characterisation of Betty, but still it flattered him to see how she entered into his thoughts. "I think you understand everything," he said.

CHAPTER VI

It was not with any intention, but solely to deliver himself from the dilemma in which he found himself—the inconceivable error he had made, imagining that it was necessary to censure, however gently, and warn against too much freedom of action, a woman so absolutely above reproach, and so full of ladylike dignity as Miss Lance—that Colonel Kingsward had named the name of Betty, his little daughter, just arrived in that immaculate stronghold of the correct and respectable Portman Square. He was a little uneasy about it when he thought of it afterwards. He was not sure that he desired even Betty to be aware of his intimacy with Miss Lance. He felt that her youthful presence would change, in some degree, the character of his relations with the enchantress who was stealing his wits away. The kind of conversation that had arisen so naturally between them, the sentiment, the confidences, the singular strain of mutual understanding which he felt, with mingled pride and bashfulness—bashfulness sat strangely upon the much-experienced Colonel, yet such was his feeling—to exist between Laura and himself, must inevitably sustain certain modifications under the sharp eyes of the child. She would not understand that subtle but strong link of friendship. He would require to be more distant, to treat his exquisite friend more like an ordinary acquaintance while under the inspection of Betty, even though he was perfectly assured that Betty knew nothing about such matters. And what, then, would Laura say? Confident as she was in her own perfect honour and candour, would she understand the subdued manner, the more formal address which would be necessary in the presence of the child? It was true that she understood everything without a word said; but then her own entire innocence of any motive but those of heavenly kindness and friendship might induce her to laugh at his precautions. Was it, perhaps, because he felt his motives to be not unmingled that the Colonel felt this? Anyhow, the introduction of Betty, whom he had snatched at in his haste to save him from the consequences of his own folly, would be a trouble to the intercourse which, as it was, was so consolatory and so sweet.

It must be added that Miss Lance, before he left her, had been very consolatory to him on the subject of Charlie, which, though always lying at the bottom of his thoughts, had begun in the midst of these new developments to weigh upon him less, perhaps, than it was natural it should have done. She had suggested that Charlie had friends in Scotland, that he had most probably gone there to avoid for a time his father's wrath, that in all probability he was enjoying himself, and very well cared for, putting off from day to day the necessity of writing.

"He never was, I suppose, much of a correspondent?" she said.

"No," Colonel Kingsward had replied, doubtfully; for indeed there never had been anything at all to call correspondence between him and his son. Charlie had written to his mother, occasionally to his sisters, but to his father, save when he wanted money, scarcely at all.

"Then this is what has happened," said Laura; "he has gone off to be as far out of the way as possible. He is fishing in Loch Tay—or he is playing golf somewhere—you know his habits."

"And so it seems do you," said the Colonel, a little jealous of his son.

"Oh, you know how a boy chatters of everything he does and likes."

Colonel Kingsward nodded his head gloomily. He did not know how boys chattered—no boy had ever chattered to him; but he accepted with a moderate satisfaction the fact that she, Laura, from whom he felt that he himself could have no secret, had taken, and did take, the trouble of turning the heart even—of a boy—outside in.

"Depend upon it," said Miss Lance, "that is where he has gone, and he has not meant to make you anxious. Perhaps he thinks you have never discovered that he had left Oxford, and he has meant to write day by day. Don't you know how one does that? It is a little difficult to begin, and one says, 'To-morrow,' and then 'To-morrow'; and the time flies on. Dear Colonel Kingsward, you will find that all this time he is quite happy on Loch Tay." She held out her hand to emphasise these words, and the Colonel, though all unaccustomed to such signs of enthusiasm, kissed that hand which held out comfort to him. It was a beautiful hand, so soft, like velvet, so yielding and flexible in his, and yet so firm in its delicate pressure. He went away with his head slightly turned, and the blood coursing through his veins. But when he thought of little Betty he dropped down, down into a blank of decorum and commonplace. Before Betty he certainly could not kiss any lady's hand. He would have to shake hands with Laura as he did with old Mrs. Lyon in Portman Square, who, indeed, was a much older friend. This thought gave him a little feeling of contrariety and uneasiness in the contemplation of his promise to take his little girl to George Street, Hanover Square.

And next morning when he went into his office, Colonel Kingsward's annoyance and indignation could not be expressed when he found once more upon his writing-table, placed in a conspicuous position so that he could not overlook it, the card of Mr. Aubrey Leigh. Who had fished it out of the waste paper basket and placed it there? He rang his bell hastily to overwhelm his attendant with angry reproof. He could not have told himself, why it made him so angry to see that card. It looked like some vulgar interference with his most private affairs.

"Where did you find this card?" he said, angrily, "and why is it replaced here? I threw it into the fire—or somewhere, yesterday—and here it is again as if the man had called to-day."

"The gentleman did call, sir, yesterday."

"What?" cried Colonel Kingsward, in a voice like a trumpet; but the man stood his ground.

"The gentleman did call, sir, yesterday. He has called two or three times; once when you were in the country. He seemed very anxious to see you. I said two o'clock for a general thing, but you have been leaving the office earlier for a day or two."

"You are very impertinent to say anything of the kind, or to give anyone information of my private movements; see that it never occurs again. And as for this gentleman," he held up his card for a moment, looked at it contemptuously and then pitched it once more into the fireplace, "be so good as to understand that I will not see him, whether he comes at two or at any other hour."

"Am I to tell him so, sir?" said the man, annoyed.

"Of course you are to tell him so; and mind you don't bring me any message or explanation. I will not see him—that is enough; now you can go."

"Shall I—say you're too busy, Colonel, or just going out, or engaged—?"

"No!" shouted Colonel Kingsward, with a force of breath which blew the attendant away like a strong wind. The Colonel returned to his work and his correspondence with an irritation and annoyance which even to himself seemed beyond the occasion. Bee's old lover, he supposed, had taken courage to make another attempt; but nothing would induce him to change his former decision. He would not hear a word, not a word! A kind of panic mingled in his hasty impulse of rage. He would not so much as see the fellow—give him any opportunity of renewing—Was it his suit to Bee? Was it something else indefinite behind? Colonel Kingsward did not very well know, but he was determined on one thing—not to allow the presence of this intruder, not to hear a word that he had to say.

And then about Betty—that was annoying too, but he had promised to do it, and to break his word to Laura was a thing he could not do. Laura—Miss Laura, if she pleased, though that is not a usual mode of address—but not Lance—how right she was! The name of Lance did not suit her at all, and yet how just and sweet all the same. Her mother had made a mésalliance, but there was no pettiness about her. She held by her father, though she was aware of his inferiority. And then he thought of her as she shook her head gently, and smiled at his awkward stumbling suggestion that the accident of the name was not irremediable. "At my age,"—what was her age? The most delightful, the most fascinating of ages, whatever it was. Not the silly girlhood of Bee and Betty, but something far more entrancing, far more charming. These thoughts interfered greatly with his correspondence, and made the mass of foreign newspapers, and the military intelligence from all over the world, which it was his business to look over, appear very dull, uninteresting and confused. He rose hastily after a while, and took his hat and sallied forth to Portman Square, where he was expected to luncheon. He was relieved, on the whole, to be thus legitimately out of the way in case that fellow should have the audacity to call again.

"I want you to come out with me, Betty," he said, after that meal, which was very solemn, serious and prolonged, but very dull and not appetising. "I want to take you to see a friend—"

"Oh, papa! we are going to—Mrs. Lyon was going to take me to see Mr. Revel's picture before he sends it in."

"To-morrow will do, my dear, equally well, if your papa wants you to go anywhere."

"Mr. Revel's picture? He is precisely a friend of the friend I am going to take you to see." For a moment Colonel Kingsward wavered thinking how much more agreeable it would be to have his interview with Laura undisturbed by the presence of this little chit with her sharp eyes. But he was a soldier and faithful to his consignee. "If it will do as well to-morrow, and will not derange Mrs. Lyon's plans, I should like you to come now."

"Run and get ready, Betty," cried the old lady, to whom obedience was a great quality, "and there will still be time to go there, if you are not very long, when you come back."

The Colonel felt as if his foot was upon more solid ground; not that any doubt of Laura had ever been in his mind—but yet—He had not suspected the existence of any link between her and Portman Square.

"Mr. Revel is a very good painter, I suppose?" he said.

"A great painter, we all think; and beginning to be really acknowledged in the art world," said the old lady, who liked it to be known that she knew a great deal about pictures, and was herself considered to have some authority in that interesting sphere.

"And—hasn't he a wife? I think I heard someone talking of his wife."

"Yes, a dear little woman!" cried Mrs. Lyon. "Her Tuesdays are the most pleasant parties. We always go when we are able. Ah! here is Betty, like a little rose. Now, acknowledge you are proud to have a little thing like that, Colonel, to walk with you through the park on a fine day like this?"

Colonel Kingsward looked at Betty. She was a pretty little blooming creature. He did not regard her with any enthusiasm, and yet she was a creditable creature enough to belong to one. He gave a little nod of approving indifference. Betty was very much admired at Portman Square—from Gerald, who kept up an artillery of glances across the big table, to the old butler, who called her attention specially to any dish that was nicer than usual, and carried meringues to her twice, she was the object of everybody's regards. Her father did not, naturally, look at her from the same point of view, but he was sufficiently pleased with her appearance. He was pleased, too, exhilarated, he could scarcely tell why, by the fact that Mrs. Lyon knew the painter's wife and spoke of her as a "dear little woman," the very words Laura had used. Did he require any guarantee that Laura herself was of the same order, knew the same sort of people as his other friends? Had such a question been put to him, the Colonel would have knocked the man down who made it, as in days when duelling was possible he would have called him out—But yet— at all events it gave him much satisfaction that the British matron in the shape of Mrs. Lyon spoke no otherwise of the lady whom for one terrible moment of delusion he had intended to warn against intercourse, too little guarded, with such equivocal men as artists. He shuddered when he thought of that extraordinary aberration.

"Who is it, papa, we are going to see?" said Betty's little voice by his side.

"It is a lady—who has taken a great interest in your brother."

"Oh, papa, that I should not have asked that the first thing! Have you any news?"

"Nothing that I can call news, but I think I may say I have reason to believe that Charlie has gone up to the north to the Mackinnons. That does not excuse him for having left us in this anxiety; but the idea, which did not occur to me till yesterday, has relieved my mind."

"To the Mackinnons!" said Betty, doubtfully, "but then I heard—" She stopped herself suddenly, and added after a moment, "How strange, papa, if he is there, that none of them should have written."

"It is strange; but perhaps when you think of all things, not so very strange. He probably has not explained the circumstances to them, and they will think that he has written; they would not feel it necessary—why should they?—to let us know of his arrival. That, as a matter of course, they would expect him to have done. I don't think, on the whole, it is at all strange; on his part inexcusable, but not to be expected from them."

"But, papa!" cried Betty.

"What is it?" he said, almost crossly. "I don't mind saying," he added, "that even for him there may be excuses—if such folly can ever be excused. He never writes to me in a general way, and it would not be a pleasant letter to write; and no doubt he has put it off from day to day, intending always to do it to-morrow—and every day would naturally make it more difficult." Thus he went on repeating unconsciously all the suggestions that had been made to him. "Remember, Betty," he said, "as soon as you see that you have done anything wrong, always make a clean breast of it at once; the longer you put it off the more difficult you will find it to do."

"Yes, papa," said little Betty, with great doubt in her tone. She did not know what to think, for she had in her blotting book at Portman Square a letter lately received from one of these same Mackinnons in which not a word was said of Charlie. Why should not Helen have mentioned him had he been there? And yet, if papa thought so, and if it relieved his mind to think so, what was Betty to set up a different opinion? Her mind was still full of this thought when she found herself following her father up the narrow stairs into the little drawing-room. There she was met by a lady, who rose and came forward to her, holding out two beautiful hands. "Such hands!" Betty said afterwards. Her own were plump, reddish articles, small enough and not badly shaped, but scarcely free from the scars and smirches of gardening, wild-flower collecting, pony saddling, all the unnecessary pieces of work that a country girl's, like a country boy's, are employed for. She had at the moment a hopeless passion for white hands. And these drew her close, while the beautiful face stooped over her and gave her a soft lingering kiss. Was it a beautiful face? At least it was very, very handsome—fine features, fine eyes, an imposing benignity, like a grand duchess at the very least.

"So this is little Betty," the lady said, to whom she was presented by that title, "just out of last century, with her grandmother's name, and the newest version of her grandmother's hat. How pretty! Oh, it is your hat, you know, not you, that I am admiring. Like a little rose!"

Betty had no prejudices aroused in her mind by this lady's name, for Colonel Kingsward did not think it necessary to pronounce it. He said, "My little Betty," introducing the girl, but he did not think it needful to make any explanations to her. And she thus fell, all unprotected, under the charm. Laura talked to her for full five minutes without taking any notice of the Colonel, and drew from her all she wanted to see, and the places to which she was going, making a complete conquest of the little girl. It was only when Colonel Kingsward's patience was quite exhausted, and he was about to jump up and propose somewhat sullenly to leave his daughter with her new friend, that Miss Lance turned to him suddenly with an exclamation of pleasure.

"Did you hear, Colonel Kingsward? She was going to see Arthur Revel's picture this afternoon. And so was I! Will you come too? He is a great friend of mine, as I told you, and he knew dear Charlie, and, of course, he would be proud and delighted to see you. Shall we take Betty back to Portman Square to pick up her carriage and her old lady, and will you go humbly on foot with me? We shall meet them, and Mrs. Revel shall give us tea."

"Oh, papa, do!" Betty cried.

It was not perhaps what he would have liked best, but he yielded with a very good grace. He had not, perhaps, been so proud of little Betty by his side as the Lyons had expected, but Laura by his side was a different matter. He could not help remarking how people looked at her as they went along, and his mind was full of pride in the handsome, commanding figure, almost as tall as himself, and walking like a queen. Yet it made his head turn round a little when he saw Miss Lance seated by Mrs. Lyon's side in the studio, talking intimately to her of the whole Kingsward family, while Betty clung to her new friend as if she had known her all her life. Old Mrs. Lyon was still more startled, and her head went round too. "What a handsome woman!" she said, in Colonel Kingsward's ear. "What a delightful woman! Who is she?"

"Miss Lance," he said, rather stupidly, feeling how little information these words conveyed. Miss Lance? Who was Miss Lance? If he had said Laura it might have been a different matter.

CHAPTER VII

While all these things were going on, Bee was left at Kingswarden alone. That is to say, she was so far from being alone that her solitude was absolute. She had all the children and was very busy among them. She had the two boys home for the Easter holidays; the house was full of the ordinary noise, mirth and confusion natural to a large young family under no more severe discipline than that exercised by a young elder sister. The big boys, were in their boyish way, gentlemen, and deferred to Bee more or less—which set a good example to the younger ones; but she was enveloped in a torrent of talk, fun, games and jest, which raged round her from before she got up in the morning till at least the twilight, when the nursery children got tired, and the big boys having exhausted every method of amusement during the day, began to feel the burden of nothing to do, and retired into short-lived attempts at reading, or games of beggar-my-neighbour, or any other simple mode of possible recreation—descending to the level of imaginary football with an old hat through the corridor before it was time to go to bed.

In the evening Bee was thus completely alone, listening to the distant bumps in the passage, and the voices of the players. The drawing-room was large, but it was indifferently lighted, which is apt to make a country drawing-room gloomy in the evening. There was one shaded lamp on a writing-table, covered at this moment with colour boxes and rough drawings of the boys, who had been constructing a hut in the grounds, and wasting much vermillion and Prussian blue on their plans for it; and near the fireplace, in which the chill of the Spring still required a little fire, was another lamp, shining silently upon Bee's white dress and her hands crossed in her lap. Her face and all its thoughts were in the shade, nobody to share, nobody to care what they were.

Betty was in town. Her one faithful though not always entirely sympathetic companion, the aunt—at all times not much more than a piece of still life—was unwell and had gone to bed; Charlie was lost in the great depth and silence of the world; Bee was thus alone. She had been working for the children, making pinafores or some other necessary, as became her position as sister-mother; for where there are so many children there is always a great deal to do; but she had grown tired of the pinafores. If it were not a hard thing to say she was a little tired of the children too, tired of having to look after them perpetually, of the nurse's complaints, and the naughtiness of baby who was spoilt and unmanageable—tired of the bumping and laughing of the boys, and tired too of bidding them be quiet, not to rouse the children.

All these things had suddenly become intolerable to Bee. She had a great many times expressed her thankfulness that she had so much to do, and no time to think—and probably to-morrow morning she would again be of that opinion; but in the meantime she was very tired of it all—tired of a position which was too much for her age, and which she was not able to bear. She was only a speck in the long, empty drawing-room, her white skirts and her hands crossed in her lap being all that showed distinctly, betraying the fact that someone was there, but with her face hidden in the rosy shade, there was nobody to see that tears had stolen up into Bee's eyes. Her hands were idle, folded in her lap. She was tired of being dutiful and a good girl, as the best of girls are sometimes. It seemed to her for the moment a dreary world in which she was placed, merely to take care of the children, not for any pleasure of her own. She felt that she could not endure for another moment the bumping in the passage, and the distant voices of the boys. Probably if they went on there would be a querulous message from Aunt Helen, or pipings from the nursery of children woke up, and a furious descent of nurse, more than insinuating that Miss Bee did not care whether baby's sleep was broken or not. But even with this certainty before her, Bee did not feel that she had energy to get up from her chair and interfere; it was too much. She was too solitary, left alone to bear all the burden.

Then the habitual thought of Charlie returned to her mind. Poor Charlie! Where was he, still more alone than she. Perhaps hidden away in the silence of the seas, or tossing in a storm, going away, away where no one who cared for him would ever see him more. The tears which had come vaguely to her eyes dropped, making a mark upon her dress, legitimatised by this thought. Bee would have been ashamed had they fallen for herself; but for Charlie—Charlie lost!—none of his family knowing where he was— she might indeed be allowed to cry. Where was he? Where was he? If he had been here he would have been sitting with her, making things more possible. Bee knew very well in her heart that if Charlie had been with her he would not have been much help to her, that he would have been grumbling over his own hard fate, and calling upon her to pity him; but the absent, if they are sometimes wronged, have, on the other hand, the privilege of being remembered in their best aspect. Then Bee's thoughts glided on from Charlie to someone else whom she had for a long time refused to think of, or tried to refuse to think of. She was so solitary to-night, with all her doors open to recollections, that he had stolen in before she knew, and now there was quite a shower of round blots upon her white dress. Aubrey—oh, Aubrey! who had betrayed her trust so, who had done her such cruel wrong!—but yet, but yet—

She was interrupted by the entrance of a servant with the evening post. Kingswarden was near enough to town to have an evening post, which is a privilege not always desirable. But any incident was a good thing for poor Bee. She drew the pinafore, at which she had been working, hastily over her knee to hide the spots of moisture, and dashed the tears from her eyes with a rapid hand. In the shade of the lamp not even the most keen eyes could see that she had been crying. She even paused as she took the letter to say, "Will you please tell the boys not to make so much noise?" There were three letters on the tray— one for her father, one for her aunt, one Betty's usual daily rigmarole of little news and nonsense which she never failed to send when she was away. Betty's letter was very welcome to her sister. But as Bee read it her face began to burn. It became more and more crimson, so that the rose shade of the lamp was overpowered by a deeper and hotter colour. Betty to turn upon her, to take up the other side, to cast herself under that dreadful new banner of Fate! Bee's breath came quickly, her heart beat with anger and trouble. She got up from her chair and began to walk quickly about the room, a sudden passion sweeping away all the forlorn sentiment of her previous thoughts. Betty! in addition to all the rest. Bee felt like the forlorn chatelaine of a besieged castle alone to defend the walls against the march of a destroying invader. The danger which had been far off was coming—it was coming! And the castle had no garrison at all—if it were not perhaps those dreadful boys making noise enough to bring down the house, who were precisely the partisans least to be depended upon, who would probably throw down their arms without striking a blow. And Bee was alone, the captain deserted of all her forces to defend the sacred hearth and the little children. The little children! Bee stamped her foot upon the floor in an appeal, not to heaven, but to all the powers of Indignation, Fury, War, War! She would defend those walls to her last gasp. She would not give way, she would fight it out step by step, to keep the invader from the children. The nursery should be her citadel. Oh, she knew what would happen, she cried to herself inconsequently! Baby, who was spoilt, would be twisted into rigid shape, the little girls would be subdued like little mice—the boys—

At this moment the old hat which served as a football came with a thump from the corridor into the hall, followed by a louder shout than ever from Arthur and Rex. Bee rushed forth upon them flinging the door open, with her blue eyes blazing.

"Do you mean to bring down the house?" she said, in a sudden outburst. "Do you mean to break the vases and the mirror and wake up the whole nursery and bring Aunt Helen down upon us? For goodness sake try to behave like reasonable creatures, and don't drive me out of my senses!" cried Bee.

The boys were so startled by this onslaught that Rex, with a final kick sent the wretched old hat flying to the end of the passage which led to the servants' hall, as if it were that harmless object that was to blame—while Arthur covered the retreat sulkily by a complaint that there was nothing to do in this beastly old hole, and that a fellow couldn't read books all the day long. Bee was so inspired and thrilling with the passion in her, that she went further than any properly constituted female creature knowing her own position ought to do.

"You have a great deal more to do than I have," she said, "far, far more to do and to amuse yourselves with. Why should you expect so much more than I do, because you are boys and I am a girl? Is it fair? You're always talking of things being fair. It isn't fair that you should disturb the whole house, the little babies, and everyone for your pleasure; and I'm not so very much older than you are, and what pleasure have I?"

The boys were very much cast down by this fiery remonstrance. There had been a squall as of several babies from the upper regions, and they had already been warned of the consequence of their horseplay. But Bee's representation touched them in their tenderest point. Was it fair? Well, no, perhaps it was not quite fair. They went back after her, humbled, into the drawing-room, and besought her to join them in a game. After they had finally retired, having finished the evening to their own partial content, Bee took out again Betty's letter and read it with less excitement than at first—or at least with less demonstration of excitement; this was what it said—

"Bee, such a delightful woman, a friend of her papa's! So handsome, so nice, so clever, so well dressed, everything you can think except young, which of course she is not—nor anything silly. Papa told me to get ready to come out with him to see an old friend of his and I wasn't at all willing, didn't like it, I thought it must be some old image like old Mrs. Mackinnon or Nancy Eversfield, don't you know. Mrs. Lyon had settled to take me out to see some pictures, and Gerald was coming, and we were to have a turn in the park after, and I had put on my new frock and was looking forward to it, when papa came in with this order: 'Get on your things and come with me, I want to take you to see an old friend.' Of course I had to go, for Mrs. Lyon will never allow me to shirk anything. But I was not in a very good humour, though they called me as fresh as a rose and all that—to please papa; as if he cared how we look! He took me to George Street, Hanover Square, a horrid little lodging, such as people come to when they come up from the country. And I had to look as serious and as steady as possible for the sake of the old lady; when there rose up from the chair, oh, such a different person, tall, but as slight as you are, with such a handsome face and such a manner. She might have been—let us say a nice, sweet aunt—but aunt is not a name that means anything delightful; and mother I must not say, for there is only one mother in the whole world; oh, but something I cannot give a name, so understanding, so kind, so nice, for that means everything. She kissed me, and then she began to talk to me as if she knew everyone of us and was very fond of us all. And then about Charlie, whom she seemed to know very well. She called him dear Charlie, and I wonder if it is she who has persuaded papa that he is with the Mackinnons, in Scotland. But I know he is not with the Mackinnons—however, I will tell you about this after.

"Dear Bee, what will you say when I tell you that this delightful woman is Miss Lance? You will say I have no heart, or no spirit, and am not sticking to you through thick and thin as I ought; but you must hear first what I have got to say. Had I known it was Miss Lance I should have shut myself close up, and whatever she had done or however nice she had been, I should have had nothing to say to her. If she had been an angel under that name I should have remembered what you had said, and I should not have seen any good in her. But I never heard what her name was till we were all in Mr. Revel's studio, quite a long time after. Papa did as he always does, introduced me to her, but not her to me. He said: "My daughter Betty," as if I must have known by instinct who she was. And, dear Bee, though I acknowledge you have every reason not to believe it, she is delightful, she is, she is! She may have done wrong. I can't tell, of course; but I don't believe she ever meant it, or to harm you, or Charlie, or anyone. Everybody is delighted with her. Mrs. Lyon, who you know is very particular, says she has the manners of a duchess—and that she is such a handsome, distinguished-looking woman. She is coming to dine here next Saturday. The only one who does not seem to be quite charmed with her is Gerald, who is prejudiced like you.

"Do try to get over your prejudice, Bee, dear—she is, she is, indeed delightful! You only want to know her. By the way, about the Mackinnons: papa has got it firmly into his head that Charlie is there; he says his mind is quite relieved about him, and that the more he thinks of it, the more he is certain it is so; now I know that it is not so. I got a letter from Helen Mackinnon the day I came here, and there is not a word about Charlie—and she would have been certain to have mentioned him had he been there. I tried to say this to papa, but his head was so full of the other idea that he did not hear me at first, and I couldn't go on. I whispered to Miss Lance in the studio, and asked her what I should do? She was so troubled and distressed about Charlie that the tears came into her eyes, but, after thinking a moment, she said, 'Oh, dear child, don't say anything. Your young friend might have been in a hurry, she might not have thought it necessary to speak of your brother. Oh, don't let us worry him now! Bad news always comes soon enough, and, of course, he will find it out if it is so.' Do you think she was right? But, oh Bee, dear Bee, I am afraid you will not think anything she says is right; and yet she is delightful. If only you knew her! Write directly, and tell me all you think."

Bee was not excited on this second reading. She did not spring to her feet, nor stamp on the floor, or feel inclined to call upon all the infernal gods. But her heart sank down as if it would never rise again, and a great pain took possession of her. Who was this witch, this magician, that everyone who belonged to Bee should be drawn into her toils—even Betty. What could she want with Betty, who was only a little girl, who was her sister's natural second and support? Bee sat a long time with her head in her hands, letting the fire go out, feeling cold and solitary and miserable, and frightened to death.

CHAPTER VIII

In the afternoon of the next day, Bee was again alone. The old aunt had come down for lunch, but gone up to her room again to rest after that meal. It was a little chilly outside. The children, of course, wrapped up in their warm things, and in the virtue of the English nursery, which shrinks from no east wind, were out for their various walks. The big boys, attended by such of the little boys as could be trusted with these athletes, were taking violent exercise somewhere, and Bee sat by the fire, alone. It is not a place for a girl of twenty. The little pinafore, half made, was on the table beside her. She had a book in her hand. Perhaps had she been a young wife looking for the return of her young husband in the evening, with all the air of the bigger world about him and an abundance of news, and plans, and life, a pretty enough picture might have been made of that cosy fireside retirement.

But even this ideal has ceased to be satisfactory to the present generation. And Bee's spirits and heart were very low. She had despatched a fiery letter to Betty, and with this all her anger had faded away. She had no courage to do anything. She seemed to have come to an end of all possibilities. She had no longer anyone to fall back upon as a supporter and sympathiser—not even Betty. Even this closest link of nature seemed to have been broken by that enemy.

To have an enemy is not a very common experience in modern life. People may do each other small harms and annoyances, but to most of us the strenuous appeals and damnations of the Psalmist are quite beyond experience. But Bee had come back to the primitive state. She had an enemy who had succeeded in taking from her everything she cared for. Aubrey her betrothed, Charlie, her father, her sister, one after the other in quick succession. It was not yet a year and a half since she first heard this woman's name, and in that time all these losses had happened. She was not even sure that her mother's death was not the work of the same subtle foe; indeed, she brought herself to believe that it was at least accelerated by all the trouble and contention brought into the family by her own misery and rebellion—all the work of that woman! Why, why, had Bee been singled out for this fate? A little girl in an English house, like other girls—no worse, no better. Why should she alone in all England have this bitterness of an enemy to make her desolate and break her heart?

While she was thus turning over drearily those dismal thoughts, there was a messenger approaching to point more sharply still the record of these disasters and their cause. Bee had laid down her book in her lap; her thoughts had strayed completely from it and gone back to her own troubles, when the door of the drawing-room opened quietly and a servant announced "Mrs. Leigh." Mrs. Leigh! It is not an uncommon name. A Mrs. Lee lived in the village, a Mrs. Grantham Lea was the clergyman's wife in the next parish. Bee drew her breath quickly and composed her looks, but thought of no visitor that could make her heavy heart beat. Not even when the lady came in, a more than middle-aged matron, of solid form and good colour, dressed with the subdued fashionableness appropriate to her age. It was not Mrs. Lee from the village, nor Mrs. Grantham Lea, nor—Yet Bee had seen her before. She rose up a little startled and made a step or two forward.

"You do not know me, Miss Kingsward? I cannot wonder at it, since we met but once, and that in circumstances—Don't start nor fly, though I see you have recognised me."

"Indeed I did not think of flying. Will you—will you—sit down."

"You need not be afraid of me, my poor child," said Mrs. Leigh.

Aubrey's mother seated herself and looked with a kind yet troubled look at the girl, who still stood up in the attitude in which she had risen from her chair. "I scarcely saw you the other time," she said. "It was in the garden. You did not give me a good reception. I should like much, sometime or other, if you would tell me why. I have never made out why. But don't be afraid; it is not on that subject I have come to you now."

Bee seated herself. She kept her blue eyes, which seemed expanded and larger than usual, but had none of the former indignant blaze in them, fixed on the old lady's face.

"Your father is not here, the servant tells me—"

"No—he is in town," she answered, faltering, almost too much absorbed by anticipation to reply.

"And you are alone—nobody with you to stand by you?"

"Mrs. Leigh," said Bee, catching her breath, "I don't know why you should ask me such questions, or—or be sorry for me. I don't need anybody to be sorry for me."

"Poor little girl! We needn't go into that question. I am sorry for any girl who is motherless, who has to take her mother's place. I would much rather have spoken to your father had he been here."

"After all," said Bee, "my father could say nothing. It is I who must decide for myself."

She said this with an involuntary betrayal of her consciousness that there could be but one subject between them, and it was not in the power of Aubrey Leigh's mother, however strongly aware she was of another theme on which she had come to speak, not to note how different was Bee's reception of her from the other time, when the girl had fled from her presence and would not even hear what she had to say. Bee's eyes were large and humid and full of an anxiety which was almost wistful. She had the air of refusing to hear with her lips, but eagerly expecting with her whole heart what was about to be said. And she looked so young, so solitary, in her mother's chair, with a mother's work lying about, the head of this silent house—that the heart of the elder woman was deeply touched. If little Betty had been like a rose, Bee was almost as white as the cluster of fragrant white narcissus that stood on the table. Poor little girl, so subdued and changed from the little passionate creature who would not hear a word, and whose indignation was stronger than even the zeal of the mother who had come to plead her son's cause!

Mrs. Leigh drew a little nearer and took Bee's hand. The girl did not resist, but kept her eyes upon her steadily, watching, her mind in a great turmoil, not knowing what to expect.

"My dear," said the old lady, "don't be alarmed. I have not come to speak about Aubrey. I cannot help hoping that one day you will do him justice; but, in the meantime, it is something else that has brought me here. Miss Kingsward—your brother—"

Bee's hand, in this lady's clasp, betrayed her in spite of herself. It became limp and uninterested when she was assured that Aubrey was not in question; and then, at her brother's name, was snatched suddenly away.

"My brother?" she cried, "Charlie!" Then, subduing herself, "What do you know about him? Oh," clasping her hands as new light seemed to break upon her, "you have come to tell me some bad news?"

"I hope not. My son found him some time ago, disheartened and unhappy about leaving Oxford. He persuaded him to come and share his rooms. He has been with him more or less all the time, which I hope may be a comfort to you. And then he fell ill. My dear Aubrey has tried to see your father, but in vain, and poor Charlie is not anxious, I fear, to see his father. Yes, he has been ill, but not so seriously that we need fear anything serious. He has shaken off the complaint, but he wants rousing—he wants someone whom he loves. Aubrey sent for me a fortnight ago. He has been well taken care of, there is nothing really wrong. But we cannot persuade him to rouse himself. It is illness that is at the bottom of it all. He would not have left you without news of him, he would not shrink from his father if he were not ill. Bee, I will confess to you that it is Aubrey who has sent me; but don't be afraid, it is for Charlie's sake—only for Charlie's sake. He thinks if you would but come to him—if you would have the courage to come—to your brother, Bee."

"He—he thinks? Not Charlie—you don't mean Charlie?" Bee cried.

"Charlie does not seem to wish for anything. We cannot rouse him. We think that the sight of someone he loves—"

Bee was full of agitation. Her lips quivered; her hands trembled. "Oh, me!" she said; "I am no one. It is not for his sister a boy cares. I do not think I should do him any good. Oh, Charlie, Charlie! all this time that we have been blaming him so, thinking him so cruel, he has been lying ill! If I could do him any good!" she cried, wringing her hands.

"The sight of you would do him good. It is not that he wants a nurse—I have seen to that; but no nurse could rouse him as the sight of some of his own people would. Do not question, my dear, but come—oh, come! He thinks he is cut off from everybody, that his father will never see him, that you must all have turned against him. Words will not convince him, but to see you, that would do so. He would feel that he was not forsaken."

"Oh, forsaken! How could he think it? He must know that we have been breaking our hearts. It was he who forsook us all."

Bee had risen again, and stood leaning upon the mantelpiece, too much shaken and agitated to keep still. Though she had thought herself so independent, she had in reality never broken the strained band of domestic subjugation. She had never so much as gone, though it was little more than an hour's journey, to London on her own authority. The thought of taking such a step startled her. And that she should do this on the word and in the company of Aubrey's mother—Aubrey, for whom she had once been ready to abandon everything, from whom she had been violently separated, whom she had cast off, flung away from her without hearing a word he had to say! How could she put herself in his way again—go with his mother, accept his services? Bee had acted quickly on the impulse of passion in all that had happened to her before. But she had not known the conflict, the rending asunder of opposite emotions. In the whirl of her thoughts her lover, whom she had cast off, came between her and the brother whom he had succoured. It was to Aubrey's house, to his very dwelling where he was, that she must go if she went to Charlie. And Charlie wanted her, or at least needed her, lying weak and despairing, waiting for a sign from home. It was difficult to realise her brother so, or to believe, indeed, that he could want her very much, that there was any yearning in his heart towards his own flesh and blood. But Mrs. Leigh thought so, and how could she refuse? How could she refuse? The problem was too much for her. She looked into Mrs. Leigh's face with an appeal for help.

"My dear," her companion said, leaving a calm and cool hand upon Bee's arm, which trembled with nervous excitement, "If you are afraid of meeting Aubrey, compose yourself. Aubrey would rather go to the end of the world than give you any pain, or put himself in your way. We are laying no trap for you—I should not have come if the case had not been urgent. Never would I have come had it been a question of my son; I would not beguile you even for his sake. It is for your brother, Bee; not for Aubrey, not for Aubrey!"

Not for Aubrey! Was that any comfort, was there any strength in that assurance? At all events, these were the words that rang through Bee's head, as she made her hurried preparations. She had almost repeated them aloud in the hasty explanations she made to Moss upstairs, who was now at the head of the nursery, and to the housekeeper below. To neither of these functionaries did it seem of any solemn importance that Bee should go away for a day or two. There was no objection on their part to being left at the head of affairs. And then Bee felt herself carried along by the whirl of strange excitement and feeling which rather than the less etherial methods of an express train seemed to sweep her through the air of the darkening spring night by Mrs. Leigh's side. A few hours before she had felt herself the most helpless of dependent creatures, abandoned by all, incapable of doing anything. And now, what was she doing? Rushing into the heart of the conflict, assuming an individual part in it, acting on her own responsibility. She could scarcely believe it was herself who sat there by Mrs. Leigh's side.

But not for Aubrey, not for Aubrey! This kept ringing in her ears, like the tolling of a bell, through all the other sounds. She sat in one corner of the carriage, and listened to Mrs. Leigh's explanations, and to the clang of the engine and rush of the train, all mingled together in bewildering confusion. But the other voice filled all space, echoing through everything. Bee felt herself trembling on the edge of a crisis, such as her life had never known. All the world seemed to be set against her, her enemy, perhaps her father, and all the habitual authorities of her young and subject life, now suddenly rising into rebellion. She would have to do and say things which she would not have ventured so much as to think of a little time ago; but whatever she might have to encounter there was to be no renewal to Bee of her own story and meaning. It was not for Aubrey that she was called or wanted—for the succour of others, for sisterly help, for charity and kindness; but not for her own love or life.

CHAPTER IX

It was to a house in one of the streets of Mayfair that Mrs. Leigh conveyed her young companion; one of those small expensive places where persons within the circle of what is called the world in London contrive to live with as little comfort and the greatest expenditure possible. It is dark and often dingy in Mayfair; nowhere is it more difficult to keep furniture, or even human apparel, clean; the rooms are small and the streets shabby; but it is one of the right places in which to live, not so perfect as it was once, indeed, but still furnishing an unimpeachable address.

It had half put on the aspect of the season by this time; some of the balconies were full of flowers, and the air of resuscitation which comes to certain quarters of London after Easter, as if, indeed, they too had risen from the dead, was vaguely visible. To be sure, little of this was apparent in the dim lamplight when the two ladies arrived at the door. Bee was hurried upstairs through the narrow passage, though she had been very keenly aware that someone in the lower room had momentarily lifted the blind to look out as they arrived—someone who did not appear, who made no sound, who had nothing to do with her or her life.

The rooms, which are usually the drawing-rooms of such a house, were turned evidently into the apartments of the sufferer. In the back room which they entered first was a nurse who greeted the ladies in dumb show, and whose white head-dress and apron had the strangest effect in the semi-darkness. She said, half by gesture, half with whispered words more visible than audible, "He is up—better—impatient—good sign—discontented with everything. Is this the lady?"

Mrs. Leigh answered in the same way, "His sister—shall I go with her?—you?—alone?"

"By herself," said the nurse, laconic; and almost inaudible as this conversation was, it occasioned a stirring and movement in the inner room.

"What a noise you make," cried a querulous, unsteady voice, "Who's there—who's there?"

The nurse took Bee's hat from her head, with a noiseless swift movement, and relieved her of the little cloak she was wearing. She took her by the arm and pushed her softly forward. "Nothing to worry. Soothe him," she breathed, holding up a curtain that Bee might pass. The room was but badly lighted, a single lamp on a table almost extinguished by the shade, a fire burning though the night was warm, and one of the long windows open, letting in the atmosphere and sounds of the London street. Bee stole in, an uncertain shadow into the shaded room, less eager than frightened and overawed by this sudden entrance into the presence of sickness and misery. She was not accustomed to associate such things with her brother. It did not seem anyone with whom she was acquainted that she was about to see.

"Oh, Charlie!" the little cry and movement she made, falling down on her knees beside him, raised a pale, unhappy face, half covered with the down of an irregular fledgling beard from the pillow.

"Hallo!" he said, and then in a tone of disappointment and disdain, "You!"

"Oh, Charlie, Charlie dear! You have been ill and we never knew."

"How do you know now? They knew I never wanted you to know," he said.

"Oh, Charlie—who ought to know but your own people? We have been wretched, thinking all sorts of dreadful things—but not this."

"Naturally," he said, "my own people might be trusted never to think the right thing. Now you do know you may as well take yourself off. I don't want you—or anybody," he added, with an impatient sigh.

"Charlie—oh, please let me stay with you. Who should be with you but your sister? And I know—a great deal about nursing. Mamma—"

"I say—hold your tongue, can't you? Who wants you to talk—of anything of that sort?"

Bee heard a slight stir in the curtains, and looking back hastily as she dried her streaming eyes saw the laconic nurse making signs to her. The sight of the stranger was more effectual even than her signs, and restored Bee's self-command at once.

"Why did they bring you here?" said Charlie. "I didn't want you; they know what I want, well enough."

"What is it you want, oh, Charlie dear? Papa—and all of us—will do anything in the world you want."

"Papa," he said, and his weakened and irregular voice ran through the gamut from a high feeble tone of irritation to the quaver of that self-pity which is so strong in all youthful trouble. "Yes, he would be pleased to get me out of the way, and be done with me now."

"Oh, Charlie! You know how wrong that is. Papa has been—miserable—"

Charlie uttered a feeble laugh. He put his hand upon his chin, stroking down the irregular tufts of hair; even in his low state the poor boy had a certain pride in what he believed to be his beard.

"Not much," he said. "I daresay you've made a fuss—Betty and you. The governor will crack up Arthur for the F.O. and let me drop like a stone."

"No, Charlie, no. He has no such thought—he has taken such trouble not to let it be known. He would not advertise or anything."

"Advertise!" A sudden hot flush came over the gaunt face. "For me!" It did not seem that such a thought had ever occurred to the young man. "Like the fellows in the newspapers that steal their master's money—'All is arranged and you can return to your situation.' By George!"

There was again a faint rustle in the curtains. Bee sprang up with her natural impatience, and went straight to the spot whence this sound had come.

"If I am not to speak to my brother alone and in freedom, I will not speak to him at all," she said.

The laconic nurse remonstrated violently with her lips and eyes.

"Don't excite him. Don't disturb him. He'll not sleep all night," she managed to convey, with much arching of the eyebrows and mouth, then disappeared silently out of the bedroom behind.

"What's that?" said Charlie, sharply. He moved on his sofa, and turned his head round with difficulty. "Are there more of you to come?"

There seemed a kind of hope and expectation in the question, but when Bee answered with despondency, "There's only me, Charlie," he broke out harshly:

"I don't want you—I want none of you; I told them so. You can go and tell my father, as soon as they let me get out I'm going off to New Zealand or somewhere—the furthest-off place I can get to."

"Oh, Charlie!" cried Bee, taking every word as the sincerest utterance of a fixed intention, "what could you do there?"

"Die, I suppose," he said, with again that quaver of self-compassion in his voice, "or go to the dogs, which will be easy enough. You may say, why didn't I die here and be done with it? I don't know—I'm sure I wanted to. It was that doctor fellow, and that woman that talks with her eyebrows, and that confounded cad, Leigh—they wouldn't let me. And I've got so weak; if you don't go away this moment I'll cry like a dashed baby!" with a more piteous quaver than ever in the remnant of his once manly voice.

All that Bee could do was to throw her arms round his neck and draw his head upon her shoulder, which he resisted fiercely for a moment, then yielded to in the abandonment of his weakness. Poor Charlie felt, perhaps, a momentary sweetness in the relaxation of all the bonds of self-control, and all the well-meaning attempts to keep him from injuring himself by emotion; the unexpected outburst did him good, partly because it was a breach of all the discipline of the sick room. Presently he came to himself and pushed Bee away.

"What do you come bothering about?" he said; "you ought to have left me alone. I've made my bed, and I've got to lie on it. I don't suppose that anyone has taken the trouble to—ask about me?" he added, after a little while, in what was intended for a careless tone.

"Oh, Charlie, everyone who has known; but papa would let nobody know: except at Oxford. We—went to Oxford—"

He got up on his pillow with his eyes shining out of their hollow sockets, his long limbs coming to the ground with a faint thump. Poor Charlie was young enough to have grown during his illness, and those gaunt limbs seemed unreasonably long.

"You went to Oxford!" he said, "and you saw—"

"Dear Charlie, they will say I am exciting you—doing you harm—"

"You saw?" he cried, bringing down his fist upon the table with a blow that made the very floor shake.

"Yes," said Bee, trembling, "we saw—or rather papa saw—"

He pushed up the shade of the lamp with his long bony fingers, and fixed his eyes, bright with fever, on her face.

"Oh, Charlie, don't look at me so!—the lady whom you used to talk to me about—whom I saw in the academy—"

"Yes?"—he grasped her hand across the table with a momentary hot pressure.

"She came and saw papa in the hotel. She told him about you, and that you had—oh, Charlie, and she so old—as old as—"

"Hold your tongue!" he cried, violently, and then with a long-drawn breath, "What more? She told him—and he was rude, I suppose. Confound him! Confound—confound them all!"

"I will not say another word unless you are quiet," said Bee, her spirit rising; "put up your feet on the sofa and be quiet, and remember all the risk you are running—or I will not say another word."

He obeyed her with murmurs of complaint, but no longer with the languid gloom of his first accost. Hope seemed to have come into his heart. He subdued himself, lay back among his pillows, obeyed her in all she stipulated. The light from underneath the raised shade played on his face and gave it a tinge of colour, though it showed more clearly the emaciation of the outlines and the aspect of neglect, rather than, as poor Charlie hoped, of enhanced manly dignity, conveyed by the irregular sick man's growth of the infant beard.

"Papa was not rude," said Bee, "he is never rude; he is a gentleman. Worse than that—"

"Worse—than what?"

"Oh, I cannot understand you at all, you and—the rest," cried the girl; "one after another you give in to her, you admire her, you do what she tells you—that woman who has harmed me all she can, and you all she can, and now—Charlie!" Bee stopped with astonishment and indignation. Her brother had raised himself up again, and aimed a furious but futile blow at her in the air. It did not touch her, but the indignity was no less on that account.

"Well," he cried, again bringing down that hand which could not reach her, on the table, "How dare you speak of one you're not worthy to name? Ah! I might have known she wouldn't desert me. It is she who has kept the way open, and subdued my father, and—" An ineffable look of happiness came upon the worn and gaunt countenance, his eyes softened, his voice fell. "I might have known!" he said to himself, "I might have known!"

And what could Bee say? Though she did not believe in—though she hated and feared with a child's intensity of terror the woman who had so often crossed her path—she could not contradict her brother's faith, though she considered it an infatuation, a folly beyond belief; it seemed, after all, in a manner true that this woman had not deserted him. She had subdued his father's displeasure somehow, made everything easier. Bee looked at him, the victim of those wiles, yet nevertheless indebted to them, with the same exasperation which her father's subjugation had caused her. What could she say, what could she do, to reveal to them that enchantress in her true colours? But Bee knew that she could do nothing, and there began to rise in her heart a dreadful question. Was it so sure that she herself was right? Was this woman, indeed, an evil Fate, or was she, was she—? And the first story of all, the story of Aubrey, was it perhaps true?

The nurse came in noiselessly, hurrying, while Bee's mind ran through those thoughts—evidently with the conviction that she would find the patient worse. But Charlie was not worse. He turned his face towards his attendant, still with something of that dreamy rapture in it.

"Oh, you may speak out," he said; "I don't mind noises to-night. Supper? Yes, I'll take some supper. Bring me a beefsteak or something substantial. I'm going to get well at once."

Nurse nodded at Bee, with much uplifting of her eyelids. "Put no faith in you," she said, working the machinery of her lips; "was wrong; done him no end of good. Beefsteak; not exactly; but soon, soon, if you're good."

CHAPTER X

Bee saw no more of Charlie that night. When she came out of his room, where there was a certain meaning in her presence, she seemed to pass into the region of dreams. She was taken upstairs to refresh herself and rest, into the smaller of two bedrooms which were over Charlie's room, the other of which was occupied by Mrs. Leigh. And she was taken downstairs to dine with that lady tête-a-tête at the small shining table. There was something about the little house altogether, a certain conciseness, an absence of drapery, and of the small elegant litter which is so general nowadays, which gave it a masculine character—or, at least, Bee, not accustomed to æsthetic young men, accustomed rather to big boys and their scorn of the decorative arts, thought so with a curious flutter of her being. This perhaps was partly because the ornamental part of the house was devoted to Charlie, and the little dining-room below seemed the sole room to live in. It had one or two portraits hung on the walls, pictures almost too much for its small dimensions. The still smaller room behind was clothed with books, and had for its only ornament a small portrait of Mrs. Leigh over the mantel-piece. Whose rooms were these? Who had furnished them so gravely, and left behind an impression of serious character which almost chilled the heart of Bee? He was nowhere visible, nor any trace of him. No allusion was made as to an absent master of the house, and yet it bore an air so individual that Bee's sensitive being was moved by it, with all the might of something stranger than imagination. She stood trembling among the books, looking at the mother's portrait over the mantel-piece, feeling as if the very mantel-shelf on which she rested her arm was warm with the touch of his. But not a word was said, not an allusion made to Aubrey.

What had she to do with Aubrey? Nothing—less than with any other man in the world—any stranger to whom she could speak with freedom, interchanging the common coin of ordinary intercourse. He was the only man in the world whom she must not talk of, must not see—the only one of whose presence it was necessary to obliterate every sign, and never to utter the name where she was. Poor Bee! Yet she felt him near, his presence suggested by everything, his name always latent in the air. She slept and waked in that strange atmosphere as in a dream. In Aubrey's house, yet with Aubrey obliterated—the one person in existence with whom she had nothing, nothing to do.

It was late before she was allowed to see her brother next day, and Bee, in the meantime, left to her own devices, had not known what to do. She had taken pen and paper two or three times to let her father know that Charlie was found, but her mind revolted, somehow, from making that intimation. What would happen when he knew? He would come here immediately; he would probably attempt to remove Charlie; he would certainly order Bee away at once from a place so unsuitable for her. It was unsuitable for her, and yet—She scarcely saw even Mrs. Leigh after breakfast, but was left to herself, with the door open into that sanctuary which was Aubrey's, with all his books and the newspapers laid out upon the table. Bee sat in the dining-room and looked into that other secluded place. In the light of day she dared not go into it. It seemed like thrusting herself into his presence who had no thought of her, who did not want her. Oh, not for Aubrey! Aubrey would not for the world disturb her, or bring any embarrassment into her mind. Aubrey would rather disappear from his own house, as if he had never existed, than remind her that he did exist, and perhaps sometimes thought of her still. Did he ever think of her? Bee knew that it would be wrong and unlike Aubrey if he kept in these rooms the poor little photograph of her almost childish face which he had once prized so much. It would have been indelicate, unlike a gentleman; and yet she made a hasty and furtive search everywhere to see if, perhaps, it might be somewhere, in some book or little frame. She would have been angry had she found it, and indignant; yet she felt a certain desolate sense of being altogether out of the question, steal into her heart, when she did not find it—in the inconsistencies of which the heart is full.

It was mid-day when she was called upstairs, to find Charlie established in the room which should have been the drawing-room, and round which she threw another wistful look as she came into it in full daylight. Oh, not a woman's room in any way, with none of those little photograph frames about which strew a woman's table—not one, and consequently none of Bee. She took this in at the first glance, as she made the three or four little steps between the door and Charlie's couch. He was more hollow-eyed and worn in the daylight than he had been even on the night before, his appearance entirely changed from that of the commonplace young Oxford man to an eager, anxious being, with all the cares of a troubled soul concentrated in his eyes. Mrs. Leigh sat near him, and the nurse was busy with cushions and pillows arranging his couch.

"My dear, you will be thankful to hear that the doctor gives a very good report to-day. He says that, though he would not have sanctioned it, my remedy has done wonders. You are my remedy, Bee. I am proud of so successful an idea—though, to be sure, it was a very simple one. Now you must go on and complete the cure, and I give you carte blanche. Ask anyone here, anyone you please, so long as it is not too much for Charlie. He may see one or two people if nurse sanctions it. I am going out myself for the day. I shall not return till late in the afternoon, and you are mistress in the meantime—absolute mistress," said Mrs. Leigh, kissing her. Bee felt that Aubrey's mother would not even meet her eyes lest she should throw too much meaning into these words. Oh, there was no meaning in them, except so far as Charlie was concerned.

And then she was left alone with her brother, the most natural, the only suitable arrangement. Nurse gave the last pat to his cushions, the last twist to the coverlet, which was over his gaunt limbs, appealed to him the last time in dumb show whether he wanted anything, and then withdrew. It was most natural that his sister, whose appearance had done him so much good, should be left with him as his nurse; but she was frightened, and Charlie self-absorbed, and it was some time before either found a word to say. At last he said, "Bee!" calling her attention, and then was silent again for some time, speaking no more.

"Yes, Charlie!" There was a flutter in Bee's voice as in her heart.

"I say, I wasn't, perhaps, very nice to you last night; I couldn't bear to be brought back; but they say I'm twice as well since you came. So I am. I've got something to keep me up. Bee, look here. Am I dreadful to look at? I know I haven't an ounce of flesh left on my bones, but some don't mind that; and then, my beard. I've heard it said that a beard that never was shaved was—was—an embellishment, don't you know. Do you think I'm dreadful to look at, Bee?"

"Oh, Charlie," said the girl, from the depths of her heart, "what does it matter how you look? The more ill you look the more need you have for your own people about you, who never would think twice of that."

Charlie's gaunt countenance was distorted with a grin of rage and annoyance. "I wish you'd shut up about my own people. The governor, perhaps, with his grand air, or Betty, as sharp as a needle—as if I wanted them!—or to be told that they would put up with me."

"Charlie," said Bee, trembling, "I don't want to vex you, you are a little—but couldn't you have a barber to come, and perhaps he could take it off."

There came a flash of fire out of Charlie's eyes; he put up his hand to his face, as if to protect that beard in which he at least believed—"I might have known," he said, "that you were the last person! A fellow's sister is always like that: just as we never think anything of a girl's looks in our own families. Well, you've given your opinion on that subject. And you think that people who care for me wouldn't think twice of that?"

"Oh, no," said Bee, clasping her hands, "how should they? But only feel for you far, far more."

Charlie took down his hand from his young beard. He looked at her with his hollow eyes full of anxiety, yet with a certain complacence. "Interesting?"—he said, "is that what you meant to say?"

"Oh, yes," cried Bee, her eyes full of pity, "for they can see what you have gone through, and how much you have been suffering,—if there was any need of making you more interesting to us."

Charlie stroked down his little tufts of wool for some time without speaking, and then he said in a caressing tone unusual to him, "I want you to do me a favour, Bee."

"Anything—anything, whatever you wish, Charlie."

"There is just one thing I wish, and one person I want to see. Sit down and write a note—you need not do more than say where I am," said Charlie, speaking quickly. "Say I am here, and have been very ill, but that the hope she'd come, and to hear that she had forgiven me, was like new life. Well! what is the meaning of your 'anything, anything,' if you break down at the first thing I ask you? Look here, Bee, if you wish me to live and get well you'll do what I say."

"Oh, Charlie, how can I?—how can I?—when you know what I feel—about—"

"What you feel—about? Who cares what you feel? You think perhaps it was you that did me all that good last night. That's all conceit, like the nonsense in novels, where a woman near your bed when you're ill makes all the difference. Girls," said Charlie, "are puffed up with that folly and believe anything. You know I didn't want you. It was what you told me about her that did me good. And your humbug, sitting there crying, 'anything, anything!' Well, here's something! You need not write a regular letter, if you don't like it. Put where I am—Charlie Kingsward very ill; will you come and see him? A telegram would do, and it would be quicker; send a telegram," he cried.

"Oh, Charlie!"

"Give me the paper and pencil—I'm shaky, but I can do that much myself—"

"Charlie, I'll do it rather than vex you; but I don't know where to send it."

"Oh, I can tell you that—Avondale, near the Parks, Oxford."

"She is not there now—she is in London," said Bee, in a low tone.

"In London?" Again the long, gaunt limbs came to the ground with a thump. "Bee, if you could get me a hansom perhaps I could go."

The nurse at this moment came in noiselessly, and Charlie shrank before her. She put him back on the sofa with a swift movement. "If you go on like this I'll take the young lady away," she said.

"I'll not go on—I'll be as meek as Moses; but, nurse, tell her she mustn't contradict a man in my state. She must do what I say."

Nurse turned her back upon the patient, and made the usual grimaces; "Humour him," her lips and eyebrows said.

"Charlie, papa knows the address, and Betty—and I ought, oh, I ought to let them know at once that you are here."

"Betty!" he said, with a grimace, "what does that little thing know?"

"She knows—better than you think I do; and papa—Papa is never happy but when he is with that lady. He goes to see her every day; she writes to him and he writes to her; they go out together," cried Bee, thinking of that invitation to Portman Square which had seemed the last insult which she could be called on to bear.

Charlie smiled—the same smile of ineffable self-complacence and confidence which had replaced in a moment the gloom of the previous night; and then he grew grave. He was not such a fool, he said to himself, as to be jealous of his own father; but still he grudged that anyone but himself should have her company. He remembered what it was to go to see her every day, to write to her, to have her letters, to be privileged to give her his arm now and then, to escort her here or there. If it had been another fellow! But a man's father—the governor! He was not a rival. Charlie imagined to himself the conversations with him for their subject, and how, perhaps for the first time, the governor would learn to do him justice, seeing him through Laura's eyes. It was true that she had rejected him, had almost laughed at him, had sent him away so completely broken down and miserable that he had not cared what became of him. But hope had sprung within him, all the more wildly from that downfall. It was like her to go to the old gentleman (it was thus he considered his father) to explain everything, to set him right. She would not have done so if her heart had not relented—her heart was so kind. She must have felt what it was to drive a man to despair—and now she was working for him, soothing down the governor, bringing everything back.

"Eh?" he said, vaguely, some time after; he had in the meantime heard Bee's voice going on vaguely addressing somebody, in the air, "are you speaking to me?"

"There is no one else to speak to," cried Bee, almost angrily. And then she said, "Charlie—how can you ask her to come here?"

"Why not here? She'll go anywhere to do a kind thing."

"But not to this house—not here, not here!"

"Why not, I should like to know—what's here?" Then Charlie stared at her for a moment with his hollow eyes, and broke into a low, feeble laugh.

"Oh," he said, "I know what you've got in your head—because of that confounded cad, Aubrey Leigh? That is just why she will come, to show what a lie all that was—as if she ever would have looked twice at a fellow like Leigh."

"He seems to have saved your life," said Bee, confused, not knowing what to think.

"You mean he gave me house-room when I was ill, and sent for a doctor. Why, any shop-keeper would have done that. And now," said Charlie, with a grin, "he shall be fully paid back."

CHAPTER XI

Betty Kingsward lived in what was to her a whirl of pleasure at Portman Square, where everybody was fond of her, and all manner of entertainments were devised for her pleasure. And her correspondence was not usually of an exciting character. Her morning letters, when she had any, were placed by her plate on the breakfast-table. If any came by other posts, she got them when she had a spare moment to look for them, and she had scarcely a spare moment at this very lively and very happy moment of her young career. Besides, that particular evening when Bee's note arrived was a very important one to Betty. It was the evening on which Miss Lance was to dine with the Lyons. And it was not a mere quiet family dinner, but a party—a thing which in her newness and inexperience still excited the little girl, who was not to say properly "out," in consequence of her mourning; still wearing black ribbons with her white frocks, and only allowed to accept invitations which were "quiet." A dinner of twenty people is not exactly an entertainment for a girl of her years, but Betty's excitement in the debût of Miss Lance was so great that no ball could have occupied her more. There was an unusual interest about it in the whole house, even Mrs. Lyon's maid, the most staid of confidential persons, had begged Betty to point out to her over the baluster "the lady, Miss Betty, that is coming with your papa."

"Oh, she's not coming with papa," Betty had cried, with a laugh at Hobbs' mistake, "she is only a great, great friend, Hobbs. You will easily know her, for there is nobody else so handsome."

"Handsome is as handsome does," said the woman, and she patted Betty on the shoulder under pretence of arranging her ribbon.

Betty had not the least idea why Hobbs looked at her with such compassionate eyes.

Miss Lance, however, did come into the room, to Betty's surprise, closely followed by Colonel Kingsward, as if they had arrived together. She was like a picture, in her black satin and lace, dressed not too young but rather too old for her age, as Mrs. Lyon pointed out, who was as much excited about her new guest as Betty herself; and the unknown lady had the greatest possible success in a party which consisted chiefly, as Betty did not remark, of old friends of Colonel Kingsward, with whom she had been acquainted all her life. Betty did not remark it, but Gerald Lyon did, who was more than ever her comrade and companion in this elderly company.

"Why all these old fogies?" he had asked irreverently, as the gentlemen with stars on their coats and the ladies in diamonds came in.

Betty perceived that it was an unusually solemn party, but thought no more of it. It was the evening of the first levee, and that, perhaps, was the reason why the old gentlemen wore their orders. Old gentlemen! They were the flower of the British army. Generals This and That, heads of departments; impossible to imagine more grand people—in the flower of their age, like Colonel Kingsward. But eighteen has its own ideas very clearly marked on that subject. Betty and Gerald stood by, lighting up one corner with a blaze of undeniable youth, to see them come in. The young pair were like flowers in comparison with the substantial size and well worn complexions of their seniors, and they were the only little nobodies, the sole representatives of undistinguished and ordinary humanity round the table. They were not by any means daunted by that. On the contrary, they felt themselves, as it were, soaring over the heads of all those limited persons who had attained, spurning the level heights of realisation. They did not in the least know what was to become of them in life, but naturally they made light of the others who did know, who had done all they were likely to do, and had no more to look to. The dignity of accomplished success filled the young ones with impulses of laughter; their inferiority gave them an elevation over all the grizzled heads; they felt themselves, nobodies, to be almost ludicrously, dizzily above the heads of the rest. Only one of the company seemed to see this, however; to cast them an occasional look, even to make them the confidants of an occasional smile, a raising of the eyebrows, a sort of unspoken comment on the fine company, which made Betty still more lively in her criticisms. But this made almost a quarrel between the two.

"Oh, I wish we were nearer to Miss Lance, to hear what she thinks of it all," Betty said.

"I can't think what you see in that woman," cried Gerald. "I, for one, have no desire to know her opinion."

Betty turned her little shoulder upon him with a glance of flame, that almost set the young man on fire.

"You prejudiced, cynical, uncharitable, malicious, odious boy!" And they did not say another word to each other for five minutes by the clock.

Miss Lance, however, there was no doubt, had a distinguished success. She captivated the gentlemen who were next to her at table, and, what was perhaps more difficult, she made a favourable impression upon the ladies in the drawing-room. Her aspect there, indeed, was of the most attractive kind. She drew Betty's arm within her own, and said with a laugh, "You and I are the girls, little Betty, among all these grand married ladies;" and then she added, "Isn't it a little absurd that we shouldn't have some title to ourselves, we old maids?—for Miss means eighteen, and it's hard that it should mean forty-two. Fancy the disappointment of hearing this juvenile title and then finding that it means a middle-aged woman."

She laughed so freely that some of the other ladies laughed too. The attention of all was directed towards the new comer, which Betty thought very natural, she was so much the handsomest of them all.

"You mean the disappointment of a gentleman?" said one of the guests.

"Oh, no, of ladies too. Don't you think women are just as fond of youth as men are, and as much disgusted with an elderly face veiling itself in false pretences? Oh, more! We think more of beauty than the men do," said Miss Lance, raising her fine head as if to expose its features to the fire of all the glances bent upon her.

There was a little chorus of cries, "Oh, no, no," and arguments against so novel a view.

But Miss Lance did not quail; her own beauty was done full justice to. She was so placed that more than one mirror in the old-fashioned room reflected her graceful and not unstudied pose.

"I know it isn't a usual view," she said, "but if you'll think of it a little you'll find it's true. The common thing is to talk about women being jealous of each other. If we are it is because we are always the first to find out a beautiful face—and usually we much exaggerate its power."

"Do you know," said Mrs. Lyon in her quavering voice, "I almost think Miss Lance is right? Mr. Lyon instantly says 'Humph!' when I point out a pretty person to him. And Gerald tells me, 'You think every girl pretty, aunt.'"

"That is because there is one little girl that he thinks the most pretty of all," said Miss Lance, with a sort of soft maternal coo in Betty's ear.

The subject was taken up and tossed about from one to another, while she who had originated it drew back a little, listening with an air of much attention, turning her head to each speaker, an attitude which was most effective. It will probably be thought the greatest waste of effort for a woman thus to exhibit what the newspapers call her personal advantages to a group of her own sex; but Miss Lance was a very clever woman, and she knew what she was about. After a time, when the first fervour of the argument was over, she returned to her first theme as to the appropriate title that ought to be invented for old maids.

"I have thought of it a great deal," she said. "I should have called myself Mrs. Laura Lance, to discriminate—but for the American custom of calling all married ladies so, which is absurd."

"I have a friend in New York who writes to me as Mrs. Mary Lyon," said the mistress of the house.

"Yes, which is ridiculous, you know; for you are not Mrs. Mary Lyon, dear lady. You are Mrs. Francis Lyon, if it is necessary to have a Christian name, for Lyon is your husband's name, not yours. You are Mrs. Mary Howard by rights—if in such a matter there are any rights."

"What!" cried old Mr. Lyon, coming in after the long array of gentlemen, "are you going to divorce my wife from me, or give her another name, or what are you going to do? We thought it was we only who could change the ladies' names, Kingsward, eh?"

Colonel Kingsward had placed himself immediately in front of Miss Lance, and Betty, looking on all unsuspicious, saw a glance pass between them—or rather, she saw Miss Lance look up into her father's face. Betty did not know in the least what that look meant, but it gave her a little shock as if she had touched an electric battery. It meant something more than to Betty's consciousness had ever been put into words. She turned her eyes away for a moment to escape the curious thrill that ran through her, and in that moment met Gerald Lyon's eyes, full of something malicious, mocking, disagreeable, which made Betty very angry. But she could not explain to herself what all these looks meant.

This curious sensation somehow spoiled the rest of the evening for Betty. Everybody it seemed to her after this meant something—something more than they said. They looked at her father, they looked at Miss Lance, they looked even at Betty's little self, embracing all three, sometimes in one comprehensive glance. And all kinds of significant little speeches were made as the company went away. "I am so glad to have seen her," one lady said in an undertone to Mrs. Lyon. "One regrets, of course, but one is thankful it is no worse." "I think," said another, "it will do very well—I think it will do very well; thank you for the opportunity." And "Charming, my dear Mrs. Lyon, charming," said another. They all spoke low and in the most confidential tone. What was it they were all so interested about?

The last of the party to go were Miss Lance and Colonel Kingsward. They seemed to go away together as they had seemed to come together.

"Your father is so kind as to see me home," Miss Lance said, by way of explanation. "I am not a grand lady with a carriage. I am old enough to walk home by myself, and I always do it, but as Colonel Kingsward is so kind, of course I like company best."

She too had a private word with Mrs. Lyon, at the head of the stairs. Betty did not want to listen, but she heard by instinct the repeated "Thank you, thank you! How can I ever express how much I thank you?" Betty was so bewildered that she could not think. She paid no attention to her father, who put his hands on her shoulders when he said "Good-night," and said, "Betty, I'll see you to-morrow." Oh, of course, she should see him to-morrow—or not, as circumstances might ordain. What did it matter? She was not anxious to see her father to-morrow, it could not be of the least importance whether they met or not; but what Betty would really have liked would have been to find out what all these little whisperings could mean.

Mrs. Lyon came up to her when the last, to wit, Colonel Kingsward following Miss Lance, had disappeared, and put her arms round the little girl. "You are looking a little tired," she said, "just this last hour. I did not think they would stay so late. It is all Miss Lance, I believe, setting us on to argue with her metaphysics. Well, everybody likes her very much, which will please you, my dear, as you are so fond of her. And now, Betty, you must run off to bed. There's hardly time for your beauty sleep."

"Mrs. Lyon," said Betty, very curious, "was it to meet Miss Lance that all those grand people came?"

"I don't know what you call grand people. They are all great friends of ours and also of your father's, and I think you know them every one. And they all know each other."

"Except Miss Lance," said Gerald, who was always disagreeable—always, when anyone mentioned Miss Lance's name.

"I know her, certainly, and better than any of them! And there is nobody so delightful," Betty cried, with fervour, partly because she believed what she said, and partly to be disagreeable in her turn to him.

"And so they all seemed to think," said old Mr. Lyon, "though I'm not so fond of new people as the rest of you. Lay hands suddenly on no man is what I say."

"And I say the same as my uncle," said Gerald, "and it's still more true of a woman than a man."

"You are such an experienced person," said the old lady; "they know so much better than we do, Betty. But never you mind, for your friend has made an excellent impression upon all these people—the most tremendously respectable people," Mrs. Lyon said, "none of your artists and light-minded persons! Make yourself comfortable with that thought, and good night, my little Betty. You must not stay up so late another night."

What nonsense that was of staying up late, when it was not yet twelve o'clock! But Betty went off to her room with a little confusion and bewilderment of mind, happy on the whole, but feeling as if she had something to think about when she should be alone. What was it she had to think about? She could not think what it was when she sat down alone to study her problem. There was no problem, and what the departing guests had said to Mrs. Lyon was quite simple, and referred to something that was their own business, that had nothing to do with Betty. How could it have anything to do with Betty?

Around the corner of the Park, Bee, too, was sitting alone and thinking at the same time, and the two sets of thoughts, neither very clear, revolved round the same circle. But neither of the sisters knew, concerning this problem, whereabouts the other was.

CHAPTER XII

And yet all this time there lay upon Betty's table, concealed under the pretty laced handkerchiefs which she had pulled out of their sachet to choose one for the party, Bee's little tremulous letter, expressing a state of mind more agitated than that of Betty, and full of wonderings and trouble. It was found there by the maid who put things in order next morning, when she called the young visitor.

"Here's a letter that came last night, and you have never opened it," said the maid, half reproachfully. She, at least, she was anxious to note, had not been to blame.

Betty took it with great sang froid. She saw by the writing it was only Bee's—and Bee's news was never imperative. There could not be much to disclose to her of the state of affairs at Kingswarden that was new, since the night before last.

But the result was that Betty went downstairs in her hat and gloves, and that Mr. Lyon and Gerald, who were both sitting down to that substantial breakfast which is the first symbol of good health and a good conscience in England, had much ado to detain her long enough to share that meal.

Mrs. Lyon did not come downstairs in the morning, so that they used the argument of helplessness, professing themselves unable to pour out their own tea.

"And what business can Betty have of such importance that she must run out without her breakfast?" said the old gentleman.

"Oh, it is news I have heard which I must take at once to papa!"

The two gentlemen looked at each other, and Mr. Lyon shook his big, old head.

"I would not trouble your papa, my dear, with anything you may have heard. Depend upon it, he will let you know anything he wishes you to know—in his own time."

"But it is news—news," said Betty; "news about Charlie!"

Then she remembered that very little had been said even to the Lyons about Charlie, and stopped with embarrassment, and her friends could not but believe that this was a hasty expedient to conceal from them that she had heard something—some flying rumour which had set her little impetuous being on fire. When she had escaped from their sympathetic looks and Gerald's magnanimous proposal to accompany her—without so much as an egg to fortify him for the labours of the day!—Betty set out, crossing the Park in the early glory of the morning, which feels at nine o'clock what six o'clock feels in the country, to carry the news to her father.

Charlie found, and ill; and demanding to see Miss Lance, his health and recovery depending upon whether he should see her or not! Betty's first instinct had been to hasten at once to George Street, Hanover Square, but then she remembered that papa presumably was the one who was most anxious about Charlie and had the best right to know, and it was perhaps better not to explain to the friends in Portman Square why Miss Lance should go to Charlie. Indeed, when she had set out, a great many questions occurred to Betty, circulating through her lively little mind without any possibility of an answer to them. Why should Charlie be so anxious to see Miss Lance? Why had he been so long there, ill, and nobody come to tell his people of it? And what was Bee doing in Curzon Street, in Aubrey Leigh's house, which was the last house in the world where she had any right to be? But she walked so fast, and the sunny air with all its movement and lightness so carried her on and filled her with pleasant sounds and images, that these thoughts, blowing like the wind through her little intelligence, had not much effect on Betty now—though there was incipient trouble in them, as even she could see.

Colonel Kingsward was seated at his breakfast when his little girl burst in upon him in all the freshness of the morning. Her youth and her bloom, and her white frock, notwithstanding its black accoutrements, made a great show in the dark-coloured, solemn, official-looking room, with its Turkey carpets and morocco chairs. The Colonel was evidently startled by the sight of her. He said, "Well?" in that tone of self-defence, and almost defiance, with which a man prepares for being called upon to give an account of himself; as if anything so absurd could be possible as that Betty, little Betty, could call upon her father to give an account of himself! But then it is very true that when there is something to be accounted for, the strongest feel how "conscience doth make cowards of us all."

"Oh," she cried, breathless, "Papa—Charlie! Bee has found Charlie, and he's been very ill—typhoid fever; he's getting better, and he's in London, and she's with him; and he wants but to see Miss Lance. Oh, papa, that's what I came about chiefly—he wants to see Miss Lance."

Colonel Kingsward's face changed many times during this breathless deliverance. He said first, "He's at Mackinnon's, I know;" then, "In London!" with no pleasure at all in his tone; and finally, "Miss Lance!" angrily, his face covered with a dark glow.

"What is all this?" he cried, when she stopped for want of breath. "Charlie—in town? You must be out of your senses. Why, he is in Scotland. I heard from—, eh? Well, I don't know that I had any letter, but—. And ill—and Bee with him? What is the meaning of all this? Are you both mad, or in a conspiracy to make yourselves disagreeable to me?"

"Papa!" cried Betty, very ready to take up the challenge; but on the whole the news was too important to justify a combat of self-defence. She produced Bee's note out of its envelope, and placed it before him, running on with a report of it while the Colonel groped for his eyeglass and arranged it upon his nose.

"A lady came and fetched her," cried Betty, hurriedly, to forestall the reading, "and brought her up to town and took her to him—oh, so bad—where he had been for weeks; and she told him you had been to Oxford, and something about Miss Lance; and he wants to see Miss Lance, and calls and calls for her, and won't be satisfied. Oh, papa!"

Colonel Kingsward had arranged his pince-nez very carefully; he had taken up Bee's note, and went over it word by word while Betty made her breathless report. When he came to the first mention of Miss Lance he struck his hand upon the table like any other man in a passion, making all the cups and plates ring.

"The little fool!" he said, "the little fool! What right had she to bring in that name? It was this that called forth Betty's exclamation, but no more was said by either till he read it out to the end. Then he flung the letter from him, and getting up, paced about the room in rage and dismay.

"A long illness," said the Colonel, "was perhaps the best thing that could have happened to him to sweep all that had passed before out of his mind; and here does this infernal little idiot, this little demon full of spite and malice, get at the boy at his worst moment and bring everything back. What right had she, the spiteful, envious little fool, to bring in the name of a lady—of a lady to whom you all owe the greatest respect?"

"Papa!" cried Betty, overwhelmed, "Bee couldn't have meant any harm."

Colonel Kingsward was out of himself and he uttered words which terrified his daughter, and which need not be recorded against him—for he certainly did not in cold blood wish Bee to fall under any celestial malediction. He stormed about the room, saying much that Betty could not understand; that it was just the thing of all others that should not have happened, and the time of all others; that if it had been a little later, or even a little earlier, it would not have mattered; that it was enough to overturn every arrangement, increase every difficulty. He was not at all a man to give way to his feelings so. His children, indeed, until very lately, had never seen him excited at all, and it was an astonishment beyond description to little Betty to be a spectator of this scene. Indeed, Colonel Kingsward awoke presently to a sense of the self-exposure he had been making, and calmed down, or, at least, controlled himself, upon which Betty ventured to ask him very humbly what he thought she had better do.

"May I go to Miss Lance and tell her? She is not angry now, nor unhappy about him like—like us," said Betty, putting the best face upon it with instinctive capacity, "and she might know what to do. She is so very kind and understanding, don't you know, papa?—and she would know what to do."

For the first time Colonel Kingsward gave his agitated little visitor a smile. "You seem to have some understanding, too, for a little girl," he said, "and it looks as if you would be worthy of my confidence, Betty. When I see you this afternoon I shall, perhaps, have something to tell you that—"

There came over Colonel Kingsward's fine countenance a smile, a consciousness, which filled Betty with amaze. She had seen her father look handsome, commanding, very serious. She had seen him wear an air which the girls in their profanity had been used in their mother's happy days to call that of the père noble. She had seen him angry, even in a passion, as to-day. She had heard him, alas! blaspheme, which had been very terrible to Betty. But she had never, she acknowledged to herself, seen him look silly before. Silly, in a girl's phraseology, was what he looked now, with that fatuity which is almost solely to be attributed to one cause; but of this Betty was not aware. It came over his countenance, and for a moment Colonel Kingsward let himself go on the flood of complacent consciousness, which healed all his wounds. Then he suddenly braced himself up and turned to Betty again.

"Perhaps," he said, in his most fatherly tone, for it seemed to the man in this crisis of his life that even little Betty's support was something to hold by, "my dear child, your instinct is right. Go to Miss Lance and tell her how things are. Don't take this odious letter, however," he said, seizing Bee's note and tearing it across with indignant vehemence, "with all its prejudices and assumptions. Tell her in your own words; and where they are—and—Where are they, by the way?" he said, groping for the fragments of the letter in his waste-paper basket. "I hope you noted the address."

He had not then, it was evident, noted the address, nor the name of Mrs. Leigh, nor in whose house Charlie was. Betty's heart beat high with the question whether she should call his attention to these additional facts, but her courage failed her. He had cooled down, he was himself again: and after a moment he added, "I will write a little note which you can take," with once more the smile that Betty thought silly floating across his face. She was standing close by the writing-table, and Betty was not aware that there was any harm in the natural glimpse which her keen eyes took, before she was conscious of it, of the note he was writing. It was not like a common note. It did not begin "Dear Miss Lance," as would have been natural. In short, it had no beginning at all, nor any signature—or rather it was signed only with his initial "F." How very extraordinary that papa should sign "F." and should not put any beginning to his letter. A kind of wondering consternation enveloped the little girl. But still she did not in the least understand what it meant.

Betty walked away along Pall Mall and Piccadilly, and by the edge of the Park to George Street, Hanover Square. It is not according to the present fashion that a girl should shrink from walking along through those busy London streets, where nobody is in search of adventures, at least at that hour of the morning. Her white morning frock and her black ribbons, and her early bloom, like the morning, though delightful to behold, did not make all the passers by stand and stare as the movements of a pretty girl used to do, if we are to credit the novels, in the beginning of the century. People, perhaps, have too much to do nowadays to give to that not unusual sight the attention which the dandies and the macaroni bestowed upon it, and Betty was so evidently bent on her own little business, whatever it was, that nothing naturally occurred to detain her.

It was so unusual for her to have a grave piece of business in hand that she was a little elated by it, even though so sorry for Charlie who was so ill, and for Bee who was so perturbed about everything. Betty herself was not perturbed; she was full of the pleasure of the morning and the long, interesting walk, and the sense of her own importance as a messenger. If there did occasionally float across her mind the idea that her father's demeanour was strange, or that it was odd that he should have signed his note to Miss Lance with an F., it was merely a momentary idea and she did not question it or detain it. And poor Charlie! Ill—not able to get out this fine weather; but he was getting better, so that there was really nothing to be troubled about.

Miss Lance was up, but had not yet appeared when Betty was shown into her little drawing-room. She was not an early riser. It was one of her vices, she frankly allowed. Betty had to wait, and had time to admire all her friend's knick-knacks, of which there were many, before she came in, which she did at last, with her arms put out to take Betty maternally to her bosom. She looked in the girl's face with a very intent glance before she took her into this embrace.

"My little Betty, so early," she said, and kissed the girl, and then looked at her again, as if in expectation of something; but as Betty could not think of anything that Miss Lance would be expecting from her, she remained unconscious of any special meaning in this look.

"Yes, I am early," she said; "it is because I have something to tell you, and something to ask of you, too."

"Tell, my dear little girl, and ask. You may be sure I shall be at your service. But what is this in your hand—a note for me?"

"Yes, it is a note for you, but may I tell you first what it is about?" Betty went on quickly with her story, though Miss Lance, without waiting for it, took the note and opened it. "Miss Lance, Charlie is found; he has been very ill, and he wants to see you."

"To see me?" Miss Lance looked with eyes of sympathy, yet great innocence, as if at an impossible proposal, at the breathless girl so anxious to get it out. "But, Betty, if he is with your friends, the Mackinnons, in Scotland—?"

"Oh, Miss Lance, I told you he was not there, don't you remember? He has never been anywhere all this time. He has had typhoid fever, and on Thursday Bee was sent for, and found him still ill, but mending. And when he heard you were in town he would give her no peace till she wrote and asked you to come and see him. And she did not know your address so she wrote to me. I went to tell papa first, and then I came on here. Oh, will you come and see Charlie? Bee said he wanted to get into a hansom and come to you as soon as he heard you were here."

"What induced them to talk of me, and why did she tell him I was here?" Miss Lance cried, with a momentary cloud upon her face, such as Betty had never seen there before. She sat down suddenly in a chair, with a pat of her foot upon the carpet, which was almost a stamp of impatience, and then she read Colonel Kingsward's note for the second time, with her brows drawn together and a blackness about her eyes which filled Betty with alarm and dismay. She looked up, however, next minute with her countenance cleared. "Your father says I am to use my own discretion," she said, with a half laugh; "that is not much help to me, is it, in deciding what is best to do? So he has been ill—and not in Scotland at all?"

"I told you he was not in Scotland," cried Betty, a little impatient in her turn. "Oh, Miss Lance, he has been ill, he is still ill, and won't you come and see him when he wants you so? Oh, come and see him, please! He looks so ill and wretched, Bee says, and weak, and cannot get back his strength; and he thinks if he could see you—"

"Poor boy—silly boy!" said Miss Lance; "why does he think it will do him good to see me? I doubt if it would do him any good; and your father says I am to use my discretion. I would do anything for any of you, Betty, but perhaps I should do him harm instead of good. Have you got your sister's letter?"

"I left it with papa—that is, he threw it into the waste paper basket," said the too truthful Betty, growing red.

"I understand," said Miss Lance, "it was not a letter to show me. Bee has her prejudices, and perhaps she is right. I cannot expect that all the family should be as nice to me as you. Have they taken him to Kingswarden? Or where is he, poor boy?"

"He is at No. 1000, Curzon Street," Betty said.

"What!" said Miss Lance. "Where?" Her brow curved over her eyes, her face grew dark as if the light had gone out of the morning, and she spoke the two monosyllables in a sharp imperative tone, so that they seemed to cut like a knife.

"At No. 1000; Curzon Street," Betty repeated with great alarm, not knowing what to think.

Miss Lance rose quickly, as if there had been something that stung her in the innocent words. She looked as if she were about to pace the room from end to end, as Colonel Kingsward did when he was disturbed. But either she did not mean this, or she restrained herself, for what she did was to walk to her writing-table and put Colonel Kingsward's note away in a drawer, and then she went to the window and looked out, and said it was a fine morning but dusty for walking—and then she returned to her chair and sat down again and looked at Betty. She was pale, and there were lines in her face that had not been there before. Her eyes were almost piteous as she looked at the surprised girl.

"I am in a very strait place," she said, "and I don't know what to do." Something like moisture seemed to come up into her eyes. "This is always how it happens to me," she said, "just at the moment, just at the moment! What am I to do?"

CHAPTER XIII

Bee had passed the whole day with Charlie, the Friday of the dinner party at Portman Square. She had resisted as long as she could writing the letter which had brought so much excitement to Betty, and the passion with which he had insisted upon this—the struggle between them, the vehemence with which he had declared that he cared for nothing in the world but to see Laura once again, to thank her for having pleaded for him with his father, to ask her forgiveness for his follies—had been bad for Charlie, who lay for the rest of the day upon the sofa, tossing from him one after the other the novels that were provided for his amusement, declaring them to be "rot" or "rubbish," growling at his sister when she continued to speak to him, and reducing poor Bee to that state of wounded imbecility which is the lot of those who endeavour to please an unpleasable invalid, with the conviction that all the time they are doing more harm than good.

Bee was not maladroit by nature, and she had the warmest desire to be serviceable to her brother, but it appeared that she always did the wrong thing, not only in the eyes of Charlie, but in those of the nurse, who came in from time to time with swift movements, bringing subordination and quiet where there had been nothing but irritation and resistance. And in this house, where she had been brought entirely for the service of Charlie, Bee did not know what to do. She was afraid to leave the rooms that had been given up to him lest she should meet someone on the stairs, or be seen only to be avoided, as if her presence there was that of a ghost or an enemy. Poor Bee—wearing out the long hours of the spring afternoon with poor attempts to be useful to the invalid, to watch his looks—which he resented by frequent adjurations not to watch him as a cat watches a mouse—to anticipate his wishes—which immediately became the last thing in the world he wanted as soon as she found out the drink or got the paper for which he was looking, heard or thought she heard steps coming to the street door, subdued voices in the hall, comings and goings half stealthily, noises subdued lest she should hear. What did it matter whether she heard or not? Why should the master of the house be banished that she, so ineffectual as she had proved, should be brought to her brother's side? She had not done, and could not do, any good to Charlie. All that she had done had been to remind him of Miss Lance, to be the medium of calling that disastrous person, who had done all the harm, back into Charlie's life—nay, of bringing her back to this house, the inmates of which she had already harmed to the utmost of her power.

That was all that had been done by Bee, and now her presence kept at a distance the one individual in the world who had the best right to be here. He came almost secretly, she felt sure, to the door in the dusk to inquire after his patient, or to get his letters; or stole in, subduing his step, that she might not be disturbed.

Poor Bee! It was very bitter to her to think that Aubrey Leigh should leave his own house because she was there. Sometimes she wondered whether it was some remnant of old, almost-extinguished feeling in his breast which had made him think that the sight of Bee would do Charlie good—the sight of Bee, for which her brother did not care at all, not at all; which was an annoyance and a fatigue to him, except when she had betrayed what was the last thing in the world she should have betrayed, the possibility of seeing again that woman who had harmed them all. If Aubrey had thought so, with some remnant of the old romance, how mistaken he had been! And it was intolerable for the girl to think that for the sake of this unsuccessful experiment he had been sent away from his own house. She placed herself in the corner of the room in which Charlie (to whom she was supposed to do good and bring pleasure) could see her least, and bitterness filled her heart. There were times in which she thought of stealing away, leaving a word for Mrs. Leigh to the effect that she was doing Charlie no good, and that Betty, who would come to-morrow, might perhaps be of more use—and returning forlorn to Kingswarden to renew the life, where perhaps nobody wanted her very much, but where, at least, there were so many things which she and no one else was there to do.

She was still in this depressed state when Mrs. Leigh (who had evidently gone away that the brother and sister might be alone and happy together) came back, looking into Charlie's room to ask how he was on her way upstairs to dress for dinner.

"Better," the nurse said, with her eyebrows. "Peevish—young lady mustn't cross him—must be humoured—things not gone quite so well to-day."

"You will tell me about it at dinner," said Mrs. Leigh, and Bee went downstairs with a heavy heart to be questioned. Aubrey's mother looked cheerful enough; she did not seem to be unhappy about his absence or to dislike the society of the girl who had driven him away. And she was very considerate even in her questions about the patient.

"We must expect these fluctuations," she said; "you must not be cast down if you are not quite so triumphantly successful to-day."

"Oh, Mrs. Leigh, I am deceiving you. I have never been successful at all. He did not want me—he doesn't care for me, and to stay here is dreadful, upsetting the house—doing no good."

"My dear, this is a strange statement to make, and you must not expect me to believe you in the face of facts. He was much better after seeing you last night."

"Doing no good," said Bee, shaking her head, "but harm, oh, real harm! It was not I that did him good, it was telling him of someone, of a lady. Oh, Mrs. Leigh, how am I to tell you?"

"My dear child, anything that you yourself know can surely be told to me. We were afraid that something about a woman was at the bottom of it, but then that is always the thing that is said, and typhoid, you know, means bad drains and not a troubled mind—though the one may make you susceptible to the other. Don't be so distressed, my dear. It seems more to your inexperience than it is in reality. He will get over that."

"Mrs. Leigh," said Bee, very pale, "he has made me write to ask her to come and see him here."

It was now Mrs. Leigh's turn to change colour. She grew red, looking astonished in the girl's despairing face.

"A woman to come and see him, here! But your brother would never insult the house and you—I am talking nonsense," she said, suddenly stopping herself, "and misconstruing him altogether. It is some lady who has jilted him—or something of that kind."

Bee had not understood what Mrs. Leigh's first idea was, and she did not see any cause for relief in the second.

"I don't know what she did to him, or what she has done to them all," the girl said, mournfully. "They are all the same. Papa, even, who does not care very much for ladies, generally—But Charlie, poor Charlie! Oh, I believe he is in love with her still, though she is twice as old as he is and has almost broken his heart.

"My dear," said Mrs. Leigh, "this must be something very different to what we thought. We thought he had got into some very dreadful trouble about a—an altogether inferior person. But as it seems to be a lady, and one that is known to the family, and who can be asked to come here—if you can tell me a little more clearly what the story is, I shall be more able to give you my advice."

Bee looked at her questioner helpless, half distracted, not knowing how to speak, and yet the story must be told. She had written that fatal invitation, and it could not be concealed who this possible visitor was. She began with a great deal of hesitation to talk of the lady whom Charlie had raved about at Oxford, and how he was to work to please her; and how he did not work, but failed in every way, and fled from Oxford; and how her father went to inquire into the story; and how the lady had come to Colonel Kingsward at the hotel, to explain to him, to excuse Charlie, to beg his father to forgive him.

"But, my dear, she can't be so very bad," said Mrs. Leigh, soothingly. "You must not judge her hardly; if she thought she had been to blame in the matter, that was really the right thing to do."

"And since then," resumed Bee, "I think papa has thought of nobody else; he writes to her and tells her everything. He goes to see her; he forgets about Charlie and all of us; he has taken Betty there, and Betty adores her too. And to-night," cried Bee, the angry tears coming into her eyes, "she is dining in Portman Square, dining with the Lyons as a great friend of ours—in Portman Square."

Mrs. Leigh drew Bee to her and gave her a kiss of consolation. I think it was partly that the girl in her misery should not see the smile, which Mrs. Leigh, thinking that she now saw through this not uncommon mystery, could not otherwise conceal.

"My poor child," she said, "my dear girl! This is hard upon you since you dislike her so much, but I am afraid it is quite natural, and a thing that could not have been guarded against. And then you must consider that your father may probably be a better judge than yourself. I don't see any harm this lady has done, except that perhaps it is not quite good taste to make herself so agreeable both to the father and son; but perhaps in Charlie's case that was not her fault. And I see no reason, my dear—really and sincerely as your friend, Bee—why you should be so prejudiced against a poor woman whose only fault is that everybody else likes her. Now isn't it a little unreasonable when you think of it calmly yourself?"

"Oh, Mrs. Leigh!" Bee cried. The situation was so intolerable, the passion of injury and misconception so strong in her that she could only gasp in insupportable anger and dismay.

"Bee! Bee! this feeling is natural but you must not let it carry you away. Have you seen her? Let me come in when she is here and give my opinion."

"I have seen her three times," said Bee, solemnly, "once at the Baths, and once at the Academy, and once at Oxford;" and then once more excitement mastered the girl. "Oh, when you know who she is! Don't smile, don't smile, but listen! She is Miss Lance."

"Miss Lance!" Mrs. Leigh repeated the name with surprise, looking into Bee's face. "You must compose yourself," she said, "you must compose yourself. Miss—? My dear, you have got over excited, you have mixed things up."

"No, I am not over-excited! I am telling you only the truth. It is Miss Lance, and they all believe in her as if she were an angel, and she is coming here."

Mrs. Leigh was very much startled, but yet she would not believe her ears. She had heard Charlie delirious in his fever not so long ago. Her mind gave a little leap to the alarming thought that there might be madness in the family, and that Bee had been seized like her brother. That what she said was actual fact seemed to her too impossible to be true. She soothed the excited girl with all her power. "Whoever it is, my dear, you shall not take any harm. There is nothing to be frightened about. I will take care of you, whoever it is."

"I do not think you believe me," said Bee. "I am not out of my mind, as you think. It is Miss Lance—Miss Laura Lance—the same, the very same, that—and I have written, and she will be coming here."

"This is very strange," said Mrs. Leigh. "It does not seem possible to believe it. The same—who came between Aubrey and you? Oh, I never meant to name him, I was never to name him; but how can I help it? Laura, who was the trouble of his house—who would not leave him—who went to your father? And now your father! I cannot understand it. I cannot believe that it is true."

"It is true," said Bee. "But, Mrs. Leigh, you forget that no one cared then, except myself; they have forgotten all that now, they have forgotten what happened. It was only my business, it was not their business. All that has gone from papa; he remembers nothing about it. And she is a witch, she is a magician, she is a devil—oh, please forgive me, forgive me—I don't know what I am saying. It has all been growing, one thing after another—first me—and then Charlie—and then papa—and then Betty. And now, after bringing him almost to death and destruction, here is Charlie, in this house, calling for her, raging with me till I wrote to call her—me!" cried Bee, with a sort of indignant eloquence. "Me! Could it go further than that? Could anything be more than that? Me!—and in this house."

"My dear child," said Mrs. Leigh, "I don't wonder, I don't wonder—it is like something in a tragedy. Oh, Bee! Forgive me for what is first in my thoughts. Was she the reason, the only reason, for your breach with my poor Aubrey? For at first you stood by him—and then you turned upon him."

"Do not ask me any more questions, please. I am not able to answer anything. Isn't it enough that all these things have happened through this woman, and that she is coming here?"

Mrs. Leigh made no further question. She saw that the girl's excitement was almost beyond her control, and that her young mind was strained to its utmost. She said, half to herself, "I must think. I cannot tell in a moment what to do. I must send for Aubrey. It is his duty and mine to let it go no further. You must try to compose yourself, my dear, and trust us. Oh, Bee," there were tears in her eyes as she came up to the girl and kissed her, "if you could but have trusted us—in all things! I don't think you ever would have repented."

But Bee did not make any response. Her hands were cold and her head hot. She was wrapt in a strange passion and confusion of human chaos and bewilderment—everything gone wrong—all the elements of life twisted the perverse way; nothing open, nothing clear. She was incapable of any simple, unmingled feeling in that confusion and medley of everything going wrong.

Mrs. Leigh, a little disappointed, went into the inner room, the little library, to write a letter—no doubt to consult or summon her son—from which she was interrupted a few minutes later by a faint call, and Bee's white face in the doorway.

"Mrs. Leigh, papa will come to-morrow, and he will take us away; at least he will take me away. I—I shan't be any longer in anyone's way. Oh, don't keep him apart from you—don't send anyone out of the house because of me!"

CHAPTER XIV

There was a great deal of commotion next morning in the house in Mayfair.

Bee was startled by having a tray brought to her bedroom with her breakfast when she was almost ready to go downstairs. "Mrs. Leigh thought, Miss, as you had been so tired last night, you might like to rest a little longer," said the maid; and Bee divined with a sharp pang through all the trouble and confusion of her mind that she was not wanted—that probably Aubrey was coming to consult with his mother what was to be done. It may be imagined with what scrupulousness she kept within her room, her pride all up in arms though her heart she thought was broken. Though the precaution was so natural, though it was taken at what was supposed to be her desire, at what was really her desire—the only one she would have expressed—yet she resented it, in the contradiction and ferment of her being. If Mrs. Leigh supposed that she wanted to see Aubrey! He was nothing to her, he had no part in her life. When she had been brought here, against her will, it had been expressly explained that it was not for Aubrey, that he would rather go away to the end of the world than disturb her. And she had herself appealed to his mother—her last action on the previous night—to bring him back, not to banish him on account of the girl who was nothing to him, and whose part it was, not his, to go away. All this, however, did not make it seem less keen a wound to Bee that she should be, so to speak, imprisoned in her own room, because Aubrey was expected downstairs. She had never, she declared to herself vehemently, felt at ease under the roof that was his; nothing but Charlie's supposed want of her would have induced her to subject herself to the chances of meeting him, and the still more appalling chance of being supposed to wish to meet him. And now this insult of imprisonment in her bedroom, lest she should by any chance come under his observation, offend his eye!—Bee was contradictory enough at all times, a rosebud set about with wilful thorns; but everything was in tumult about her, and all her conditions nothing but contradictions now.

Thus it happened that while Betty was setting out with much excitement, but that all pleasurable, walking lightly among undiscovered dangers, Bee was suddenly arrested, as she felt, imprisoned in the little room looking out upon roofs and backs of houses, thrust aside into a corner that she might not be seen or her presence known—imperceptibly the force of the description grew as she went on piling up agony upon agony. It was some time before, in the commotion of her feelings, she could bring herself to swallow her tea, and then she walked about the room, gazed out of the window from which, as it was at the back of the house, she saw nothing, and found the position more and more intolerable every minute. A prisoner! she who had been brought here against her will, on pretence that her presence might save her brother's life, or something equally grandiose and impossible—save her brother's life, bring him back from despair by the sight of some one that he loved. These were the sort of words that Mrs. Leigh had said. As if it mattered to Charlie one way or the other what Bee might think or do! As if he were to be consoled by her, or stimulated, or brought back to life! She had affected him involuntarily, undesirably, by her betrayal of the vicinity of that woman, that witch, who had warped his heart and being. But as for influencing in her own person her brother's mind or life, Bee knew she was as little capable as baby, the little tyrant of the nursery. Oh! how foolish she had been to come at all, to yield to what was said, the flattering suggestion that she could do so much, when she knew all along in her inmost consciousness that she could do nothing! The only thing for her to do now was to go back to the dull life of which in her impatient foolishness she had grown so weary, the dull life in which she was indeed of some use after all, where it was clearly her duty to get the upper hand of baby, to preserve the discipline of the nursery, to train the little ones, and keep the big boys in order. These were the elder sister's duties, with which nobody could interfere—not any ridiculous, sentimental, exaggerated idea, as Charlie had said, of what a woman's ministrations could do. "Oh, woman, in our hours of ease!" that sort of foolish, foolish, intolerable, ludicrous kind of thing, which it used to be considered right to say, though people knew better now. Bee felt bitterly that to say of her that she was a ministering angel would be irony, contumely, the sort of thing people said when they laughed at women and their old-fashioned sham pretences. She had never made any such pretence. She had said from the beginning that Charlie would care for none of her ministrations. She had been brought here against her judgment, against her will, and now she was shut up as in a prison in order that Aubrey might not be embarrassed by the sight of her! As if she had wished to see Aubrey! As if it had not been on the assurance that she was not to see Aubrey that she had been beguiled here!

When a message came to her that she was to go to her brother, Bee did not know what to do. It seemed to her that Aubrey might be lurking somewhere on the stairs, that he might be behind Charlie's sofa, or lying in wait on the other side of the curtain, notwithstanding her offence at the quite contradictory idea that she was imprisoned in her room to be kept out of his way. These two things were entirely contrary from each other, yet it was quite possible to entertain and be disturbed by both in the tumult and confusion of a perverse young mind. She stepped out of her room as if she were about to fall into an ambush, notwithstanding that she had been thrilling in every irritated nerve with the idea of being imprisoned there.

Charlie had insisted on getting up much earlier than usual. He had not waited for the doctor's visit. He was better; well, he said, stimulated into nervous strength and capability, though his gaunt limbs tottered under him and his thin hand trembled. When he got into his sitting-room he flung away all his cushions and wrappings as soon as his nurse left him and went to the mirror over the mantel-piece and gazed at himself in the glass, smoothing down and stroking into their right place those irregular soft tufts growing here and there upon his chin, which he thought were the beginnings of a beard.

Would she think it was a beard, that sign of manhood? They were too downy, fluffy, unenergetic, a foolish kind of growth, like a colt's, some long, some short, yet Charlie could not help being proud of them. He felt that they would come to something in time, and remembered that he had often heard it said that a beard which never had been shaved became the finest—in time. Would she think so? or would she laugh and tell him that this would not do, that he must get himself shaved?

He would not mind that she should laugh. She might do anything, all she did was delightful to poor Charlie, and there would be a compliment even in being told that he must get shaved. Charlie had stroked his upper lip occasionally with a razor, but it had never been necessary to suggest to him that he should get shaved before.

He had to be put back upon his sofa when nurse re-appeared, but he only remained there for the time, promising no permanent obedience. When Laura came he certainly should not receive her there.

"When did your letter go? When would Betty receive it?" he said, when Bee, breathless and pale, at last, under nurse's escort, was brought downstairs.

"She must have got it last night. But there was a dinner party," said Bee, after a pause, "last night at Portman Square."

"What do I care for their dinner parties? I suppose the postman would go all the same."

"But Betty could not do anything till this morning."

"No," said Charlie, "I suppose not. She would be too much taken up with her ridiculous dress and what she was to wear"—the knowledge of a young man who had sisters, pierced through even his indignation—"or with some nonsense about Gerald Lyon—that fellow! And to think," he said, in an outburst of high, moral indignation "that one's fate should be at the mercy of a little thing like Betty, or what she might say or do!"

"Betty is not so much younger than we are; to be sure," said Bee, with reflective sadness, "she has never had anything to make her think of all the troubles that are in the world."

Charlie turned upon her with scorn.

"And what have you had to make you think, and what do you suppose you know? A girl, always protected by everybody, kept out of the battle, never allowed to feel the air on your cheek! I must tell you, Bee, that your setting yourself up for knowing things is the most ridiculous exhibition in the world."

Bee's wounded soul could not find any words. She kept out of the battle! She setting up for knowing things! And what was his knowledge in comparison with hers? He had but been deluded like the rest by a woman whom Bee had always seen through, and never, never put any faith in; whereas she had lost what was most dear, all her individual hopes and prospects, and been obliged to sacrifice what she knew would be the only love of her life.

She looked at Charlie with eyes that were full of unutterable things. He was reckless with hope and expectation, self-deceived, thinking that all was coming right again; whereas Bee knew that things would never more be right with her. And yet he presumed to say that she knew nothing, and that to think she had suffered was a mere pretence! "How little, how little," Bee thought, "other people know."

The house seemed full that morning of sounds and commotions, unlike ordinary times. There were sounds of ringing bells, of doors opened and shut, of voices downstairs. Once both Charlie and Bee held their breath, thinking the moment had come, for a carriage stopped at the door, there was the sound of a noisy summons, and then steps coming upstairs.

Alas! it was nothing but the doctor, who came in, ushered by nurse, but not until she had held a private conference with him, keeping them both in the most tremendous suspense in the bedroom. It is true this was a thing which happened every morning, but they had both forgotten that in the tension of highly-wrought feeling.

And when the doctor came he shook his head. "There has been too much going on here," he said. "You have been doing too much or talking too much. Miss Kingsward, you helped us greatly with our patient yesterday, but I am afraid you have been going too far, you have hurried him too much. We dare not press recovery at railway speed after so serious an illness as this."

"Oh, I have not wished to do so," said Bee. "It is some friends that we are expecting."

"Friends? I never said he was to see friends," the doctor said.

"Come doctor," said Charlie, "you must not be too hard upon me. It's—it's my father and sister that are coming."

"Your father and sister are different, but not too much even of them. Recollect, nurse, what I say, not too much even of the nearest and dearest. The machinery has been too much out of gear to come round all in a moment. And, Miss Kingsward, you are pale, too. You had better go out a little and take the air. There must not be too much conversation, not too much reading either. I must have quiet, perfect quiet."

"Am I to do nothing but think?" said Charlie. "Is that the best thing for a fellow to do that has missed his schools and lost his time?"

"Be thankful that you are at a time of life when the loss of a few weeks doesn't matter, and don't think," said the doctor, "or we shall have to stop even the father and sister, and send you to bed again. Be reasonable, be reasonable. A few days' quiet and you will be out of my hands."

"Oh, Charlie, then you have given up seeing anyone else," said Bee, with a cry of relief as the doctor, attended by the nurse, went downstairs.

"I have done nothing of the kind," he cried, jumping up from the sofa and going to the window. "And you had better tell that woman to go out for a walk and that you will look after me. Do you think when Laura comes that I will not see her if fifty doctors were to interfere? But if you want to save me a little you will send that woman out of the way. It is the worry and being contradicted that does me harm."

"How can I, Charlie—oh, how can I, in the face of what the doctor said?"

He turned back upon her flaming with feverish rage and excitement.

"If you don't I'll go out. I'll have a cab called, and get away from this prison," he cried. "I don't care what happens to me, but I shall see her if I die for it."

"Perhaps," said Bee to herself, trembling, "she will not come. Oh! perhaps she will not come!" But she felt that this was a very forlorn hope, and when the nurse came back the poor girl, faltering and ill at ease, obeyed the peremptory signs and frowns of Charlie, once more established on the sofa and seeming to take no part in the negotiation.

"Nurse, I have been thinking," said Bee, with that talent for the circumstantial which women have, even when acting against their will, "that you have far more need of a walk and a little fresh air than I have, who have only been here for a day, and that if you will tell me exactly what to do, I could take care of him while you go out a little."

"Shouldn't think of leaving him," said nurse, with her eyebrows working as usual and a mocking smile about her lips. "Too much talk; doctor not pleased."

"But if I promise not to talk? I shall not talk. You don't want to talk, do you, Charlie?"

Charlie launched a missile at her in his ingratitude, over his shoulder. "Not with you," he said.

"You hear?" cried Bee, now intent upon gaining her point, and terrified lest other visitors might arrive before this matter were decided; "we shall not talk, and I will do all you tell me. Oh, only tell me what I am to do."

"Nothing to do," said the nurse, "not for the next hour; nothing, but keep him quiet. Well, if you think you can undertake that, just for half an hour—"

"I will—I will—for as long as you please," cried Bee. It was better, indeed, if there must be this interview with Laura, that there should be as few spectators as possible. She hurried the woman away with eagerness, though she had been alarmed at the first suggestion. But when she was alone with him, and nobody to stand by her, thinking at every sound she heard that this was the dreaded arrival, Bee crept close to him with a sudden panic of terror and dismay.

"Oh, Charlie, don't listen to her, don't believe her; oh, don't be led astray by her again! I have done what you told me, but I oughtn't to have done it. Oh, Charlie, stand fast, whatever she says, and don't be led astray by her again."

The only sign of Charlie's gratitude that Bee received was to be hastily pushed away by his shoulder. "You little fool, what do you know about it?" her brother said.

CHAPTER XV

But the nurse went out for her walk and came in again and nothing happened, and Charlie had his invalid dinner, which in his excitement he could not eat, and Bee was called downstairs to luncheon, and yet nobody came. The luncheon was a terrible ordeal for Bee. She attempted to eat, with an eye on the window, to watch for the arrival of the visitors, and an ear upon the subdued sounds of the house, through which she seemed to hear the distant step, the distant voice of someone whose presence was not acknowledged. She repeated with eagerness her little speech of the night before. "Something must have detained papa," she said, "I cannot understand it, but he is sure to come, and he will take me away."

"I don't want you to be taken away, my dear," said Mrs. Leigh. "I should not let you go if I could help it."

"Oh, but I must, I must," said Bee, trembling and agitated. She could not eat anything, any more than Charlie, and when the nurse came downstairs, indignantly carrying the tray from which scarcely anything had been taken, Bee could make no reply to her remonstrances. "The young lady had better not come upstairs again," said nurse; "she has done him more harm than good, he will have a relapse if we don't mind. It is as much as my character is worth." She talked like other people when there was no patient present, and she was genuinely afraid.

"What are we to do?" said Mrs. Leigh. "If this lady comes he ought not to see her! But perhaps she will not come."

"That is what I have hoped," said Bee, "but if she doesn't come he will go out, he will get to her somehow; he will kill himself with struggling—"

At the suggestion of going out the nurse gave a shriek and thrust her tray into the servant's hands who was waiting. "He will have to kill me first," she said, rushing away.

And immediately upon this scene came Betty, fresh and shining in her white frock, with a smile like a little sunbeam, who announced at once that Miss Lance was coming.

"How is Charlie?" said Betty. "Oh, Mrs. Leigh, how good you have been! Papa is coming himself to thank you. What a trouble it must have been to have him ill here all the time. Mrs. Lyon, whom I am staying with, thinks it so wonderful of you—so kind, so kind! And Bee, she is coming, though it is rather a hard thing for her to do. She says you will not like to see her, Mrs. Leigh, and that it will be an intrusion upon you; but I said when you had been so good to poor Charlie all along, you would not be angry that she should come who is such a friend."

"Any friend, of course, of Colonel Kingsward's—" Mrs. Leigh said stiffly, while little Betty stared. She thought they all looked very strange; the old lady so stiff, and Bee turning red and turning white, and a general air as if something had gone wrong.

"Is Charlie worse?" she said, with an anxious look.

And then Bee was suddenly called upstairs. "Can't manage him any longer," the nurse said on the landing. "I wash my hands of it. Your fault if he has a relapse."

"Who is that?" said Charlie, from within, "Who is it? I will see her! Nobody shall interfere, no one—doctor, or nurse, or—the devil himself. Bee!"

"It is only Betty," said Bee, upon which Charlie ceased his raging and flung himself again on his sofa.

"You want to torment me; you want to wear me out; you want to kill me," he said, with tears of keen disappointment in his eyes.

"Charlie," said Bee, "she is coming. Betty is here to say so; she is coming in about an hour or so. If you will eat your dinner and lie quite quiet and compose yourself you will be allowed to see her, and nurse will not object."

"Oh, Miss Kingsward, don't answer for me. It is as much as his life is worth."

"But not unless you eat your dinner and keep perfectly quiet."

"Give us that old dinner," said Charlie, with a loud, unsteady laugh, and the tray was brought back and he performed his duty upon the half-cold dishes with an expedition and exuberance that gave nurse new apprehensions.

"He'll have indigestion," she said, "if he gobbles like that," speaking once more inaudibly over Charlie's shoulder. But afterwards all was quiet till the fated moment came.

I do not think if these girls had known the feelings that were within Miss Lance's breast that they would have been able to retain their respective feelings towards her—Betty of adoration or Bee of hostility. She had lived a life of adventure, and she had come already on various occasions to the very eve of such a settled condition of life as would have made further adventure unnecessary and impossible—but something had always come in the way. Something so often comes in the way of such a career. The stolid people who are incapable of any skilful combinations go on and prosper, while those who have wasted so much cleverness or much wit, so much trouble—and disturbed the lives of others and risked their own—fail just at the moment of success. I am sometimes very sorry for the poor adventurers. Miss Lance went to Curzon Street with all her wits painfully about her, knowing that she was about to stand for her life. It seemed the most extraordinary spite of fate that this should have happened in the house of Aubrey Leigh. She would have had in any case a disagreeable moment enough between Charlie Kingsward and his father, but it was too much to have the other brought in. The man whom she had so wronged, the family (for she knew that his mother was there also) who knew all about her, who could tell everything, and stop her on the very threshold of the new life—that new life in which there would be no equivocal circumstances, nothing that she could be reproached with, only duty and kindness. So often she seemed to have been just within sight of that halcyon spot where she would need to scheme no more, where duty and every virtuous thing would be natural and easy. Was the failure to come all over again?

She was little more than an adventuress, this troubled woman, and yet it was not without something of the exalted feeling of one who is about to stand for his life, for emancipation and freedom to do well and all that is best in existence, that she walked through the streets towards her fate. Truth alone was possible with the Leighs, who knew everything about her past, and could not be persuaded or turned from their certainty by any explanations. But poor Charlie! Bare truth was not possible with him, whom she had sacrificed lightly to the amusement of the moment, whom she could never have married or made the instrument of building up her fortune except in the way which, to do her justice she had not foreseen, through the access he had given her to his father. How was she to satisfy that foolish, hot-headed boy?—and how to stop the mouths of the others in the background?—and how to persuade Colonel Kingsward that circumstances alone were against her—that she herself was not to blame? She did not conceal from herself any of these difficulties, but she was too brave a woman to fly before them. She preferred to walk, and to walk alone, to this trial which awaited her, in order to subdue her nerves and get the aid of the fresh air and solitude to steady her being. She was going to stand for her life.

It seemed a good augury that she was allowed to enter the house without any interruption from the sitting-room below, where she had the conviction that her worst opponents were lying in wait. She thought even that she had been able to distinguish the white cap and shawl of Mrs. Leigh through the window, but it was Betty who met her in the hall—met her with a kiss and expression of delight.

"Oh, I am so glad you have come," said Betty, "he is so eager to see you." The people in ambush in the ground floor rooms must have heard the exclamation, but they made no sign. At the door upstairs they were met by the nurse, excited and laconic, speaking without any sound.

"No worry—don't contradict. Much as life is worth," she said, with emphatic, silent lips. Miss Lance, so composed, so perfect in her manner, so wound up to everything, laughed a little—she was so natural!—and nodded her head. And then she went in.

Charlie on the sofa was of course the chief figure. But he had jumped up, flinging his wrappings about, and stood in his gaunt and tremulous length, with his big hollow eyes and his ragged little beard, and his hands stretched out. "At last!" he said, "at last—Laura!" stumbling in his weakness as he advanced to her. Bee was standing up straight against the window in the furthest corner of the room, not making a movement. How real, how natural, how completely herself and ready for any emergency this visitor was! She took Charlie's hands in hers, supporting him with that firm hold, and put him back upon his couch.

"Now," she said, "the conditions of my visit are these: perfect quiet and obedience, and no excitement. If you rebel in any way I shall go. I know what nursing is, and I know what common-sense is—and I came here to help you, not to harm you. Move a toe or finger more than you ought, and I shall go!"

"I will not move, not an eyelid if you tell me not. I want to do nothing but look at you. Laura! oh, Laura! I have been dead, and now I am alive again," Charlie said.

"Ill or well," said Miss Lance, arranging his cushions with great skill, "you are a foolish, absurd boy. Partly it belongs to your age and partly to your temperament. I should not have considered you like your father at the first glance, but you are like him. Now, perfect quiet. Consider that your grandmother has come to see you, and that it does not suit the old lady to have her mind disturbed."

He had seized her hand and was kissing it over and over again. Miss Lance took those caresses very quietly, but after a minute she withdrew her hand. "Now, tell me all about it," she said; "you went off in such a commotion—so angry with me—"

"Never angry," he said, "but miserable, oh, more miserable—too miserable for words. I thought that you had cut me off for ever."

"You were right so far as your foolish ideas of that moment went, but I hope you have learnt better since, and now tell me what did you do? I hoped you had gone home, and then that you had gone to Scotland, and then—. What did you do?"

"I don't know," said Charlie, "I can't tell you. I suppose I must have been ill then. I came up to town, but I don't know what I did. And I was brought here, and I've been ill ever since, and couldn't seem to get better until I heard you had been speaking for me. You speaking for me, Laura! Thinking of me a little, trying to bring me back to life. I'll come back to life, dear, for you—anything, Laura, for you!"

"My dear boy, it is a pity you should not have a better reason," she said. The two girls had not gone away. Betty had retired to the corner where Bee was, and they stood close together holding each other, ashamed and scornful beyond expression of Charlie's abandonment. Even Betty, who was almost as much in love with Miss Lance as Charlie was, was ashamed to hear him "going on" in this ridiculous way. What Miss Lance felt to have these words of devotion addressed to her in the presence of two such listeners I will not say. She was acutely sensible of their presence, and of what they were thinking, but she did not shrink from the ordeal. "And you must not call me Laura," she said, "unless you can make it Aunt Laura, or Grandmother Laura, which are titles I shouldn't object to. Anything else would be ridiculous between you and me."

"Laura!" the young man said, raising himself quickly.

"Say Aunt Laura, my dear, and if you move another inch I will go away!"

"You are crushing me," he cried, "you are driving me to despair!"

"Dear Charlie," said Miss Lance, "all this, you know, is very great nonsense—between you and me; I have told you so all along. Now things have really become too serious to go on. I want to be kind to you, to help you to get well, and to see as much of you as possible; for you are a dear boy and I am fond of you. But this can't be unless you will see things in their true light and acknowledge the real state of affairs. I am most willing and ready to be your friend, to be a mother to you. But anything else is ridiculous. Do you hear me, Charlie?—ridiculous! You don't want to be laughed at, and you don't want me to be laughed at, I suppose?" She took his hands with which he had covered his face and held them in hers. "Now, no nonsense, Charlie. Be a man! Will you have me for your friend, always ready to do anything for you, or will you have nothing to do with me? Come! I might be your mother, I have always told you so. And look here," she said, with a tone of genuine passion in her voice and a half turn of her flexible figure towards the two girls, "I'm worth having for a mother; whatever you may think in your cruel youth, I am, I am!" Surely this was to them and not to him. The movement, the accent, was momentary. Her voice changed again into the softness of a caress. "Charlie, my dear boy, don't make me ridiculous, don't make people laugh at me. They call me an old witch, trying to entrap a young man. Will you let people—nay, will you make people call me so?"

"I make anyone call you—anything but what you are!" he cried. "Nobody would dare," said the unfortunate fellow, "to do anything but revere you and admire you so long as I was there."

"And then break out laughing the moment your back was turned," she said. "'What a hold the old hag has got upon him!' is what they would say. And it would be quite true. Not that I am an old hag. No, I don't think I am that, I am worse. I'm a very well preserved woman of my years. I've taken great care of myself to keep up what are called my personal advantages. I have never wished—I don't wish now—to be thought older than I am, or ugly. I am just old enough—to be your mother, Charlie, if I had married young, as your mother did—"

He drew his hands out of her cool and firm grasp, and once more covered his face with them. "Don't torture me," he cried.

"No, my dear boy, I don't want to torture you, but you must not make me, nor yourself—whom I am proud of—ridiculous. I am going probably—for nothing is certain till it happens," she said, with a mournful tone in her voice, slightly shaking her head, "and you may perhaps help to balk me—I am probably going to make a match with a reasonable person suited to my age."

Poor Charlie started up, his hands fell from his face, his large miserable eyes were fixed upon hers. "And you come—you come—to tell me this!" he cried.

"It will be partly for you—to show how impossible your folly is—but most for myself, to secure my own happiness." She said these words very slowly, one by one—"To secure my own happiness. Have I not the right to do that, because a young man, who should have been my son, has taken it into his foolish head to form other ideas of me? You would rather make me ridiculous and wretched than consider my dignity, my welfare, my happiness—and this is what you call love!" she said.

The girls listened to this conversation with feelings impossible to put into words, not knowing what to think. One of them loved the woman and the other hated her; they were equally overwhelmed in their young and simple ideas. She seemed to be speaking a language new to them, and to have risen into a region which they had never known.

CHAPTER XVI

She left Charlie's room, having soothed him and reduced him to quiet in this inconceivable way, with a smile on her face and the look of one who was perfectly mistress of the situation. But when she had gone down half-a-dozen steps and reached the landing, she stood still and leaned against the wall, clasping her hands tight as if there was something in them to hold by. She had carried through this part of her ordeal with a high hand. She had made it look the kindest yet the most decisive interview in the world, crushing the foolish young heart, without remorse, yet tenderly, kindly, with such a force of sense and reason as could not be resisted—and all so naturally, with so much apparent ease, as if it cost her nothing. But she was after all, merely a woman, and she knew that only half, nay, not half, not the worst half of her trial was over. She lay back against the wall, having nothing else to rest upon, and closed her eyes for a moment. The two girls had followed her instinctively out of Charlie's room, and stood on the stairs one above the other, gazing at her. The long lines of her figure seemed to relax, as if she might have fallen, and in their wonder and ignorance they might still have stood by and looked on letting her fall, without knowing what to do. But she did not do so. The corner of the walls supported her as if they had made a couch for her, and presently she opened her eyes with a vague smile at Betty, who was foremost. "I was tired," she said, and then, "it isn't easy"—drawing a long breath.

At this moment the trim figure of Mrs. Leigh's maid appeared on the stairs below, so commonplace, so trim, so neat, the little apparition of ordinary life which glides through every tragedy, lifting its everyday voice in announcements of dinner, in inquiries about tea, in all the nothings of routine, in the midst of all tumults of misery and passion. "If you please, madam—my lady would be glad if you would step into the dining-room," she said.

Miss Lance raised herself in a moment from that half-recumbent position against the wall. She recovered herself, got back her colour and the brightness of her eyes, and that look of being perfectly natural, at her ease, unstrained, spontaneous, which she had shown throughout the interview with Charlie. "Certainly," she said. There did not seem to be time for the twinkling of an eyelid between the one mood and the other. She required no preparation or interval to pull herself together. She looked at the two sisters as if to call them to follow her, and then walked quietly downstairs to be tried for her life—like a martyr—oh, no, for she was not a martyr, but a criminal. She had no confidence of innocence about her. She knew what indictment was about to be brought against her, and she knew it was true. This knowledge, however, gives a certain strength. It gives courage such as the innocent who do not know what charge may be brought against them or how to meet it, do not possess. She had rehearsed the scene. She knew what she was going to be accused of, and had thought over, and set in order, all the pleas. She knew exactly what she had done and what she had not, which was a tower of strength to her, and she knew that on her power of fighting it out depended her life. It is difficult altogether to deny our sympathy to a brave creature fighting for bare life. However guilty he may be, human nature takes sides with him, hopes in the face of all justice that there may be a loophole of escape. Even Bee, coming slowly downstairs after her, already thrown into a curious tumult of feeling by that scene in Charlie's room, began to feel her breath quicken with excitement even in the hostility of her heart.

There was one thing that Miss Lance had not foreseen, and that burst upon her at once when the maid opened the door—Colonel Kingsward, standing with his arm upon the mantel-piece and his countenance as if turned to stone. The shock which this sight gave her was very difficult to overcome or conceal, it struck her with a sudden dart as of despair; her impulse was to fling down her arms, to acknowledge herself vanquished, and to retreat, a defeated and ruined adventuress, but she was too brave and unalterably by nature too sanguine to do this. She gave him a nod and a smile, to which he scarcely responded, as she went towards Mrs. Leigh.

"How strange," she said, "when I come to see a new friend to find so old a friend! I wondered if it could be Mr. Leigh's house, but I was not sure—of the number."

"I am afraid I cannot say I am glad to see you, Laura," said Mrs. Leigh.

"No? Perhaps it would have been too much to expect. We were, so to speak, on different sides. Poor Amy, I know, was never satisfactory to you, and I don't wonder. Of course you only thought of me as her friend."

"If that were all!" Mrs. Leigh said.

"Was there more than that? May I sit down? I have had a long walk, and rather an exhaustive interview—and I did not expect to be put on my trial. But it is always best to know what one is accused of. I think it quite natural—quite natural that you should not like me, Mrs. Leigh. I was Amy's friend and she was trying to you. She put me in a very false position which I ought never to have accepted. But yet—I understand your attitude, and I submit to it with respect—but, pardon me—sincerely, I don't know what there was more."

Miss Lance had taken a chair, a perfectly upright one, on which few people could have sat gracefully. She made it evident that it was mere fatigue which made her subside upon it momentarily, and lifted her fine head and limpid eyes with so candid and respectful an air towards Mrs. Leigh's comfortable, unheroic face, that no contrast of the oppressed and oppressor could have been more marked. If anyone had suffered in the matter between these two ladies, it certainly was not the one with the rosy countenance and round, well-filled-out figure; or so, at least, any impartial observer certainly would have felt.

Mrs. Leigh, for her part, was almost speechless with excitement and anger. She had intended to keep perfectly calm, but the look, the tone, the appearance of this personage altogether, brought before her overpoweringly many past scenes—scenes in which, to tell the truth, Miss Lance had not been always in the wrong, in which the other figure, now altogether disappeared, of Aubrey's wife was the foremost, an immovable gentle-mannered fool, with whom all reason and argument were unavailing, whom everybody had believed to be inspired by the companion to whom she clung. All Amy's faults had been bound upon Laura's shoulders, but this was not altogether deserved, and Miss Lance did not shrink from anything that could be said on that subject. It required more courage to say, "Was there anything more?"

"More!" cried Mrs. Leigh, choking with the remembrance. "More! My boy's house was made unsafe for him, it was made miserable to him, he was involved in every kind of danger and scandal, and she asks me if there was more?"

"Poor Amy," said Miss Lance, with a little pause on the name, shaking her head gently in compassion and regret. "Poor Amy put me in a very false position. I have already said so, I ought not to have accepted it, I ought not to have promised; but it was so difficult to refuse a promise to the dying. Let Colonel Kingsward judge. She was very unwise, but she had been my friend from infancy and clung to me more, much more than I wished. She exacted a promise from me on her death-bed that I would never leave her child—which was folly, and, perhaps more than folly, so far, at least, as I was concerned. You may imagine, Colonel Kingsward," she added, steadfastly regarding him. He had kept his head turned away, not looking at her, but this gaze compelled him against his will to shift his position, to turn towards the appellant who made him the judge. He still kept his eyes away, but his head turned by an attraction which he could not withstand. "You may imagine, Colonel Kingsward—that I was the person who suffered most," Miss Lance said after that pause, "compelled to stay in a house where I had never been welcome, except to poor Amy, who was dead; a sort of guardian, a sort of nurse, and yet with none of their rights, held fast by a promise which I had given against my will, and which I never ceased to regret. You are a man, Colonel Kingsward, but you have more understanding of a woman's feelings than any I know. My position was a false one, it was cruel—but I was bound by my word."

"No one ought to have given such a promise," he said, coldly, with averted eyes.

"You are always right, I ought not to have done so; but she was dying, and I was fond of her, poor girl, though she was foolish—it is not always the wisest people one loves most—fond of her, very fond of her, and of her poor little child."

The tears came to Miss Lance's eyes. She shook her head a little as if to shake them from her eyelashes. "Why should I cry? They have been so long happy, happier far than we—"

Mrs. Leigh, the prosecutor, the accuser, gave a gulp, a sob; the child was her grandchild, her only one—and besides anger in a woman is as prone to tears as sorrow. She gave a stifled cry, "I don't deny you were good to the child; oh, Laura, I could have forgiven you everything! But not—not—"

"What?" Miss Lance said.

Mrs. Leigh seized upon Bee by the arm and drew her forward—Aubrey's mother wanted words, she wanted eloquence, her arguments had to be pointed by fact. She took Bee, who had been standing in proud yet excited spectatorship, and held her by her own side. "Aubrey," she said, almost inarticulately, and stopped to recover her breath—"Aubrey—whom you had driven from his home—found at last this dear girl, this nice, good girl, who would have made him a new life. But you interfered, you wrote to her father, you went—I don't know what you did—and said you had a claim, a prior claim. If you appeal to Colonel Kingsward, he is the best judge. You went to him—"

"Not to me, I was not aware, I never even saw Miss Lance till long after; forgive me for interrupting you."

Miss Lance turned towards him again with that full look of faith and confidence. "Always just!" she said. And this time for a tremulous moment their eyes met. He turned his away again hastily, but he had received that touch; an indefinable wavering came over his aspect of iron.

"Yes," she said, "I do not deny it—it is quite true. Shall I now explain before every one who is here? I think," she added, after a moment, "that my little Betty, who has nothing particular to do with it, may run away."

"I!" said Betty, clinging to the back of a chair.

"Go," said her father, impatiently, "go!"

"Yes, my dear, run away. Charlie must want some one. He will have got over me a little, and he will want some one. Dear little Betty, run away!"

Miss Lance rose from her seat—probably that too was a relief to her—and, with a smile and a kiss, turned Betty out of the room. She came back then and sat down again. It gained a little time, and she was at a crisis harder than she had ever faced before. She had gained a moment to think, but even now she was not sure what way there was out of this strait, the most momentous in which she had ever been. She looked round her at one after another with a look that seemed as secure and confident, as easy and natural, as before; but her brain was working at the most tremendous rate, looking for some clue, some indication. She looked round as with a pause of conscious power, and then her gaze fixed itself on Bee. Bee stood near Mrs. Leigh's chair. She was standing firm but tremulous, a deeply concerned spectator, but there was on her face nothing of the eager attention with which a girl would listen to an explanation about her lover. She was not more interested than she had been before, not so much so as when Charlie was in question. When Mrs. Leigh, in her indictment, said, "You interfered," Bee had made a faint, almost imperceptible movement of her head. The mind works very quickly when its fate hangs on the balance of a minute, and now, suddenly, the culprit arraigned before these terrible judges saw her way.

"I interfered," Miss Lance said, slowly, "but not because of any prior claim;"—she paused again for a moment—"that would have been as absurd as in the case Colonel Kingsward knows of. I interfered—because I had other reasons for believing that Aubrey Leigh was not the man to marry a dear, good, nice girl."

"You had—other reasons, Laura! Mind what you are saying—you will have to prove your words," cried Mrs. Leigh, rising in her wrath, with an astonished and threatening face.

"I do not ask his mother to believe me. It is before Colonel Kingsward," said Miss Lance, "that I stand or fall."

"Colonel Kingsward, make her speak out! You know it was because she claimed my son—she, a woman twice his age; and now she pretends—Make her speak out! How dare you? You said he had promised to marry you—that he was bound to you. Colonel Kingsward, make her speak out!"

"That was what I understood," he said, looking out of the window, his head turned half towards the other speakers, but not venturing to look at them. "I did not see Miss Lance, but that was what I understood."

Laura sat firm, as if she were made of marble, but almost as pale. Her nerves were so highly strung that if she had for a moment relaxed their tension, she would have fallen to the ground. She sat like a rock, holding herself together with the strong grasp of her clasped hands.

"You hear, you hear! You are convicted out of your own mouth. Oh, you are cruel, you are wicked, Laura Lance! If you have anything to say speak out, speak out!"

"I will say nothing," said Miss Lance. "I will leave another, a better witness, to say it for me. Colonel Kingsward, ask your daughter if it was because of my prior claim, as his mother calls it, that she broke off her engagement with Aubrey Leigh."

Colonel Kingsward turned, surprised, to his daughter, who, roused by the sound of her own name, looked up quickly—first at the seemingly composed and serious woman opposite to her, then at her father. He spoke to her angrily, abruptly.

"Do you hear? Answer the question that is put to you. Was it because of this lady, or any claim of hers, that you—how shall I say it?—a girl like you had no right to decide one way or the other—that you broke off—that your mind was changed towards Mr. Aubrey Leigh?"

It appeared to Bee suddenly as if she had become the culprit, and all eyes were fixed on her. She trembled, looking at them all. What had she done? She was surely unhappy enough, wretched enough, a clandestine visitor, keeping Aubrey out of his own house, and what had she to do with Aubrey? Nothing, nothing! Nor he with her—that her heart should now be snatched out of her bosom publicly in respect to him.

"That is long past," she said, faltering, "it is an old story. Mr. Aubrey Leigh is—a stranger to me; it is of no consequence—now!"

"Bee," her father thundered at her, "answer the question! Was it because of—this lady that you changed your mind?"

Colonel Kingsward had always the art, somehow, of kindling the blaze of opposition in the blue eyes which were so like his own. She looked at him almost fiercely in reply, fully roused.

"No!" she said, "no! It was not because of—that lady. It was another—reason of my own."

"What was your reason?" cried Mrs. Leigh. "Oh, Bee, speak! What was it, what was it? Tell me, tell me, my dear, what was your reason? that I may prove to you it was not true."

"Had it anything to do with—this lady?" asked Colonel Kingsward once more.

"I never spoke to that lady but once," cried Bee, almost violently. "I don't know her; I don't want to know her. She has nothing to do with it. It was because of something quite different, something that we heard—I—and mamma."

Miss Lance looked at him with a smile on her face, loosing the grip of her hands, spreading them out in demonstration of her acquittal. She rose up slowly, her beautiful eyes filled with tears. She allowed it to be seen for the first time how she was shaken with emotion.

"You have heard," she said, "a witness you trust more than me—if I put myself into the breach to secure a pause, it was only such a piece of folly as I have done before. I hope now that you will let me withdraw. I am dreadfully tired, I am not fit for any more."

She looked with that appeal upon her face, first at one of her judges, then at the other. "If you are satisfied, let me go." It seemed as if she could not say a word more. They made no response, but she did not wait for that. "I take it for granted," she added, "that by that child's mouth I am cleared," and then she turned towards the door.

Colonel Kingsward, with a little start, came from his place by the mantel-piece and opened it for her, as he would have done for any woman. She let it appear that this movement was unexpected, and went to her heart; she paused a moment looking up at him—her eyes swimming in tears, her mouth quivering.

"How kind you are!" she said, "even though you don't believe in me any more! but I have done all I can. I am very tired, scarcely able to walk." He stood rigid, and made no sign, and she, looking at him, softly shook her head—"Let me see you at least once," she said, very low, in a pleading tone, "this evening, some time?"

Still he gave no answer, standing like a man of iron, holding the door open. She gave him another look, and then walked quietly, but with a slight quiver and half stumble, away. They all stood watching until her tall figure was seen to pass the window, disappearing in the street, which is the outer world.

"Colonel Kingsward—" said Mrs. Leigh.

He started at the sound of his name, as if he had but just awakened out of a dream, and began to smooth his hat, which all this time he had held in his hands.

"Excuse me," he said, "excuse me, another time. I have some pressing business to see to now."

And he, too, disappeared into that street which led both ways, into the monotony of London, which is the world.

CHAPTER XVII

Those who were left behind were not very careful of what Colonel Kingsward did. They were not thinking of his concerns; in the strain of personal feeling the most generous of human creatures is forced to think first of their own. Neither of the women who were left in the room had any time to consider the matter, but if they had they would have made sure without hesitation that nothing which could happen to Colonel Kingsward could be half so important as that crisis in which his daughter was involved.

Mrs. Leigh turned round upon the girl by her side and seized her hands. "Bee," she cried, "now we are alone and we can speak freely. Tell me what it was, there is nobody here to frighten you, to take the words from your mouth. What was it, what was it that made you turn from Aubrey? At last, at last, it can be cleared up whatever it was."

Bee turned away, trying to disengage her hands. "It is of no consequence," she said, "Oh, don't make me go back to those old, old things. What does it matter to Mr. Leigh? And as for me—"

"It matters everything to Aubrey. He will be able to clear himself if you will give him the chance. How could he clear himself when he was never allowed to speak, when he did not know? Bee, in justice, in mere justice! What was it? You said your mother—"

"Yes, I had her then. We heard it together, and she felt it like me. But we had no time to talk of it after, for she was ill. If you would please not ask me, Mrs. Leigh! I was very miserable—mother dying, and nowhere, nowhere in all the world anything to trust to. Don't, oh! don't make me go back upon it! I am not—so very—happy, even now!"

The girl would not let herself be drawn into Mrs. Leigh's arms. She refused to rest her head upon the warm and ample bosom which was offered to her. She drew away her hands. It was difficult, very difficult, to keep from crying. It is always hard for a girl to keep from crying when her being is so moved. The only chance for her was to keep apart from all contact, to stand by herself and persuade herself that nobody cared and that she was alone in the world.

"Bee, I believe," said Mrs. Leigh, solemnly, "that you have but to speak a word and you will be happy. You have not your mother now. You can't turn to her and ask her what you should do. But I am sure that she would say, 'speak!' If she were here she would not let you break a man's heart and spoil his life for a punctilio. I have always heard she was a good woman and kind—kind. Bee," the elder lady laid her hand suddenly on the girl's shoulder, making her start, "she would say 'speak' if she were here."

"Oh, mamma, if you were here!" said Bee, through her tears.

She broke down altogether and became inarticulate, sobbing with her face buried in her hands. The ordeal of the last two days had been severe. Charlie and his concerns and the appearance of Miss Lance, and the conflict only half understood which had been going on round her, had excited and disturbed her beyond expression, as everybody could see and understand. But, indeed, these were but secondary elements in the storm which had overwhelmed Bee, which was chiefly brought back by that sudden plunge into the atmosphere of Aubrey. The sensation of being in his house, which she might in other circumstances have shared with him, of sitting at his table, in his seat, under the roof that habitually sheltered him—here, where her own life ought to have been passed, but where the first condition now was that there should be nothing of him visible. In Aubrey's house, but not for Aubrey! Aubrey banished, lest perhaps her eyes might fall upon him by chance, or her ears be offended by the sound of his voice! Even his mother did not understand how much this had to do with the passion and trouble of the girl, from whose eyes the innocent name of her mother, sweetest though saddest of memories, had let forth the salt and boiling tears. If Mrs. Leigh had been anybody in the world save Aubrey's mother, Bee would have clung to her, accepting the tender support and consolation of the elder women's arms and her sympathy, but from Aubrey's mother she felt herself compelled to keep apart.

It was not until her almost convulsive sobbing was over that this question could be re-opened, and in the meantime Betty having heard the sound of the closing door came rushing downstairs and burst into the room: perhaps she was not so much disturbed or excited as Mrs. Leigh was by Bee's condition. She gave her sister a kiss as she lay on the sofa where Mrs. Leigh had placed her, and patted her on the shoulder.

"She will be better when she has had it out," said Betty. "She has worked herself up into such a state about Miss Lance. And oh, please tell me what has happened. You are her enemy, too, Mrs. Leigh—oh, how can you misjudge her so! As if she had been the cause of any harm! I was sent away," said Betty, "and, of course, Bee could not speak—but I could have told you. Yes, of course, I knew! How could I help knowing, being her sister? I can't tell whether she told me, I knew without telling; and, of course, she must have told me. This is how it was—"

Bee put forth her hand and caught her sister by the dress, but Betty was not so easily stopped. She turned round quickly, and took the detaining hand into her own and patted and caressed it.

"It is far better to speak out," she said, "it must be told now, and though I am young and you call me little Betty, I cannot help hearing, can I, what people say? Mrs. Leigh, this was how it was. Whatever happened about dear Miss Lance—whom I shall stick to and believe in whatever you say," cried Betty, by way of an interlude, with flashing eyes, "that had nothing, nothing to do with it. That was a story—like Charlie's, I suppose, and Bee no more made a fuss about it than I should do. It was after, when Bee was standing by Aubrey, like—like Joan of Arc; yes, of course I shall call him Aubrey—I should like to have him for a brother, but that has got nothing to do with it. A lady came to call upon mamma, and she told a story about someone on the railway who had met Aubrey on the way home after that scene at Cologne, after he was engaged to Bee, and was miserable because of papa's opposition." Betty spoke so fast that her words tumbled over each other, so to speak, in the rush for utterance. "Well, he was seen," she resumed, pausing for breath, "putting a young woman with children into one of the sleeping carriages—a poor young woman that had no money or right to be there. He put her in, and when they got to London he was seen talking to her, and giving her money, as if she belonged to him. I don't see any harm in that, for he was always kind to poor people. But these ladies did, and I suppose so did mamma, and Bee blazed up. That is just like her. She takes fire, she never waits to ask questions, she stops her ears. She thought it was something dreadful, showing that he had never cared for her, that he had cared for other people even when he was pretending, I should have done quite different. I should have said, 'Now, look here, Aubrey, what does it mean?'—or, rather, I should never have thought anything but that he was kind. He was always kind—silly, indeed, about poor people, as so many are."

Mrs. Leigh had followed Betty's rapid narrative with as much attention as she could concentrate upon it, but the speed with which the words flew forth, the little interruptions, the expressions of Betty's matured and wise opinions, bewildered her beyond measure.

"What does it all mean?" she asked, looking from one to another when the story was done. "A sleeping carriage on the railway—a woman with children—as if she belonged to him? How could a woman with children belong to him?" Then she paused and grew crimson with an old woman's painful blush. "Is it vice, horrible vulgar vice, this child is attributing to my boy?"

The two girls stared, confused and troubled. Bee got up from the sofa and put her hands to her head, her eyes fixed upon Mrs. Leigh with an appalled and horrified look. She had not asked herself of what Aubrey had been accused. She had fled from him before the dreadful thought of relationships she did not understand, of something which was the last insult to her, whatever it might be in itself. "Vulgar vice!" The girls were cowed as if some guilt had been imputed to themselves.

"You are not like anything I have known, you girls of the period," cried the angry mother. "You are acquainted with such things as I at my age had never heard of. You make accusations! But now—he shall answer for himself," she said, flaming with righteous wrath. Mrs. Leigh went to the bell and rang it so violently that the sound echoed all over the house.

"Go and ask your master to come here at once, directly; I want him this moment," she said, stamping her foot in her impatience. And then there was a pause. The man went off and was seen from the window to cross the street on his errand. Then Bee rose, her tears hastily dried up, pushing back from her forehead her disordered hair.

"I had better go. If you have sent for Mr. Leigh it will be better that I should go."

Mrs. Leigh was almost incapable of speech. She took Bee by the shoulders and put her back almost violently on the sofa. "You shall stay there," she said, in a choked and angry voice.

What a horrible pause it was! The girls were silent, looking at each other with wild alarm. Betty, who had blurted out the story, but to whom the idea of repeating it before Aubrey—before a man—was unspeakable horror, made a step towards the door. Then she said, "No, I will not run away," with tremendous courage. "It is not our fault," she added, after a pause. "Bee, if I have got to say it again, give me your hand."

"It is I who ought to say it," said Bee, pale with the horror of what was to come. "Vulgar vice!" And she to accuse him, and to stand up before the world and say that was why!

It seemed a long time, but it was really only a few minutes, before Aubrey appeared. He came in quickly, breathless with haste and suspense. He expected, from what his mother had told him, to find Miss Lance and Colonel Kingsward there. He came into the agitated room and found, of all people in the world, Bee and Betty, terrified, and his mother, walking about the room sounding, as it were, a metaphorical lash about their ears, in the frank passion of an elder woman who has the most just cause of offence and no reason to bate her breath. There was something humorous in the tragic situation, but to them it was wholly tragic, and Aubrey, seeing for the first time after so long an interval the girl he loved, and seeing her in such strange circumstances, was by no means disposed to see any humorous side.

"Here, Aubrey!" said his mother, "I have called upon you to hear what you are accused of. You thought it was Laura Lance, but she has nothing to do with it. You are accused of travelling from Germany, that time when you were sent off from Cologne—the time those Kingswards turned upon you"—(the girls both started, and recovered themselves a little at the shock of this contemptuous description),—"travelling in sleeping carriages and I know not what with a woman and children, who were believed to belong to you! What have you to say?"

"That was not what I said, Mrs. Leigh."

"What have you to say?" cried Mrs. Leigh, waving her hand to silence Betty; "the accused has surely the right to speak first."

"What have I to say? But to what, mother? What is it? Was I travelling with a woman and children? I suppose I was travelling—with all the women and children that were in the same train. But otherwise, of course you know I was with nobody. What does it mean?"

Bee got up from the sofa like a ghost, her blue eyes wild, her face pale. "Oh, let us go, let us go! Do not torment us," she said. "I will acknowledge that it was not true. Now that I see him I am sure that it was not true. I was mad. I was so stung to think—Mrs. Leigh, do not kill me! I did him no harm; do not, do not go over it any more!"

"Go over what?" cried Aubrey. "Bee! She can't stand, she doesn't see where she is going. Mother, what on earth does it matter what was against me if it is all over? Mother! How dare you torture my poor girl—?"

This was naturally all the thanks Mrs. Leigh got for her efforts to unravel the mystery, which the reader knows was the most innocent mystery, and which had never been cleared up or thought of since that day. It came clear of itself the moment that Aubrey, only to support her, took Bee into his arms.

CHAPTER XVIII

The Sorceress walked away very slowly down the street.

She had the sensation of having fallen from a great height, after the excitement of having fought bravely to keep her place there, and of having anticipated every step of a combat still more severe which yet had not come to pass after her previsions. It had been a fight lasting for hours, from the moment Betty, all unconscious, had told her of the house in which Charlie was. That was in the morning, and now it was late afternoon, and the work of the day, the common work of the day in which all the innocent common people about had been employed, was rounding towards its end. It seemed to her a long, long time that she had been involved, first in imagination, in severe thought, and then in actual conflict—in this struggle, fighting for her life. From the beginning she had made up her mind that she should fail. It was a consciously losing game that she had fought so gallantly, never giving in; and indeed she was not unaware, nor was she without a languid satisfaction in the fact that she had indeed carried off the honours of the field, that it would not be said that she had been beaten. But what did that matter? Argument she knew and felt had nothing to do with such affairs. She had known herself to have lost from the moment she saw Colonel Kingsward standing there against the mantelpiece in the dining-room. It had not been possible for her then to give in, to turn and go forth into the street flinging down her arms. On the contrary, it was her nature to fight to the last; and she had carried off an apparent victory. She had marched off with colours flying from the field of battle, leaving every enemy confounded. But she herself entertained no illusion in the matter. It was possible no doubt that her spell might yet be strong enough upon her middle-aged captive to make him ignore and pass over everything that told against her—but, after considering the situation with a keen and close survey of every likelihood, she dismissed that hope. No, her chance was lost—again; the battle was over—again. It had been so near being successful that the shock was greater perhaps than usual; but she had now been feeling the shock for hours; so that her actual fall was as much a relief as a pang, and her mind, full of resource, obstinately sanguine, was becoming ready to pass on to the next chance, and had already sprung up to think—What now?

I am sorry that in this story I have always been placed in natural opposition to this woman, who was certainly a creature full of interest, full of resource, and indomitable in her way. And she had a theory of existence, as, it is my opinion, we all must have, making out to ourselves the most plausible reasons and excuses for all we do. Her struggle—in which she would not have denied that she had sometimes been unscrupulous—had always been for a standing-ground on which, if once attained, she could have been good. She had always promised herself that she would be good when once she had attained—oh, excellent! kind, just, true!—a model woman. And what, after all, had been her methods? There had been little harm in them. Here and there somebody had been injured, as in the case of Aubrey Leigh, of Charlie Kingsward. To the first she had indeed done considerable harm, but then she had soothed the life of Amy, his little foolish wife, to whom she had been more kind than she had been unkind to him. She had not wanted to be the third person between that tiresome couple. She had stayed in his house from a kind of sense of duty, and had Aubrey Leigh indeed asked her to become his second wife she would, of course, have accepted him for the sake of the position, but with a grimace. She was not particularly sorry for having harmed him. It served him right for—well, for being Aubrey Leigh. And as for Bee Kingsward, she had triumphantly proved, much to her own surprise it must be said, that it was not she who had done Bee any harm. Then Charlie—poor Charlie, poor boy! He thought, of course, that he was very miserable and badly used. Great heavens! that a boy should have the folly to imagine that anything could make him miserable, at twenty-two—a man, and with all the world before him. Miss Lance at this moment was not in the least sorry for Charlie. It would do him good. A young fellow who had nothing in the world to complain of, who had everything in his favour—it was good for him to be unhappy a little, to be made to remember that he was only flesh and blood after all.

Thus she came to the conclusion, as she walked along, that really she had done no harm to other people. To herself, alas! she was always doing harm, and every failure made it more and more unlikely that she would ever succeed. She did not brood over her losses when she was thus defeated. She turned to the next thing that offered with what would have been in a better cause a splendid philosophy, but yet in moments like this she felt that it became every day more improbable that she would ever succeed. Instead of the large and liberal sphere in which she always hoped to be able to fulfil all the duties of life in an imposing and remarkable way, she would have probably to drop into—what? A governess's place, for which she would already be thought too old, some dreadful position about a school, some miserable place as housekeeper—she with all her schemes, her hopes of better things, her power over others. This prospect was always before her, and came back to her mind at moments when she was at the lowest ebb, for she had no money at all. She had always been dependent upon somebody. Even now her little campaign in George Street, Hanover Square, was at the expense of the friend with whom she had lived in Oxford, and who believed Laura was concerting measures to establish herself permanently in some remunerative occupation. These accounts would have to be settled somehow, and some other expedient be found by which to try again. Well, one thing done with, another to come on—was not that the course of life? And there was a certain relief in the thought that it was done with. The suspense was over; there was no longer the conflict between hope and fear, which wears out the nerves and clouds the clearness of one's mental vision. One down, another come on! She said this to herself with a forlorn laugh in the depths of her being, yet not so very forlorn. This woman had a kind of pleasure in the new start, even when she did not know what it was to be. There are a great many things in which I avow I have the greatest sympathy with her, and find her more interesting than a great many blameless people. Poetic justice is generally in books awarded to such persons. But that is, one is aware, not always the case in life.

While Miss Lance went on quietly along the long unlovely street, with those thoughts in her mind, walking more slowly than usual, a little languid and exhausted after her struggle, but as has been said frankly and without arriere penseé giving up the battle as lost, and accepting her defeat—she became suddenly aware of a quick firm footstep behind, sounding fast and continuous upon the pavement. A woman like this has all her wits very sharply about her, the ears and the sight of a savage, and an unslumbering habit of observation, or she could never carry on her career. She heard the step and instinctively noted it before her mind awoke to any sense of meaning and importance in it. Then, all at once, as it came just to that distance behind which made it apparent that this footstep was following someone who went before, it suddenly slackened without stopping, became slow when it had been fast. At this, her thoughts flew away like a mist and she became all ears, but she was too wise to turn round, to display any interest. Perhaps it might be that he was only going his own way, not intending to follow, and that he had slackened his pace unconsciously without ulterior motives when he saw her in front of him—though this Miss Lance scarcely believed.

Perhaps—I will not affirm it—she threw a little more of her real languor and weariness into her attitude and movements when she made this exciting discovery. She was, in reality, very tired. She had looked so when she left the house; perhaps she had forgotten her great fatigue a little in the course of her walk, but it now came back again with double force, which is not unusual in the most matter of fact circumstances. As her pace grew slower, the footstep behind became slower also, but always followed on. Miss Lance proceeded steadily, choosing the quietest streets, pausing now and then at a shop window to rest. The climax came when she reached a window which had a rail round it, upon which she leaned heavily, every line of her dress expressing, with a faculty which her garments specially possessed, an exhaustion which could scarcely go further. Then she raised her head to look what the place was. It was full of embroideries and needlework, a woman's shop, where she was sure of sympathy. She went in blindly, as if her very sight were clouded with her fatigue.

"I am very tired," she said; "I want some silk for embroidery; but that is not my chief object. May I sit down a little? I am so very tired."

"Certainly, ma'am, certainly," cried the mistress of the shop, rushing round from behind the counter to place a chair for her and offer a glass of water. She sat down so as to be visible from the door, but still with her back to it. The step had stopped, and there was a shadow across the window—the tall shadow of a man looking in. A smile came upon Miss Lance's face—of gratitude and thanks to the kind people— also perhaps of some internal satisfaction. But she did not act as if she were conscious of anyone waiting for her. She took the glass of water with many acknowledgments; she leant back on the chair murmuring, "Thanks, thanks," to the exhortations of the shop-woman not to hurry, to take a good rest. She did not hurry at all. Finally, she was so much better as to be able to buy her silks, and, declaring herself quite restored, to go out again into the open air.

She was met by the shadow that had been visible through the window, and which, as she knew very well, was Colonel Kingsward, stiff and embarrassed, yet with great anxiety in his face. "I feared you were ill," he said, with a little jerk, the words coming in spite of him. "I feared you were fainting."

"Oh, Colonel Kingsward, you!"

"Yes—I feared you were fainting. It is—nothing, I hope?"

"Nothing but exhaustion," she said, with a faint smile. "I was very tired, but I have rested and I am a little better now."

"Will you let me call a cab for you? You don't seem fit to walk."

"Oh, no cab, thanks! I would much rather walk—the air and the slow movement does one a little good."

She was pale, and her voice was rather faint, and every line of her dress, as I have said, was tired—tired to death—and yet not ungracefully tired.

"I cannot let you go like this alone." His voice softened every moment; they went on for a step or two together. "You had better—take my arm, at least," he said.

She took it with a little cry and a sudden clasp. "I think you are not a mere man, but an archangel of kindness and goodness," she said, with a faint laugh that broke down, and tears in her eyes.

And I think for that moment, in the extraordinary revulsion of feeling, Miss Lance almost believed what she said.

CHAPTER XIX

What more is there to say? It is better, when one is able to deal poetic justice all round, to reward the good and punish the evil. Who are the good and who are the evil? We have not to do with murderers, with breakers of the law, with enemies of God or man. If Aubrey Leigh had not been exceedingly imprudent, if Bee had not been hot-headed and passionate, there would never have been that miserable breach between them. And the Sorceress, who destroyed for a time the peace of the Kingsward family, really never at any time meant that family any real harm. She meant them indeed, to her own consciousness, all the good in the world, and to promote their welfare in every way by making them her own. And as a matter of fact she did so, devoting herself to their welfare. She made Colonel Kingsward an excellent wife and adopted his children into her sedulous and unremitting care with a zeal which a mother could not have surpassed. Her translation from scheming poverty to abundance, and that graceful modest wealth which is almost the most beautiful of the conditions of life, was made in a way which was quite exquisite as a work of art. Nobody could ever have suspected that she had been once poor. She had all the habits of the best society. There was nowhere they could go, even into the most exalted regions, where the new Mrs. Kingsward was not distinguished. She extended the Colonel's connections and interest, and made his house popular and delightful; and she was perfect for his children. Even the county people and near neighbours, who were the most critical, acknowledged this. The little girls soon learned to adore their step-mother; the big boys admired and stood in awe of her, submitting more or less to her influence, though a little suspicious and sometimes half hostile. As for baby, who had been in a fair way of growing up detestable and a little family tyrant, his father's new marriage was the saving of him. He scarcely knew as he grew up that the former Miss Lance was not his mother, and he was said in the family to be her idol, but a very well disciplined and well behaved idol, and the one of the boys who was likely to have the finest career.

Charlie, poor Charlie, was not so fortunate, at least at first. The appointment which Colonel Kingsward declared he had been looking out for all along was got as soon as Charlie was able to accept it, and he left England when he was little more than convalescent. People said it was strange that a man with considerable influence, and in the very centre of affairs, should have sent his eldest son away to the ends of the earth, to a dangerous climate and a difficult post. But it turned out very well on the whole, for after a few years of languor and disgust with the world, there suddenly fell in Charlie's way an opportunity of showing that there was, after all, a great deal of English pluck and courage in him. I do not think it came to anything more than that—but then that, at certain moments, has been the foundation and the saving of the British Empire in various regions of the world. There was not one of his relations who celebrated Charlie's success with so much fervour as his step-mother, who was never tired of talking of it, nor of declaring that she had always expected as much, and known what was in him. Dear Charlie, she said, had fulfilled all her expectations, and made her more glad and proud than words could say. It was a poor return for this maternal devotion, yet a melancholy fact, that Charlie turned away in disgust whenever he heard of her, and could not endure her name.

Bee, whose little troubles have been so much the subject of this story, accomplished her fate by becoming Mrs. Aubrey Leigh in the natural course of events. There was no family quarrel kept up to scandalise and amuse society, but there never was much intercourse nor any great cordiality between the houses of Kingswarden and Forestleigh. I think, however, that it was against her father that Bee's heart revolted most.

Margaret Oliphant – A Short Biography

Margaret Oliphant Wilson was born on April 4th, 1828 to Francis W. Wilson, a clerk, and Margaret Oliphant, at Wallyford, near Musselburgh, East Lothian.

She spent her childhood at Lasswade, near Dalkeith, Glasgow before moving to Liverpool.

Her youth was spent in establishing a writing style so much so that, in 1849, she had her first novel published: Passages in the Life of Mrs. Margaret Maitland based on the Scottish Free Church movement. It met with some success and was a good start to her career.

Two years later, in 1851, her third book Caleb Field was published. It was also now that she met the publisher William Blackwood in Edinburgh and was asked to contribute to his well-received Blackwood's Magazine. It was to be a lifetimes endeavor. Over the course of the relationship she would have well over 100 articles published.

In May 1852, Margaret married her cousin, Frank Wilson Oliphant, at Birkenhead, and they settled at Harrington Square, Camden, London. He was an artist working primarily in stained glass. With the marriage she became Margaret Oliphant Wilson Oliphant.

Their marriage produced six children but three tragically died in infancy.

When her husband developed signs of the dreaded consumption (tuberculosis) they moved, on the advice of doctors, to warmer climes. In January 1859 it was to Florence, and then to Rome where, sadly, he died.

Margaret was naturally devastated but was also now left without support and only her income from her writing. She returned to England and took up the task of supporting her three remaining children by her literary activity.

By now she was being published both as an established novelist and regularly in Blackwood's Magazine, amongst others. Her incredible and prolific work rate increased both her commercial reputation and the size of her reading audience.

Against this her domestic life continued to be tragic, full of sorrow and disappointment.

In January 1864 her only remaining daughter Maggie died and was buried in her father's grave in Rome. Her brother, who had emigrated to Canada, was shortly afterwards involved in financial ruin. Margaret generously offered a home to him and his children, adding another demand to her already heavy responsibilities.

In 1866 she settled at Windsor to be closer to her sons, who were being educated at near-by Eton School. That year, her second cousin, Annie Louisa Walker, came to live with her as a companion-housekeeper. Windsor was now to be her home for the rest of her life.

Her literary career for three decades was one of constant delivery and success. Whether she wrote historical works or across several genres in fiction: domestic realism, historical, romance or supernatural she was successful.

For more than thirty years she pursued a varied literary career but family life continued to bring problems.

The literary ambitions she wished for her sons were unfulfilled. Cyril Francis, the eldest, died in 1890, leaving a Life of Alfred de Musset, incorporated in his mother's Foreign Classics for English Readers. The younger, Francis, who she nicknamed 'Cecco', collaborated with her in the Victorian Age of English Literature and won a position at the British Museum, but was rejected by Sir Andrew Clark, a famous physician. Cecco died in 1894.

With the last of her children now lost to her, she had but little further interest in life. Her health steadily and inexorably declined.

Margaret Oliphant Wilson Oliphant died at the age of 69 in Wimbledon on 20th June 1897. She is buried in Eton beside her sons.

At her death, Margaret was still working on Annals of a Publishing House, a record of Blackwood's Magazine with which she had enjoyed such a successful relationship.

Her Autobiography and Letters, which present a thoughtful picture of her domestic anxieties, was published in 1899. Only parts were written with a wider audience in mind: she had originally intended the Autobiography for her son, but he died before she could finish it.

Opinions on Oliphant's work are split, with some critics seeing her as a 'domestic novelist', while others recognize her work as influential and important to the Victorian literature canon. Critical reception from her contemporaries is also divided. John Skelton took the view that Oliphant wrote too much and too quickly. Writing a Blackwood's article called 'A Little Chat About Mrs. Oliphant', he asked, "Had Mrs. Oliphant concentrated her powers, what might she not have done? We might have had another Charlotte Brontë or another George Eliot." However not all of the contemporary reception was negative. The esteemed M. R. James admired Oliphant's supernatural fiction, concluding that "the religious ghost story, as it may be called, was never done better than by Mrs. Oliphant in 'The Open Door' and 'A Beleaguered City'. Mary Butts lavished praise on Oliphant's ghost story 'The Library Window', describing it as "one masterpiece of sober loveliness".

More modern critics of Oliphant's work include Virginia Woolf, who asked in Three Guineas whether Oliphant's autobiography does not lead the reader "to deplore the fact that Mrs. Oliphant sold her brain, her very admirable brain, prostituted her culture and enslaved her intellectual liberty in order that she might earn her living and educate her children."

Whatever the merits of their cases Margaret Oliphant has been shamefully neglected in modern years. She is now becoming more widely recognised as a leading writer of her day.

A canon of more than 120 works, including novels, travel books, histories, and volumes of literary criticism.

Novels

Margaret Maitland (1849)
Merkland (1850)
Caleb Field (1851)
John Drayton (1851)
Adam Graeme (1852)
The Melvilles (1852)
Katie Stewart (1852)
Harry Muir (1853)
Ailieford (1853)
The Quiet Heart (1854)
Magdalen Hepburn (1854)
Zaidee (1855)
Lilliesleaf (1855)
Christian Melville (1855)
The Athelings (1857)
The Days of My Life (1857)
Orphans (1858)
The Laird of Norlaw (1858)
Agnes Hopetoun's Schools and Holidays (1859)
Lucy Crofton (1860)
The House on the Moor (1861)
The Last of the Mortimers (1862)
Heart and Cross (1863)
Salem Chapel (1863)
The Rector (1863)
Doctor's Family (1863)
The Perpetual Curate (1864)
Miss Marjoribanks (1866)
Phoebe Junior (1876)
A Son of the Soil (1865)
Agnes (1866)
Madonna Mary (1867)
Brownlows (1868)
The Minister's Wife (1869)
The Three Brothers (1870)
John: A Love Story (1870)
Squire Arden (1871)
At his Gates (1872)

Ombra (1872
May (1873)
Innocent (1873)
The Story of Valentine and his Brother (1875)
A Rose in June (1874)
For Love and Life (1874)
Whiteladies (1875)
An Odd Couple (1875)
The Curate in Charge (1876)
Carità (1877)
Young Musgrave (1877)
Mrs. Arthur (1877)
The Primrose Path (1878)
Within the Precincts (1879)
The Fugitives (1879)
A Beleaguered City (1879)
The Greatest Heiress in England (1880)
He That Will Not When He May (1880)
In Trust (1881)
Harry Joscelyn (1881)
Lady Jane (1882)
A Little Pilgrim in the Unseen (1882)
The Lady Lindores (1883)
Sir Tom (1883)
Hester (1883)
It Was a Lover and his Lass (1883)
The Lady's Walk (1883)
The Wizard's Son (1884)
Madam (1884)
The Prodigals and their Inheritance (1885)
Oliver's Bride (1885)
A Country Gentleman and his Family (1886)
A House Divided Against Itself (1886)
Effie Ogilvie (1886)
A Poor Gentleman (1886)
The Son of his Father (1886)
Joyce (1888)
Cousin Mary (1888)
The Land of Darkness (1888)
Lady Car (1889)
Kirsteen (1890)
The Mystery of Mrs. Biencarrow (1890)
Sons and Daughters (1890)
The Railway Man and his Children (1891)
The Heir Presumptive and the Heir Apparent (1891)
The Marriage of Elinor (1891)
Janet (1891)
The Cuckoo in the Nest (1892)

Diana Trelawny (1892)
The Sorceress (1893)
A House in Bloomsbury (1894)
Sir Robert's Fortune (1894)
Who Was Lost and is Found (1894)
Lady William (1894)
Two Strangers (1895)
Old Mr. Tredgold (1895)
The Unjust Steward (1896)
The Ways of Life (1897)

Short stories
Neighbours on the Green (1889)
A Widow's Tale and Other Stories (1898)
That Little Cutty (1898)
The Open Door (1918)

Selected Articles

Mary Russel Mitford (Blackwood's Magazine, Vol. 75, 1854)
Evelin and Pepys (Blackwood's Magazine, Vol. 76, 1854)
The Holy Land (Blackwood's Magazine, Vol. 76, 1854)
Mr. Thackeray and his Novels (Blackwood's Magazine, Vol. 77, 1855)
Bulwer (Blackwood's Magazine, Vol. 77, 1855)
Charles Dickens (Blackwood's Magazine, Vol. 77, 1855)
Modern Novelists—Great and Small (Blackwood's Magazine, Vol. 77, 1855)
Modern Light Literature: Poetry (Blackwood's Magazine, Vol. 79, 1856)
Religion in Common Life (Blackwood's Magazine, Vol. 79, 1856)
Sydney Smith (Blackwood's Magazine, Vol. 79, 1856)
The Laws Concerning Women (Blackwood's Magazine, Vol. 79, 1856)
The Art of Caviling (Blackwood's Magazine, Vol. 80, 1856)
Béranger (Blackwood's Magazine, Vol. 83, 1858)
The Condition of Women (Blackwood's Magazine, Vol. 83, 1858)
The Missionary Explorer (Blackwood's Magazine, Vol. 83, 1858)
Religious Memoirs (Blackwood's Magazine, Vol. 83, 1858)
Social Science (Blackwood's Magazine, Vol. 88, 1860)
Scotland and her Accusers (Blackwood's Magazine, Vol. 90, 1861)
The Chronicles of Carlingford (Blackwood's Magazine 1862–1865)
Girolamo Savonarola (Blackwood's Magazine, Vol. 93, 1863)
The Life of Jesus (Blackwood's Magazine, Vol. 96, 1864)
Giacomo Leopardi (Blackwood's Magazine, Vol. 98, 1865)
The Great Unrepresented (Blackwood's Magazine, Vol. 100, 1866)
Mill on the Subjection of Women (The Edinburgh Review, Vol. 130, 1869)
The Opium-Eater (Blackwood's Magazine, Vol. 122, 1877)
Russian and Nihilism in the Novels of I. Tourgeniéf (Blackwood's Magazine, Vol. 127, 1880)
School and College (Blackwood's Magazine, Vol. 128, 1880)

The Grievances of Women (Fraser's Magazine, New Series, Vol. 21, 1880)
Mrs. Carlyle (The Contemporary Review, Vol. 43, May 1883)
The Ethics of Biography (The Contemporary Review, July 1883)
Victor Hugo (The Contemporary Review, Vol. 48, July/December 1885)
A Venetian Dynasty (The Contemporary Review, Vol. 50, August 1886)
Laurence Oliphant (Blackwood's Magazine, Vol. 145, 1889)
Tennyson (Blackwood's Magazine, Vol. 152, 1892)
Addison, the Humorist (Century Magazine, Vol. 48, 1894)
The Anti-Marriage League (Blackwood's Magazine, Vol. 159, 1896)

Biographies

Edward Irving (1862)
Francis of Assisi (1871)
Count de Montalembert (1872)
Dante (1877)
Cervantes (1880)
Life of Sheridan in the English Men of Letters series (1883)
John Tulloch (1888)
Laurence Oliphant (1892)

Historical & Critical Works

Historical Sketches of the Reign of George II (1869)
The Makers of Florence (1876)
A Literary History of England from 1760 to 1825 (1882)
The Makers of Venice (1887)
Royal Edinburgh (1890)
Jerusalem (1891)
The Makers of Modern Rome (1895)
William Blackwood and his Sons (1897)
The Sisters Brontë. In: Women Novelists of Queen Victoria's Reign (1897)

www.ingramcontent.com/pod-product-compliance
Lightning Source LLC
Chambersburg PA
CBHW052034020726
47501CB00004B/1397